W9-ANR-688

OWE IT TO
THE WIND

*Sarah
Jarosz*

OWE IT TO THE WIND

THREE LIVES, TWO LOVES, ONE PACT

J.R. ARMSTRONG

Willowrose Publishing
Fowlerville, Michigan

ACKNOWLEDGMENTS: I would like to thank my husband, Will, and friends Joy Bell, Susan Perrone, and Mark Armstrong for reading my manuscript and giving me valuable input. And Mary Jo Zazueta of To The Point Solutions for her immense help in putting this book together.

Copyright © 2009 J.R. Armstrong

All rights reserved. No part of this publication may be reproduced or transmitted in any form or by any means, electronic or mechanical, including photocopying, recording, or any information storage and retrieval system, without written permission from the publisher. Exceptions are made for brief excerpts used in published reviews.

Willowrose Publishing
P. O. Box 1187
Fowlerville, MI 48836
www.jrarmstrong.net

Armstrong, J.R. (Janice R.)

    Owe it to the wind : three lives, two loves, one pact / J.R. Armstrong. — Fowlerville, Mich. : Willowrose Pub., c2009.

    p. ; cm.

    ISBN: 978-0-9822299-0-3

    1. High school students—Fiction. 2. Man-woman relationships—Fiction. 3. Love stories. 4. Bildungsromans. I. Title.

PS3601. R5761 O94 2009   2008941613
813/.6—dc22   0906

Printed in the United States of America

10 9 8 7 6 5 4 3 2 1

This is a work of fiction. Names, characters, places, and incidents either are the product of the author's imagination or are used fictitiously, and any resemblance to actual persons, living or dead, businesses, companies, events, or locales is entirely coincidental.

Cover and interior design by To The Point Solutions
www.tothepointsolutions.com

To Mom, Dad

&

Will

OWE IT TO THE WIND

CHAPTER 1

1963

THE FOUR BROTHERS PLAYED FOOTBALL IN THE YARD. ALL of them knew they were too close to the house, especially the large sliding-glass door their mom and dad always warned them about—but this was where the open space was—where they could run far and wide. Besides, Michael always caught the ball. Even though the ball had hit the house a couple of times over the years, nothing serious had happened. Parents always worried about nothing.

"Michael! Michael!" Michael looked and saw the panic on his brother's face. He was about to be tackled, which he hated. His brother quickly threw the football to save himself.

"Michael, get it!" yelled their oldest brother, Dave.

Michael ran hard, praying the ball would drop. It was too high. Even for the tallest of them, it was too high. "Michael!" All three were screaming now. Instinctively, he threw his arms over his head as he heard the shattering of glass.

Silence.

Slowly Michael brought his arms down. The four brothers were rooted to their own spots. He looked at the three of them. They were as white as he was. They were in trouble now, big trouble.

Michael did the only thing he could think of. He stepped through the broken glass door, grabbed the football, and stepped back outside. Incriminating evidence. If it wasn't there, they could certainly come up with a good cover story. Lightning, the neighbor's horse got loose again and kicked it in . . . anything. As Michael started to run towards his brothers, they all bolted away from him, faster than he'd seen any of them run before.

"Mike!"

He stopped and slowly turned around to face their father, who had come around the side of the house. "How many times have you been told not to play ball here?" his father roared. Michael could hear his mother crying. She was standing in the kitchen, staring at the broken glass, his baby sister on her hip.

"A—a lot." *Say sir, you know he likes it when you show him respect.* "Sir."

The two of them stared at each other. "Do you know how much that window's gonna cost?"

"No, no, sir."

"Do you know what 'laid-off' means?"

"Yes, sir."

"Where do you think the money is gonna come from to pay for this?"

"I don't know, sir. I'll . . . I'll do what I can."

Slowly his father undid his belt buckle and started pulling the leather strap through the loops. "Come here."

"Oh, God! Dan! No!" his mother screamed out the window.

"You shut up! Come here, Mike."

It wasn't that he didn't want to obey his father; he was simply too scared to move. *Had he been drinking yet? Or, more importantly, how much had he had to drink?* Michael threw a pleading look over his shoulder and saw his brothers hiding behind the barn. Three sets of wide-opened eyes looked back at him. Michael turned around to face his father. He was going it alone.

"Dan, he's only fourteen! Please!"

"Shut up! How many times has he been told?"

"You know the rest of the boys were playing, too. Michael wouldn't be out back playing football by himself. If you're going to punish him, you have to punish all of them."

"I don't see anybody else here. Do you? Come here, boy. I'm gonna teach you to never play ball out back here again. In fact, when I'm done, you ain't never gonna want to play football again."

"Gosh Mom, don't you think you should take him to a doctor? He needs stitches or something," Michael could hear his brother Darrell whispering.

His mother hadn't stopped crying since walking into the kitchen. She shook her head. "There's nothing to stitch to." Michael could feel her gently pulling pieces of his shirt off. Carefully she washed his back. He tried not to cry, but everything hurt. His back was on fire. There was no position he could get into to lessen the pain. He didn't know if he had passed out or fallen asleep, but the next thing he knew it was dark outside and his younger brother was watching him.

"Here. Look what I got." Michael turned to see his brother holding out a candy bar. They never had candy in the house. Candy was a treat for good children. When were they ever good?

Michael could barely move, but he managed to wrap his hand around it. "Where did you get this?" he asked.

"I ran down to Jim's. I thought you might like it. You know, cheer you up a bit."

"You didn't tell—"

"No."

Michael heard his mother walk into the room. He couldn't move fast enough to hide the candy bar, but she didn't seem to notice. Softly she smoothed his hair back. "How are you feelin', baby?"

He looked at her. Slowly he took a bite, chewed it, and then said, "I hate him. I'm gonna keep on playing football. Someday I'm gonna be better than he ever thought of being. And when I leave here . . . I'm never coming back."

"Honey, please, don't talk like that—"

"Nothin' is gonna hold me here."

CHAPTER 2

2001

JEFF WATCHED HIS GODDAUGHTER WALK THROUGH THE RESTAURANT. Sadness tugged at his heart as he thought about how much Robin looked like her mother at that age. She was taller, she had gotten height from her father; but her chestnut hair, straight nose, and wide smile were from her mother. Robin had been dancing since she was four, which was evident in the way she walked: straight and graceful. Her hair was pulled loosely back in a tortoise-shell clip. She gave Jeff an affectionate kiss on his cheek and slid quietly into her seat.

"Hello," she smiled at him.

"Hi, Princess." As her godfather, he over-indulged her. Robin was the only girl—he had three sons and two nephews. In reality, all of the boys pampered her too much; but things are rough when you grow up without a mother, he told himself. And now . . .

"How are you holding up?" he gently asked.

She shrugged. "Okay, I guess. I must admit, I never thought I'd be orphaned at twenty-three. Well, I guess technically I'm not an orphan. My stepmother's still around."

"You know, you're not alone. I'll always be here for you. And, you have your brother, don't forget."

She waved a hand. Gary—who actually held the impressive name of Benjamin Gerald Beechum IV—was her half-brother and a sore subject. Not that he was a bad kid; just self-centered and unmotivated. He had decided not to go to college. They had money, why should he waste four years studying for a degree he didn't want? "I'd just be wasting our money, Dad."

"Well, let's look at it this way," their father had said. "It's not *our* money. It's *my* money. And if you ever want to see any of it when I'm gone, you'll get yourself a college degree. You need to be able to take over the business when your mother and I are gone."

Sadly, one of Gary's first reactions upon hearing their father had been killed in a plane crash was that he wouldn't have to get that college degree after all. Look at all that money he would be inheriting. Life was good. Sorry, Dad. Thanks, Dad.

Robin looked at the menu. "I, um," Jeff stopped. *Am I doing the right thing?* He had argued back and forth with himself, and had finally decided on a course of action, but was now debating with himself again.

She looked up at him. *Yes, it is the right thing. She needs something new to occupy her thoughts.* "I have something . . . I thought you might like."

"Oh, you . . ." she shook her head. Robin knew he spoiled her.

"Your Grandmother Becktame gave it to me a long time ago, for safe keeping. She wanted you to have it someday."

She remembered Grandmother Becktame. Probably jewelry. Her grandmother had had money. A piece of jewelry would be nice.

Robin hoped her disappointment didn't show as Jeff slid a book over to her. She looked up at him. "It's . . . a diary." *Grandmother Becktame's diary? Well . . . okay . . . I guess it will be interesting. What was she thinking before she died?*

"Don't look so disappointed," he said. "It was your mother's."

"My mother's? My real mother?"

"Yeah."

Robin picked up the diary and looked at it with genuine interest. The mention of her mother's name was taboo in her house. Only at her godfather's, when her father wasn't around, was she ever allowed to talk about her birthmother. Godfather and his sister, Aunt Mandy, would share pictures and stories with Robin. They had known her mother from when they were little to her passing. They knew all sorts of things about her. They talked about her mother freely. On occasion, Aunt Mandy had gotten choked up. "Oh, Robin. Honey, I'm so sorry," she would say.

"It's okay, Aunt Mandy," Robin would reply, which only seemed to distress her aunt even more.

"I, um, took the liberty," continued Jeff, "of reading it."

"You read this?"

He chuckled. "Trust me, if Meg knew I'd read her private diary, she'd kill me. But I wanted to know what you were going to find out."

"Censor it, you mean?"

"Well," he reddened slightly. "I gave it to you intact. I just . . . didn't want there to be any . . . surprises. Actually, it was kind of fun going down memory lane from your mom's perspective. I thought I might explain to you first what your mom meant by 'new blood' though."

"New blood?"

"Yeah. You know, your mom, Aunt Mandy, and I grew up in Lyons, back when it was a small town. Between us, we knew everybody. I would have guys over all the time, and your mom and Aunt Mandy would be right in there, playing football or baseball, or whatever us guys decided to do. When we got to high school, your mom didn't feel like dating any of those guys. 'How can I date somebody I used to beat up?'" he used a falsetto voice, mimicking her mother. "But, when I was a senior and your mom and Aunt Mandy were juniors, our small high school consolidated with two other school districts to make one large school system. That's why the Lyons School District is so big. Hence, 'new blood.' Some new guys for Megan to meet. That's why she bought the diary. She felt she was finally going to have something to write about."

"Did she?"

Robin thought his face suddenly looked sad. As he took a sip of water and avoided looking into her eyes, he nodded. "Oh, yeah."

CHAPTER 3

1966

MEGAN STUDIED HERSELF IN THE MIRROR, FIRST WITHOUT makeup and then with. Her chestnut hair was long and curled nicely on its own at the ends. Her face had a few freckles, but she liked them. "A hint of tease" she had read somewhere. Megan immediately latched onto the phrase, since she couldn't get rid of them anyway. Green eyes and well, what could she say about her body? "Short but tough" was the boys' unanimous description. She definitely looked more feminine with the makeup.

She considered her best friend, Mandy. Stringy blonde hair and the skinniest legs you ever saw. A long face on a long frame. Megan couldn't understand why the guys thought Mandy "had filled out nicely."

"So," Megan asked the mirror, "why did Mandy have more dates than I did last year?" Not that she had had a lot, but . . . *Mandy isn't as picky as I am. She isn't holding out for the perfect man to walk her way.* Megan wasn't even jealous about the number of dates Mandy had—they were with "nobodies"—however, she had to admit to a twinge of envy when they argued about Mandy's steady through the summer. "How can you go out with him? I bloodied his nose!"

"You did that years ago, Meg! Besides, you definitely couldn't bloody his nose today. You're not even tall enough to reach it! And let me tell you," Mandy got a dreamy look in her eyes, "can he kiss. I mean, my stomach was doing flip-flops."

"Ew, yuck! My stomach's doing flip-flops, too—as in barf!" Meg had had her share of kisses, though none she could brag about. *How dare Mandy have a real good kisser! And in Joey, yet!* Now she was jealous.

Megan snapped her fingers. *A diary! I need a diary. This is my year to shine and I want to remember all of it.*

September 4, 1966: My dreams have come true! My wish has been granted! New blood! Finally, the chance to meet some new guys! I lost ten pounds over the summer, Mom let me get my hair styled, and I did my nails. I think I've talked her into allowing me to wear makeup this year, too. I am all set for school tomorrow—"Opening Day" (now I know why hunters are so happy to hear those words). Surely there has to be some new guys that are good-looking, possibly with some intelligence, and somebody who can beat me in arm wrestling (I can't very well respect a guy that I am capable of beating up). Jonesy and Mandy will pick me up first thing in the morning! Brand-new school—here I come.

On the first day of school, Megan checked out every new guy. On the whole, the other two school districts had a lot of good-looking boys to pick from. *This should be a fun year. I will have to ask Jonesy to introduce me to the football players.*

And then, suddenly interrupting her daydream, Adonis appeared. He was walking down the hall towards her. Megan couldn't take her eyes off him. The other boys were good-looking—but . . . So intently was she staring, that she lost her grip on her books and they all hit the floor. Embarrassed, she quickly bent down to pick them up, as other students also helped her. As Megan reached for some loose papers, long legs stepped over them. She glanced up to see him staring down at her. Their eyes met and then . . . he kept on walking.

September 5, 1966: I saw him today. The man of my dreams! Tall, blonde, built, short hair, which I don't care for, but that only means he's a football player! Yes! I know he saw me! He's just beautiful. I have to be in the same spot tomorrow so that our eyes can meet again.

September 12, 1966: So far I have not seen "Him" again. Where can he be? Was it just a fluke that I saw him that first day? I was so glad that we had a big new school and now it may prove my undoing! What if I never see him again? He has to be here. He also has to be a football player. Friday Mandy and I are going to the football game. Hopefully, I'll see him then. I know Jonesy would introduce us, but I don't want to be set up. I want a guy of my own. Jonesy has a habit of assuming I don't mind always "filling in" for one of his friends when they can't get a date.

My other sore subject with Jonesy is the co-captain. When we were a small school we had one captain. Jonesy would have been it this year. But, now that we are bigger, they decided to have two co-captains. And, from what I have heard about this guy, he has to be the "all brawn, no brains" type. He eats and sleeps football. Jonesy says he's an All-American and he doesn't mind sharing the title—he's happy he still has a title. I don't care what Jonesy says. He should have that title all to himself. So . . . I want to see who this Michael MacKenzie is, so I can snub him. Jonesy found this humorous: "You're going to snub him? That's funny. Do you know anything about the guy?" No. Apparently, he's pretty good at snubbing people himself. Keeps to himself mostly, although Jonesy says he can be decent and a lot of fun when he's not in one of his moods. But, by and large, Jonesy says the guys steer clear of him. I guess he's pretty big and our guys are glad they don't have to play against him. Jonesy says MacKenzie is never going to notice me, for me to snub him. Still, I want to see what this creep looks like.

Also, I need to see "my guy" and find out his name, without anybody suspecting that I have a crush on him. He is without a doubt the most handsome guy I have ever seen.

⇒   ⇐

The girls were at the Hill's house, getting ready to go to the football game. Jonesy had left ages ago. Mandy had a date and Megan was helping her put her makeup on. Megan could have had a date, too; and it was beyond Jonesy as to why she had said no.

"He needs a date for the dance. You need a date. I don't see—"

"I do not need a date for the dance!" she had yelled indignantly.

"Who asked *you* out?" asked Jonesy, not realizing how he sounded. He was simply curious. Now he was getting the look. "What? I just asked a simple question."

"Nobody. But I don't need you setting me up all the time like . . . like, like I'm desperate." There, she'd said it.

"Nobody thinks you're desperate," he said confidently, "they just think you're dateless." Meg glared at him, so he left.

The two girls sat behind the football players. Meg scanned them endlessly. She knew who Michael MacKenzie was right away as the announcer said his name over and over again. *Honest to Pete! Is he the only one playing? Excuse me, Jonesy was the one who threw him the ball.*

Mandy leaned into her. "I think somebody is watching you."

"Who?"

"Jim Wagner."

"Who?"

"You don't know who Jim is?" Megan shook her head. "He's really cute. Look, over there."

They both tried to casually glance over to the right. "The one who just turned around. Number 48."

"He did look cute, from what I saw. He couldn't have been staring at me though."

"Yeah, I think he was. I talked to him a little bit yesterday. Seems really nice."

"He's in one of your classes?"

"No, he was over to the house. A bunch of the players were."

Megan gave her a full stare. "You are my best friend and you didn't call me?"

Mandy looked down. "Jonesy wouldn't let me."

If truth be told, Megan would have called Jonesy her best friend, so she was stunned at hearing this. She finally found her voice. "Why?"

"Because . . ." Mandy continued to stare at the people in front of them, "Michael MacKenzie was there and Jonesy was afraid you might say something to him."

"Like what?"

"I don't know; but you've been pretty vocal about wanting to tell the guy off. He didn't bump Jonesy out of being captain. The administration decided they wanted two co-captains. He and Jonesy were elected. You act like we're the head school and we've allowed these visitors to come here. We," she put her hands out, "are three separate schools that are now under one roof. We're all here equally, even though we brought in the most students. It doesn't bother Jonesy. Why does it bother you?"

Megan stared at her. "I guess I hadn't looked at it that way. I mean, we donated the land . . . it's called Lyons High, just like it's always been. I just hadn't looked at it that way before." *But, I am really sick of hearing Michael MacKenzie's name . . . again.*

"And," Mandy chuckled, "the other reason is, I think Jonesy's a little bit afraid of him. He really didn't want to have to defend you if you said or did something that ticked the guy off."

They looked at each other and started to laugh. At six foot, one hundred eighty pounds, and very popular, they had never known Jonesy to be afraid of anybody. "I really think Jim is trying to get your attention," said Mandy.

"Oh my God! There he is," Megan said excitedly, sitting up straight.

"Who?"

"Who? Huh? What?" How could Mandy miss Mr. Adonis? There he was, standing next to Jonesy. They were both talking with the coach.

After several moments of silence, Mandy said, "I don't think your heart is racing for Jonesy, so . . . are you by any chance interested in the tall blonde next to him?"

"Oh God, Mandy, he's the one I saw in the hall last week. He's gorgeous, don't you think? I haven't seen him since then. If Jonesy's going to set me up, he can set me up with him."

"Ah, you're not gonna like this."

"No . . ." Megan looked at Mandy, ". . . don't tell me that he was my date for tonight?"

"Well—"

"No!" she yelled loud enough so that several people turned their way. "Oh, why didn't I ask Jonesy who he was setting me up with before I blew up at him?"

"Meg—"

"Oh, it doesn't matter. I still don't know his name. But you do, don't ya?"

"Yeah."

"Well?" she nearly screamed again.

"That's—"

But Meg had turned around to look at him again. He was just putting his helmet back on as he jogged onto the field. "Oh, no." Along with the player's number, the co-captains had the honor of having their last names emblazoned on the back of their jerseys. "That's not—"

"Michael MacKenzie," said Mandy. "On the bright side, he wasn't your date."

September 15, 1966: Last night was our football game. What can I say? We won and I found out who the co-captain is. What a disappointment. My dream guy is the same guy I've sworn to snub: Michael MacKenzie.

"Excuse me. It's Megan, right?"

She looked up. "Yeah. Um, Jim . . . Wagner, right?" He smiled, obviously pleased that she knew who he was. *I have absolutely no idea why this guy is at my classroom door.*

"Last week I asked Jonesy to introduce us, so I could ask you out.

Instead he told me he'd just set us up. Apparently you didn't like that idea so . . . I'm here to ask if you'd like to go out with me this Saturday."

"Oh." She stood there for several seconds. *Gosh, a real live date. He's actually pretty cute. A football player. I could do worse.* "Okay." *Mandy was right, he was trying to get my attention on Friday night.*

"We don't have practice after school today, just a meeting. Would you like a ride home? Give us a chance to get to know each other?"

Not have to ride the bus home? Yes! "Okay."

"The meeting will last about a half hour. If you want to meet me at the locker room door, I'll be out as soon as it's over."

"Okay."

Megan was standing outside the boys' locker room at the appointed time when someone opened a door, letting in a blast of air from outside. The breeze that came down the hallway felt cold on her bare legs, so she tried to move away from it at the same time the locker room door opened. She collided with the first guy out. "I'm sor—" She turned to see Michael MacKenzie staring down at her.

"What is your problem?" he asked her.

"I . . . I . . . what?" she was too stunned to get anything more out.

"The first day of school you nearly broke my neck, dumping all your books at my feet. You were staring at me so hard I thought my fly was open." Her jaw dropped. "And now you're here and you just happen to bump into me. I'll tell ya right now: I'm not interested, honey."

Her jaw was still hanging open as he turned to walk away. *Nobody talks to me that way!* "You conceited horse's ass! I'm not here for you!"

He turned around, gave her a look that could kill, and started back towards her. Megan was not sure what he had planned for her, but she stood her ground. She had never backed down from anyone and she wasn't going to start now. Suddenly she felt a presence beside her. "She's here for me."

Michael stopped and looked at Jim. He glanced back and forth between the two of them. Slowly the anger left him. "Sorry," he said to Jim, and then he looked at Megan. He seemed to be mulling something over. *What?* "I'm sorry I spoke to you that way." He walked off.

Megan realized she had been holding her breath. Until a few moments ago, she had not realized how big and solid Michael was. Although she was glad she had stood up to him, he had unnerved her. "You okay?" she heard Jim ask. They started walking down the hallway.

"Yeah, I just . . . never met anybody like him." She looked at Jim with renewed interest. "I thought a lot of the guys were scared of him. You didn't seem to be."

He opened the door for her and they walked out to the parking lot. "Michael and I are neighbors. We used to be good friends."

"Used to be?"

He nodded. "He has a lot of family problems. Mainly his dad, who is drunk most of the time. I don't know what it is. His dad just doesn't seem to like him. A few years back, Michael was out of school for a week. His brothers said he was sick. They were real hush-hush and acted odd about it. When Michael came back, he was a different person. Didn't want to hang out, didn't laugh, didn't smile. He just focused on athletics, football primarily, and he's just kept his distance from everybody since then. He really hasn't spoken much to me—or to anybody, for that matter. I can still remember when he was a lot of fun."

"I doubt that," muttered Megan.

Jim chuckled. "I know what you mean, but it's true. Now, tell me about you."

September 18, 1966: I met a new guy in school today: Jim Wagner. He seems really nice, cute. I have a date with him on Saturday. I guess I'm excited. He drove me home. I am so disappointed in "my guy". He's so good-looking and as I found out today, very rude.

At least I stood up to him, which is more than I can say about a lot of the guys.

15

CHAPTER 4

September 19, 1966: Why does that SOB Michael keep coming to mind? He is rude, conceited, arrogant, and gorgeous. When he was looking at me, just before he apologized, I felt like I was seeing someone totally different. Like, I was seeing the real person. That his rudeness was the acting part. What makes a person be that nasty? I've heard some of the girls who have gone to school with him all these years talking. They too said he used to be a lot of fun, when they were younger. How does a person change like that?

Jim seems like a nice guy. He walked me to a couple of my classes today and I'm actually looking forward to going out with him on Saturday. The guys have an away football game and he won't be home much before midnight on Friday, which is why we're not going out then.

HOW IS THIS POSSIBLE? SHE SCREAMED INSIDE. HOW? MEGAN always enjoyed study hall—but now this! Her friend Trish sat kitty-corner from her, near the back of the room. Megan had just finished telling Trish about her encounter with "that conceited SOB of a co-captain", when Michael MacKenzie himself sauntered into the room, tossed a piece of paper at Miss Quinn without even looking at her, and then turned to some of the guys who asked him what he was doing there. "Got kicked out of the other study hall and sent down here."

The guys hooted. Michael laughed with them and Megan felt her heart skip a beat. *He is so gorgeous when he smiles. He is arrogant. He's an ass. Okay, he's good-looking; get over it. That's all he's got to offer.* But, somewhere deep down inside, she believed otherwise. Something about when he had looked at her outside the locker room door . . . it was as if his mask had fallen away for one brief instant.

Michael saw her. The surprise on his face quickly vanished and his eyes narrowed. Most everyone in the room had heard about their encounter.

"Welcome to our study hall, Michael," said Miss Quinn. "You can have the cherished seat behind Miss Becktame."

There was a hush in the room as Michael calmly turned towards Miss Quinn and, with mock expression, said, "And who might that be?" Little ripples of laughter went through the room.

Miss Quinn smiled back and pointed down the row saying, "Oh, my mistake. I thought you two had already met."

Now there was feigned coughing mixed in with the suppressed laughter. As Michael moved towards her, Meg could feel her face growing warmer by the second. She heard Trish mutter, "Uh-oh." *Yeah, uh-oh is right.*

Michael slammed his books down behind her, which made her jump. "I told you she was in for it now," someone whispered.

By the end of the study period Megan hadn't turned a single page of her book.

September 20, 1966: I cannot believe my luck! Michael got booted out of his other study hall and was sent to mine! And guess where Miss Quinn put him? Right behind me. You should have seen the look he gave me. Six of the football players are also in there and you could hear them snickering. How am I supposed to concentrate with him sitting behind me all year? This is just great.

September 24, 1966: I went out with Jim on Saturday. He's really pretty cute and very nice. We went to the show and grabbed a burger afterwards. We made out in the driveway, until Mom realized I was home and started flashing the outside light at us. That was embarrassing! But, he asked me to the dance next Friday after the game. I said yes, of course.

A few days had passed and everyone was disappointed that nothing had come of Meg and Michael sitting by each other. Those who had placed bets as to who would start something first had given up on making easy money. It was pretty much forgotten—except by one person—Meg.

It was bad enough that every other day he sat behind her and ignored her. At least before, it was just his looks that had gotten to her. Now it was his constant pencil tapping. Tap, tap, tap, tap, tap, tap. *Did he ever use the stupid thing?*

At first, Meg thought it was a nervous habit of his and that eventually he would either stop or she'd get used to it—but she was now convinced Michael was doing it simply to bug her. And he was succeeding, which really burned her.

Meg had an assignment due next hour, and she knew she'd never get it done with him making noise behind her.

"Would you please stop that?" she whispered.

The pencil stopped in midair. "What?" Total innocence.

"You know what!" she hissed. "Your pencil."

"That bothers you?"

"Yes!"

"Finally." He continued tapping and went back to reading.

Meg smoldered in front of him. She saw her chance when Miss Quinn left the room. As everybody started talking, she whirled around in her chair. "I'm warning you to stop the pencil tapping. I can't concentrate."

"And what are you gonna do about it? Sic Jim on me?"

Growing up, she had played football, baseball, wrestled, and bloodied a few noses. She had been a regular tomboy. Meg hadn't needed anybody to defend her then, and she didn't need anybody to defend her now. She balled up her fist and brought it to his attention. "I can take care of myself! Stop the tapping!" She was furious.

"Meg," Trish warned. This was not the guy to pick on. What was Meg thinking? Trish knew Meg had heard the stories about him: he was mean and nasty. Everybody, including the football players, left Michael alone.

"Uh-oh." He pretended to be scared and stopped. Meg sighed and turned back around. Thirty seconds later, the tapping started up again—louder and more furious. Soon, students began to place their bets. Then, Miss Quinn returned.

She found what she was looking for and left again.

Megan whipped around in her seat, ripped the pencil out of his hand, and snapped it in two. She slammed the two pieces back down on his desk. "I warned you," she glared at him.

Michael was too astonished to say anything. Trish slapped both hands over her mouth. The room had gone completely quiet. "I suggest you turn around," he finally said.

Meg wasn't about to let him tell her what to do, so she continued to remain turned in her seat and stared at him as coldly as she could. "Miss Becktame, what are you doing?" yelled Miss Quinn. "You know my rules. No talking. You will stay after school one day next week. Now, turn around." Meg quickly did as she was told and tried to concentrate.

Michael, who had been lazily stretched out in his chair, sat up. Meg heard him move as he leaned on his desk. "I warned you," he whispered.

She placed her hand behind her head and gave him the finger. She heard him chuckle and say, "I love a challenge."

Meg sat up straight in her chair. *What the heck did that mean? Maybe this time I went too far.*

September 27, 1966: I have had it with pretty boy MacKenzie sitting behind me in study hall. The guy drives me nuts. I fixed him today, though. He had better understand who he's dealing with. I'm not afraid of him, like most of the school is. I can be mean, too. You should have seen the look on his face today when I snapped his pencil in two.

September 29, 1966: I met Jim after the football game on Friday (varsity won again!) and we went to the dance. I looked around, but didn't see Michael there. That was fine with me. I had a very pleasant evening with Jim. We made out again in the driveway.

Mandy had been out most of the week with the flu. Megan had stayed after for her detention with Miss Quinn and was just finishing cleaning out the locker she shared with Mandy. Meg hoped Mandy wouldn't notice all the papers and gum wrappers she had thrown out. *There, it looks pretty decent.* Meg glanced at her watch. *Oh, no. How did thirty minutes go by so fast?* Jonesy was her ride home and he was probably pacing the floor by now. She was grabbing Mandy's books and her own when she recognized Jonesy's footsteps coming down the hallway. "I'm coming!" she hollered.

Meg hauled out two history books, two English books, one French book, and a Spanish book.

"Meg," Jonesy came whirling around the corner. "I can't take you home tonight. Sorry. Call your mom and have her come get you, okay? Thanks. See ya."

"No! Jonesy, wait! Mom's gone. She's visiting friends for the day. You're my only ride home."

He stood there for a second. "If you run quickly, maybe you can catch up with Jim." She stood with her armload of books and looked at him. He started backing away from her. "I'm really sorry, Meg."

"Where are you going?" she started to follow him. "Jonesy, don't you dare leave me stranded here." He suddenly turned and took off running. "Jeffrey Hamilton Hill! I'll tell your mother you deserted me!"

"Tell her I won't be home for dinner," echoed down the hall.

The books already felt heavy in her arms. *Surely he isn't going to leave me here. This is not like Jonesy. He didn't even offer to take any of the books. What is up with him?* Meg couldn't run, but she sped up as best she could. "Jeff—"

Meg felt the wind get knocked out of her as she went sprawling backwards, books and papers flying. She sat up, dazed for a minute, wondering when they had erected a brick wall around the corner. Then Michael's face came into focus.

"That was cute," he sneered. She glared up at him, waiting for an apology. It never came. He leaned against the wall, arms folded across his chest, and watched as she picked up papers, examining each one before putting it back in its place. Meg was livid. Here she was, on her hands and knees, while he stood there just watching. And grinning. If he wasn't gentleman enough to help, the least he could do was leave! But no, he was enjoying this way too much. And to think this was his fault. She finally got the books all stacked and stood up. "Thanks for the help."

"Was I the one running in the hall? Was I the one not looking where I was going? Was I the one with an armload of—"

"Are any of the other guys still around?" she asked through gritted teeth.

"Nope. I was the last one out." His clear-blue eyes seared through her and it slowly dawned on Meg that they were alone. Mandy had told her that the overall consensus about why Michael hadn't hit her for the backtalk and breaking his pencil wasn't the fact that she was a girl, but rather that there were too many witnesses. He had beaten up guys who had said far less to him. *Is he standing around because he has something nasty planned for me?* Meg had just decided she'd better hurry up and find somebody else in the building, when he walked across the hallway. She watched him stop at a locker and dial the combination.

"Is that your locker?" she asked.

"No," he turned and gave her a look. "My locker is clear on the other side, so I thought I'd just stop here, break into somebody else's locker, and steal their books," he held one up to her, "so as to save me the trouble of walking." He pulled out his jacket and put it on. "Wow, their jacket is just my size, too." He slammed the door shut.

Meg burned; not because he'd been sarcastic with her but at her own foolishness. In the beginning, when she had wanted to find out who her Adonis was, she had hurried out of Jonesy's car every morning, ran to her locker, leaving Mandy in the dust, got what she needed for the morning, and had traveled all over the school in hopes of getting a glimpse of him—and here his locker was almost directly across from hers.

He came up to her and stopped. "Those books look heavy. You want some help?"

Well, maybe he isn't so bad. "Yes, please." Michael took the top one and walked off. She should have known! He was a moron, an idiot! She had let him get the best of her again.

Michael turned and smiled at her. "I was just teasing. Here," he held the book out to her, "I'll trade ya."

Even though his smile seemed genuine, Meg was now furious. "Forget it!" He had already started to take the books from her and she jerked them away. No! No! Don't fall over! She danced in the hallway, trying to steady the stack of books in her arms. Meg jammed her chin down on them. Steady, steady. Big sigh of relief.

"Suit yourself."

Meg headed for the parking lot. There had to be somebody else here. She didn't like hearing Michael directly behind her.

They reached the parking lot. It was a depressing and lonely scene. Michael stood beside her and scanned the vacant lot. "Gosh, I don't see another soul here," he commented, setting the book back on her stack.

Meg nodded her head towards the one car that was in sight. "Is that rusted heap of junk yours?"

He shook the keys in his hand. "It'll get me home." He walked off. "See ya."

What am I going to do now? I will ring Jonesy's neck. No, I'll tear him apart limb by limb. Well, I could wait another couple of hours for Mom to get home. What about asking Mrs. Hill to come and get me? Then I could really get even with Jonesy.

Michael pulled up alongside her. He opened the driver's door and got out. "Do you want a ride home?"

No, not really. But, what are my options? Two to three hours waiting for Mom? Call Mrs. Hill, who may or may not come because Mandy's sick or . . . a twenty-minute ride with asshole here? "With you?" she said nastily.

He put up his hands and got in. *No, wait. I don't want to sit around here. I'm going to drop these books any second.* Meg hurried over and grabbed the door handle as best she could. She pulled and strained as the door gave slightly. Two books fell. She jerked it hard at the same time Michael pushed from inside. The door flew open. Books and papers once again hit the ground—but this time the wind took what it could. "No!" she screamed. Meg ran through the parking lot swearing, grabbing, and stomping on any piece of paper she could reach. She turned to see if Michael was helping. No, he was still in the car, laughing. She watched the rest of the papers dance across the street. Slowly she returned to the car. Michael was trying his best not to laugh in front of her, as she had not looked very ladylike in a skirt with the wind blowing. Meg picked up the books one at a time and tossed them in the car.

"You do seem to have a problem with books," he said. She picked up the last one and sent it flying through the air, hitting him squarely on the shoulder. He seemed not to notice.

Meg finally got in and slammed the door. She was going to boil Jonesy in hot oil. "Ya know," he said amiably, "maybe I could save you some books by pointing out that the ones that have the same cover are what we call

22

duplicates. You aren't going to get any more facts out of this history book than you are the other one."

"I know that!" she screeched. "Some of these are Mandy's, you stupid ass. She's been out sick all week."

"You seem to have a bit of a temper."

"You ain't seen nothin' yet. Wait 'til you see what I do to Jonesy when I get a hold of him."

He nodded. "In all fairness, I think I'm to blame for him leaving you like he did."

"What are you talking about?" She eyed him suspiciously.

"Well, he ... I ... hmm."

"Let's not forget that my having to stay after school today was *your* fault!"

"No. I told you to turn around. You just refused to listen to me. I do, however, take responsibility for Jonesy."

She had heard stories about Michael: the gals loved him, the guys feared him. Even Jonesy seemed intimidated by him. Had they had some falling-out she didn't know about? She was too concerned now for Jonesy to argue with him about herself. "What did you do to Jonesy?"

"I introduced him to Suzann Cochran."

"Who?"

"Suzann—I know her from my school. But, in all fairness to me, Jonesy has asked me several times to introduce him. Today, all three of us just happened to be in the hall at the same time—and she had told me she was interested, so ... sorry."

She sat back in the seat. "I don't understand. If he was taking her home, what was the big deal about me riding along?"

"No, no," he shook his head. "I ... I think Jonesy was planning, was hoping for something ... more than just taking her home."

"A date *after* school?" To her, dates were done on the weekend, not during the week—and certainly not in the middle of the day. "What kind of a date is that? What do you do? Go for a walk in the park?" She envisioned Jonesy strolling along with a girl on his arm, like in Victorian times. *No, that wasn't Jonesy.* "The show's not open. I suppose you could go for a hamburger."

He chuckled. "You are such an innocent."

"What's that supposed to mean?"

"Does the name Suzann Cochran mean anything to you?"

"No. Should it?"

"She was quite well-known at my old school. She has become, shall we say popular, here . . . with the guys."

He watched Meg mull this over. "Are you saying that she . . .?"

"Puts out," he filled in.

"Well, thank you for introducing Jonesy to *that*!"

"Oh," he looked concerned. "Is this his first time?"

"My God!" she yelled. "I don't know! I don't *want* to know! I don't even want to imagine! I'm sorry you told me!" She stared out the side window. *What did you and Michael talk about on the way home from school today, dear? Well, we talked about sex, Mom. Yeah, I'm going to say that to the woman who can't even discuss it with me. Thank goodness I've got Mrs. Hill. The first time I have this gorgeous hunk all to myself, we talk about sex. Or, would it be more accurate if I told everyone we talked about Jonesy having sex?*

He pulled into her driveway. "I don't know what you're getting upset about. I mean, it's not like it's going to happen to *you*."

Slowly Meg turned to face him. She gave Michael as cold a stare as she could. "Of course not," she said softly. "Nobody would ever find me attractive enough to want to do anything with *me*."

"Okay, that came out wrong. I didn't mean, I didn't mean to insinuate . . . that . . . that you weren't attractive . . ." *What is she doing to me? I've always had the upper hand with girls.* He couldn't think straight. "I don't want you to think that *I'm* interested in you."

She grabbed the door handle and shoved. The door didn't budge. She continued pulling on the handle and slamming her shoulder into the door while she yelled, "You pompous son of a —! You think I'm interested in you and you're letting me down easy? You sit behind me in study hall and bug the living daylights out of me—and for that I'm supposed to find you irresistible? I am dating Jim Wagner, in case nobody informed you. I find him cute, well-mannered, and he's nice to me." She slammed her shoulder into the door again. As he reached over, Meg balled up her fist and shook it at him, "Don't come near me."

"I was only going to help—"

"Shut up! You conceited, arrogant piece of dog tur —" the door flew open and she tumbled onto the stone driveway. Meg landed on her side. Ow! She looked at her hand and arm. Blood oozed out. One foot was still in the car and she was sure her thigh looked like her hand and arm. Meg glanced at Michael and saw him staring out the front window with his right hand held up over the side of his face.

"I didn't see anything," he offered. *What? You didn't see me tumble out the door and land on my butt? Let's add dense and stupid to the list I started.* Slowly Meg sat up and then realized her skirt was around her waist. *Oh, no! Could I be any more humiliated? Clearly he saw everything. I will be the laughing stock of the school. From beginning to end, this has been one big mistake.* She pulled her foot out of the car and carefully stood. This was supposed to be her year to shine. This was her year to meet new blood—to have a boyfriend or just play the field. Meg had so looked forward to this year, and now she would be laughed at. She burst into tears. *Oh, this is great! NOW my humiliation is complete.*

Michael peeked out from behind his hand. Seeing her standing, he immediately jumped out of the car. "Let's get you in the house," he moved her aside while he gathered up the books. They walked up the sidewalk, while Meg fumbled for her house key. Michael stared at the huge wooden door with the brass knocker. It looked like something you would see in a movie. He walked in with her and set the books down on the nearest table.

"You really need to get that cleaned up," he said.

"As soon as you leave, I will."

He looked around. "Where's your mom?"

"She's not here."

"Oh. Do you want me to clean it for you?"

"Yeah. You'd love that, wouldn't you?" Michael didn't understand why she was yelling at him. He thought he had been doing the right thing by offering to help. "I'm sure you'd especially love to clean the back of my thigh because it hurts all the way up my backside! You know," she could feel fresh tears forming, which made her madder still. She didn't want to give him any more satisfaction than she had already. "It's true. That first day of school, I was gawking at you. You were the most handsome guy I'd ever laid eyes on. But ya know what? That's all you have to offer. You're rude, you're arrogant, and you're conceited. You've got nothing to offer except your looks. Trust me when I say I'm not interested in you! Now, get out!" she screamed.

"Meg I—"

"Get out!" Using her good hand, she shoved him out the door and slammed it shut.

October 4, 1966: I don't know that I can go to school tomorrow. Jonesy decided he couldn't take me home after school for reasons I will not mention here! I will simply say that I am not speaking to him! I was completely humiliated in front of Michael. It's not my fault that his stupid car door wouldn't open properly and it dumped me out. He must have loved seeing ALL OF ME! I'm sure he's calling every player on the team right now and telling them everything that happened. I can't face that.

By morning, Meg had decided to face the music. Might as well get it over with. She couldn't hide out at home for the next two years. She called Jonesy to tell him she was taking the bus. "You don't want a ride to school?" he asked incredulously.

"No. I'm so furious with you. Don't even speak to me."

Meg got through the morning without anybody saying anything or laughing at her. That just meant Michael hadn't hurried home and called everybody. Wait until after lunch. She snubbed Jonesy, who gave her a perplexed look. She wondered what Michael had dreamed up for her in study hall and thought about not going. Another first, skipping class. No, she was not giving him that satisfaction.

She already had her head in a book when he walked by her in study hall and sat down. She kept waiting for something, anything, from him. It wasn't until she was in her next class that it dawned on her: Michael hadn't tapped his pencil. In fact, he had been very quiet.

Jonesy came over to her house after football practice. "What's the matter with you?" He couldn't remember the last time Megan had been this mad at him.

She was sitting in her bedroom, staring out the window. "How do you think I got home last night?" she asked quietly.

"Listen, I'm sorry about that." He came in and sat down on the bed across from her. "Did you have to wait long for your mom?"

He seemed genuine. *Could it be possible that Michael never told anyone? But, why wouldn't he?* "No. Michael drove me home," she watched his face carefully.

"Oh, well, that was nice of him. So, what's the problem?"

"He didn't mention it to you? To anyone?"

He shrugged. "No, not that I'm aware of. He didn't . . . did he do something he shouldn't have?"

"No. No. I just thought . . . he might have mentioned it."

Jonesy looked at her. "Is there anything I need to know?"

"No. I'd like a ride in the morning, okay?"

He got up. "Okay. Meg, if he did anything—"

She smiled and shook her head. "Everything's fine." *But why didn't Michael tell somebody? Everybody?*

October 6, 1966: Jim asked me to go steady and I said yes. At least this way I won't be sitting at home on the weekends. I could do worse.

They had both gotten to study hall early. Miss Quinn hadn't arrived yet, so everyone was talking. Megan turned around and faced Michael. He looked up at her. "You never told anybody, did you?" she asked.

"Never told anybody what?"

"You know. About giving me a ride home . . . and bragging about what happened."

"What did you think I would brag about? That I gave you a ride home and made you cry?"

"I'm sure the guys would have gotten a good laugh out of that."

"Yes, I'm sure some of them would have; but it wouldn't have gone down well with Jim and Jonesy and some of the other guys you grew up with. I'm not quite the asshole you think I am. I saw no reason for you to be the joke of the school. I'm sorry you fell out."

"Well, it was an accident."

"Yeah, I know. There's a little trick to the door. I was gonna help ya."

She remembered shoving her fist in his face. "I'm sorry. And, thank you for not saying anything to anybody."

"No problem. Listen . . ." She waited while he looked down at his book. "I wanted to clear up something with you. Would it be all right if I came over to your house tonight after practice?"

"Sure."

"Miss Quinn."

Meg quickly turned around, her heart pounding. *Why is he coming over to my house? What in the world does he have to say to me? And thank you, God, he didn't tell anyone—although I still can't believe it.*

"Have you lost your mind?" demanded Mandy.

"What? He's just coming over to talk."

"Yeah, I know. And look at you. Changing your clothes, redoing your hair, your makeup. I thought you said it wasn't a date."

"It's not. I always change out of my school clothes."

"And now, perfume. You don't do this much for Jim—who you are going steady with, let's not forget."

Meg looked at her. "I have not forgotten," she flashed Jim's ring in Mandy's face. "I do too get this ready for him. Has Jonesy mentioned a date with Suzann Cochran to you?"

"That slut? No," Mandy made a face. "Jonesy wouldn't be caught dead with someone like her. I thought you knew him better than that."

"Yeah, I thought I did, too," muttered Meg.

"Megan, tell me what's going on here."

"I told you. He's coming over to clear up something."

"Like what?"

"I don't know, but I'm dying to find out," she held one sweater up against her and then another. She looked at Mandy questioningly.

"Okay," Mandy nodded. "You do put makeup and perfume on for Jim, but you're never this excited."

Meg glanced at her and then looked away. "I'm not excited."

"When you first saw Michael, all I heard about was how handsome he was. He was your dream man. The best I have ever heard you say about Jim is that he's nice."

"I think he's cute."

"There are a lot of girls who would love to be in your shoes. But Jim doesn't do anything for you, does he?"

"I'm going steady with him."

"But he doesn't do anything for you, does he? No, it's the arrogant, conceited idiot. I don't understand you." Meg didn't answer. "I'm going to leave before Michael gets here. Call me after he leaves. I want to know what he wanted to talk to you about."

Meg sank down on the bed and surveyed her room. Mandy was right. There were clothes thrown all over from her going through her closet and dresser. She had tried extra hard to get the makeup just right. *What is it about Michael that makes my stomach always do flip-flops?* The few times he had smiled at her, she had been glad she was sitting down. Meg broke away from her thoughts the second she heard a car coming up the driveway. She flew down the stairs and then stopped. No, she really didn't act this way for Jim. She waited for the knock at the door and then took her time getting there.

"Hi."

"Hi," she stepped out and shut the door. "Nobody's home, so I'm not allowed to have guys in the house. Want to go for a walk in the woods?"

"Okay." As they meandered through the trees, they both looked in opposite directions. Neither one spoke. *This is not what I call a comfortable silence. When is he going to tell me what he came over for?* He stopped walking and cleared his throat. *Ah, here it comes.*

Michael took a deep breath. "Listen, about the other day. When I said . . ." he stopped and she looked at him. "When I said, 'It's not gonna happen to you,' I wasn't implying what you think I was implying. I mean, we'd been talking about Suzann and Jonesy and I didn't want you to think that I'd offered to take you home for some ulterior motive, like I know Jonesy had Suzann." She could see him start to redden and he shook his head. "I'm not any good at this." He abruptly turned and started back through the trees.

"Michael," she had to run to keep up with him. "That was really sweet of you."

"Oh, God. You're not going to tell anybody that, are you?" he looked horrified.

She laughed. "Who would believe me?"

He smiled. "I guess I have kind of a rough reputation."

"You know, when you smile—" *There's a shift in the universe. All right. Get over this guy right now. He is not the one for you. Admit you have a crush on him and get over it.* "—you look nice. You should do it more often."

"Gnaw, my mother always tells me that. Not gonna happen."

"Come on," she motioned with her hand and started down the trail.

He stood uncertainly. "What?"

"Come on." Seeing him hesitate, she smiled. "Maybe I have an ulterior motive."

"Yeah, you did say you found me awfully handsome."

"No, just handsome, not awfully handsome."

"Oh, I see," slowly he followed her. They eventually came to a stream. Michael saw a wool blanket hanging on a tree branch. Megan reached up and pulled it down. She gave it a few shakes and spread it out on the ground.

"Sit," she patted the spot next to her. He sat down reluctantly. She could sense his uneasiness. "My parents own fifty acres here, but it's my woods. My folks don't come out here at all. I can tell you the names of all the trees and plants. I have most of the animals named." She talked quietly. "There's a rabbit . . . see how the leaves rustle? I bet there's a little vole or snake—"

"A vole? You mean mole?"

"No, a vole. Moles tend to stay underground. Voles are similar to mice."

"Okay, but I don't see any leaves rustling."

"Right there." He looked where she was pointing, but shook his head. She got up and carefully made her way over. "There, see." He watched as a snake made its way across.

"Eagle eyes, huh?"

She shrugged and sat down again. He watched her as she looked around. "I come here a lot; particularly when I'm upset. When I need to relax. When I want to just be by myself. It's a nice peaceful and restful place to be. I thought maybe," she turned and looked at him, "you needed that."

They stared at each other. Suddenly he stood up. "I need to get home." He took off at a fast pace. Upon reaching his car, he looked behind him. Meg had not followed him. He got in and sat for a few seconds. *What are you thinking, MacKenzie? What are you doing? What is the Number One Rule that you have lived by for four years? Never get close to anyone. Don't let anybody in. It has served you well, don't blow it now. You know how Jim feels about her. He was your best friend once. If nothing else, don't do this to him. But when have you ever met anyone who stood up to you?*

October 9, 1966: Michael said he wanted to come over to my house today after football practice. I couldn't imagine what he wanted to say to me, but guess what? He apologized to me! I couldn't believe it and trust me, nobody else will either, so I'll just keep it to myself. I took him out in my woods and we sat down on the blanket that I keep out there. He got nervous and left. I wonder if he's not used to girls.

CHAPTER 5

I just want you to tell me how you did it." megan glanced up to see Michael and Chris coming through the study hall door.

"I told you, I knew the answer," said Michael.

"But, you couldn't have. How did you guys do it? Just tell me."

Michael stopped and turned to Chris. "Are you calling me a liar, a cheat, or both?" Megan noticed that Michael didn't raise his voice. Standing a good head taller than small-boned, tiny Chris, Michael was already intimidating. Even though everyone who was listening hoped Chris would just give it up, Chris was too distraught to notice he was in any danger.

"Come on, Chris. You lost fair and square," one of the football players said.

"No! You guys cheated somehow. I want to know how you did it because I was watching. Just tell me. I'm not going to tell on you. I just want to know."

Megan wanted to tell Chris to shut up. He had been a friend of hers since elementary school. After Jonesy and Mandy, Chris had probably tramped through her woods with her more than anybody. Since entering high school, they had gone their separate ways, but the affection she had for him then was still with her. If Chris wasn't careful, Michael would take him down in one blow—and Meg felt helpless to do anything.

Another girl chimed in. "Chris, you got beat by a bunch of jocks, just accept it."

"No! You," he bent his head back to look up at Michael, "couldn't possibly know that answer."

"Because I'm a jock and, therefore, too stupid?"

Please, Michael. Please don't hit him, Meg pleaded inwardly. *Do something, think of something. Miss Quinn get in here.*

"Meg." She sat up straight as she heard Michael spit out her name.

"Yes?" She hoped her voice didn't shake.

He continued staring down at Chris as he spoke. "Name a small rodent that starts with the letter 'v'."

"Vole?"

"Thank you."

"Jonesy had the answer, too," added the football player. "Michael just said it first."

Chris whirled around. "I know Meg would know the answer. And with Jonesy living next door to her, I can see how he might know; but how would Mich—" he stopped and looked at Meg. She shook her head furiously. Slowly Chris looked up at Michael and sat down at his desk.

Michael went to his seat at the back of the room while Meg kept her face in her book. She knew everyone was looking their way. For not having a teacher in the room, it was deathly quiet. "Does anybody have anything they want to say?" asked Michael.

Miss Quinn was surprised to find all of the students quietly studying when she arrived five minutes after the bell.

Jim called Meg after dinner, like he did most nights. As they chatted, Meg had the feeling that his mind was someplace else. Finally, he said, "What exactly happened in study hall today?"

Why does he care about this? "You mean between Michael and Chris?"

"Yeah."

"Well, actually I don't know what they were arguing about; but Chris seemed to think Michael was too stupid to answer a question."

"So, how was it Michael dragged you in on the conversation?"

"Cuz he knew I'd know the answer."

"Why would he think you'd know the answer? Were you in class with him and Chris?"

"No." She explained about Michael being over and how the word *vole* came up. Silence followed. "Oh, I found my homecoming dress—"

"Why was Michael over at your house to begin with?"

"He wanted to apologize for a misunderstanding we had. What color is your—"

"Michael *apologized* to you?"

"Oh, no. I wasn't supposed to tell anybody," she started to laugh. "He's afraid it'll ruin his reputation. Now, I need to know what color your suit is." Dead silence. "Jim? I haven't bought the dress yet, if you're worried."

She could hear the frustration in his voice, but didn't understand where it was coming from. "What misunderstanding would the two of you have that he felt he needed to apologize for? To come over to your house and apologize?"

"He insulted me, or at least I thought he had insulted me." Meg explained about Jonesy abandoning her and how Michael had ended up driving her home.

"You never told me he drove you home."

"It wasn't any big deal."

"Oddly enough, he never mentioned it either. When I asked you why you were all scraped up, somehow I never got the impression you fell out of Michael's car."

"You are making a bigger deal out of this than necessary." *Jealousy is not something I've seen in Jim before.*

"Why is it neither one of you mentioned it . . . to anybody, as far as I can figure?" The rest of their conversation was brief. Jim was clearly upset and Meg couldn't see the big deal.

When the phone rang again, a half hour later, Megan assumed it was Jim with more questions. "Hello," she was ready to fight.

"Can you believe that little twerp? Chris? Where does he get off saying that I cheated or that I was too stupid to know the answer?"

"Michael?"

He went on for another five minutes, clearly needing to blow off steam. Finally, he stopped. "You're smiling, aren't you?" he asked.

"Yes."

"Why?" he growled.

"Because you're mad that Chris thought you were a dumb jock and until two days ago you didn't know what a small rodent was that started with a 'v'."

"I'll have you know I have a 3.8 grade point average."

"Do you really?" she asked, obviously surprised.

"Yes."

"What started this to begin with?" She had never found out.

"You know, Mr. Alderson hates jocks, and he decided to have a contest. I think he was out to humiliate us, but it just didn't go the way he expected it to. There were five of us athletes on one team and five people with 3.7 or above on the other. Mr. Alderson fired questions at us--and we held our own," he softly chuckled. "I think everybody was surprised, even us."

She thought of all the games Mandy, Jonesy, and she had played growing up. "Jonesy's no slouch. He can actually be intelligent when he wants to be."

"Chris seemed to know you."

"Oh, yes. Chris and I were great friends when we were little. And, I want to thank you for not killing him. He's very excitable and often doesn't realize what he's saying."

"He wasn't worth my time or energy," he said disgustedly. Apparently he was done blowing steam. "Has he been in your woods?"

"Several times."

"Jim hasn't though, has he?"

She hesitated for a moment. "No, as a matter of fact, he hasn't." Actually she'd never thought much about it. He came and picked her up, dropped her off, and that was that. "Who's smiling now?"

"Mike!" she heard someone yell in the background.

"See ya." The line was dead before she could say anything. Slowly she put down the phone. *What was that all about?* Then, she smiled. Michael

35

MacKenzie had called her! All the girls said he was made of stone. There were several who had chased after him and had nothing to show for it. *Well, well, well. Hmm. What can I wear tomorrow that will catch his eye?*

> *October 10, 1966: Michael and Chris were having an argument in study hall today. And then Michael called on me (!) to set Chris straight. The whole place went dead, I swear.*
>
> *Jim phoned me after dinner, but all he wanted to talk about was what happened in my study hall. He seemed jealous. I'm not liking that side of him. There's nothing going on between Michael and me. But—wait 'til you hear this!*
>
> *Michael called me! I wonder where he got my phone number. I know it's no big deal, but still: Michael MacKenzie, my Adonis called me! I still think he's arrogant and conceited but HE CALLED ME!*

Megan could hardly contain herself. The ride to school was quiet. She wanted to tell Mandy about the phone call, but didn't dare say anything in front of Jonesy. She knew he would immediately tell Jim. There wasn't anything going on—but she sure wished there was!

Meg had forgotten that today the senior class would nominate five girls and five boys to serve on the Homecoming Court. On Friday, the entire school would vote for one of each. Then, at halftime, the king and queen would be crowned.

During study hall, the president of the Student Council came over the loudspeaker: "Listen up! Here are the seniors who have made the Homecoming Court . . ." As he read the list of females, Meg knew two of them. He read the male list. She was not surprised that Jonesy made it; but was stunned when Jim's name was called. *I had no idea my steady was that popular. Hmm, I wonder if I need a different dress. Mine is not fancy enough for the court.*

Meg's attention was drawn to the conversation behind her. She could hear Michael complaining to Randy, another football player. "Just put in your time and leave," Randy said.

"I will . . . but still . . ."

Michael stormed out as soon as the bell rang. "What is he pouting about now?" Megan caught up to Randy. She did not know him well, but she was dying to know what they had been talking about.

"Coach says we all have to attend the dance. The school has been supportive of us, we need to give back, that sort of thing."

"Hasn't he ever been to a dance before?" Meg smirked.

"I don't think it's that as much as that he has to get dressed up. Suit and tie."

"Ah."

October 12, 1966: Today the seniors announced their Homecoming Court. No surprise that Jonesy made it, he's always been popular; but I was really stunned when Jim made it. I had no idea. Mandy thinks the dress I picked out for the dance will be fine. I don't know. When I bought it, I wasn't planning on being a "court" date.

I also found out that all the football players have to attend the dance in a suit and tie. I wonder what Michael looks like dressed up. I can't wait to see.

Friday dawned. Students were keyed up. So far, the varsity team had won all of its games—and tonight, victory was expected. This was the coach's dream team. He had been able to handpick the cream of the crop from the three high schools that were now joined as one. He had four All-Americans and several Honorable Mentions on the varsity squad. There had only been a few injuries this season—nothing was going to stand in their way.

School was dismissed after the pep rally. Mandy and Megan started to get ready for the evening as soon as they got home. The Hills always went to the games to watch their son play; tonight the Becktames would join them.

"Don't you look lovely," said Megan's father as she came down the stairs. "Jim will be totally captivated when he sees you."

She smiled. *Actually, I dressed with Michael in mind.* She went over to the Hill's ahead of her parents, so she could talk to Jonesy before he left for the game.

Meg knocked on Jonesy's bedroom door. When she was sure he was decent, she let herself in. "Good luck tonight."

"Thanks," he tied his shoes and stood up. "What's that look for?"

"I just . . . no look . . . I was just wondering why Michael doesn't date."

"Don't tell me you're interested," he said with surprise in his voice.

"No, I'm just curious."

"Oh, God. I can see that look on your face. Are you crazy?"

"I am *not* interested!"

"I demand that you *not* be interested in Michael. I don't believe this. What's wrong with Jim? He's a nice guy."

"I like Jim. He's okay."

"Okay? You're going steady with him and the best that you can come up with is okay?"

"I said I liked him. Just tell me why Michael doesn't date. I'm curious."

"What makes you think he doesn't date?"

"I never hear about it. He never shows up at any of the parties or dances."

"He dates. He dates a certain type of girl. One-nighters. Get my drift?"

"Oh," she headed out the door, "that would explain the conversation I had with him."

"What? Megan, get back here!"

It was a brisk October night. Mandy and Megan sat frozen in the bleachers, along with all the other girls dressed to the hilt. They sat away from their parents, with Mandy's date. Finally, it was halftime and the Homecoming Court lined up on the field. "This has to be tough for you," said Mandy. "Dare I ask who you voted for today?"

"I voted for Jonesy, of course. I've known him a heck of a lot longer than I've known Jim." Mandy nodded.

There was a scream as the queen was crowned. Megan and Mandy jumped up and down with the crowd. Tracey was a friend of theirs. ". . . and her king is . . . Pat Gleason."

Meg let out a disgusted, "Oh." She leaned over and yelled in Mandy's ear above the whistles and clapping. "Another thing that Jonesy was robbed of because those stupid schools came over here."

"Meg—"

"First, he has to share being captain of the football team—and now this. God, he's having a rotten senior year."

"The college that he's been dying to go to offered him a football scholarship. He's got a bunch of new girls to date. He is co-captain of a football team that will probably win the state championship, and he's on the Homecoming Court. I'm thinking he's happy with his senior year."

They barely won the game. It was the closest the team had come to losing; most likely because all the guys on the Homecoming Court were football players and their minds weren't entirely on the game that night.

Even though Jim was on the court and had to escort one of the girls and dance the first dance with her, Megan still waited for him outside the locker room door. The hallway was filled with excitement as the queen and her court waited also.

The door slammed back and Michael stepped out. He was dressed in a suit.

Michael watched Megan as she looked him up and down. "Do I meet with your approval?" he growled.

"Your tie is crooked."

He took a deep breath and let it out loudly. "Are you going to fix it or just stare at me for the evening?" *If you want to know the truth—stare at you for the evening.*

Meg turned and handed her corsage and purse to Tracey. As she straightened Michael's tie, he stood still. Meg could feel his eyes on her. She hoped she gave the impression of boredom—she was anything but. She felt a presence next to her—Jim. His eyes shifted back and forth between her and Michael. Megan grabbed her corsage from Tracey. "Here, could you put this on me, please?" At first, Jim thought she was asking Michael, but then realized she was facing him. Jim pinned it on her.

Nobody could go out onto the dance floor until the court arrived. Jim was expected to escort Nancy onto the floor and have the first dance with her. Megan had gone to school with the petite brunette for five years. She knew Nancy had a solid track record of going through guys; and like Megan, Nancy was happy about having some new blood in the school. She swayed over, smiling. Batting her well-made up eyes, she said, "I hope you don't mind that Jim is escorting me."

Meg shrugged her shoulders. "No, not at all." This seemed to irritate Jim. *I'm sorry if I'm not the jealous type.* Nancy had slipped her hand through Jim's arm and was talking to him. Meg turned to see Michael still standing beside her. Arms across his chest, he glared at the clock in the hallway.

"What's the matter?" she asked.

"I hate this," he growled. "I don't care to be dressed up. I don't want to dance . . . I don't want to be here. One hour. That's all anybody else has to put in. I got an hour and five dances, seeing as how I complained so loudly. Where are those other three idiots?" he ended, referring to the football players on the court who had not as yet made an appearance. Before Megan could say anything, he headed for the locker room. He and Jonesy, who was just coming through the door, nearly collided.

"I thought he got all his aggression out while on the field," Jonesy mumbled. Several standing near him shook their heads.

The door flew open. Pat, his shirt still unbuttoned, carried his tie. Neal was carrying his shoes. "Let's go," ordered Michael. Nobody thought to oppose him; but they did move slowly in the hopes that Pat and Neal would be presentable by the time they arrived at the doors to the gym where the dance was held. Behind the court walked the football players with their dates. Meg waited thinking she would step in line soon when it hit her: she didn't have an escort and Michael didn't have a date. Slowly the two of them stepped in line behind everyone else.

"Great," she heard him mutter.

"What?"

"Thanks to Jim being popular, I get to escort *you* in."

"Don't bother!" she flared. "God, would it really hurt you to be pleasant and polite for one hour?"

As Meg tried to bypass the people in front of them, Michael grabbed her elbow. He leaned over to whisper in her ear, so as not to be heard. "Jim has to dance the first dance and more with Nancy. Coach is chaperoning. I have to dance at least five times. Might as well be with you."

"Gee, thanks. I feel so special."

"You're . . . I feel comfortable with you, okay?"

"Oh . . . okay." They walked quietly down the hall for a minute, then Meg turned to him and said, "Maybe you should date. Then you wouldn't feel so uncomfortable around girls."

Michael laughed so hard a dozen heads turned around. He looked at Mark, who was walking in front of him. "She thinks I should date. It would make me comfortable around girls." The hallway filled with laughter. *What did I say that is so funny?*

Through the whole first number, all Meg saw was Jim glaring at her and the only thing she could feel was the pressure of Michael's hand on her back pulling her into him. Her one hand rested in his and she prayed he couldn't feel her sweating.

"You do know," Michael said after some time, "that Nancy is trying to get her hooks into Jim tonight?"

"Yeah, let her."

"What?"

"I don't care. I mean—that's not what I meant. Of course, I care. I mean . . ." *No, I really don't care. She doesn't stand a chance though, from the way he's been talking to me.*

Michael studied her. "Did you vote for him for king?"

"No, I voted for Jonesy. Oh!" He couldn't stop himself from smiling, seeing her eyes big with horror. "Don't you dare tell Jim I said that!"

He chuckled. "Nice girlfriend he's got himself."

"I've known Jonesy a whole lot longer—" She did not need to defend herself.

The dance ended. Although he let go of her, Michael stayed by Meg's side. He looked around and saw that Jim was still engaged in court duties. "Do you want me to get you something to drink?"

He said it gruffly. Obviously he wanted her to say no. Meg smiled pleasantly. "Yes, thank you. That would be nice."

He glared at her and then walked off to get some punch. Meg's eyes followed him the entire length of the gym as he made his way back to her. "What are you staring at?" he asked, not handing her the glass until she answered.

"You look so handsome," she teased.

He leaned over and whispered in her ear, "Yes, you've always thought so." She felt her face redden.

Megan and Jim spent most of the night arguing. "You have to divide your time up between Nancy and me," she pointed out. "You don't see me asking you a hundred questions about it."

"You know very well why I have to spend time with her. And I'm not complaining about you dancing with her boyfriend or any other guy. I just don't see how it is that you are so chummy with Michael. What do you have on him?"

"Nothing. We're just friends. The coach said he had to dance five times—"

"I know! I was there! But every dance doesn't have to be with you. And, what was that crack about him dating?"

"I just thought he wouldn't feel so uncomfortable around girls if he dated—"

"Uncomfortable?" Meg thought Jim was going to come unglued. He bent down and whispered in her ear. "There isn't a guy here who isn't intimidated by him. By the same token, do you know how many girls have given their all to him? Michael is quite charming when he wants something. There isn't a girl who's been with him who doesn't talk about how sweet and kind he *really* is. He's just *misunderstood*. Trust me, the only complaint he's gotten is that he dumps them afterwards."

"Oh. Jonesy did mention—"

"So, what? Are you hoping to be added to his one-night stand list tonight?" Jim realized he'd gone too far when he saw the livid look on her face.

"How dare you speak to me like that!"

"God, Meg! I'm sorry, I'm sorry." He grabbed both her arms to hold her in place. She refused to look at him.

"It's just that . . . it's embarrassing for me. When you're not with me, you're with him— "

"Michael is keeping me company so that you can do your court duties. He's doing you a favor."

"Yeah, he's doing me a real favor."

Meg walked off, milling with the crowd. She was mad at Jim, but more than anything, she was mad at herself. She knew Jim was serious about her. He had told her enough times. She never reciprocated the feelings, but she hadn't discouraged him either. She wasn't being fair to him. Not that Meg felt she had a chance with Michael, but it wasn't fair to lead Jim on. He was a great guy; he just didn't set off any sparks for her.

Meg felt a hand encompass her elbow and felt herself being pulled to the dance floor. It was Michael. *Did he purposely choose another slow dance?*

He smiled. "Last dance and I am out of here."

"Lucky you." *I should have known.*

"What? You're not having a good time tonight?"

"Jim is just . . . he's driving me crazy."

Michael hesitated. "He does care about you, you know."

"How would you know?"

"You're all he talks about." *Great, wonderful.*

They danced in silence until Michael said softly, "You look beautiful tonight."

She looked up in surprise, "Thank you."

"You told me to be polite."

"Ah." *Yes, of course.*

As the music faded, Michael leaned over to whisper in her ear, his cheek barely brushing against hers. "Doesn't mean it isn't true though. Good night." He walked away and, with a wave to his coach, he walked out the door, leaving her alone on the dance floor.

October 14, 1966: I feel terrible! Tonight was Homecoming (we won again) and I broke up with Jim. It was awful. He kept telling me he loved me and he was sorry he had yelled at me all night about Michael. He told me I was breaking his heart. I feel terrible. He is a decent guy. I don't think anybody could treat me better, but I just don't feel anything when I'm with him.

Michael, on the other hand, puts butterflies in my stomach. Long after he left me on the dance floor, I could still feel his hand pressing into my back. His mouth against my ear sent a jolt through me that I want to feel again. I want to feel all of it again. But--who am I fooling? I know I don't stand a chance with him. Still, it's not right to lead Jim on just so I have a date every weekend.

Meg was surprised when she pulled into her driveway at five-thirty on Tuesday to see Michael's car parked there. She could feel her heart beat faster. *Stop it! There is some logical explanation for his being here. It's no big deal.*

Michael was just coming down the walk when he spotted her. "Hey, what are you doing here?" she smiled at him.

He took her in. He admired her long chestnut hair that would never let him study. Tight jeans, bulky sweater, high boots; he sighed inwardly. "I came to talk with you about something that's been on my mind. Where have you been?"

"I volunteer in town a couple of days a week at the veterinarian's office. What do you want to talk about that you couldn't say in study hall?" she screwed up her face. She couldn't imagine. He didn't answer. "Want to go for a walk?"

"I don't know. Maybe I should just mind my own business." He glanced over at his car. *No, don't go. Stay here with me.* "Yeah, okay." Instead of heading out to the woods, Meg started for the house. "Where are you going?" he asked.

"It's cold out. I'll make us some hot chocolate and popcorn to take with us."

They went into the kitchen, where her mother was cooking dinner. "You'll spoil your supper."

"Mom! You know I give most of the popcorn to the animals. I mainly want the hot chocolate because it's so cold out."

"Then stay inside. You can start a fire in the fireplace."

"Have you met Michael?" Her mother had her back to him.

She turned around. "Oh, hi. Yes, I had a very nice chat with him before you got here." She could tell her daughter was trying to get a message across to her, but she wasn't sure what it was. Mrs. Becktame looked at Michael and saw him casting his eyes around the kitchen. "Would you like to stay for supper?" She saw the startled look on Meg's face. *Okay, that wasn't what she was fishing for. She really just wanted the hot chocolate and popcorn?*

Michael hesitated, uncertain how to respond. "Why don't you stay?" said Meg. *Actually Mom, that's not a bad idea.* "What are we having, Mom?"

"Chicken fricassee with rice, green beans with almonds, and homemade crescent rolls."

Mother and daughter waited. Neither could read his expression. Finally, he realized they were waiting for an answer. "That sounds really good, Mrs. Becktame."

"Meg, set another plate. I have plenty of food," she assured him.

Michael made no protest and Meg got out another plate and some silverware. She was just setting it on the table when the front door opened. "I'm home!"

"Hey, Daddy."

Michael immediately came off the stool he was sitting on and was standing nearly at attention when Meg introduced her dad. "I read about you in the paper. You boys are having a great season this year."

"Yes, sir."

"I bet you've been offered some fine college scholarships."

"Yes, sir."

"Picked one yet?"

"No, sir."

It was obvious Michael was uncomfortable. "Well," said Mr. Becktame, "do I have time to change my clothes before dinner?"

"Yep."

As her dad took off upstairs, Michael headed for the front door. "I'm sorry. I can't stay, Mrs. Becktame. My mom expects me home for dinner."

Megan walked Michael out to his car. "What was that all about?"

45

"What?"

"You were fine 'til my dad got home." He shrugged his shoulders. She remembered Jim telling her that Michael's father drank. She thought of the voice yelling Mike in the background the one time he called. The voice did not sound like it belonged to a pleasant person. Is that why Michael was nervous? "My dad is a very nice guy."

"I'm sure he is." He hesitated a moment. "Your parents are a lot older than I expected."

"Yeah, I hear that a lot. My mom had several miscarriages before she had me. Why don't you come back in?"

"No!" he said sharply, then his face softened. "Food sure smelled good. Although I don't even know what chicken fricassee is."

She explained what it was. "My mom's a gourmet cook."

"Well, thank you; but I really need to get going."

"What is it you wanted to say to me?" He looked around and then proceeded to get in his car. "Michael."

He rolled down his window and she leaned in. Still not looking at her, he said, "I know it's none of my business but . . . I understand you broke up with Jim after the dance. I hate to think that it's because . . . well, because I danced with you. Some of the guys overheard Jim yelling at you."

"You had nothing to do with it. Jim is a great guy, he just isn't the one for me. He was getting too serious."

"He is nuts about you, though." *I feel so much better now, thank you.*

"Personally, I can't see the attraction," he smiled up at her. "See ya later, eagle eyes."

October 17, 1966: Michael came over after practice. He wanted to talk about me breaking up with Jim. He seemed concerned that he was responsible. Surely that means something. I mean, why would he care? Mom invited him to stay for dinner but he didn't. I can't believe he came over to the house just to discuss that.

It surprised no one that the varsity football team went on to become state champs. Michael was awarded Most Valuable Player and named to the All-Conference Team and the All-State Team. This surprised no one either, especially Michael, since he had won several awards and trophies in athletics already.

CHAPTER 6

November 10, 1966: It snowed for the first time. We got just a little. Michael helped me with my homework in study hall but he wouldn't even look at me.

November 14, 1966: Michael just sits behind me and doesn't offer anything. He barely speaks to me and when he does it's only to answer my question. Jonesy says he always shuts people out. I've known that from the beginning, but somehow I thought I was different.

November 21, 1966: Another week of being ignored by Michael. I wonder what he would say if I asked him out, seeing as how he's never going to do it. I see Jim with that puppy dog look and I feel just awful. There are plenty of girls who like him--why doesn't he ask one of them out?

November 25, 1966: Over Thanksgiving vacation I went out with Mandy's cousin Aaron. He's not too bad looking. I haven't seen him in about five years. We went to the show with Jonesy and his latest fling, Jill. I wonder what Michael is doing over vacation. I walk around in my woods and just dream about him. It's not fair. I think about him way too much and he doesn't think about me at all!

December 1, 1966: I know that girls don't ask guys out, but I am seriously toying with the idea of asking Michael. What harm could it do if I ask him to just come over and go for a walk with me in my woods? That wouldn't really be considered a date, would it? Every time I think about him whispering in my ear Homecoming night I get butterflies in my stomach. He doesn't tap his pencil behind me anymore. Surely that means something.

December 3, 1966: Michael, Michael, Michael. I am in love with Michael MacKenzie and he doesn't even know I exist. Mrs. Megan MacKenzie. I think that has a nice ring to it.

Meg felt a tap on her shoulder the second Miss Quinn walked out the door. She leaned back. "What?"

"Do you ever walk in your woods in all this snow?" There was a good foot of snow on the ground.

"Sure, all the time."

"Are you going tonight?"

"After I get back from the vet's."

"You're still working there?"

"I volunteer there." He said nothing more, so she turned in her chair to see his head in his book. "Would you like to come over tonight?"

He didn't look at her. "What would be a good time, if I decided to do that?"

"I have my mom's car today, so I'm going directly from school. I'll be home around five, five-thirty. Why not come then?"

"That's dinnertime."

"No, not tonight. My dad won't be home until late, so mom and I will just eat leftovers whenever we both feel like it. You could eat with us."

"No, that's all right. Maybe I'll be over."

"Okay, suit yourself."

Six-thirty found Megan wandering alone in the woods. She had walked past the stream and was deep into the acreage. If Michael showed up, her tracks would be easy to follow in the snow. She was crying, when she heard the snap of a twig. *No!* She had not wanted Michael to find her like this. Indeed, she had given up on him coming at all. She quickly blew her nose, dabbed her eyes, and turned around. *Where is he?* She was sure she had heard a twig break. *There he is. Headed back the other way.* "Michael!" she yelled.

He kept walking at a fast pace, so she ran after him. "Michael! Would you stop? I know you can hear me!"

He stopped, but kept his back to her. She walked around him, out of breath. "Why are you leaving?"

"Oh, come on, Meg," he said disgustedly. "I'm an hour later than I said I would be and you're out here blubbering away." He took off walking.

She was too flabbergasted to do anything but stand there with her mouth open. "You are really something, you know that?" she finally managed to get out. "I knew you had a big head, but I didn't realize it was that big! Did I not say I was going to the vet's today after school? I've been helping out with a sick dog for over a week. When I left him two days ago he seemed to be getting better. Today, he died when I got there—like he was waiting for me to say . . ." her eyes welled up again. "Just get out of here!"

Meg headed back into the woods. She had cried for a short while at the vet's office, but not wanting Michael to have to wait for her, she had hurried home. And, not wanting Michael to see her sobbing, she had only allowed herself a short cry in the woods; holding it in as best she could so that if he showed up, she could pull herself together quickly. Now that he was gone, she sobbed loudly, her whole body shaking.

Meg didn't know how long she had been crying when she felt hands on her shoulders slowly massaging her. *Forget it, Michael!* She kept on crying.

"I'm sorry," Michael turned her around and wrapped his arms around her. She cried into his jacket while he held her.

"It wasn't your dog, was it?" he finally asked, as she continued to cry.

"No, but he was so young and friendly. He was so cute," she started up again.

"Oh, honey, you shouldn't—" he stopped. *No, she's crying too hard to have heard me.* Eventually she stopped and he let go.

Meg blew her nose. "Do you want to walk some?"

"Sure."

They walked quietly. Occasionally she would point out an animal or a familiar spot. "Did Jonesy ever tell you about the time . . ." Meg was daydreaming when suddenly her foot shot out from under her and she fell. She buried her face in her hands. *Why do I make a complete fool out of myself every time I am with him? This never happened when I was dating Jim or out with Mandy's cousin! I am an absolute klutz with this guy. It's not fair. No, no, do not start crying again.*

Michael stood over her. "I guess this is one of those walks where I should have offered my arm."

Slowly she looked up at him. "Yes. This is all your fault." Michael grinned and held out his hand. He helped Meg to her feet and she slipped her arm through his. They continued walking.

"Michael, why do you shut people out?"

He was silent for a long time and then said, "As an only child, do you ever wonder why you're here?"

"What?"

"I mean, maybe you aren't supposed to be here. Maybe you're a mistake, maybe you're a surprise." She stopped and stared at him, dumbfounded. "I guess you've never thought that way."

"No, I haven't!"

"Well, I don't mean . . . I'm sure your parents love you. They at least treat you decently. Don't they?"

"Yes."

He looked around to avoid eye contact. "I personally don't think that way, because I'm one of ten, but . . . I do wonder why I'm the hated one."

"What do you mean? I don't think any of the guys hate you. Scared of you, maybe but . . . the guys say you're a lot of fun when you want to be."

"No, no," he shook his head. "Never mind. Forget it. And please don't think anything about being an only child. It's quite obvious *your* parents care about you."

"Why would you think your parents don't care about you?"

"Because they don't!" he yelled. "Well, my mom does; but my dad— it's getting dark out. I've got to go." He took off at a brisk pace.

She hurried after him. She had almost caught up with him when he swung back around. "Don't, Meg! Don't!" She stopped. "Rule Number One: Don't get close to anyone, don't let anybody in. Just stay away from me. For your own good, stay away from me."

"That's an awfully lonely road," she said. "I have Mandy . . . and Jonesy, actually. I tell him a lot of stuff. And some of the other girls that I hang out with at school. But to not have anybody to confide in. You have to have somebody, Michael. I'm not implying me—just somebody. I know you used to be good friends with Jim, he told me so. Jonesy is a good listener—"

"You don't understand."

"I would be willing to listen."

No," he got in his car and left.

December 7, 1966: I had a bad day at the vet's. A dog that I've been helping with died. I was crying when Michael showed up. We went for a walk. He actually comforted me, hugged me, and I swear he called me honey. In the end, though, he left in a huff. He told me Rule Number One was don't let anyone in. Is that why he acts so mean and rude? And the times that he's fun and friendly are when he's let his guard down? Why would you want to live like that? I get these little glimpses of a really great guy and then 'slam' I'm out in the cold. I think if he would just stay mean and rotten I could get him out of my system. As it is, when he hugged me, it was wonderful, even though I was bawling my eyes out. I just don't understand him.

December 8, 1966: Michael didn't come to study hall today, although I know he was in school. Surely he is not skipping class because of me?

December 19, 1966: Last day before school is out for Christmas. Michael has been in and out of study hall. He does not speak to me. I did ask him what he'd been doing and I got a very curt "I'm busy." I have two weeks to get him out of my system, and as rude as he's been, I should be able to do that. But can I?

"I'm bored!" Meg yelled at the house in general.

"You've only been out two days. Go over to the Hill's," her dad hollered, and then went back to reading his newspaper.

"I just came from the Hill's. They're dull. You want to play cribbage?"

"Boy, you are desperate. Go get the board."

An hour later Mandy called. "Get ready, we're going tobogganing."

"And tell her to be ready when I get there!" Jonesy hollered in the background.

Meg gave her dad an affectionate hug, so he wouldn't complain about her leaving in the middle of a game, then she ran to get ready.

As it turned out, several of their friends were also there. Megan spotted Lydia, Jonesy's latest heartthrob, whom she didn't trust. So far, he had not made much headway with her; but today it looked like he was getting some place. *Oh no, you don't,* thought Megan as she watched Lydia. *I know your game. The guy you're after isn't here, so Jonesy will do nicely for the day. Well, you can't have him.* Meg snuck up behind Jonesy and with a yell jumped on his back. The two of them slid down the hill, arms and legs flying. Jonesy was furious. "See what you did?" he yelled at Meg as they watched Lydia sail by with a guy on a saucer.

"She's not for you," said Meg. "She's just using you for the day. There are girls here who are actually interested in you—go after one of them."

"And why don't *you* go back to Jim or one of the other guys I know who would like to take you out—instead of running after Michael?" Meg stormed off in a huff.

"It's our turn!" yelled Mandy, flagging them both. The toboggan held eight. Six people were yelling for the two of them to hurry up. Meg scrambled up the hill and waited for Jonesy. She felt him wrap his legs and arms around her.

She turned her head slightly, "I'm sorry. You're right. Cripe, am I that obvious? If you noticed, that means everybody knows." *Great.* "Hey, who wants to ask me out?"

"Ready?" someone up front questioned.

"Ready!" Megan hollered.

"Give us a push, Jonesy," she heard behind her.

Give us a push Jonesy? Who am I leaning on? She carefully tilted her head back to see Michael smiling at her upside down.

"Hi."

She bolted upright. When had he arrived? And what exactly had she just said? The ride down was a complete blur. He got off and helped her up. "What are you being obvious about?"

She was glad her cheeks were already red from the cold; otherwise he would see her blushing. "Something stupid Jonesy said, that's all."

"See the guy over there, in the gray jacket?" He pointed.

"Yeah."

"He wants to ask you out." She glared at him. "Do you want me to introduce you?"

"No!"

"Why not?"

"I'm not interested, thank you." She started up the hill.

He walked beside her. "Well, I guess I'm stuck with you for the rest of the day with that attitude."

"What?"

"You don't want to meet him and with me nearby he won't dare come over and introduce himself or . . ." he indicated with his head, "have Jonesy do it." Meg looked over to see Ron (she at least knew his name) and Jonesy talking as they looked in her direction.

"Why would your presence stop him?" she demanded.

He smiled. "You know very well, everybody's scared of me." She made a face at him and walked off.

Michael was still standing beside her, waiting for the next ride, when she realized someone was talking to him. Megan slapped the back of her hand against Michael's arm. "He's cute. Introduce me to him." She had meant it as a joke, but the look Michael gave her was not one of amusement.

Michael turned to the guy next to him, who was grinning from ear to ear. His eyes were on Megan as he ignored the grilling look. "Yes, Michael. Introduce us."

"Fine. This is Meg. This is my brother Josh."

"Your brother?" Michael had told her he was one of ten; however, it had never occurred to her that she went to school with any of his siblings. "What grade are you in?"

"Sophomore."

"I'm a junior."

"Yeah, I know." Unlike Michael, he smiled readily. She could see the family resemblance now. The blonde hair, the straight nose, the blue eyes. He was a smaller version of his older brother.

"How do you like going to Lyons?"

"Are we going down again or not?" Michael asked her gruffly.

She glanced from one to the other. "Sure."

She was pleasantly surprised to find that Michael stayed with her the entire time they were at the park. Josh soon disappeared with his own set of friends. By the time it was getting dark, everyone was wet and cold. It was decided that they would all descend on the Hill's house. Their door was always open to the kids and Mrs. Hill could be counted on to have snacks and soft drinks in the house.

An hour later, the kids were sitting by the fireplace with hot chocolate in their hands, eating popcorn, and waiting for brownies to come out of the oven. Everybody was in good spirits. Music was playing, the pool table was in use—it was a party. Megan looked at her watch. She was expected home for dinner. She would love to have Michael walk her home, but she knew if she asked him in front of anyone it would be an immediate no.

Mrs. Hill appeared with warm brownies. As the kids gathered around her, Meg turned to Michael, "Would you mind walking me home? Mom's waiting dinner."

Michael looked at the brownies, which were quickly being devoured. "You live next door. Don't tell me there's something in your woods that you're afraid of when it's dark."

"Never mind." Meg started to walk out of the room, with her feminine intuition telling her that Michael would follow. She turned to see him head for the brownies. *That's it! That's the last straw! Brownies, over me? When am I ever going to learn? What was that guy's name? Ron? He was cute. I'll have Jonesy introduce us. I am not sitting around anymore! This is my year to shine. Michael's number one rule is don't let anybody in. Mine is meet new blood. And I haven't been doing a very good job of it.*

Meg jammed her arms in her jacket sleeves and swore under her breath when she heard it rip. *Look what he's done now. Ripped my favorite jacket!*

"Here, I got you one; but it's still pretty hot. Trust me." Meg turned to see Michael holding out a brownie to her. He was running his tongue along the roof of his mouth where he'd burned himself.

"The cold air will do that good." She held onto both brownies while he got his varsity jacket on.

"It's really neat through here," Michael said as they walked along a well-worn path in the snow. Jonesy, Mandy, and Meg had blazed a trail between the two houses years ago, and it was still regularly used. The moon was out, so they could see clearly.

Michael stopped just before the glow of her porch light. It was snowing and Meg opened her mouth, stuck out her tongue, and tried to catch snowflakes. He watched her and said unexpectedly, "Do you ever wonder what you'll do after high school?"

"No, I don't wonder. I know."

"Oh?"

"Yeah. I'm going to go to college and become a veterinarian."

"That's why you volunteer at the vet clinic?"

"Yeah."

"I didn't realize you were into it that much. Why don't you have any dogs or cats of your own?"

"I've always been told it's because my mom is allergic; but a few years ago Jonesy said something to me about how my mom comes over and she never seems fazed by their two dogs and cat, except for the fact that she has a fit about all the hair. She doesn't sneeze, she doesn't swell up, she doesn't take anything for them so . . . I guess I don't have any pets because my mom is kind of a clean freak. I enjoy the Hill's pets." He nodded. "Do you have any pets?"

"We have a dog, an old mongrel that came one day and never left."

They stared at each other. "Okay, well, I'll see ya. Thank you for the brownie and walking me home. I appreciate it."

"Meg? Are you . . . busy Saturday night?"

She thought for a moment. "I imagine Mandy and I will find something to do. We talked about going to the show." She shrugged her shoulders. "I guess that's what I'll be doing."

He looked at her and then nodded. "Okay, see ya."

Wait a minute. Wait a minute! "You weren't insinuating that you . . ."

No, he will just laugh at me. As if he would ask me out. But, what if that's what he meant and I blew it? I'll kill myself.

He turned around and looked at her. "What did you think I was getting at?"

"I know you! I could very well see you saying, 'Oh, nothing to do? I'll go back and tell Ron. He was asking me to find out.'"

He chuckled. "Well, I'd ask you; but you've got big plans with Mandy."

"Mandy who?" He stared at her. He was beginning to regret his impulsive question. "Honest to Pete! That is what you were going to say, isn't it? I knew it! Good-bye Michael."

"No, Meg. Wait! I was not! Would you please go out with me Saturday night?" She had disappeared into the shadows, but he was relatively certain she was still there.

"Yes."

"I'll call you."

"Okay. Bye."

"Bye."

December 21, 1966: We went tobogganing today with a bunch of kids from school. Had a great time because Michael showed up and stayed with me the whole time. Went to Hill's afterwards and he walked me home. I think he likes it out in my woods. But the big news is: He asked me out! I can't believe it! I was so excited I tripped and landed on the sidewalk. I know he couldn't see me, so hopefully he didn't hear me. The butterflies in my stomach won't go away. I'm so excited! Also met his brother Josh at the park. Cute, but he's only a sophomore.

By Saturday morning, Meg decided she had dreamt the whole thing. Michael hadn't called. *He said Saturday night, didn't he? Maybe he meant in a couple of years.*

In the afternoon, Meg went skating with Jonesy, only to come home and have her mom tell her that Michael had called. *Of course, I wait for days and nothing. The minute I step outside . . . With my luck, he won't call again.*

But, he did, an hour later. "About tonight . . ." Her heart sank. He was calling it off, she could tell. Rule Number One was going to prevail. "Would you like to go to a movie?"

"Yeah."

"What would you like to see?" *He's going to let me pick?* She named a show she'd seen advertised that sounded good. She heard a rustling of newspaper.

"I found it. It's showing at the Twin Stars. Do you know where that's located?"

"Yeah."

"Okay. I'll meet you there."

"What?" *He couldn't have said--*

"I'll meet you there."

She was confused. "Why?"

"I'll meet you at seven, okay?"

"No, not okay. Just come here and get me." *Was this his way of not having to pay? How can I tell people I went out on a date with Michael when I had to drive myself there, pay for it, and drive myself home? I am so glad I didn't call up my friends, except Mandy, and tell them I was going out with him. They would love to hear this story.*

"I'm not going to."

"Why not?" She could feel her anger start to rise.

"You'd be ten minutes late just sitting upstairs already to go and I'd have to sit and make small talk with your parents. Then I'd have to bring you all the way home, which is out of my way. It's just easier my way. So, no hassle, okay?"

"Look, if you don't have the money to pay for me, I understand. I'll pay, but—"

"No, that's not it. I plan on paying for both of us."

"Well, thank you for that. I tell ya what. I'll meet you halfway. I'll be ready and downstairs when you get here and I'll instruct my parents to keep to simple questions that are within your intelligence range."

"Cute," he sneered. "Just meet me there, okay?"

"No," she was mad now. *I'm not worth driving all the way here for? Jim never had a problem.* "If you're not man enough to come and get me, then you're not man enough to take me out!"

She heard a sharp intake of breath. "Is that so?"

"Yes, that's so."

"Very well then. Good-bye." The dial tone buzzed in Meg's ear.

The nerve! She slammed down the phone. *Who does he think he is?* She thought about when she had told Mandy that Michael had asked her out. Mandy had been excited for her, but apprehensive. "I know he has his rude moments; but gosh, is he gorgeous. Jonesy says he keeps to himself. Why do you think that is? But then I hear some of the girls say he's really nice when they've been alone with him. I don't know, Meg. I know you're excited; but Jonesy will have a fit." *Yeah, well, if they find out about this, they will be laughing at me. 'She actually thought she had a date with him? That'll be the day!'*

She ran through the woods to Mandy's house. "Can you believe it?" she ended.

Mandy looked at her. "You turned down a date with Michael MacKenzie? Jonesy will be relieved."

"You can't call that a date." They stared at each other. "Can you?"

"Well, he was going to pay, sit next to you, and maybe get you something to eat afterwards. Do you know how many girls are after him?"

Megan flopped down on the bed. "Yeah, I know. He's never going to ask me out again, is he? Why do I always let my temper get the best of me?"

She sat in her room, alone, and heard the hall clock chime eight times. Deep down she knew Michael wouldn't show up, although she had hoped he'd be mad enough to prove her wrong.

Megan was bored, so she got out some of her homework. Her dad came into her room. "I thought you had a date tonight, kitten."

"Oh, Daddy. I'm afraid I let my pride get in the way and I said something I shouldn't have." She told him what happened.

"You did the right thing," he said.

"You say that because I'm your little girl and nobody's good enough to take me out."

He chuckled. "I wouldn't have let you go out and meet him at some show—even if you had told him yes. There'll be plenty of others."

"Nobody's like Michael."

"I don't know. He seemed pretty stiff to me. Jim would at least talk to me."

"I think he has some family problems, mainly his dad. At least that's the rumor."

"Meg," her mother hollered up the stairs. "Michael's here!"

Her eyes grew wide and she ran to the window. That heap of junk had never looked so good. "Oh, Daddy! He came! He really came! When you go downstairs please be pleasant! No, maybe you'd better stay up here! No, Michael has to learn how to talk to you. No, maybe another day. No, he's got to learn that you're a good guy . . . but maybe not tonight—"

"Megan," her dad butted in. "Get ready. I've already made *my* decision. I'm going down and talking to him. Bye."

"Daddy. Daddy, wait." *Oh. I better hurry.* She was already dressed and had on her makeup. Meg ran a brush through her hair. It would have to do. She didn't want her dad running Michael off before the date even started. However, she did take a quick detour to her parents' room and whispered into the phone to Mandy, "He's here! He really came. I'll call ya tomorrow."

She was glad to see that Michael was a bit more relaxed tonight. Apparently her Dad had found the right topic to discuss—sports.

Michael didn't smile at her, but he stood up when she entered the room. "Sorry I'm late." It was all he offered and she knew he didn't mean it, but she didn't care. She told him it was all right. A few minutes later, they were out the door. He gave her no further explanation and she did not ask for one. It was enough that he had come.

"I think we can make the nine o'clock showing," he offered.

"Okay." Usually she sat close to her date, but with Michael she felt uneasy. More than likely he'd tell her to sit on her own side, so that was where she stayed.

He never looked at her or said anything. *So, this is my date with Michael MacKenzie.* Finally, Meg broke the silence by asking, "You're still mad at me, huh?"

"If I was, I wouldn't have shown up."

"Well then, would it be too much to ask you to turn on the heat?"

"That's one of the things I didn't get to tell you this afternoon. This car has no heat."

"You're trying to get back at me, aren't you?"

"Try it yourself." She leaned over and flipped all the switches. Nothing. "There's a blanket in the back." She got it out and wrapped it around her. "It's not that cold," he said as her teeth started to chatter.

"It's freezing! Did you know it's winter out?" *Some date. At least I will remember this one.*

"Should have met me," was his only comment.

They arrived in time for the show. Standing in the lobby, Michael took off his varsity jacket and wrapped it around her shoulders. They found two seats and sat down. He handed her a soft drink, but she shook her head. "I'm not taking a cold drink until my hands warm up."

"Oh, honestly. Give 'em to me," he said. She smiled slightly. He made it sound like they were detachable.

He set down the popcorn and drinks and took her hands in his, rubbing them together. "They feel like ice. Don't you know enough to wear gloves in the winter time?"

"I wore my mittens." She stared at him. She still found it hard to believe she was out with him. His hands were rough but warm and she loved the feel of them. Now that football season was over, he was letting his blonde hair grow. *Not bad, not bad at all.* He dropped her hands abruptly when the movie started. He handed her the drink, offered her popcorn, and then leaned as far away from her as possible.

They finished the popcorn and he moved the bag. *Will he hold my hand now? No, apparently not, since his arm is on the armrest.* As engrossed as Meg was in him, that's how engrossed Michael was in the movie. *Should I put my arm next to his? I can't tell my friends that he didn't even hold my hand. This is like going out with Jonesy or his cousin. And, if he isn't going to hold my hand in the theater, obviously I'm not going to get a kiss at the end of the night either. That will be humiliating. I can hear it now.*

Okay, I can't possibly embarrass myself more than I already have with this guy. The most that will happen is he'll tell me no. Why can't this be a scary movie? Then I'd have some justification. What if this is my one and only date with him? Might as well make the most of the night. Here goes. Cautiously Meg slipped her hand under his elbow and slid her hand down his arm. Michael shifted towards her, taking her hand in his. "You still cold?" he whispered.

"Yeah."

He smiled and rubbed her hand. "It feels awfully warm to me."

Embarrassed at being found out, Meg tried to pull her hand away, but Michael wouldn't let go. Instead, he chuckled and held her hand throughout the rest of the movie. She couldn't concentrate on the screen at all. *Now, this is a date.*

Back out in the cold, he insisted she continue to wear his jacket. And, once they were in the car, he bundled her up in the blanket as well, pulling her next to him.

Even though Meg wasn't as cold as before, she was not going to make out in his car. But she was going to get a kiss—even if she had to make the first move. Meg hadn't come this far just to hold hands.

When they arrived at her house, Michael walked her to the door. "Why don't you come in for a little bit?" she offered.

"No, that's okay. I should get going," he backed away from her.

You are not leaving until I get a kiss. "My parents are upstairs and won't disturb us. We can sit by the fireplace and get warm. I'll fix us some hot chocolate."

He wavered for a moment and then stepped inside. Her mom called down once to make sure it was them and then they were left alone.

When Meg entered the living room with their drinks, Michael had a fire roaring. He must have been colder than he had let on because he was practically sitting in it. She could sense his uneasiness as he looked around the room.

"What's wrong?" she asked.

"I just feel very uncomfortable here."

"Why?" She was hurt.

"I . . . I just . . . don't fit in here. I mean, I look at this place and think of what I have to go home to. There's a bit of a contrast. It must be nice to have money."

"Don't make me feel bad because my dad can provide for me." She sat down on the sofa. He made her feel uncomfortable with his talk.

"I didn't mean that."

"I know you didn't, but you mustn't look at everything so materialistically."

"Why is it always the ones with money who say that?" She started to retort, then realized she had no answer; so she quickly shoved the mug to her open mouth.

He suddenly turned to her. "Come here." She looked up at him, startled. The tone was anything but inviting. She half expected him to snap his fingers at her, as if she was his pet dog.

"No."

They stared each other down. She had never had a date like him before. And she wasn't about to let Michael get the best of her, especially in her own home.

Finally he said, "It's warm by the fire. Why don't you come sit here?"

She shook her head. "I'm comfortable."

He turned back around to face the fire and she could hear herself screaming inside. *Stupid, stupid, stupid! What am I trying to prove, sitting over here by myself? I have dreamed of this moment for months—to do what? To tell him no and let him figure out that I really mean yes? Well, I can hardly get up and sit next to him now. Why can't I ever act normal around him? It's the darn butterflies in my stomach.* She tried to think of something to say to break the silence. "You come from a large family. That's something I've always wanted."

"Whatever for?" he snarled.

"It's not fun being an only child."

"Yeah, I can see it's killing you," he mumbled. He suddenly stood up. "Time to go."

She nearly spilled her drink hurrying to get up. "Wait!" *Darn, I am going to have to make the first move. If only I had sat by him.*

"What?" he asked, while throwing on his jacket and putting his hand on the door knob.

Surprising herself, since she did not consider herself a forward person, Megan wrapped her arms around his neck. Michael made no protest, yet he did not move towards her either. There was an awkward silence. Slowly she brought her arms down.

"Meg," he said quietly, looking at the floor. "I have tried so hard to freeze you out. You don't want to become involved with me."

"Yes, I do," she said, before she could even think.

He looked at her and cupped his hands around her face. "I guess winter has to yield to spring sometime." Before she could ask what he meant, Michael brought his lips down on hers. His arms came around her shoulders, pulling her into him. This wasn't a young boy's gentle virginal kiss. It was hard and rough and had fire flowing through it.

"Don't go," she said, feeling him release her.

"I have to. It's late."

"Will I see you later this week? Over vacation?"

"Meg . . . don't expect anything from me. I can't deliver. I'm sorry." He shook his head. "You sit in front of me with that gorgeous hair and I wonder what it would be like to run my fingers through it, to kiss you . . . to take long walks with you in your woods . . . I have to go," he said abruptly.

"Michael —"

He was gone.

December 23, 1966: I went out with Michael tonight. It didn't start out great, seeing as how he has no heat in his car--but it ended just fine, I think. He came and picked me up and we went to the show. He got me popcorn and a drink, held my hand and gave me his varsity jacket to wear! Then, we sat romantically by the fire. It was wonderful when he kissed me! But after that, he acted strangely. I don't understand him. I just know I'm madly in love with him.

That was the only date Meg had with Michael for the rest of Christmas vacation. Jonesy did ask her about going out with Ron. "You are not setting me up," she complained.

"No, I'm not setting you up. He wanted to meet you when we went tobogganing, except Michael never left your side," he added disgustedly.

"Yes, that was a shame, wasn't it?" she grinned. Jonesy did not smile back.

She wondered what Michael was up to. In reality, he probably hadn't given her a second thought the minute he was out her door—and she knew it. That's what really burned her. Here she was, spending every waking minute thinking of him, and for all she knew, he was dating someone else.

"I have had a dismal Christmas," moaned Megan.

"Yeah, it must be tough getting only one present," sneered Jonesy.

Megan glanced out the window at her new car. "Well, what else was there to get me? It's the only thing I wanted." *Besides Michael.*

"Then stop complaining," yelled Mandy.

Megan started to explain that getting one present wasn't the issue. She was disappointed that Michael hadn't come around or called since their first date. She asked Jonesy why he was so against her dating him. "Because Michael only dates one type of girl—easy. And I don't want you to get that kind of reputation."

"I don't think that's true. Those are just rumors."

"Meg," he looked at her, "I've played football with the guy all season, talked to his friends that he grew up with, and I think I know him a little bit better than you. Don't date him; you'll get yourself a reputation. Don't do this to yourself. He'll be gone in another few months and you still have a year of high school left. Forget him. He's not worth it." *Easy for you to say. You didn't kiss him.*

December 25, 1966: I got a car! It's the only present I got, but I don't care. I have my own car! Haven't heard a word from Michael since our date. All I do is dream about that man. I have a car!

CHAPTER 7

I T FELT GREAT DRIVING TO SCHOOL IN HER SHINY NEW CAR. NO more riding the bus or catching a ride with Jonesy! All of the guys came over to look at it—except Michael. Megan saw him briefly as he got out of his car and, without even looking her way, went into the building. Still, she was undaunted.

When Megan got to study hall, Michael was already sitting at his desk with his head in a book. "Hi," Meg sat down, hoping she sounded friendly and nothing more.

Michael didn't look at her, although he did raise a hand in acknowledgment. *Well, at least he didn't totally ignore me.* "I see you're in one of your more friendly moods today."

This produced a sheepish grin. "How was your vacation?" he asked, still without looking up.

"Fine. And yours?"

"So-so. Miss Quinn is getting ready to yell."

"Becktame turn around! MacKenzie, must you always be talking?" Thus ended their conversation.

"I'll meet you at my car!" Megan hollered to Mandy at the end of the day. When she went out, Michael was propped against it.

"Is this a joke or is it really yours?" he asked upon seeing her.

"It's all mine. You like it?"

"Very nice. God, it's rough being an only child with money."

She could feel her temper start to rise, but she didn't want that. "My mom is tired of me either asking for the car or having to take me someplace when she wants to use the car also. This was just a solution to a problem."

"Yeah."

"Would you like to take it for a spin?" She didn't know what she was thinking. The words came out before she could stop herself.

He suddenly perked up. "Yeah." *Now what am I going to say? Dad has told me a hundred times that nobody, but nobody, is to drive my car. I haven't even let Mandy or Jonesy drive it in the driveway. They will be furious if they find out Michael has driven it.* She threw him the keys.

They drove off as Mandy emerged from the school. "Hey!" Megan heard Mandy yell, yet she chose to ignore her friend. They left her standing in the bitter cold—and Megan felt guilty twice over.

"A bunch of us are going tobogganing tonight. You going?" he asked.

"No, I wasn't invited."

"So, now you're invited. Want to go?"

"Is this a pick-me-up or a meet-you-there invitation?"

He smiled. "I never did get that heater fixed in my car."

She considered her options. Her dad wouldn't let her drive around alone at night and she had no idea what Jonesy's plans were for the evening—the future did not look good. "All right. No use in both of us freezing. You drive to my house and then we'll go in my car from there."

"Such a bargain. I drive."

"Not with my dad watching out the window you won't," she retorted.

He looked at her with the realization that he wasn't supposed to be driving her car now. "Fine. But when we're out of sight, we're switching drivers. I am not being chauffeured by you."

"Okay." She would be in so much trouble if Jonesy or Mandy got mad enough to tell on her. He pulled up next to Mandy and got out.

"Thanks for leaving me," Mandy complained as soon as she had the door open.

"I'm sorry, but I forgot you," Megan said. *Whoops!*

"Thanks! And what's the idea of letting him drive?" Megan ignored the rest of the conversation.

Later in the evening, Megan was surprised to open the front door to Michael but no car. She looked around. "Where'd you come from?"

"You didn't think I'd freeze my tail off for you, did you? I got a ride to Jonesy's and then I walked through your woods."

She told her parents good-bye and they walked out the door. Megan drove the car down the driveway when Michael said, "Okay, my turn." They switched seats.

Since it was a school night, there weren't nearly as many kids as before and when the temperature started to drop, everybody decided to call it an early night. Jonesy had finally made an impression on Lydia, so he wasn't happy with this turn of events. Plus, he didn't like Megan being alone with Michael. So, to kill two birds with one stone, he suggested they all go out for pizza, knowing full well that Megan would pick up on it.

"Sounds good to me," Meg said, and then realized that Michael had hesitated. "Well, whatever you want to do."

"No, that's fine."

Inside the pizzeria Megan blew on her hands and rubbed them. "I've never seen anybody get so cold so fast," Michael said, shaking his head.

"She's actually gotten better," offered Jonesy.

When their order was announced, Jonesy was too taken up with Lydia to hear; and since Megan and Michael had been looking everywhere except at each other, Michael was relieved to get up from the table to retrieve it. However, that left Megan alone to watch Jonesy nibble on Lydia's ear. *Oh, how gross! Hmm. What is taking Michael so long?* She turned to see that he was surrounded by four girls, all of whom were tossing their shiny locks, batting their eyes, and giggling. *How revolting!* One girl even went so far as to rest her hand on Michael's arm. Megan must have said something out loud because the next thing she knew Jonesy had kicked her under the table. He gave her a look and then, peering over Lydia's head, hollered, "Let's go, Michael! I'm starving!"

When Michael returned to the table, he said nothing—no explanation or apology to Meg. The two of them ate in silence, while Jonesy and Lydia laughed and talked. At one point Meg caught Michael's eye and rolled hers. He just smiled.

When they were finished eating, they left the pizzeria and went out to their cars. Michael immediately got in the driver's seat. "I'm thinking tomorrow I'd like to take your car for a spin, Meg," Jonesy grinned. They both knew he had her over a barrel.

"Fine," she growled. *See what you did now, Michael? And I'm still waiting for an explanation about the four girls that you seemed to be having a fine time with.* She was so steamed it took her a while to realize that they were headed in the opposite direction of her home. Meg sat up. "Where are we going?"

"My house," he answered matter-of-factly.

"Come again?"

"Well, Dale gave me a ride to Jonesy's and I intended to get a ride back with him. But I think he got way laid, so to speak, because he didn't show up at the pizzeria like he said he would. Seems you are once again the victim of Suzann Cochran. So, you are taking me home."

"Suzann? What? Oh! Well . . . what about me? How am I getting home?"

"This is your car. I would hope you knew how to drive it."

"I'm not driving home in the middle of the night by myself! What if something happens?"

"It's not the middle of the night. Nothing's going to happen to you. Nothing ever happens around here. Besides, I've found you to be a very resourceful person—"

"I'm not driving home alone in the dark."

"You know everybody along the way. What's going to happen?"

"I could get killed!"

"If you're that poor of a driver you shouldn't have your own car."

"I'm a great driver!"

"So, you should have no problem."

"Michael, you picked me up. It's your responsibility to see me safely home to my door."

"There's no reason for you to be so insistent. I'm not driving you home and then hitchhiking back. Why should I freeze? Or did you mean I could drive you home and then take your car to my house?" He started to slow down. "I could give it back to you in the morning, at school."

My God, he is serious! Take my car? Take my brand-new car that he isn't even supposed to be driving and do God knows what with it? How stupid does he think I am? Does he think Dad won't notice my car missing first thing in the morning? "No! What I mean is—"

"Then, there's no discussion. It's not as if I planned this. I did try to get a ride home. I'm simply not going to take you—and that's that. Unless you can come up with a better, warmer idea."

"You . . . bastard!" He laughed. "What's so funny?"

"You're the only person I know who has the guts to swear at me to my face," he paused and then looked at her, "and get away with it."

She tossed her head. "I'm not afraid of you."

He looked in the side view mirror, pulled out around a car that she thought was going fast enough, and after he got back in the lane said, "If you continue to say yes every time I ask you out, you will be."

She started to make a retort. Even had her mouth open, but something about the way he spoke made her stop. At that moment, she was afraid of him. When she thought about it, she knew little about Michael, except what Jonesy and Jim had told her. She knew plenty of guys who stayed clear of him. *Get real. He's not going to beat me up or something. Probably break my heart, but . . .* "What, what do you mean by that?"

"You know you're being unreasonable," he spoke calmly. "My plan is the only one that will get us both home warmly. You've got a brand-new car, so it's unlikely it will break down. You know plenty of people along the way. If you get stuck, walk to their house and call your father. He'll come get you. Or, if you're that scared, drive to your nearest friend's house and call your dad and have him come get you."

"I see. Well, look at it from my point of view. First, you take me tobogganing and I nearly freeze to death. Then, you yak it up with a bunch of girls while I'm left sitting in a pizzeria, hungry and getting nauseated watching Jonesy go through his routine. And now I have to drive home alone in the dark."

"What girls?" He seemed interested in this.

"The four girls at the pizzeria. Don't tell me you've forgotten them already?"

"Oh, those girls," he laughed. "One date and you're jealous."

"I am not!" she cried indignantly. "Besides, this is our second date."

"Our second? Oh, now we're keeping track. Are we going steady yet?"

"Certainly not! I had enough of that with Jim."

He shook his head. "I never understood why you broke up with him. He was nuts about you and I have to think, knowing him as well as I used to, that he would have been a decent boyfriend."

"He was a decent boyfriend. I still think he's a great guy . . . he just wasn't the one for me."

"And who do you think is?" she saw him glance at her out of the corner of his eye.

She paused, "I don't know. I imagine I'll meet him in college." She could feel her face start to turn red and was glad it was dark in the car. "What do you know about me anyway?"

It was some time before he answered, "You'd be surprised at what I know about you."

"Like what?" *Dare I hope this means he actually has an interest in me?*

"None of your business." He turned down a long driveway and drove up to the house. He backed it up, drove it part way down the drive and stopped. They both got out. "You should be able to manage from here."

She looked around and saw a big two-story house with tall columns supporting a second-floor porch. "Neat house."

"It's dark out," he sneered.

There were trees in rows that ran the length of the driveway. "You've got your own woods."

He shook his head. "It's called an apple orchard."

"Oh. Is that what your dad does?"

"No," he snorted, "he's a factory rat."

"Well, still," she looked around, "you've got acreage here."

"Ten."

"The way you talked, I thought . . ." *Your house was in a long line of dumpy little houses.* ". . . this is nice. This isn't what I imagined at all."

"Go home, Meg," he said gruffly, walking toward the house.

"Why do you get like that?" she hollered after him. "You can be so nice and then, bam, you're rude. I don't deserve it."

He stopped and looked at her. "You're right, you don't. So, why do you keep hanging around me?"

"Because I want to. Michael, don't shut me out. I'm not the enemy."

Hands jammed in his pockets, he walked up to her. "Meg," he said softly, "don't get involved with me. I promise you, I'm not worth it."

She smiled and wrapped her arms around his waist. *I just want another of those gorgeous kisses of yours.* "You realize . . . don't you . . . that come fall I'll be long gone. I'm going someplace. I don't know where yet, but I've been offered some nice football scholarships."

"Okay."

"Do you understand what I'm saying?"

"Yes." She lifted her chin up. "Do you understand what I'm thinking right now?"

He smiled down at her and slowly brought his arms around her. He bent down and kissed her. "What am I going to do with you?" he asked, holding her.

"Just let me be the one person you let in."

She liked the way his eyes roved over her face. Then, abruptly, it was gone and his face was hard. He unfastened her hands from around his waist. "You need to go."

"What? What just happened here? I don't understand you."

"Don't try. Just go." He took off at a run for the house. *What did I say? What did I do? You're the one who left me stranded out here in this god-forsaken country! I should be the one who's mad! And, darn it, I am!* She jumped in her car and tore off down the driveway.

Meg knew she could get home safely. *But what had he been jabbering about? First it sounded like he cared and then the next minute he is pushing me away. I don't understand him—will I ever?* It had been snowing off and on all evening and she knew she should slow down, but she was too worked up. She didn't see the patch of ice on the road until it was too late. She spun around in a complete circle and landed in the ditch. Meg swore, banged on the steering wheel until her hands hurt, cried for ten seconds, and then tried to get the car out. She slid further into the ditch. More swearing. She got out and tried to survey the damage, but it was too dark to see anything. *This is why Daddy told me to buy a flashlight for the car. Well, tomorrow I'll do it.*

Meg calmed down enough to look around. Not a car in sight. This was a section of the county that she knew little about, yet it looked familiar. *Ah, yes. The light burning in that window over there is Jim's house. That would be just dandy knocking on his door. "Hello Jim, I've just spent the evening with Michael. How would you like to dig me out of a ditch and I'll tell you all about it?"* It was cold. She envisioned the school bus driving by in the morning. *"Hey, isn't that Meg, frozen to her car? They make a nice couple, don't they? Michael must have dumped her. She's so close to his house—and yet so far."*

Well, Michael got me into this; he can jolly well get me out. Stomping with fury all the way to his house, she was beginning to get warm. *If there's so much as a scratch on my beautiful, shiny car I'm holding him responsible*, she thought to herself. She also thought of all the unpleasant things she was going to say and do when she got a hold of him.

By the time Meg pounded furiously on his door, she was actually hot. For whatever reason, she assumed Michael would answer, and was ready to assault him, when a woman opened the door. Meg found herself at a loss for words. *Michael's mother?*

"Yes?"

"Ah . . . Mrs. MacKenzie?"

"Yes."

"Ah . . . I'm a friend . . . er, I was . . . anyway, until a few, ah, minutes . . . it's a long story . . . of Michael's . . . is Michael here?"

"Yes." She seemed hesitant about letting Meg in. She looked around, "Come in." She grabbed a little girl running by and said quietly, "Go find Michael and ask him to come here." The little girl ran up a flight of stairs and Megan followed her with her eyes. It was some time before she saw Michael emerge. He started down the stairs and then saw her. He stopped. Teeth clenched, he gave her an intimidating stare. This had been a bad idea. "What are you doing here?"

"I . . . well, I got stuck . . . down the road."

"Are you kidding me?" he roared.

"Michael," his mother hissed. Though it sounded like a warning rather than reprimanding him for his rudeness.

"I'll get my jacket," he said disgustedly and disappeared.

"Hello." Meg turned to see his younger brother.

"Hi." *Darn, what is his name?*

"Stuck, huh?"

In more ways than one. "Yeah."

"I'll go help Michael. You can stay warm in the den," he motioned towards a room.

"Oh, Josh. I don't know," his mother's hands were clasped and she kept working the thumbs back and forth against each other.

"It's okay. I checked." She seemed relieved and smiled at Megan for the first time. Megan introduced herself.

"Let me show you to the den," she offered.

"Maybe I should go with the guys—"

"No reason for you to get cold," said Josh. "We'll take care of things."

She followed Mrs. MacKenzie into the den. She must have been a beautiful woman in her day, as Michael and Josh had a lot of her looks, the blonde hair, the blue eyes. Walking into the den, Megan found five pair of eyes fastened on her, all younger than herself. Being an only child, she was overwhelmed. She had never been around small children before and she found it disconcerting to have them stare at her. *Am I the one who said I wanted to be in a large family? No wonder Michael sneered at me.*

Meg was at a complete loss for words when two little girls crawled into her lap. She could hear Michael and Josh going out the door. She started to holler to them that she was coming along also, when she heard Michael say, "Didn't I tell you they were a pain in the butt?"

She sat back down. Mrs. MacKenzie gave her a weak smile. "He has a little bit of a temper."

"Yes, he does, doesn't he?" Megan smiled back and wondered what on earth she was smiling about. *Why do I always let my temper get the best of me? I should have gone to Jim's.*

Megan had grown up around adults, so she never felt uncomfortable in their presence—before tonight. In fact, she'd been a big hit with Jim's parents. Even if Jim had been less than happy to see her had she arrived at his house unannounced, his temper wouldn't have surfaced. Jim would probably have offered to follow her home in his car. But Michael? A line of cuss words would probably follow her home.

Megan looked around the room. *This isn't a bad house. Maybe it needs a little paint here and there, but so what? The way Michael talks, I thought it was a dump. It has character. Michael should also take into consideration how many children his father has to support compared to my dad.*

Suddenly, the mood in the room changed. Megan saw a shadow looming in the doorway and Mrs. MacKenzie stiffen. "To bed."

There was a mad dash by all of the children to turn off the TV, put the toys in a box, and get out of the room. None of them spoke or kissed him goodnight. In fact, they all left through a different door than the one he was occupying. And occupying it he was. *So, this is where Michael gets his build.* Michael was considered one of the biggest guys in the high school, and this was one of the largest men she'd ever seen.

Mrs. MacKenzie appeared immobile, so Megan decided to keep her mouth shut. There was something else Michael had inherited from his father. A long, cold stare.

"What are you doing here?" Each word came out slowly and was carefully enunciated. *Definitely Jim's place would have been the better idea.*

"The roads are bad and she went in a ditch. She saw our light on and came and asked for help. The boys are digging her out." This quick explanation came from Mrs. MacKenzie.

"You from around here?" he asked.

Meg could see the pleading look on Mrs. MacKenzie's face—but pleading her to say what? Meg had been brought up to respect her elders and not to lie; plus she wasn't good at lying.

"No, I live on the other side of town."

"Really? Do you happen to go to . . ." they both waited, "that new high school?"

He doesn't know the name of the high school his kids go to?

"Yes."

"Then, you must know my boys," he smiled for the first time. It did not make Meg feel any better.

"Josh and Michael? Yes, I know them."

"Which one are you here to see?"

"Dan please—"

"I asked the young lady a question. I expect an answer." Megan could feel her heart pounding. *Why didn't I listen to anybody when they said Michael had family problems? No wonder he doesn't let anybody in.*

She hoped her voice stayed even as she said, "I'm not here to see anybody. My car went in a ditch. I go to school with both your sons. I figured as big as they are, the two of them could get my car out a lot easier than I could by myself." She stood up. She was getting out of here, no question about it. She turned to Michael's mother. "Thank you for allowing me to get warm. I'll go see how the guys are coming along."

The outside door suddenly opened and they could hear Josh's cheery voice, "Okay, you're all set—" Seeing his father he went silent.

"Where have you been?" Mr. MacKenzie swayed as he walked towards Josh and grabbed a chair for support.

"I was outside, getting Meg's car out of a ditch."

His father flung his hand in her direction. "Is this your girlfriend?"

"I go to school with her, that's all."

"So, she must be Mike's. Where is that no good brother of yours?" Meg remembered the look on Michael's face when he had asked her, "Why am I the hated one?"

"I am not anybody's girlfriend." Like the children who had left the room ahead of her, Meg looked for a different door to go out, so that she didn't have to pass him, but she wasn't familiar with the house.

She jumped when he hollered at Josh, totally ignoring her, "Where's Mike?"

"He's in the garage, putting the shovels away," answered Josh.

"Go get him!" Josh hesitated and glanced at Meg. "I told you to go get him!"

Josh took off, and so did Meg. She squeezed past Mr. MacKenzie while he focused his attention on Josh's departing back. As she went past him, she got a whiff of something—though she didn't know what. "Where are you going?" he barked.

"To my car," and she was out the door. She was shaking as she ran down the driveway after Josh. He definitely wasn't headed for the garage.

Hearing someone behind him, Josh turned around and stopped. He waited for Meg to catch up. "Michael's waiting for you at your car."

"Oh, God. Have I got him in a ton of trouble?"

"Don't worry about it, just go." He headed for the house.

She ran all the way down the long driveway without stopping. *What have I done?* She had never experienced anything like this in her life. All the adults she knew were nice, decent people. She was running on empty. She could see the headlights of her car and wished Michael would drive down and pick her up, which she knew very well he wouldn't do. She stopped in the glow of the headlights, utterly exhausted. *Run me over. Please, run me over and I won't have to say a word about my conversation with your dad.* "Let's move it!" hollered Michael.

She stumbled to the driver's side where he was sitting. "I'll drive now," she panted.

"Forget it. You proved your point. Get in and I'll drive you home."

"No, no," she was still panting, hands on knees.

Michael pointed to Jim's house. "Gee, I wonder whose house that is? The one that has a driveway only ten feet from your car. I guess you couldn't see the house because of all the lights that are on."

"I'm really, really sorry."

"Just get in."

She pointed back down the road and took a deep breath. "I think your dad wants to talk to you now."

"My *dad?*" She thought he was going to come at her through the open window. "You spoke to my father?"

"Sort of."

"What the hell does 'sort of' mean?" He jumped out of the car.

"He wanted to know what I was doing at your house. I told him my car went in the ditch."

"Mike!" They could hear his name being yelled across the night air.

"Does he know we were together tonight?"

"No. I told him I went to school with you and Josh and I was driving by and went in the ditch."

"Mike!" The voice was louder.

Michael grabbed her arm and shoved her into the car. "I'm sorry. You've got to leave *right now*. You're going to have to get home by yourself."

"I'll be all right. God, I'm sorry Michael!"

"I'm sorry I didn't see you home."

"I'll see that she gets safely home."

Michael whirled around with his fists up; then relaxed when he recognized Jim.

"Go on," they could all hear Mr. MacKenzie getting closer.

Michael nodded. "Thanks." He took off at a dead run in the snow.

"Thank you for the offer, but I'll be all right."

"I'll follow in my car."

"Jim, that's not necessary; but thank you."

"I'm going to do it anyway, so get moving." Jim followed her home and got out of his car when they arrived. She was still shaking.

"Michael's going to be okay, isn't he?" she asked.

Jim hesitated. "I suppose."

"What does that mean?"

He shrugged. "I don't know how much Michael has told you and I don't know how much I should tell you. But, the next time you're stuck out our way, come to my house."

She laughed sarcastically. "You don't need to worry about me showing up at Michael's doorstep again." She looked at him. She knew he still felt the same way about her. "Jim, I couldn't come to your house. I'd just spent the evening with Michael. It wouldn't have been right. His dad drinks, right?"

"Yeah."

"You told me that before and . . . I just didn't think. A lot?"

"Yeah."

"What will happen to Michael tonight?" She wasn't sure she wanted to know the answer.

"I can only imagine."

"Michael told me once he was the hated one. Why is that?"

Jim was uneasy, wondering how much he should tell her. "Back when Michael and I were friends . . . I don't mean that we're not friends now, it's just that . . . Michael doesn't talk to me anymore. I know what you're asking though. He said that to me too, once. I don't know, Meg. His dad really has it in for him. He's abusive and he seems to have a personal grudge against Michael. Michael always got it worse than the rest of them. His dad goes out of his way to look for things to accuse him of."

They stood quietly, both staring at the ground. Jim sighed. "You know, Meg, people who are abused . . ." He didn't know how to phrase it. " . . . can abuse other people in their lives . . . I would hate to think that . . . he . . ."

"Michael hasn't done anything to me."

"For about the last three or four years, he hasn't talked to anybody much. He seems to have let you in though. If he should ever . . ."

"I'll be fine," she offered, "you and Jonesy worry too much."

"Meg, if you ever get tired of him . . ." He looked at her directly for the first time.

"Jim," she felt terrible. He looked so lost. "I think you are a terrific guy. I truly do. I'm sorry."

"Yeah, a lot of good it's done me, huh?" he got in his car and left.

January 3, 1967: What has my temper gotten me into now? Michael invited me tobogganing tonight. I let him drive my car. If Daddy ever finds out, he'll kill me. And now, Jonesy and Mandy are going to be bugging me because they know he's driving it.

Anyway, I did something really stupid. We went tobogganing, went out for pizza with Jonesy and his latest love interest, and then Michael ended up driving my car to his house because he didn't have any other way of getting home. I was really mad at him for leaving me stranded clear on the other side of town. I went in the ditch. I should have walked to Jim's house, but I couldn't do that. So, I went to Michael's. It was terrible! His dad drinks (a lot from what I hear) and he was very rude to me. I got out of there with his dad practically chasing me down the driveway. Michael and Josh had gotten my car out of the ditch and

I got in and left. I hope nothing bad happens to Michael because of me. Jim saw me home in his car. Why do I always let my temper get the best of me?

Megan tossed and turned all night. She dreaded going to school; yet at the same time she was anxious to get there to make sure Michael was okay. *Of course he will be okay,* she assured herself. *What's the big deal? He helped a stranded motorist get her car out of a ditch. What is so bad about that? Michael would just explain everything to his dad and that would be that, right? I mean, what is there to be mad about?* she asked herself for the hundredth time.

Meg was at her locker when a sudden hush fell over the hallway. She felt someone stop behind her and caught Mandy's expression out of the corner of her eye. Slowly Meg turned around and her jaw dropped.

"Mornin'."

"Oh, Michael." He was sporting a colorful shiner. She started to bring her hand up to touch it when he grabbed her wrist.

"It's very tender. Come on, I'll walk you to class."

"I don't understand. Why? For rescuing a damsel in distress?"

He shook his head. "Forget about it, Meg. I take it you got home all right last night?"

"Yes, but . . ." They were at her homeroom door and he turned to leave. "Wait," she ran after him, not knowing what she was going to say. "Listen, my folks are going over to the Hill's house tonight, to play bridge. Why don't you come over?" She expected him to turn her down, but he seemed to be considering it.

He shrugged his shoulders. "Why not? I've got no place else to go."

"Oh, God. Michael!"

"Meg, you're putting too much on yourself. What happened last night wasn't just you. In fact, it wasn't you at all. Things have been building up for several months now—last night they just came to a head. Don't worry about it."

"I feel so bad."

"Forget about it, Meg. I'll see you tonight, okay?"

She didn't see Michael for the rest of the day. She wondered if he would really show up and had to beg Mandy not to tell what she was doing. "I don't trust him," wailed Mandy. "What if something happens to you?"

"Nothing is going to happen to me. Just remember, you and I had a big fight, we're not speaking to each other, and that's why I'm not coming over with my parents tonight, okay?"

"I don't like this. I'll call you every half hour."

"No."

"Every hour—"

"No!"

"Just to see if you're all right . . ."

"I'll be fine. He got in a fight with his dad, not me."

"Yeah, but you were the reason. Maybe he's going to get his revenge on you—"

"He's not like that."

"Jonesy says he's a real loner. He's strange."

"He's fine. I'm going to be fine."

"You know you're not allowed to have boys over to your house when your parents aren't there."

"I am well aware of my own house rules, thank you."

"If it were somebody like Jim, then I wouldn't—"

"Well, it's not Jim!" Meg exploded. "You know that big fight that we are supposed to have so that I don't come over tonight? I think we're having it now!"

"Megan Anne Becktame," Mandy was getting hot now. "If—"

"Nothing is going to happen! You don't understand him the way I do."

"—you forget to pick me up tomorrow morning, your name is mud."

"Why do you girls have to fight?" Her mother sighed.

"I guess it's part of growing up."

Her mom looked at her. "Maybe I should invite the Hills over here."

"No!" *Stay calm; she'll get suspicious.*

"Honestly, Josephine," said her dad, coming into the room. "I think Megan's old enough to stay home alone. She's driving that car of hers all over the countryside and we don't even know where she is half the time. We'll be right next door. She can call if she needs us."

Meg wrapped her arms around her dad and gave him a peck on the cheek. "I think I've been pretty good about telling you where I'm going."

"I know," he smiled. "I trust you."

Yeah, lay the guilt on tonight of all nights.

"I'll send Jeffrey over to check on you later," was her mother's parting shot.

"No!" *If Jonesy finds out what I'm up to, there is no telling what he'll do.* "Don't embarrass me by sending Jonesy over to check on me like I am a baby. I will be the laughing stock of the school."

"I'll handle it," said her dad as he left.

Megan left off cleaning the kitchen, which was her job, until Michael arrived. That way she would have something to do. She couldn't imagine them sitting in the living room chitchatting while she stared at his black-and-blue eye.

She wandered through the house, half praying he would show up, half praying that he wouldn't. She would be in so much trouble if her parents ever found out. *Hmm, why do I always seem to be doing stuff I shouldn't where Michael is concerned?* She saw headlights coming up the driveway. *Here he is! He came! He came!*

Michael sat on a barstool at the kitchen counter while she cleaned dishes. He seemed as uncomfortable as she did. They spoke very little.

When she was finished with the kitchen and wondered what on earth she was going to do with him, he cleared his throat. "Could I ask you for a big favor?"

She smiled. "Of course."

"Could you fix me a sandwich or something to eat?"

"Didn't you have any dinner?"

"No." *What was his mother doing? Starving him?*

"Did you go home after school today?"

"No."

"Michael!"

"What do I want to go home for?" She pulled a steak out of the refrigerator. "Just a sandwich will be fine, thank you."

"I'll fix you a steak sandwich."

"Don't do that. A peanut butter and jelly sandwich is all I need."

"I am hardly going to fix you that for dinner. This is a leftover. I'm just going to warm it up. Would you like some French fries?"

"No." She pulled them out anyway.

"Megan."

"Have no fear. I am a pretty decent cook."

"I'm not worried about that."

"My mom is a great cook and I've learned a lot from her. Even Jonesy eats my cooking. I just hope that by heating this back up I don't make it too well-done—or do you like it that way?"

"How would I know? My family doesn't eat steak."

She started to make a wisecrack and then caught herself. He was serious. It had never dawned on her that not everyone ate steak. "You don't eat steak?"

"It's not something poor people buy." She blushed. *Of course, with umpteen people in the house I should have realized that. Why does my brain always work below sea level when I am around him?*

She added a salad along with the steak and fries. She set it all down in front of Michael and then started naming several flavors of pop they had in the house and ended with, "And of course, we've got milk."

His eyes lit up. "Real milk?"

"Real milk?" *Come on brain, kick in. Was this another trick question? Come on, think. I function fine around Jim. What would I answer if Jim asked me this question? He never would.* "As opposed to ... unreal milk?"

"We have powdered milk at my house. It's cheaper. I used to get the real stuff at Jim's all the time, though."

Poor. That's how I have to think. Poor. "Yes, we have real milk."

"I'd like a glass of that. A tall glass, please? This steak is really good. My compliments to the chef."

"Dah!" she waved her hand. "That's nothing."

After Michael polished off three glasses of milk and the last two pieces of chocolate cake, they retired to the living room. The cake—not the steak—would take some explaining. It was her dad's favorite but . . . Michael needed it.

He sat down on the sofa, one arm draped across the back. Meg wasn't sure if he meant that as an invitation or not, but she wasn't playing any silly games with him tonight. She sat down next to him, her face inches away from his, while he stared off into space. "What?" Michael finally asked, turning towards her.

"Shouldn't I get something for your face?"

"No. You're not going to baby me. That's my mom's department, and she doesn't get anywhere with me either," he growled. Slowly he pulled her to him and kissed her. He pulled away and stared at Meg.

"What? What'd I do now?" she asked. *Can't I do anything right around him?*

"Well, I just never thought I'd say this."

"What?"

"It hurts to kiss you."

She felt the giggles coming on, but sobered up when he touched his cheekbone. "My face is still thumping. That damn bastard."

"You want an ice pack?"

"I had one on most of the night." Seeing her doubtful look he added, "The swelling's gone down a lot."

"Why did he do this to you? I didn't tell him that we were together," she was almost in tears. "I tried to make him think that I had just arrived—"

"Meg, stop. It's not you and it's not the first time. This is just a way of life for me. Don't worry."

"Have you had anybody look at you?"

"You mean a doctor?" She nodded. "Now who would foot the bill for that?"

"I will."

"Meg, trust me, you are not responsible for this. Look," he sat for several seconds, wrestling with himself. "My father was a really good football player in his day. He was sure that he was headed for the big time. Well, my sister ruined all his plans." He gave a slight laugh. "Apparently he didn't learn his lesson though, seeing as how he had nine more of us! Anyway, my two older brothers came along and my father was determined that his sons would be football players. Live out his dream through us. However, my brothers didn't care for football, but, I did. I love it. My father went to every one of their games and they got a lot of verbal abuse because they weren't very good—but nothing more. But hey, I love the game and I was going to make him so proud. Finally, a son who would follow in his footsteps.

"In the beginning, he went to my games; but as time went on and people congratulated him on how good I was, that I was a chip off the old block, that it looked like I could go far playing ball . . . well, I could see that it only made him angry at me. I didn't understand why. He even told me to quit.

"Obviously, I have refused to do that and it's been a living nightmare ever since. The only explanation I have ever been able to come up with is that he can't stand to see me go where he didn't get to go. He's tried to stop me, tried to break my arm or my leg."

She stared at him, horrified. This was something that was beyond her comprehension. *Who would do something like that to another human being? To their own child?*

"My older brothers have been there, and they've tried to protect me, but they're gone now. Darrell's married and Dave's in the service. Right now, it's not too bad. He always lets up after football season and he's working the graveyard shift, so I'm able to sleep at night without being rudely awakened."

"I understand that you love football," she spoke softly, "but, wouldn't it be easier if you didn't play?"

"And let him win?" Michael yelled. "No, this is my ticket out of here! I only have a few months to go and I'm gone. I have some very nice football scholarship offers and I'm going to take one of them—and then I'm never coming back. Don't make any plans with me, Meg," he added sternly.

"I'm not! God, you're arrogant. Just because I'm nice to you, you think I want a lifelong commitment? Get real."

They both fell silent. Her dad had gotten a fire going in the fireplace before he left, knowing how much Meg enjoyed them. She got up and poked at it. She threw another log on and turned around. Michael had both feet flat on the floor, his hands pressed against his forehead, elbows on his knees. She thought about hugging him, he looked so lost and alone. Suddenly he sat straight up. "God, I should never have told you! What was I thinking?" he yelled. "You and your woods and always being nice to me. It's peaceful here, it's relaxing, and you make me say stuff that I've never told another soul. Oh Meg, you can't tell anybody what I told you."

"I won't."

"No, Meg. You've got to promise me," he grabbed her arms, "not anybody!"

"Michael, I promise. You need to have somebody to talk to. You can't keep it all bottled up inside. I understand. Your secret is safe with me; although . . . everybody that I talk with seems to know you have . . . family problems. I mean, how are you explaining your face to people?"

"I don't owe anybody an explanation. You promise?"

"Yes, Michael," she looked up at him. "I promise you."

He relaxed, but didn't let go. "I think about you way too much." It was almost a whisper.

"I'll always be here if you need me."

"No! That's just it!" He let go and headed for the door, almost forgetting his jacket on the way out. "I don't need you! I don't need anybody!" He disappeared out the door. It opened briefly. "Thanks for dinner." Then, he was gone.

January 4, 1967: Michael came to school today with a beautiful black eye, compliments of his dad. I felt terrible, so I invited him over to the house tonight since Mom and Daddy were going over to the Hill's for cards. I fixed him dinner and we sat by the fire. He told me some things about his dad that he swore me to secrecy about. Then he got mad and walked out. I know he can be rude and arrogant but there is just something about him. And, if I'm not mistaken, I think he cares about me, too. He just seems unwilling to admit it.

It was Friday. They were in study hall and Meg could hear Michael complain to his football pals how he had to break his date with Valerie because he couldn't very well let her see him like this.

All right, who's Valerie? I don't care. I don't care, she kept repeating to herself. *We're just friends. He means nothing to me.* She felt a lump start in her throat. *Why am I so crazy about this guy?*

"Hey, Meg," she felt his pencil tap her on the shoulder, "you've already seen me at my worst. Want to go out tonight?" She could see his friends trying not to laugh.

"No, thank you."

"Got a big date tonight, huh?" The guys snickered.

"Actually," she said putting on a fake air, "I can't decide between Barry and the ballet, Paul and his play, or Opie and the opera." They all laughed and she turned back around.

"Don't forget to add Mean Michael with his . . . and the . . . hmm," she heard Michael say. She bit her lip, realizing he was stuck. The guys soon chimed in to help.

"Mean Michael with the monster movies."

"Mean Michael with his mud-wrestling team."

"Mean Michael and his motor machine."

"Thanks guys, thanks a lot!" Michael said, while everybody within hearing distance laughed.

Michael was waiting for her, at least it looked that way, when Meg and Mandy walked out of school at the end of the day. He fell in step with her and Mandy quickly moved ahead. "Listen," Michael said, when he was sure everybody was out of earshot. "I'd really like to repay you for the other night. My big problem is that I'm a little low on cash at the moment. Would you mind just going for a ride?"

"I told you, I'm busy tonight. Thank you."

"Oh, come on. Forget the play, the ballet, and the opera. The mud wrestling guy with the monster machine has got to be more interesting."

She smiled. "I'm so glad I get to have the chance to be with you because you don't want to scare off Valerie and because I'm considered a cheap date."

"You're not number two on my list, if that's what you're thinking."

"I'm not?"

"No. You're like four or five."

With eyes blazing, Meg stomped off. He caught up with her and said, "But after dinner the other night, you're moving up fast."

She practically screamed. "You are the most conceited—" she groped for an adequate word, "child I've ever met!"

"Fine. I'll pick you up what? About seven?"

"I am not going out with you."

She almost made it to the car when she felt his hand take her arm and jerk her around. "You know I was only joking."

"Who's Valerie?"

"She's somebody I went to school with last year. Don't get any ideas about 'us' because there is no 'us'. I just want to thank you for the other night."

"You're welcome." She considered herself a fairly strong girl and was surprised and annoyed to realize she couldn't shake his hand off. Indeed, she could hardly move her arm. "I don't like being used, so don't bother coming over, *ever*." He released her. Back straight, head held high, she threw her books in the backseat and flew out of the parking lot.

She heard Mandy heave a sigh of relief. "I'm glad that's over," she said. "Jonesy will be happy."

Megan said nothing the entire drive home but as soon as she dropped off Mandy, she lowered her forehead to the steering wheel. *How could I have done that? What do I care if I'm far down on his list, as long as I get to go out with him? I have too much pride. He will never speak to me again, let alone ask me out. Probably nobody will ever ask me out again. Sixteen and I am destined to be a spinster. I'll be known as Megan the Snot. That doesn't go together. Megan the Menacing, Megan the Monster, Megan the Mobster? Megan the . . . Miserable.*

Seven o'clock. *I could be out having a wonderful time right now; but no, I have pride. Aren't I having fun with my pride? Why can't girls call boys? Just to say I'm sorry? No, I am not sorry. He was rude. Made fun of me in front of his friends. This one evening it would not have killed me to say yes. Or I could have given him a flippant, "If you feel like coming over, fine. I don't care." Or I could have said, "No, thank you. Not tonight, maybe another night." But, no, I had to tell him off.*

At seven-fifteen, Meg decided to take a walk. It was the usual January thaw so she decided to try out her new boots. The stream was her favorite place to go, even though it was too wet to sit on the ground. She finally stretched herself out on a log, clasped her hands over her stomach, and stared up at the night sky. *So, this is what it is like to be dead. Cold, dark, miserable. Nobody here to mourn my passing. I am a mean, morbid, miserable monster who —*

"What are you doing?"

She screamed, sat up, lost her balance, and fell splat in the mud. She glared at him. "Sorry I'm late," Michael offered.

Meg slowly got up without his help.

"Ready to go for a ride?" His face was still black and blue, but the swelling had left and he could now manage a decent smile.

"I'm caked with mud, in case you didn't notice!"

"Hey, ya know what? I saw a house a little ways back. Maybe the people there will let you change. I guess you didn't see it, because all the lights are on."

She clenched her hands into fists. "Oh! If your face wasn't already . . ."

"You'd do what?" he challenged.

She struck off for home with him trailing behind.

"Ya know," he finally volunteered, "I think the advertisements are all wrong."

"What advertisements?"

"That blondes are more fun."

"It's 'blondes HAVE more fun'."

"Well, I have to agree, seeing as how I'm blonde and I do have fun. However, I'm beginning to think redheads are more fun."

"What's that crack supposed to mean?"

"It's not a crack; it's a compliment."

"Uh-huh." She got to her house and expected him to follow her in.

"I'll wait for you in the car."

"You can come in. I'll just be a minute."

"I'll wait for you in the car," he said tersely.

It wasn't until she had changed and was running downstairs that she suddenly realized she had never said she would go out with him. *The nerve!* Even though she was deliriously happy that he had showed up, he shouldn't just assume— *Oh, give it a rest, Becktame. Look at it from old maid Valerie's viewpoint. He dumped her just to be with me, Megan Becktame.*

"Where did you get this car?" she asked when she got in.

"It's my mom's. I thought you'd be happy to know my car is being repaired."

She shrugged her shoulders. *What do I care? I have a perfectly good new car.* "The heater," he said.

"Oh!"

"That's why I'm a little low on cash at the moment." He drove. She listened to the radio.

After driving along several dirt roads they ended up back at her place. *Well, he said he was taking me for a ride. He did, guess that's it.* He turned off the engine, but left the radio on. *Am I supposed to get out?* Neither one had spoken much during the ride. *Is this the end of our date?*

"Well . . .thank you for a lovely . . . trip."

She started to get out when he grabbed a hold of her wrist and pulled her to him. "You don't have to go already, do ya?"

"No."

He kissed her hesitantly and then harder. He drew back. "Still hurts." She started to pull away, but he held onto her. "Not as bad as it did, though."

"I'm sorry you can't be with Valerie tonight."

She watched his eyes examine her face. "I didn't really care to go out with her, that's the real reason I cancelled."

"Why not?"

"Meg," he frowned, "I meant what I said earlier about there is no 'us.' But I do enjoy being with you. You said you didn't like being used and I can understand that. I just wanted to be with you tonight. Another night it will be somebody else," he added quickly. "You understand?"

"Yeah. You want to play the field. And I do understand, which is why I told Jonesy to introduce me to Ron."

"What? What for?" he yelled.

"Well, my thinking is this: if he wants to meet me, maybe he's thinking about asking me out, and I would like to go out and do something." *Granted, I talked to Jonesy when I found out about Valerie and was furious with you. Now, I don't want to meet Ron, but it's too late.*

"I don't believe you!"

"I'm sorry. But, who keeps saying there is no us? Who had a date with Valerie?"

"Oh," he sat up straight and smiled. "You did it for spite. You were jealous."

Dang. "I was not!" she hotly denied. "But, if you think I'm going to sit by the phone every night waiting for you to call, you're wrong."

He kissed her. "I thought that hurt your face," she said.

"I don't care."

January 7, 1967: I was so mad at Michael yesterday. He had a date! Some girl named Valerie. I was so mad I told Jonesy I wanted to meet Ron who has been asking about me. Then, Michael showed up at the house! As if I didn't have a date! He just thinks he can show up any time he wants and I'm just going to be sitting here waiting for him! The nerve. But I am so happy when I see him. We drove around and then we made out in his mom's car. His face is still black and blue but that didn't seem to bother him. Or maybe it did because after awhile he just held me. He held me tight for a long time and I loved it. I could have held onto him all night. I know he's going to break my heart, but I can't tell him to get lost. I just want to be with him all the time, even though there are times when he pushes me away. I don't understand him.

As I sit here and write this on a lonely Saturday night.

⇒　⇐

"Let's go do something!" screamed Mandy. "You've got a car, you've got no date, and us girls want to go someplace."

Meg stared at the girls surrounding her car in the school parking lot on Friday afternoon. "Yeah, come on Meg, you've been no fun lately."

They had been on her for weeks to do something and she could hardly tell them she wanted to sit by the phone instead, in the hope that Michael would call. He certainly had given no indication that he would be doing any such thing. In fact, he had basically ignored her all week. She had enjoyed going out with the girls before . . . *Oh, what the heck?*

"All right, all right," Meg said.

The evening found four girls in Meg's car complaining to each other about why they didn't want to go here or there--and they still had to pick up Marcy.

"I don't want to just cruise," said Meg.

"That's what's fun!"

"I say, let's go to the show. Even if we don't see any cute guys, at least we'll see a decent movie."

"There's nothing I want to see."

Marcy got in the car, giggling. "Wait 'til you guys hear."

"What?" yelled all four girls.

"I overheard Mark say his parents were going to be gone tonight and he invited a bunch of the guys over for a poker game." The girls squealed in delight.

"We're not going," said Meg.

"Oh, don't be such a spoil sport!"

"You've been a grouch for the last month."

"We'll just look in the window."

"Yeah, just the window."

"I have grown up with you guys. I know it's not going to be 'just the window.' You're all going to do something stupid," Meg said.

"If you feel that way, you can sit in the car."

Yeah and drive away.

"This is a bad idea," muttered Megan as they drove past Mark's house. She had the headlights off and parked several yards away. Before she could say anything else, her companions piled out, and were giggling as they ran up the slope towards Mark's house. "Be quiet!" hissed Meg, even though they couldn't hear her.

The girls were gathered around a basement window when Megan came trudging up from behind. "Michael's here," Patti taunted.

"Meg doesn't care, they're just friends," said Trish. The girls sniggered.

"So, this is where Jonesy took off to," muttered Mandy in Meg's ear. And then she smiled. "Wait 'til I tell Mom."

"He's playing cards, so what?"

"They've also raided the liquor cabinet."

There were a number of guys in the basement, drinking, playing cards, and making a general uproar. The guys were making so much noise that the girls stopped whispering and began to talk and laugh out loud as they watched the boys. In their carelessness, they didn't see Tim, one of their classmates, leaning against the wall directly below the window. He stood, moving his index finger up and down. It was Jonesy who finally saw him, "What are you doing?" he asked.

A few of the guys turned to look Tim's way. "I've only had one beer, but I swear—"

"So, stop looking like a jerk," offered someone.

"— I hear giggling."

The girls immediately froze when they noticed several pairs of eyes looking up to the window. Mark jumped out of his seat and doused the lights—all the lights, inside and out. The girls screamed. They heard other screams from the far side of the house. "What was that?" yelled Trish.

"I don't want to find out!" Marcy bolted.

Pandemonium broke loose. Nobody could remember which way the car was, they all collided with each other, and suddenly the guys were running outside from two different doors.

"I knew it! I knew it!" yelled Megan. She ran straight for the trees. Surely she could hide behind one until things settled down. She had the keys, so she didn't have to worry about being left behind.

"There's one there, one over there, there!" Someone was having the time of his life pointing out girls.

Suddenly, Megan heard someone directly behind her. She nearly shrieked. She had been sure she was far enough away so that nobody could see her. As she felt arms come around her legs, she screamed and they both fell to the ground. "Beautiful tackle!" someone yelled. *Oh God, a football player. Please let it be Jonesy.* He had her pinned, face to the ground.

"Get off me!" she yelled.

"Meg?"

She stopped struggling. "Michael?" He released her enough so that she could turn over; but he didn't get off her.

"You just can't keep away from me, can you?" he smiled.

"Oh, blow it out your—" his mouth came down hard on hers. It was not what she was expecting. Half of her struggled and half of her couldn't get enough.

"My face doesn't feel half bad," he said as he ran his mouth down along her neck. She was shocked at the feelings it sent through her. It had never been like this with other guys.

"Michael, stop," Meg did her best not to moan. "There are people around."

He looked up. "Nobody's paying any attention. In fact, all I see are a bunch of people just like us." He started unzipping her jacket.

She thought of Jonesy telling her how Michael would ruin her reputation. "What do you think you're doing?"

"It's what you came for, isn't it?"

"No!"

He heard her anger and felt her struggle under him. "Okay, okay, don't get excited. I'm not going to hurt you." She stopped struggling as she felt his tongue against her skin. "I could never hurt you, Meg."

"Where's Michael?" they heard someone yell. "Michael?"

He stood up and helped Meg to her feet. He put his arm around her shoulders and the two of them walked back to the house. "Ah-ha, got one!" yelled Mark. "To the dungeon!"

All the girls had been rounded up, including four others from school who had been at a different window. "So, that's what we heard." Each pointed at the other group. "You scared the life out of us when you screamed."

"Well, look what the cat dragged in," said one of the girls as Megan came down the stairs.

Megan smiled as Michael walked in behind her and she saw Justine's face. Justine had been going to school with Michael since seventh grade and chasing him since ninth—with no success. Megan had already butted heads with Justine in art class. "I just couldn't get away," said Megan innocently. She saw Jonesy seething. Her friends laughed though, and as Patti walked by she whispered, "I want details."

The music started, as the cards had long since disappeared, and everyone seemed to be pairing off. Mandy came up to Meg, "If we don't leave now, I'm going to wind up with Larry."

But Meg didn't want to leave, not if she was going to end up with Michael. And if she left, would he pair up with somebody else? Justine? So far, he had stuck near her; but not that near. "Surely you can stand Larry for one night," she said quietly, even though Larry was one of her least favorite guys.

"Meg, I'll never forgive you if you leave me with him. You know he's got traveling hands!"

"One swift kick in the right place ought to do the trick. Then he'll leave you alone all night."

"Take me home and then come back if you want."

"Have Jonesy take you."

"Meg!"

"Let's get out of here." Meg turned to see Michael standing next to her.

"Ah, well," Meg looked from one to the other. "Mandy wants me to take her home." She could feel Mandy start to slink off, knowing she would never say a word to Michael. Megan could kick herself. She had known Mandy all her life and yet she was ready to dump her for an hour or two because Michael snapped his fingers. *What kind of friend am I?*

"Okay," said Michael. "Let's all leave. Drop Mandy off at her place and I'll be in your driveway."

"Okay." She saw the surprised look on Mandy's face. "Everybody else has a ride home, don't you think?"

"I'd say so," answered Michael, looking around.

Megan was able to catch Trish's eye and pointed to the door that they were leaving. Trish nodded in acknowledgment. Michael and the girls left. The two girls rode in silence. Mandy was mad that she didn't get paired up with who she wanted and she was irritated that Meg seriously considered that she should be paired up with Larry. Megan felt guilty that she would have deserted Mandy if push came to shove.

"Ya know," Mandy finally ventured, "I've heard stories about Michael—and not just from Jonesy. He seems to date, well, the fast kind. So, why is he seeing you?"

Megan turned and looked at her. "I haven't done anything with him that I can't tell you about. He's kissed me, and that's been it."

"What are you gonna do if he wants more?"

"I'll tell him no. Don't worry, I'm not going to do anything stupid."

"You look at him different than you have other guys."

"Do I need to tell you that I have a horrible crush on him?"

"No. I know you do. I just hope you can tell him no when the time comes."

"Yes, I can. We're basically friends, and on occasion he kisses me."

"Uh-huh. Remember Marcy—the guy she met at the fair and was so in love with?"

"Yeah."

"How she got caught up in the moment and it just happened?"

"It was Marcy's idea to go to Mark's house tonight," said Megan.

"What's that got to do with—?"

"She's an idiot!" yelled Megan. "Look, I'm not stupid. I am not going to let Michael use me, dump me, and then talk about me. You will remember that Marcy's boyfriend dumped her just a few days later. I haven't forgotten that. I am sure that in the end Michael will dump me, but I'm just going to have fun with him for now and when he leaves, I promise I'll still have my virginity intact. If not for myself, then for you and Jonesy."

"I'm just trying to be a friend. Which is a lot more than I can say for you, seeing as how you didn't mind leaving me with leechy Larry! Oddly enough, I have Michael to thank for getting me out of that one."

Megan swallowed hard. "I really wasn't going to leave you with him. I would have worked something out." She dropped Mandy off at her house and met Michael in her driveway.

He was leaning against his car, arms folded across his chest. He motioned with his hand, "Got my car out of the shop."

"I see. Heater's fixed, huh?"

"Yeah but . . . I still don't have any money."

She grinned and shook her head. It was inconsequential to her, she just wanted to be with him. "Do you want to come inside? I'll make some popcorn and we can watch TV."

"No," slowly he smiled.

"Want to go for a walk in my woods?"

"You're getting warmer." She struck the same pose as he: she leaned up against her own car, folded her arms across her chest, and smiled back at him. He chuckled, "Ever make out in the backseat of your new car?"

"No, can't say I have." He took her by the elbow and opened the back door for her. She crawled in, trying not to think about Marcy's long tale of the "ecstasy of the moment;" and instead tried to concentrate on the bawling and screaming Marcy did when he said good-bye and the agony she was in until her period finally started.

Is this what being in love is like? she wondered, as Michael crawled in after her. They were both stretched out on the backseat, their arms wrapped around each other. She loved the feel of his body pressed up against hers, his arms around her, his fingers running through her hair, his mouth on hers. Before she knew it, he had her jacket unzipped, his hand where it shouldn't be. "Don't," she whispered, not even convincing herself.

He continued and it wasn't until he started to unbutton her blouse that she said anything more. Of course her moans didn't help. "Michael, stop."

"You know, you don't mean it," he whispered.

"Yes, I . . ." *Oh that feels good.* "Michael you really have to stop."

"Baby, I want you."

"I bet you say that to all the girls."

She meant it as a joke and was surprised when she heard him say, "It's a line that hasn't failed me yet."

He was surprised at her strength as she struggled against him. "Get off me!"

"Meg. Hey, hey. Okay, I'll stop," he leaned away from her. "I thought . . . you were enjoying it."

She was glad it was dark as her face was red. "I was, but that didn't mean . . . I said no."

"Yeah, but you didn't *mean* no."

"Yes, I did Michael! Yes, I enjoyed it but . . . I . . . don't want to end up like that."

"Well, then, we need to sit up." She expected him to leave, but they both sat up and he wrapped his arm around her.

She laid her head on his shoulder. It was silent for a long time. Finally Meg asked, "What do you plan on doing when you graduate?"

"After I decide which college I'm going to, I'll go there and find out what job makes a whole lot of money and study for that."

"Money's important to you, huh?"

"Yep. It sure hasn't been much fun without it. And, I suppose by next year you'll have found your high school sweetheart who you can marry and have ten kids with before you're thirty."

She nearly came out of her seat. "Spare me! We are entering the seventies. I'm going to be a veterinarian and be my own boss."

"You're serious about that?" He looked amused.

"Yes."

"Well . . . I think that's great. You certainly seem to care about animals. You'll be very good at it I'm sure." Another long stretch of silence.

"I do love your kisses," she glanced up at him. He said nothing, just stared at her. Slowly she lay across his lap, facing him. "You have nothing to say about that, huh?"

"Nope."

Tentatively she kissed him, and then harder. His arms encircled her waist. "You don't get to kiss me like that and then tell me no. Hmm, maybe that's what I should do—tell you no."

She smiled and laid her head on his chest. Softly he stroked her hair. "Things are so much better when I'm with you," he whispered.

She looked up in surprise, "Thank you."

"It doesn't mean anything. Don't get any ideas—"

"Why do you always do that?" she asked.

"I just don't want you thinking—"

"You give me a nice compliment and then you ruin it. Michael, you are such a great football player. Of course, there wasn't much competition this year, seeing as how the really big guys were your teammates instead of on the opposing team."

"Okay, I get the message." They stared each other down. "I suppose this means I have to kiss and make up."

"No." She continued to gaze at him, only inches from his face.

Softly he kissed her, not sure if he would be rebuffed or not. He wasn't, so he kissed her some more. "See," he said, "I can't say no to you."

January 14, 1967: I ended up with Michael last night, although I started out with the girls. We went to Mark's house because his parents weren't home and the guys all were. They heard us outside and chased us down. Michael tackled me! But it was fun as he kissed me. We decided to leave after that. I dropped Mandy off at her house and Michael and I made out in the back of my car. I did have to tell him no a couple of times as he wanted to go further than just kissing. Let me tell you, it was hard. I am so crazy about him and I don't know why. One minute he can be so sweet, and the next minute he's shooting me down.

CHAPTER 8

As she walked past the gym, Megan decided to watch Jonesy and the guys practice basketball. She enjoyed the sport and had been to all the home games since entering high school. When the whistle blew, Jonesy came over and collapsed on the bench next to her. "Don't tell me your car broke down?"

"No, I don't need a ride home. Yearbook staff meeting got out early, so I thought I'd just watch you guys for a few minutes, that's all."

"Well, if that's the case, I'm surprised you're not up top, watching Michael." He pointed to the deck above them.

"What's he doing up there?"

"Practicing," he made it sound like a stupid question. The whistle blew and he left.

She walked to the top of the bleachers and, even though she knew better, she burst out laughing. The guys turned to stare at her. "Get lost!" they yelled.

"I'm sorry. What are you doing?"

"What does it look like?"

"Hey, Captain, throw her out of here."

"I'll take care of her." She looked to see Michael walking towards her, unsmiling. She burst out laughing again, seeing him in a skin-tight blue-and-white striped outfit. "What are you doing here?"

"I came to watch. But watch *what*, I'm sure I don't know. What do you call that ridiculous looking outfit?"

"I call it a wrestling outfit."

"You wrestle?"

"Looks that way, I'd say."

"Why didn't you tell me?"

"I didn't know it was any of your business."

Undaunted she continued. "You any good?"

"No."

"Then why do it?"

"To keep in shape."

"When's your next game?"

He rolled his eyes. "It's called a match, and it's tomorrow."

"Here?"

"Yeah."

"Hmm, okay."

"Hmm, okay, what?"

"I'll come."

"I don't recall inviting you."

"Do I need an invitation?" He continued to stare at her. "I go to all of Jonesy's home basketball games, why not your home wrestling ga— matches?"

He came closer to her. "You're making it sound like 'us.' Remember, there is no 'us.'"

"There is no 'us' between Jonesy and me either, except that we are friends. You and I are friends, aren't we?"

"Suit yourself," he said, before walking off.

The next afternoon Meg found herself going it alone as none of her girlfriends found wrestling interesting. Basketball yes, but not wrestling. Megan discovered she hated it. Guys grunting and groaning, grabbing each other here and there. It took her awhile to realize the competition went by weight. Obviously Michael would be the last to wrestle. She wanted to leave, but how to do so graciously? She felt someone sit down beside her. "Don't look so worried."

She knew the face, but it took a minute to come up with a name. "Hi, Josh." She never saw Michael's younger brother around school. "Michael told me he wasn't any good, but is it possible his opponent is even worse, so he has a chance of winning?"

Josh gave her a funny look and didn't say anything for several seconds. "Well, I like to think Michael always has a chance." *Oh, that was a nice way of looking at it.*

Finally, it was time for Michael's match. "I can't watch this," she said. Instead Megan focused on Josh's face, which pretty much told her how it was going. When the crowd yelled to signify the end of the match, Josh had an unhappy look on his face. "Don't tell me he lost."

"Yep." *Great. I can't very well congratulate Michael on a job well done— and it wouldn't be nice to slink off just because he lost. Well, maybe I can cheer him up.*

Standing outside the locker room door with Josh she found him quite different from his older brother. He had an easy manner, smiled a lot, and made her laugh.

Michael came out, took one look at Meg, and immediately snapped, "What are you standing around here for? I hope not for me!"

"I just thought . . ." she looked from him to Josh and back again. "I'm sorry you lost."

"I wouldn't have lost if you'd stayed away like I told you to."

"Wh—what?"

"You made me nervous. I couldn't concentrate."

"Aw, Michael, don't tell her something like that," said Josh, "she's liable to believe you."

"Shut up!" he roared at Josh.

"I— I'm sorry," she managed to get out, stunned by his accusation.

"It's all your fault!" his eyes bore into hers.

"Michael, cut it out!" yelled Josh. "Just because you lost, don't take it out on her. That guy had you out-weighed, out-classed —"

"I told you to shut up! Go get in the car!" He whirled on Megan again. She noticed that Josh didn't budge. So, there was someone else who didn't jump every time Michael said to. She appreciated the support, though it did her little good. "Why don't you get lost and leave me alone?"

Humiliated she turned and ran out the door.

January 17, 1967: I found out Michael wrestles, which is a nasty sport. I don't think I can stand to see another one. Guys grabbing each other in places where they shouldn't. It was awful. Michael lost, but he had already told me he wasn't any good. So, imagine my surprise when he blamed me for him losing! I couldn't believe it! Said he couldn't concentrate with me there.

He was really yelling at me. It was embarrassing, really embarrassing with his brother Josh there, trying to defend me. He told me to get lost and leave him alone.

Megan skipped study hall the next day. She just couldn't face Michael. Not that she felt she should apologize, but she knew Michael wouldn't. Instead, he would probably harass her in front of his friends. It was bad enough being totally humiliated in front of Josh, quite another to be humiliated in front of the whole class.

As she sat in the bathroom, berating herself and watching cigarette smoke circle above her head from the next stall, she wondered again what the appeal was to skipping class. *On the other hand, maybe I am supposed to go someplace more exciting than the bathroom. Like where?* Siberia came to mind.

She was working in the back of the vet clinic when the doctor's wife came breezing through the door. "Meg, the most gorgeous guy is out in the lobby asking for you."

Megan looked at her. Jonesy was cute, but definitely not gorgeous. Besides, Mrs. Thomas knew Jonesy. "Are you sure he wants me?"

"Asked for you by name."

As Mrs. Thomas swung back out the door, Megan caught a glimpse of Michael. Her heart gave a leap. *What is he doing here? Wait a minute. I sense a rat. Since he couldn't embarrass me in front of the class, is he going to do it in front of my co-workers? He certainly wouldn't be here to apologize, don't even entertain the thought, Becktame. So, why is he here? He must have tracked me down through Mandy or Jonesy, one of the other girls I hang out with . . . has he been to the house? Mom told him where I am? So that . . . what? He wants me to apologize to him? I don't think so!*

Megan could feel herself getting madder by the second. She had nothing to be sorry about. *He is a big jerk!* She would handle him just like she had all the others. She'd been handling guys all her life, why let Michael get to her? Anybody—even Larry the Leech—was nicer! She'd kick him where it hurts! *Make me apologize? I don't think so! He totally humiliated me. How many other guys in the locker room heard him?*

Both Mrs. Thomas and Michael were startled when the door slammed open and Megan yelled, "What do you want?"

Michael glanced uncertainly at Mrs. Thomas, who had never seen Meg like this. Hopefully she didn't act this way with the clients, who on occasion weren't the nicest. "I wondered if you'd be having a break soon and we could talk for a minute."

Meg looked at Mrs. Thomas, who had no idea if Meg wanted permission for a break or to use her for an excuse to not have one. Mrs. Thomas decided on a hasty retreat to the backroom, saying that she thought Dr. Thomas wanted her.

"Can you come outside for a minute?" asked Michael.

Meg crossed her arms over her chest, just like she'd seen Michael do to intimidate people, and stalked out while he held the door open for her.

"You weren't in study hall today," he said pleasantly, and then waited for an explanation that was not forthcoming.

She continued to stare at him. He smiled slightly. "So, you really do work here, huh?"

"No. I pay them a large sum of money to allow me to sit in the backroom in the off-chance you show up to check on me."

"Well, we're certainly pleasant today," he mumbled, and instantly regretted it.

"Don't you dare talk to me about being pleasant you SOB!"

"I'm sorry."

"How did you find me?"

"I drove out to your house. Your mom said you were here."

"That's who I have to thank, huh?"

"Look, I didn't come here to argue. I came to see if you wanted to go to the basketball game on Friday with me." She waited to see if he was going to say anything more. "You said you went to all of Jonesy's home games."

"That's it? You treat me like dirt and then expect me to go out with you? Aren't you the same person who just yesterday yelled at me to get lost and leave you alone? It was embarrassing enough with Josh standing there; but I'm sure other people heard you, too."

"You know, I'm no good at apologies. This is as good as it gets. Do you want to go out with me on Friday or not? Yes or no?"

It was his arrogance that really got to her. Leaning against his car, head cocked to one side, he was so sure she was going to say yes.

"No."

"Fine, suit yourself." He got in his car and she could hear him swearing as she walked away. Her hand was almost on the clinic door when she heard him get back out, slamming the car door hard. "Damn it, Megan! All right!" he stormed up to her. "I'm sorry!" She waited. "I apologize!" There seemed to be something more she wanted him to say, and he ran an exasperated hand through his hair. "I, I'm sorry. I shouldn't . . . I shouldn't have said the things I said. I don't know what else you want me to say." He saw her face soften.

"You really should learn to control your temper."

"I know."

"Someday saying you're sorry isn't going to fix things."

"I know. So, what about Friday?"

She thought about the few guys she had dated. There hadn't been that many, but she'd grown up with guys and they all had pretty much treated her decently. She didn't need what Michael was dishing out, she knew that. "I'll go if you promise to pamper me."

"*Pamper* you?" She thought he was going to come unglued. "You live in a huge house and probably have your mattress stuffed with bills and you want *me* to pamper *you?*"

"It doesn't cost you anything to be nice, to have some manners and to treat me with some respect."

"Pamper you?" he walked towards his car. "You don't know what you're asking." He got in, started the engine, and then pulled up next to her. "If I'm nice to you, and I'm saying *if*, you can't tell anybody. I mean, I have a reputation to uphold." She laughed. "I'm serious now. You don't know what you're asking."

She walked over to him, ducked her head inside, and gave him a quick kiss. "Yeah, I'll go with you Friday."

"I need you, Meg," he said softly, looking at her. "But . . . you've come at the wrong time in my life. And I am really sorry about that."

She frowned as she watched him drive away.

January 18, 1967: After Michael told me off, I just couldn't go to study hall and sit there with him behind me. However, he tracked me down at the vet clinic. He apologized for his rude behavior and asked me out for Friday's basketball game. I was going anyway to see Jonesy play, but I decided after all is said and done I'd rather go with Michael. Then he told me he needed me but that I'd come into his life at the wrong time. What does that mean?

She smiled as Michael opened all the doors for her on their way to the game. The house door, the car door, the school door. He brought up topics for conversation that she was sure he had had to ask somebody about. This wasn't him, she knew, but at least he was making an effort. "Michael, you don't have to chit-chat with me about animals. I know you'd rather hunt them than save them."

He seemed relieved. "What do you want to talk about then?"

She shrugged. "We don't *have* to talk."

"Oh . . . good." She shook her head and he was sure she was going to blast him, but before she turned her head away, he saw her smile.

The game was exciting. At halftime the score was tied. She leaned against Michael. "I'm hungry."

"Again? You're worse than I am. What do you want this time?"

"Popcorn."

"A large, I suppose."

"Yeah, I could go for a large."

"Okay. Sit tight." He got up to go.

"A Coke, too?"

"A large, I know." He disappeared in the crowd.

By the time the game resumed, Michael had not returned. Some minutes passed and a few of Meg's friends sitting several rows down hollered up to her, "Where's Michael?"

"He's getting us something to eat."

They frowned at each other and then one ventured. "He left the concession stand before we did."

"He's probably talking to some of his old friends that he hasn't seen all year." They accepted this and turned back to the game.

Michael's former school district had been split. The majority of the students had come to the new high school, but the rest were attending the opposing team's school. "I take it you don't get excited at games," she had said to him earlier, as she jumped up and down and screamed, while he just sat there.

"I'm a little torn," he had answered. "I grew up with a lot of these guys, so I hate cheering against them. But, on the other hand, I've made new friends here and I don't want to cheer against them either."

She thought for a moment. "Was it like this for you in football?"

He smiled. "No, that was different. It was my job to beat them. I'll just watch. You go ahead and cheer."

The third period came and went. Halfway through the fourth period one of the wrestlers hollered to her, "Where's Michael?"

"Went to get us something to eat."

"They just closed the concession stand. I didn't see him down there."

"Must have gone out for it," she laughed, dying inside. *Where can he be? Is this his revenge? Dumping me here, for everybody to see? But, he's been so pleasant all evening.* She scanned the crowd—and then her heart stopped. There he was. Sitting across the court opposite her a few rows up, talking to a blonde bombshell. They were laughing. Why had this not dawned on her? If Michael knew some of the guys from the other school, he would certainly know some of the girls.

She watched as the girl flipped her long hair and dipped her hand down into the popcorn bag—way down. Meg jumped up with a yell as Michael offered the blonde a drink. Fortunately, at that point, the rest of the crowd jumped up with her.

She could well imagine Michael making a date with the girl. Like, maybe right after the game? *Should I ask my girlfriends for a ride? Leave before he has the chance to snub me? "Oh, you thought you were going to show her up by leaving with blondie? She left your sorry ass a long time ago." Okay, stop. I am acting like a jealous, possessive girlfriend, which I have no right to do. So, we've gone out a few times. Big deal. He's talking to a girl he grew up with, big deal. But, this is embarrassing. How many other people see him across the way? "Don't get any ideas about us, there is no us." How many times has he said that to me? We're just friends. And as a friend, I will sit here and wait until he returns. We'll see what kind of a friend he is.*

Concentrating now on Michael instead of the game, Megan saw him glance up at the scoreboard and a horrified look crossed his face. "I gotta go," she could see him mouth. *Yeah, Michael, it's that time already!* He got up, looked at the popcorn in his hand, and then handed it to the girl. Obviously there wasn't enough to bother with. He shook the drink and must have decided there was some redemption there, as he kept it. He got down from the bleachers and then turned as he heard the girl yell his name. Even from where she sat, Megan could see the girl put a hand to her mouth and shout, "Call me." Michael nodded. Megan fanned herself as she felt blood rush up her face. She tried to concentrate on the game so that Michael would think she hadn't noticed he had been gone for most of the second half.

He sat down next to her. As he offered her the drink, she saw that he looked as red as she felt. "It doesn't look exactly full," she commented. "No, thank you."

He didn't look at her. "I changed the straw."

"That was thoughtful. But, no thank you." She turned back to the game. She wondered if Michael had heard the rumors about them and if so, what he thought. Even though she had told Jonesy and Mandy that she didn't know what they were talking about, she did as of yesterday when she had been in the bathroom stall before classes started. . . .

The outside door had opened with several girls laughing and chatting, ". . . I mean, I don't get it. This isn't like him at all."

"It has to be her car and her money. What else has she got to offer?"

"Yeah, I don't think her looks are that hot."

"A lot of the guys would disagree with you there. Cripe, look at Jim. I think he's still hung up on her."

"She has to be putting out. I don't care what anybody else says."

"Yeah, but he never stays. It's like . . . he really likes her." It was quiet for two seconds and then they all burst out laughing.

"But, you know what?" another one of them ventured. "He seems more like he used to be. Ya know, when we were kids?"

"What are ya sayin'? She's good for him?" More snickers.

"Haven't the rest of you noticed it? He smiles, he laughs. Not a lot, I admit; but more than he has in the last few years. He's . . . more relaxed."

"It's all the tension release he's getting!" They all hooted and Megan had had enough. They were talking about Michael and her! The nerve! From their voices she knew these were not girls she knew. How dare they be discussing her virginity—or lack there of. How disgusting. She felt dirty . . . and mad.

She snapped the bar back on the stall door and stepped out. The place went dead. At least Michael had taught her how to stare. They all looked elsewhere—except one. She was propped up against the sink. She took a long drag on her cigarette and then slowly let it out, glaring at Megan the whole time. *Okay, Michael. What does one do when someone stares you back equally? No, she was not giving ground.*

She smiled, "You have as good a stare as I have. Are you one of Michael's one-night stands?" She stuck her chin out and the two girls closest to the smoker stepped back. Megan had never been in a fight, but she had wrestled and played hard with the boys she had grown up with. *Come on, honey, bring it on.*

The girl tapped some of her ash into the sink, "And here I thought you were the shy, timid type."

"Guess you were wrong," answered Megan. "Like you were about everything else."

They all stood silently for several more seconds. Megan finally walked across to the sink. The other girls moved out of the way. She took her time washing and drying her hands and, as she was going out the door, heard the girl who hadn't moved from her post say, "I like your car."

Megan turned around, stone-faced. "Thank you." It wasn't until she sat down in homeroom that she suddenly felt queasy. *You idiot! What was I thinking? Taking on five hoods! They could have beaten the crap out of me! Don't use that bathroom again!*

She felt Michael tug on her sleeve. He was standing. Everyone else was walking down the bleachers. "The game's over?" she asked, startled. "Who won?"

"Who won?" he asked incredulously. He had discovered that Megan knew as much about basketball as he did. She had really been into the game.

She glanced quickly at the scoreboard. Guest: 79. Home: 81. "Oh. Thank goodness, we won. That was close, huh?"

"Yeah." They started down the bleachers. "Just in case Jonesy should say anything to you—he saved the day for us."

"Please, don't tell him I missed it."

"Your secret is safe with me." They got into his car. "Would you like a burger or something?"

"Yeah. I didn't get much to eat at the game," she said dryly.

"Sorry about that. I ran into some old friends. I didn't realize the time until the game was nearly over."

Get off your high horse, Becktame. He's not your property. At least he came back to get you. The smokers in the bathroom will have a field day with this. "It's nice you got to see some of your old friends."

"I'm sorry I was gone so long. What were you thinking about, that you didn't notice the game had ended? It was a real cliff-hanger."

"I was just thinking about . . . stuff."

"I suppose you're wondering what happened to the popcorn," he said.

"No. I could see my popcorn and drink disappearing from where I was sitting. She's pretty." Silence. Too long a silence. An embarrassed silence. She looked at him. "Do you have a date with her?" Longer silence. "I see." She swallowed hard. "Well, I do appreciate you at least taking me home instead of telling me to find a ride. Thank you for that."

He looked at her. "I don't have a date with her tonight. Is that the type of guy you think I am? It's for next weekend."

"Oh. Okay." They went into the restaurant and sat down.

He still couldn't look at her. "You . . . don't mind . . . do you?"

"You having a date with another girl? No. You have always told me there is no us. We're friends. And as a friend I say, go for it. I'm sure she'll give you what I won't." *All right. My voice is starting to rise. It's starting to sound a little angry, a little jealous. We're friends. I knew all along he would dump me. At least it's for somebody who is really good-looking.* She took a deep breath. "Hey, I know," she had his attention now, "there were two really cool looking guys down on the court. I got their names. Maybe you could introduce me and I could get a date with one of them and we could double."

"Are you going to order?"

Yes, let me see. One of everything on the menu. That will take him what, a week to work off? The only talking the two of them did was to order. They ate in silence and rode to her house the same way. As soon as he put the car in park, she had the door open. "Meg, wait," he grabbed her arm.

"Michael, I'm sorry I acted the way I did," she sighed. "You are certainly free to do whatever you want. I'm sorry."

"Meg," he said softly and turned the car off. "You and I . . . are becoming too close. I . . . don't want . . . I don't want to be close to anybody. Can you understand that?" He looked at her.

She shook her head. "No."

"The guys won't come near you as long as they know I'm interested in you. If I start dating somebody else then . . . I'm sure they'll come calling. Things are better this way, Meg. You'll see . . . someday."

"Yeah, okay." He didn't walk her to the door.

January 19, 1967: I can't believe I was stupid enough to take on five hoodlums in a bathroom that hardly anybody uses! What was I thinking? Defending my honor, I guess. How dare they discuss what I am doing alone with Michael.

Mandy had a fit when I told her. "Look what this guy is doing to you! You had detention for the first time in your life because of him, you skipped class, which you've never done before. You let Michael drive your car, you have him inside your home when your parents aren't there, and then you were almost in a catfight with a bunch of girls that we would never associate with! He's no good for you! Dump him before he dumps you." Yeah, like I could ever dump Michael.

January 20, 1967: Michael took me to the basketball game. And here I thought we were getting along so well. He dumped me. I'm watching the game, enjoying myself, and then I see him across the court with this gorgeous blonde. The two of them ate all my popcorn and drank most of my pop (but Michael did think of me—he changed the straw). He made a date with her for next weekend. How do I know this? He told me so himself!

He dropped me off at home saying we were getting too close for his comfort. Like he cared or something. I am just crushed. I am so hung up on him. I am never going to feel this way about another guy, ever. Sixteen and I'm ruined for life. There will never be another Michael.

January 26, 1967: Michael had the gall to ask me today if I was coming to his wrestling match. NO! I don't need to watch him grope some other guy. It's bad enough that come Friday night I'll be imagining him groping Blondie.

CHAPTER 9

S o, how did your match go last night?" not that Megan was terribly interested, but she did want to keep the lines of communication open with him.

"I won."

"Good. Congratulations."

"Thank you."

"Good thing I didn't show up. Then you'd have probably lost."

"You know very well I didn't mean that when I said it. Do you pay any attention to wrestling?"

"No. Why would I? I think it's an awful sport. It's . . . ishy."

"Ishy?" He screwed his face up. "Is that really a word?"

"You got my meaning, didn't you?" He thought about this and then nodded. "Why do you ask?"

"Just wondered."

"Talk about wondering, what happened to your car? I noticed you haven't driven it all week." *Maybe it's busted and he can't take his date out tonight.*

"Oh, my father and I play this little game on occasion called hide-

Michael's-car-keys-until-he-finds-them. But, at the moment, I am one up on him because I've found my keys."

"So, why not drive?"

"If I had taken them earlier in the week, he might have decided to hide them again and then I might not be able to find them in time for tonight. And I really need to get away tonight."

"I see. Well, you have fun."

"Thank you. What are you doing tonight?"

Nothing! "I, um, have a couple of choices. Haven't decided on what I want to do yet."

"Well, whatever you decide, have fun."

"Thanks." *Ringing your neck comes to mind. That would be fun.*

Friday night came and went. Mandy and Patti had dates. Meg didn't bother to ask Trish and Marcy what they were doing. She tried to occupy her mind with other things instead of thinking about Michael and what he was doing on his date. She didn't care if they were just out walking. She was deprived of his company, and that hurt. *Be glad he dumped you now,* she told herself. *Be glad he dumped you before something happened.* She loved his kisses, she loved the way his hands felt moving over her. *Better that nothing had happened. How would I be feeling now, if I hadn't said no to him? At least I can still look him in the eye.* She tried knitting, reading, watching TV, and sewing. But all she saw was Michael's face.

Megan was surprised when Michael phoned on Saturday. "You doing anything tonight?" he asked.

"Yeah, I'm going out . . ." *Forget it. He knows I'm lying.* "No."

She expected him to laugh and make a sarcastic remark. Instead she heard him ask, "What would you like to do?"

"Oh, I don't know. Go bowling?"

"Do you know how to bowl or is throwing your ball in the gutter considered bowling?"

"I do not throw my ball in the gutter."

"Yeah, we'll see. Seven?"

"Okay. Are you all right?" She waited for him to answer. "How was your date last night?"

"I'll see you at seven."

Knowing how uncomfortable Michael was around her dad, Megan was dressed and waiting for him when he knocked. "I'm leaving!" she hollered and headed for the door.

"Wait! Is Michael here?" Her dad came in the room and she saw Michael stiffen. Just like Megan couldn't understand why Michael's father treated him so, Michael couldn't believe that her father was a gentle soul. To him, all fathers were to be closely watched in case they made a sudden move to strike. "Mrs. Becktame wants some furniture moved. Do you think you could help me with some of the heavier pieces?"

"Yes, sir."

She grabbed Michael's arm as he started to follow her dad into the living room. "You don't need to 'sir' him," she whispered. "He's my dad. He likes you." His look told her he didn't believe her.

She followed behind and the three of them moved furniture from here to there, from there to here. Each time her mom shook her head. "No, it's just not working. I was so sure I'd like it this way."

"How many times have you said that now?" asked Megan.

"Tell me," said her dad as he looked at Michael, "is my daughter this indecisive?"

"No," answered Michael, "she knows exactly what she wants and is very good at letting me know it."

"Very funny," Megan said.

Her mom started to laugh and Meg looked at her. "He thinks you're a brat."

"He does not!" Meg looked over to see Michael grinning. "You are so dead when we go bowling."

"Okay," her mom said, "I've made my decision. I don't need a new arrangement, I need new furniture." *Why did Mom have to say that in front of Michael?* Megan groaned inwardly.

Mr. Becktame didn't help either when he said, "Fine, my dear. Tomorrow we'll go to the store and see if we can't find something to your liking." Michael didn't say a word.

Megan only added to Michael's quiet mood when she beat him the first game in bowling. "I told you I don't throw my ball in the gutter."

Some of his friends came in and ribbed him when they saw the score. She expected Michael to say, "I let her win," but instead she saw him look at her. It clearly said, "You're not winning again." She returned the cool stare. Michael was an All-American football player—a star. If he thought she was going to back down for one frame, he was wrong. His ego could just take a bruising for a change. They both summed each other up—and the race was on, with his friends cheering Meg on.

Michael won the second game by two pins. "Okay, we're even. Let's quit," she offered. He nodded. But his friends wouldn't hear of it. They had money riding on this. They needed a tiebreaker. She could see the steam rising off Michael, couldn't they?

"Fine," he muttered and glared at her.

What? Does he want me to throw a few gutters? No, I wasn't raised that way. I've beaten Jonesy plenty of times and he survived. Maybe this will be his first humbling experience. Do him some good.

However, as the game went on, Meg began to think maybe she should throw a few gutters. They were neck and neck and his friends were getting louder and cruder. *Knock it off,* she wanted to say, *I have to go home with him.* Michael wasn't speaking to her at all now. *Okay, this isn't worth it.* Her ego would not be upset if she lost; but if her ball landed in the gutter they'd all know what she was doing. Carefully she took out three pins and turned around to find Michael right behind her.

"Don't you dare throw this game," he hissed.

"I wasn't!" she hotly denied.

"That's the first time you've missed your mark."

How does he know where my mark is? Although it was true. "I'm getting tired, okay?"

He threw three strikes in a row and she breathed a sigh of relief.

The guys still congratulated her, even though she lost.

"Don't you ever play down to me," he growled when they got to his car.

"I wasn't. You *need* your ego burst." She was plainly disgusted.

"It was the only time you missed your mark. How is it you're such a good bowler?"

"My parents' friends used to own the bowling alley. I've been bowling there since I was five."

"A little piece of information you forgot to tell me," he accused.

"I didn't want to scare you off." He glared at her.

They drove to her place in silence. "You coming in?" she asked as she fiddled with the car door and finally got it open. He sat there. *Okay.* She got out and walked up to her door. She turned to see him still sitting there. She walked back and got in the car. They sat.

"I suppose you'll be getting new bedroom furniture tomorrow, along with your mom's living room furniture."

She chose to ignore this and instead said, "Do you want to go for a walk in the—"

"No."

"Do you want me to get out?" He didn't answer, so she opened the door.

He grabbed her wrist. "No." She slammed the door shut and waited.

It was a long time and it came out haltingly, but at last he spoke. "Why . . . why do you have to be so . . . why do you stand up to me? Cuz if you didn't . . . I'd never have paid any attention to you. You're different. I . . . like the fact that . . . everybody's scared of me. They leave me alone. I want that. But you . . . I've never had anyone stand up to me. Tell me off. I don't want this!" he suddenly yelled.

"You don't want what?"

"I don't want to think about you! I don't want to think about you all the time, like I do now! You want to know about my date last night with Wendy?"

So, that's what her name is. "Yeah, sure."

"It ended rather early. After the third time I called her Meg she asked me to take her home." Megan quickly turned her head, so he wouldn't see the smile. "I don't want this. Do you understand?"

116

"Well, no. I can't say that I do. I think about you, too; but I find that it's a nice feeling."

"I don't have nice feelings! I just want . . ." His voice got louder, but as she brought her face closer to his, he stopped. He couldn't very well tell her off when she was so close. "I just want you to understand . . ." She brushed her lips across his. "I just . . . want you to . . ."

She moved her lips along his cheek until she got to his ear. "Tell me what you want."

He grabbed her up in his arms and kissed her. "I just want you."

January 28, 1967: Michael took me bowling. I beat him the first game but he beat me the next two. Some of his friends showed up and they were really giving him a hard time. Guess we won't do that again!

Michael acted funny all night. Barely spoke to me and I wondered why he asked me out at all. I was dying to know how last night's date went, but I didn't dare ask. We got back to my place and then he started yelling. It sounded like he didn't want to see me anymore, and then he told me he wanted me! I think he really, REALLY likes me!!!! We made out and I let him go a little bit further this time before I said no. I want to tell him that I love him but I know that will drive him away for sure.

February 14, 1967: Today was Valentine's Day. Michael made no mention of it at all in school, so neither did I. However, he came over to the vet clinic and handed me a single rose. I was so pleased and then he had to ruin it by saying, "It's all I could afford." I wish he didn't have this hang-up about money.

Friday they went to the basketball game. Megan could tell something was wrong and asked him. "Nothing!" he yelled. "Would you stop harping on me?"

Megan jumped up and down, screamed, clapped, cheered, and booed throughout the first half. Michael never moved a muscle. In fact, he looked bored. She slipped her hand through his arm and was dismayed when he disentangled himself from her and stared out over the court. During the third quarter they both just sat. "We're leaving," he suddenly said, stood up, and took off down the bleachers. He stopped at the bottom and waited. For a few seconds, Meg was too stunned to move. Slowly she got up and followed him out. He opened the car door for her, but he didn't say a word.

He drove up her driveway. "We're done," he said.

She sat still, not quite understanding. "For the night? For the . . ." she couldn't bring herself to say it.

"We're done . . . done." He couldn't look at her. He quickly got out, came around to her side, and opened the door. She just sat there. "Please. Don't prolong this. Please just . . . Meg, don't. Don't cry, Megan." Swearing, he slammed the door, got back in, and jammed the car in reverse. They took off down the driveway. She had no idea where they were going. Neither did he.

Finally, he pulled into one of his old make-out haunts, killed the lights and engine, and they just sat. Meg had gotten herself under control by now. *You knew this time would come,* she kept yelling at herself.

"I told you not to get involved with me."

"Yeah, I know," she sniffed. "You also told me you wanted me. Is it because I keep saying no to you?"

"Give me a little credit."

"I thought . . . I thought we really had something. I'm okay now. You can take me home. I guess deep down inside I've always known that I cared more for you than you for me. I thought I'd at least get this year out of you. I'm sorry. This is my fault. You've always told me you didn't want to get involved and . . . it's my own fault."

"God, Meg, if you only knew," he said.

"Well then, tell me."

"Why? What good will it do me? What good will it do either one of us?" For the first time he looked at her.

"I love you," she said. He was leaving anyway, what did she have to lose?

"Meg, you're only sixteen," he said softly. "There will be others."

"Not like you."

He smiled slightly and glanced at her, then looked away. "Not like you either."

"So . . . why? Why now?"

"Come on, Meg. It should be obvious by now. Especially after Valentine's Day."

"What? You remembered. You brought me a rose."

"Yeah, one."

"So? I agree it was kind of late in the day for you to remember; but I figured you didn't want to bring a flower to school." She smiled at him.

"Look, I didn't have the money. I don't have the money. I . . . it's not that I don't want to take you places—I just don't have any money! Don't you get it? I can't afford you!" He went to start up the car but she grabbed his wrist.

"Are you telling me," she started out slowly, "that you are breaking up with me because of a cash problem? Look at me! Is this an excuse to dump me or are you telling me the truth? *Look at me!* Because I'm getting really mad! You don't need to worry about me breaking down again and crying! You look at me and you tell me the truth!"

"Look at you," he sneered, "you have no concept. You sit in your fancy house, have your own private woods, and drive a new car. While I don't have two pennies to rub together. What could the two of us possibly do together? Walk in your woods? Sit and talk? Go at it in the backseat of my car? You're not comfortable with that and, quite frankly, neither am I."

"Oh, I see. I've got all the money; but I'm not good enough to be in your backseat. Thank you very much."

He finally turned and looked at her. "You're not trash."

"Oh." They both stared out their side windows. Megan cleared her throat. "I do have money for us to go—"

"Don't even think it!"

"If you would please let me finish. I have the money, but would guess you would be uncomfortable with that. And I don't know if I would eventually feel I'm being used or not. Why . . . don't you just get a job?"

"I've thought of that. But between sports and studying, I don't really have the time. My goal has always been to get *the hell out of here!*" He suddenly flared, and then as quickly calmed down. "To get into a really good college. I am going to make a lot of money someday, Meg. I am never living like this again. But . . . you need somebody who can take you out every weekend. You need somebody who has money now."

"No. I just need you."

"I'm no good for you."

"Well, let's see. You're talented, ambitious, and honest. You've been decent to me. A little moody perhaps . . ." *There, I got one smile out of him.* "We're teenagers. We're not supposed to have a lot of money."

"You do. Jonesy does."

"Jonesy works for his dad. He makes his own hours and, quite frankly, he only works when he feels like it. Ya know," she said slowly, "I was a little miffed on Valentine's Day when you didn't say anything, didn't do anything, but then I thought, okay, that's just you. But when you came to the clinic . . . it was the thought that counted, Michael. You cared enough about me to do something. I wouldn't have been any happier if you had given me a dozen roses. It was the fact that you went and got me a rose and drove to where I worked and gave it to me. I love being with you. That doesn't cost you anything. And yes, I like to go to the movies and bowling and stuff like that, and maybe sometimes I could offer to pay, and if you felt okay with that, we could go. And if you had a problem with me paying, then I guess I'll go with the girls. You need to be straight with me, though. Is this an easy excuse for you to dump me or is this really the problem? We can work out the problem, but if you don't want to date me anymore then be man enough to tell me."

She sat and waited for what seemed like an eternity, her heart in her throat. He started up the car and drove to her house. He turned and looked at her. "Meg," and she knew then what he was going to say, she could see it in his face, "I'm going to leave you someday, that's a sure thing. Don't you think it would be better, easier for you . . . for both of us, if we just did it now? Before we get . . . personally involved?"

"I'm already personally involved."

"No, I mean . . . intimate. Really intimate. I don't want . . . you to think I'm using you."

She nodded. "I was thinking I couldn't feel any worse; but you're right. If we had gone all the way and then you told me good-bye I'd feel like trash, used, really stupid. This way I just feel heartsick. But, I can forgive you that. You've always been up front with me. Thank you for that."

"I'm sorry, Meg."

"Me too," he brought his hand up around her neck to pull her towards him. Meg shook him off. "I don't want a good-bye kiss. See ya around."

February 17, 1967: Why is it that whenever I think things are going great with Michael, he lets me down? He broke up with me. This time for good. I hurt so bad. I told him I loved him and he just sat there, not saying a word. Just because I have money and he doesn't. Or at least that's what he says. I'm not sure I believe him. I don't know what to think, except that I just hurt. How am I supposed to go to school every day and see him and pretend that everything's okay? I am so glad I didn't go all the way with him. That would have been worse. I can just imagine the guys talking. They'll be talking anyway, but at least Michael and I know nothing like that happened.

Late in the evening, her mom knocked on Megan's bedroom door. "What?" yelled Megan.

Her mom let herself in. "What are you crying about?"

"Michael broke up with me."

"Oh, good. Then you won't mind me telling him off. Nobody should be calling at this ungodly hour." Her mom started back out the door.

"What are you talking about?"

"He's on the phone. No polite boy would call after nine." Megan pushed past her mom in the narrow hallway.

"Michael?"

"Yeah, hi. I'm sorry to call so late—"

"It's all right. Mom and Daddy are watching TV."

"I was just . . . missing you. Will you take me back?"

"You are such an idiot!" she screamed.

"I know. See ya tomorrow?"

"Yeah. Okay."

P.S. Michael called. He wants me back! He can't live without me.

They stayed at her house all Sunday afternoon. "Let's bake some cookies," Meg offered.

"I'll eat cookies. I am *not* baking any." He hopped onto a barstool to watch her.

"Jonesy used to bake with me."

Slowly he grinned. "Really?"

She was hauling the ingredients out of the cupboard when she turned around and looked at him. "You don't need to spread that around. We were little kids. Trust me, he has not baked with me in years."

"What else can you tell me about Jonesy?"

"Nothing of interest to you."

Later, she suspected that he actually liked the milk better than the cookies, although Michael told her they were good. He apologized to Mrs. Becktame for calling so late.

"It would be best if you didn't call after nine," she reprimanded.

"Yes, ma'am." *Way to be, Mom. He was comfortable around you at least, now he's not.*

They walked around in the woods. "Do you remember anything I've taught you?" Meg asked, as she pointed out the different trees and flowers and named them.

"I didn't know this was biology class."

"Oh, look, here comes Stanley!"

"Who?"

He would have warned her, but it was too late. The raccoon came right up to her and stood on its haunches.

"Let's see what I've got," Meg reached a hand into her pocket and then knelt down.

"You're not gonna—" but the raccoon had already reached his paw out and taken what she offered. He sniffed it and then waited. She scratched behind Stanley's ears and talked soothingly to him. Michael didn't dare move. "He could have rabies," he whispered.

"I don't allow that in my woods," Meg stated. She stood up and Stanley waddled off.

"Do you do that with all the animals here?"

"Not all, but a lot of them."

"I don't think that's wise."

"I've been doing it for years. Don't worry. I know what I'm doing. Why do you think I want to be a vet?"

He looked thoughtful and then nodded. "I wish I knew what I wanted to do. You're lucky." He changed the subject abruptly. "You going to come to my wrestling match this week? It's at home."

"No, thank you."

"I'm sorry I yelled at you. It wasn't your fault. I was just blowing off steam. I should be able to beat this guy. I'd like you to see me win instead of you thinking of me as a loser."

"I have never thought of you as a loser."

"Please, will you come?"

"I don't think so." How could she kindly tell him what a gross sport it was? "I'm going to be at the vet clinic all week."

"You've managed to go to all of Jonesy's home basketball games. You've only been to one of my wrestling matches."

"Guess you should have played basketball. I'd have seen you then. Maybe that is a sport you could have excelled in."

"I don't care for basketball that much."

"You might have liked it, if you'd played. Surely you could have done better there than wrestling."

He stared at her and then glanced at his watch. "Walk me to the car. I need to get home."

She slipped her hand through his arm and he did not pull away. "You don't read the newspaper, do you?" he asked when they got to his car.

"No. Why?"

"Just wondered. See ya."

March 13, 1967: I will kill Michael with my bare hands when I get a hold of him! When I think about the things I said! And he just stood there, staring at me. All day long I heard the kids congratulating Michael. I know that he's been to the district tournament and regionals; but doesn't everybody go? I asked him the other day if he was done. He said no, he still needed to go to the state finals. How long does this groping contest drag on for?

Then Jonesy stops me in the hall and says, "Which are you feeling, proud or scared?"

"Proud or scared about what?"

"Michael." I had no clue what he was talking about. Get this! Am I proud of Michael for winning BOTH the district and regional tournaments or scared because in the state finals he has to go up against the one guy he lost to early in the season? Apparently the time I saw him was the only match he lost! I feel like a fool! Telling Michael he should have gone out for the basketball team! Maybe he could have excelled there! He must have laughed all the way home.

I will kill him with my bare hands when he shows up here since I can't do it in public.

CHAPTER 10

HOW COULD YOU *NOT* KNOW?" HE YELLED BACK. "THE ENTIRE school knew!"

"You could have told me."

"Why? You were never interested. If *only* I'd been on the *basketball* team."

"Well, I'm sorry. But watching guys grunt and groan and grope each other—I'm sorry! It's disgusting!"

He got in her face. "Maybe if you'd stop saying no, you'd enjoy it."

"Very funny. I must be the laughing stock!"

"How do you think I feel? My own girlfriend thinks I'm no good at wrestling and that I should have gone out for another sport."

"I'm sorry! Had I known . . . I don't know why it's such a big deal if I went or not anyway."

He didn't say anything for a long time. "I guess you're right."

"No, tell me, please."

"It's just that . . . other than Josh, nobody has ever bothered to come and watch me wrestle. I thought, ya know, that it might be nice if my girlfriend came and supported me. But *nooo* she thinks I should try out for the basketball—"

"I'm sorry. Okay? I'm really sorry. Surely your parents—mom—came and watched a few times."

"No. My older brothers always said they would, but they never did. And I was never really sure if Josh came to support me or if he just wanted to get away from home for awhile."

"Oh, Michael. I'm sorry."

"Is there anything else you can say?"

"Yeah, what's with you calling me your girlfriend?"

"Oh, well, this is just great. On top of everything else, you don't want me? I guess that explains everything!" He turned and walked off through the woods.

"Michael! Stop! Michael! That's not what I meant!" She ran after him. Meg thought about tackling him the way he had tackled her but all she could envision is that she'd get the back of his heel in her face. Instead, she grabbed the back of his belt with both hands.

Michael dragged her along without slowing down, but she hung on. She tried getting one arm around him and getting a foot in front of him to trip him. She tried various other moves to get him to either slow down or stop. Finally, he did. "You're not thinking of wrestling me to the ground, are you? And winning?"

She came around to face him and wrapped her arms tightly around him. He rested his hands on the top of her shoulders but wouldn't look at her. "I would love to be your girlfriend, but which one of us is always saying 'there is no us. Don't get any ideas. Don't get close to me'? I don't dare think of you as my boyfriend because you'd have a fit. You have a reputation for going through a lot of girls. You never stay. Look how many times you've dumped me. What about Valerie? What about Wendy? What are you pouting about?"

"You. Just like the wrestling, you're the last to know you're mine. You know . . . you know how I feel about you."

"No. Tell me."

"I'm not gonna. You should know."

"From all the times you've told me good-bye?"

"You know I never mean that. I always come back."

"Ya know, when you say girlfriend . . . that's kind of a commitment. Like . . . no more Valerie, no more Wendy, no more . . . anybody."

He looked at her, his hands playing along her back. "Yeah, I know."

"Is that . . . what you're saying?"

"I haven't been with anybody else, have I? And I don't want to be."

She smiled. "When do you go to the state finals?"

"Friday. I'll be gone all weekend." *Finally, I can go out with the girls and see a movie.*

She wrapped her arms around his neck and drew him to her, kissing him. "How about if your girlfriend fixes you a great big meal on Thursday night?"

"You've got to stop kissing me like that."

"Why?"

"It might land you in trouble."

"With you, that might not be a bad thing."

March 14, 1967: I don't know if he'll ever say it, but Michael loves me. I know he does. He's just too bullheaded to admit it. He did call me his girlfriend though, and he walks me to a lot of classes during the day. People talk to me like they think we're a couple. I know I'm only sixteen, but I have met the man I'm going to marry. I just know it.

"Where are your parents?" asked Michael, looking around the kitchen.

"They are safely over at the Hill's playing bridge," she answered.

"I'm going home—"

"No, you're not!" she bristled. "I spent two week's allowance and quizzed Mom as tactfully as I could on how to make roast duck. She thinks I'm doing this as a home economics project. Let's hope she doesn't remember I'm not taking that class."

"Megan, if your parents find me here or find out that I've been here, you're going to be in trouble."

"Yeah? What are they going to do to me? Lecture me at the most. I can handle it."

"What if they ground you? Then we can't go out."

She laughed. "I've never been grounded in my life. Don't worry. Go sit in the dining room and I'll bring it out."

"I can eat at the counter." He remained on the barstool that he always sat on.

"Michael," he could see a speech coming, "this is my contribution to your wrestling. I'm sorry I've been a flop at it. I'm going to make it up to you as best I can. I have made dinner, with all the trimmings. This is not a counter dinner. This is dinner dinner. Go to the dining room, please."

Slowly he slid off the stool and went around the corner. She saw him stop as his eyes took in the table. "Oh, God, not candlelight."

"Yep," she answered.

He threw her a glance, but dutifully went and sat down. He was amazed at the meal she had prepared. Roast duck, a salad that had tons more than just lettuce in it, steamed vegetables, rolls, and an entire gallon of milk.

"Meg, I can't believe you did all this. I'm stunned. You fixed this yourself?"

"I love to cook. I think I was born in the wrong century. I love to sew—I make a lot of my own clothes--to knit, to do all those things that girls my age aren't supposed to like anymore."

She saw him look down at the formal setting. "Do I really need this many forks and knives?" he asked.

She lit the candles and sat down across from him. "My parents love to go to their country club. I go sometimes and . . . I'd like to take you there." *Actually I'm thinking of the prom.* "I figure you should know how, so you won't be embarrassed. So, this is how it works." She went through everything. At first, he started to get mad. But then he decided that maybe Meg was right. His own mother wouldn't know one fork from the other. This was the world that Megan lived in. If he truly believed that one day he'd be making a lot of money and living like this, he should learn a few things from someone who knew.

"God, Meg, this is excellent," he said as he ate. He didn't mind his own mother's cooking; but this, this was like nothing he'd ever had before.

"Thank you. We don't have this often, but it's one of my favorites." For dessert she brought out homemade cheesecake. "What would you like on top of it? Chocolate, raspberries, or strawberries?"

"I wouldn't know what goes on top. I'm getting full."

She hoped her face didn't register surprise as she realized he never had cheesecake before. "Well, personally, I prefer chocolate."

"I'm not a chocolate person."

She made a face. "That's one strike against you." She put strawberries on his, chocolate on hers. They finished eating and then they cleared the table. "I need to clean up in here so my parents don't suspect."

He stepped away from her. "I don't do dishes."

She chuckled. "Just sit on the stool and keep me company. Tell me what I need to know about wrestling, so that when I come to the finals I know what's going on."

"You're not coming to the finals," he stated flatly.

"Yes, I am," she challenged.

"No, Meg. The time to have seen me was before. When I was pretty sure of winning. The guy you saw me lose to—I'll probably be facing him again. I don't want you there. I'll use you as an easy excuse, even though I know perfectly well that you have nothing to do with it. And, don't think about sneaking in either," he warned. He saw the surprised look on her face. *How does he know what I'm thinking?* "I need to be able to concentrate. I won't be able to, if I think about you." She smiled. "Don't think you have me wrapped around your little finger."

"I didn't say anything."

"I saw that look. Promise me you won't come to the finals."

"Do I have to?"

"Please . . . for me."

She looked at him. "I'm sorry I wasn't supportive. I won't make that mistake again. If you are that worried, then I promise I won't come; but if you change your mind, please call me and tell me that I can come, okay?"

"Okay, but I won't. This guy will be really tough for me to beat. I need to be able to concentrate. You don't like wrestling; I accept that. I don't really want to sit around and watch you sew or knit or whatever you said you did. We're even, okay?"

"Okay."

They talked for a few more minutes and then he slid off the barstool. "I've got to go."

"What? Now? No."

"The team will be leaving after school tomorrow, but I'll see you before I go."

She walked over to him and he wrapped his arms around her. They held onto each other, her head against his chest, his chin resting on her head. She could stay like this all night. Slowly he let her go, bringing his hands up under her chin and kissing her. "Don't go," she whispered.

"Don't make this hard on me," he kissed her some more.

"Let's go in the living room." She tried moving him in that direction.

Between kisses he told her no. She continued to try to move him towards the couch. Finally, he held her at arms length. "I have to go. Don't do this." Then, he smiled. "It's not fun when someone says no, is it?" She pouted. He grabbed her up for one final, long kiss and said, "Who knows. Maybe I'll bring you back a present."

March 18, 1967: This has been a very long weekend, although Friday I went out with the girls and saw a movie. Jonesy and a few of the other guys went up Saturday to cheer our wrestlers on. I told him to call me as soon as Michael's match was over. He never called. Well, at least Michael can't blame me for losing; however, I think I will steer clear of him on Monday.

Sunday afternoon Megan was heading outside when she heard a car door slam. She looked up to see Michael. He stood beside his car, staring unhappily at her. She walked over and hugged him. "Going for a walk?" he asked.

"Yeah." They walked with their arms around each other. She wanted to ask how it went, but was afraid to. *Better to let him tell me in his own good time. But then, that looks like I don't care.* "You okay?" she asked.

"Yeah. Did Jonesy give you the blow by blow?"

"No, he never called me. Nobody called me. Do you want to talk about it?"

"Not really."

"Okay . . . I'm here though, if . . ."

"What did you do this weekend?"

There wasn't much to tell, but she thought of as many things as she could. Silence descended as she frantically thought of something else to say. "How are you going to feel tomorrow?" he asked.

"About what?"

"Are you going to want to be seen with me? Do you want to be seen with a loser?"

"You are not a loser!" she hotly stated. "And you're never going to be a loser!"

He smiled, bending down to kiss her. "Keep your eyes closed." She did as she was told and felt something go over her head and then weight around her neck. "Okay, you can look."

She looked down to see a heavy medallion on a multicolored ribbon. She picked it up and read it. "You won?" she looked to see him grinning down at her.

"It was close; but I pulled it out."

"But Jonesy didn't call me."

"No. I asked him not to. I wanted to be the one to tell you."

"Oh, God. This is so neat!" She threw herself at Michael and he swung her around.

"I promised you a present. I had to come back with something."

"What do you mean?"

"That's yours."

"This medal? No. I'm not keeping it."

"Yes, you are."

"Michael, this is yours. I'll wear it for the rest of the day; but you need to take it home with you when you go."

"Meg," he looked down at her, "I can't afford to buy you stuff. Let me give you something that I worked for. I have a trophy to go with that, which I'll keep. And I have three other medals, so don't worry about it."

"Three other medals . . . from football, you mean?"

"No, wrestling."

"What are they for?"

"From other years."

She stared at him. Something . . . she was not getting something. "Okay. You're a senior. It makes sense that you would have played other years. How did you do before this year?"

"I came in second as a freshman."

She nodded. "And the other two years?"

"I was . . . state champ."

He didn't like the look he was getting. "You've been state champ in wrestling for the last two years and you let me say all those things—and you *never* said a word?" she ended up yelling.

"If only you had asked me questions instead of assuming I was bad at it. It's your own fault."

"The first day I saw you at wrestling practice and somebody hollered for the Captain to get rid of me . . . you said you'd take care of it."

"And I did."

"But I thought you were telling the Captain . . . *you're* the Captain of the wrestling team, aren't you?" He grinned.

"Don't do that to me again," she said.

"Don't do that to me again," he countered.

"Come on, I want to show Mom and Daddy." She grabbed his arm and felt him stiffen. "Michael, don't be this way around my parents, please."

"Your mother hates me after I called —"

"She does not hate you. We were all up. She's big on etiquette. She said what she wanted to say and now it's forgotten. Come on."

Her parents were duly impressed and congratulated him. "She moped around here all last night," offered her dad. "It was hard for me to keep it a secret."

"*You* knew?" Meg whirled on him.

"Yeah. Michael was afraid Jeff would tell you, so he asked Jeff not to. And Jeff took it upon himself to tell me. I was the one who got to tell you if Michael lost, though."

"But, how would you have known?"

"I listened to it on the radio. Close match."

As she slowly turned towards Michael, he was making his getaway. "I need to get going," he said.

"It was on the radio?" She gritted her teeth.

"You really should learn to ask questions."

March 19, 1967: Michael won! He's State Champ! And as I found out—has been for the last two years! How could he keep it a secret all this time? And then to find out Daddy listened to it on the radio and didn't tell me! Jonesy and the guys went up and watched it and nobody told me a thing! Michael gave me his medallion to keep. He cares. He really cares about me.

March 26, 1967: Michael is acting his strange self again. Now that he's given me his medallion I've barely seen him. He hardly talks to me in study hall, doesn't walk me to my classes, doesn't come over, nothing. In fact, I spent this last weekend by myself. One, I hoped that he would call so I stayed close to the phone and two, I couldn't let the girls know that he hadn't asked me out.

April 2, 1967: I guess I've been dumped. I just haven't been told.

April 5, 1967: Michael asked me out for Saturday night. I didn't dare ask what's wrong with Friday. I gave him an off-handed 'yeah.' Why does he do this to me? Maybe this time I should dump him. I'm getting tired of always being on his yo-yo where he decides whether or not we're going together. My heart can't take this. Better to be permanently through with him.

CHAPTER 11

MEG WAITED TO HEAR FROM MICHAEL ALL DAY SATURDAY. Nothing. Sunday came and went. Nothing. She expected he would at least have had the decency to call and tell her he wasn't coming. Monday Meg walked into study hall to find Michael already at his desk. Never a good sign. She slammed down in her seat and stared at him. He ignored her.

"I thought we had a date Saturday," Megan said.

"Did I show up?"

"No."

"Then I guess we didn't have one." He was engrossed in his book.

She wanted to give him a stinging retort, but turned around when she could think of nothing. When the hour was done and the bell rang, they both stood up. "Hate me?" he asked.

She looked up at him. "No, I don't hate you. I just don't understand."

"Well, learn to!" he yelled and walked off.

April 10, 1967: Michael humiliated me in study hall today. He asked if I hated him and I told him no. That seemed to make him mad and he hollered at me in front of everybody. Why would he want me to hate him?

Coming home from the vet's office, Meg turned down her road to see Michael parked along the side. As soon as she drove past, he fell in behind her. *What does he want?*

They both got out of their cars in her driveway and stared at each other. He finally broke the silence. "I suppose you want an explanation."

"No, not anymore. I don't hate you, but I don't care anymore, either." *Let's see if you can hurt. Cuz it hurt me to say that.* Meg thought his face looked sad—or was she just hoping? "You treat me like crap," she continued, when he didn't offer anything. "How am I supposed to feel?" He looked at the ground. There were a million things she wanted to say, but she was afraid she'd burst into tears. The best she could do was walk away.

"I saw you at track practice yesterday," he ventured.

"Yes, believe it or not I went to watch Jonesy. I was just as surprised to see you there. Although, I guess I shouldn't have been; just like I wasn't surprised when I found out you hold most of the track records at your old high school. You're one superb athlete, aren't you? Must be nice. Maybe that's why you feel it's all right to act the way you do. Jonesy used to be the only pole-vaulter we had, so I used to go out on the field during practice and he'd try to teach me how to do it. Guess I won't be doing that this year, thank you very much. I have watched Jonesy for two years now. But, of course, yesterday I was just there for you. I finally left when I heard some girl say, 'When is she going to get the message? He's *doing* somebody else.' And then I saw they were all looking at me." This time, Meg planned on making it to the house.

She was almost to the door when she heard him say, "I'm not *doing* anybody else." He got in his car and left.

April 11, 1967: I don't know why Michael even bothered to come over today. I hear rumors that he's seeing somebody else, but nobody wants to actually confirm it for me. He confirmed just the opposite—said he wasn't seeing anybody. I don't really think I believe him. I just know that I ache all over. I hurt so bad because of him. Love shouldn't hurt this much.

Meg was walking down the deserted hallway before homeroom when a pencil suddenly hit her shoulder. "Ow!" she yelled, rubbing where she'd been hit. She whirled around to find Michael, his face inches from hers, his blue eyes unblinking. "Did you go out with Presulski this last weekend?"

"Yeah." *What's it to you?*

He towered over her, so she leaned away from him. He looked anything but pleasant. "That medal I gave you says you're *mine!*"

"You haven't taken me out in a couple of weeks. You haven't *spoken* to me in a couple of weeks! Make up your mind, Michael, because it's killing me."

"Okay. I will make up my mind." *God, don't start crying! Not here! I knew he would break my heart.* "I made up my mind a long time ago. Will you go to the prom with me?"

"The prom?" After the way he'd been acting it was the last invitation she expected to come out of his mouth. *Does he have a clue how expensive it is? Or will I have to pay for it? Cripe, I don't care—as long as I get to be with him. But, he is one weekend too late.* "Gosh, Michael . . . I'm sorry. I can't." She tried to walk around him, but he blocked her path.

"Did that . . . did Presulski . . . ask you to the prom?" He could tell by the look on her face that it was so. "No," he said. "You tell him no."

"Michael, I can't do that," she said softly.

"Would you rather go with him?"

"No, but . . . do you realize how much the prom costs?"

He suddenly exploded. "Yes, I do! What do you think I've been doing for the last three weeks? I've been working!"

"Working?" She couldn't get any other words out.

"Yes, working. I wanted to take you to the prom, but I didn't have the money. So, I got a job. And then you go out with somebody else while I'm working my ass off?!"

"You know what might have helped? If you'd talked to me! You don't walk me to class anymore, you don't talk to me in study hall, you don't come over. How was I supposed to know you were doing something nice?"

"You should know me by now!"

"No, Michael. That doesn't cut it. I don't know what to say. I am . . . amazed that you would do something like that for me. If only you had told me. I would much rather go with you . . . but I've already accepted someone else's invitation." *And it will absolutely kill me to see you there with someone else.*

Slowly she made her way around him. He didn't stop her this time. Halfway down the hall she heard, "Meg." She stopped. "You either tell him today that you're going with me, or I will. A hint: it will be a whole lot kinder and easier on him if you do it. I'll be over tonight to see what you decided." She listened to his footsteps echo down the hall in the opposite direction.

April 17, 1967: I must have the weirdest and strangest relationship of anybody I know—and don't know. Now Michael tells me he's been working so that he can take me to the prom. I already accepted another invitation, since he's been giving me the silent treatment. I told Paul that I couldn't go with him because if I didn't Michael would have, and I can't imagine that would have been pleasant for Paul. Now, I'm afraid that Michael is going to stand me up. Maybe that was the plan all along. It's nine-thirty. He said he would come over today and he never showed. And I know he won't dare call after Mom yelled at him. But he could have called before nine!

At lunch Jim stopped her. "Have you seen Michael today?"

"No, but I don't usually see him until late in the day. Why?"

"It was just . . . awfully loud at the MacKenzie's last night. I have first and third hour with Michael, he wasn't there. And Josh has avoided me like the plague. This is just like the last time."

"Last time what?"

"Nothing." Jim started to walk away.

"Last time . . . when I went to his house? When I put my car in the ditch?"

"No. That was mild compared to last night. Forget I said anything."

"Jim, Michael was planning on coming over to my house last night and he never showed. He never called. Should I be worried?" *So far, I've just been mad.*

"He was coming over . . . I thought you two had broken up."

"Yeah, well," she threw her hands up, "who knows with Michael?"

"I don't know what to tell ya, Meg." Jim walked off.

When Meg got home she wondered what she should do, like she could do anything. She didn't dare call Michael's house. The problem was finally solved when the phone rang. She picked it up. "Thank you for answering the phone," she heard.

"Michael? Where are you?"

"I'm at Jonesy's. Could you meet me at the end of your driveway?"

"Yeah, sure. Are you all right?" He hung up and she wondered if Jonesy was having a fit at the other end, thinking about her meeting Michael. "I'm going for a walk," she hollered to her parents. Her dad waved in acknowledgement.

He was sitting in his car, waiting for her. She tried to tell herself everything was fine, even though she didn't feel it. He didn't help her with the door and when she finally got it open she saw why. In addition to a black eye, that she had prepared herself for, he also had his hand in a cast and a split lip, which she wasn't prepared for. "Oh, God, Michael." She wanted to hold him. He didn't say anything; he just drove.

They ended up down a road that was overgrown. Twenty feet in, Michael stopped the car and turned off the motor. It was completely isolated. They certainly wouldn't be disturbed out here.

"Oh, honey," was all she could say. He looked so battered.

"I've had all I can take Meg," he said.

"What can I do to help?" He only shook his head. She had racked her brain and couldn't see how this might be her fault, but she asked anyway.

"No, Meg. This is just the asshole I live with. This is my life."

"Tell me what happened."

"Actually, getting a job has helped me avoid him," he sighed. "I . . . don't particularly want to go to the prom, but I knew you would. And I knew I wouldn't have the money –"

"Oh, God. This *is* my fault!"

"No, Meg. This was a decision I made. I remembered what you said about Jonesy working for his dad and making his own hours. My uncle runs his own shop, so I called him and he said he'd take me on. So, I've been working a few hours after track practice. I still wasn't going to have enough money, but then some of the men that work there wanted weekends off, so I've been filling in for them. That's why I haven't been around to take you out."

"Why didn't you tell me?"

He shrugged. "It scares me . . . how I feel about you. I mean look at me—you've got me working and going to the prom. I've avoided both of those my whole life. And then I find out you're going out with somebody else!"

"If you had told me what you were doing, I would never have gone out. He means nothing to me. I told you, I love you." He leaned over to give her a kiss, but it hurt too much. They agreed to get more comfortable in the backseat. He opened the back door, picked up a bag, heaved it forward, and got in. Carefully she hugged him. "So, what exactly happened with your dad?"

"I came home. Somehow he'd found out that I was working. Seven o'clock at night and he's already drunk. Starts demanding that I give him my paycheck. One, I didn't have it; and two, I wouldn't have given it to him if I had. We got to arguing . . . guess you could hear us all over the countryside. At least this time, I gave as good as I got."

"What? What do you mean?"

"I'm tired of him beating on me, Meg. I've had all I can take. I'm done being his punching bag. I decided to fight back." He could see by the look on her face that this was beyond her comprehension. "You, with the perfect parents. You've got no clue what my life is like. What it's been like for years. I don't need you feeling sorry for me, Megan."

"I'm not."

"I only have a few more months and then I'm out of here! Do you hear me?"

"Why are you turning on me? Why do you do this to me all the time? I'm the one that is on your side!"

"You don't understand."

"Well, I'm trying. How did you break your hand, your arm, whatever you broke?" She indicated the cast.

"I've been going to school, doing track, working, finding out that my girlfriend is running around on me —"

"I was not running around on you."

"— and then that bastard demands that I give him my paycheck! I'm done!"

"Okay, Michael, okay. Calm down. It's me you're yelling at." She tried another question. "Why do you have a packed bag?" She indicated the suitcase he'd thrown in the front seat. *You're not thinking of coming to my house, are you? My parents will flip.*

"Well, as I said, we were pretty loud. Jim's mom called mine this morning, wanting to know what was going on. They both agreed I couldn't stay at home anymore, so I'll be staying at Jim's, probably for the rest of the school year."

"That's good, isn't it? Jim's parents seemed nice to me."

"Oh, I'd forgotten you'd met them. Yeah, they're nice. That part's fine. I just worry about Josh, although he gets along with our father better than most of us. He should be okay."

"You'll be close by . . . if he's not." Michael nodded. "How did you break your hand?"

"I'd gotten a couple of good punches in, when he ducked . . . I hit a brick wall."

"Oh, baby," she hugged him gently and then kissed him.

"God, if the two of us didn't look like a pair of bookends sitting at opposite ends of the emergency room last night. I don't like you going out with other guys," he said suddenly.

She smiled. "You have nothing to worry about. And if you hadn't yelled at me and then given me the silent treatment, I would never have gone out."

"How far did he get?"

She chuckled. "You have nothing to worry about."

"How far?"

"He held my hand in the show and gave me one kiss good-night before I ducked in the house."

"You didn't sit and make out with him?"

"I didn't want to. I wanted to hurry in and see if you'd called."

"But, you were going to go to the prom with him?" He looked at her. "You did tell him . . . didn't you?"

"Yes, I told him I was going with you. Remember, I had no idea you would ask me and I would really like to go. I am very, very happy to be going with you. We are . . . still going . . . aren't we?"

It was his turn to laugh. With his one good hand he brushed her hair back. "If you want to go with me looking like this, then yes, we'll go."

"Kiss me," she whispered. He did so, carefully. It didn't take long before she realized that feeling as bad as she did for him, she was letting him go further than she had ever gone before. "Michael, stop."

"Come on, honey. Stop telling me no. I need this. Do you understand what I'm saying?"

"Yes, I do—but *I* don't. I don't need this. Mich—" All he had to do was kiss her again and she lost all resolve. No, she had to get back on track. "Michael, I mean it, please. I don't want that kind of reputation. Your cast hurts against my skin and, quite frankly, this isn't very comfortable for me all the way around."

He stopped. "I'll take you home."

He drove up her driveway and let her out. "Michael, I know you're mad at me—"

"Actually, Meg I'm not. I understand. You were right to stop me. I'm not happy, but I'm not mad either. Just be there for me, Meg. That's what I really need."

"I'm here whenever you need me."

April 18, 1967: Michael wasn't in school today. He met me afterward, though. He looked awful. He and his dad beat the crap out of each other and he's gone to stay with Jim for the rest of the school year. I don't understand people like this. Anyway, I felt bad for him and we went kind of far in the backseat. Not all the way, but headed in that direction. I wanted to ask him about his back, but didn't think it was the time to. I had his shirt off with my hands on his back, and it is all rippled. It was weird. His entire back seemed to be that way, from what I could tell. But, Michael says we are going to the prom!

Michael walked down to the stream and then slowly made his way to where he knew Meg would be. Granted, he had lost a race today because of the cast, but she shouldn't have run off like she had. He won two others.

She could have stayed and seen what kind of a mood he was in. He slowed his gait and looked around. This piece of land really was beautiful.

He had to admit Megan had a way with animals. She would make an excellent veterinarian. He had come upon her several times to find animals within inches of her. Gradually his uneasiness about the animals getting so close to her had diminished. Jonesy had told him she had always fed and played with the wild creatures. They hadn't harmed her yet, so why try to stop her—she didn't pay any attention to him anyway.

Michael stopped. Just ahead was a raccoon. He wondered if it was the same one he had seen with Meg a few times. The animal sensed his presence and sat back on its hind legs. For a moment, they locked eyes and then Stanley raised one paw and was off. Michael smiled and continued on his walk. He knew Meg was out here somewhere. He had to admit this was relaxing. He felt at peace here.

He finally found her walking back and forth, a notepad and pencil in hand. She would look up, shake her head, and then march off. She would then stretch her legs way out while walking and he could hear her counting. She would then look up, shake her head, and walk off— repeating the same routine all over again.

Michael propped himself against a tree and watched her. *Does she have any clue how gorgeous she is?* She was not like the other girls who flirted and spent all morning in the bathroom checking on their makeup. Her chestnut hair was silky to the touch. He was always afraid that one day he'd come to school to discover she had cut it. Not that she had ever mentioned doing that, but still, it was something he worried about. She was turning around for the sixth time when she caught sight of him. "How long have you been standing there?" she demanded.

"Long enough," he smiled. "What are you doing?"

She pouted for a moment and then turned her back on him. He had seen her turn red, so he walked over and wrapped his good arm around her, kissing the top of her head. "You're gorgeous."

"Knock it off," she said.

"Don't believe me? Would I date someone who's not gorgeous?" She continued sketching on her pad of paper.

"You seem to be in a good mood for having lost a race," she obviously wanted to change the subject.

"You shouldn't have left so soon," he said. "I won two others."

"Oh," she looked up at him. "Well, good for you. I could see you getting mad. I know you can't run as well with your cast . . ."

"No, I can't. The son of a bitch has ruined my track career; but thankfully I didn't make that a priority. I did okay today."

"Well, good."

"So, what have you got there?"

She finished drawing, looked at him, and hesitantly showed him. "It's my log cabin." She saw the questioning look. "I was thinking for a graduation present—high school or college—that Daddy might give me some land."

"And . . . you're thinking this would be a nice piece of land to put your cabin on?" She could see he was only humoring her.

"I think this is a nice spot. There are plenty of trees here to cut to build with, so I wouldn't have to have them hauled in—but the size doesn't fit."

"What do you mean?"

"If I start here and mark off so many yards, then I hit that tree—and that's where the squirrels live. Now, if I move down here, then I run into that tree—and that's where the owls live."

"You can't tear down either one of those trees?"

"Heavens no, they know me. I couldn't uproot them!"

"Meg, you need a ton of trees to build a cabin. You're going to uproot a lot of animals, I imagine."

"Oh." She hadn't thought of that. "Hmm. There's a clearing down a ways. Maybe I should have the logs brought in, instead of chopping down my own, huh? That way I wouldn't uproot anybody I know."

He burst out laughing and saw that her feelings were hurt. "I think it's a fine idea," he bent to kiss her. "Explain the rest of your plan to me."

"You're not interested," she pouted.

"I am, too. Now here, what's this, the kitchen?"

"This is the kitchen. That is the bedroom."

"That's an awfully large kitchen."

"I need room to create."

"And, what's this?"

"A ladder."

"What for?"

"To get to the loft."

"A ladder? What's wrong with stairs?"

"You can't have stairs! How many pioneers do you know who have stairs in their cabins?"

"None."

"They have ladders, right?"

"Yep. Now that you mention it, all my pioneer friends have ladders in their cabins."

She glared at him. "You know what I mean." She turned her back on him and he put his arm around her waist, resting his chin on her head.

"And this?" he pointed.

"A fireplace. You have to have a fireplace."

"Yes, I know; but your sketch leaves something to be desired."

"It's a rough draft," she protested. "This is the guest bedroom or den, the dining area, kitchen, then up in the loft is the master bedroom and a smaller room for storage or sewing or something."

"And what's this?" He pointed to a square placed a short distance from the cabin. "Your outhouse?"

He had meant it as a joke and was surprised when she said, "No, that's the barn. Here's the outhouse." She drew another box.

"You're not serious about an outhouse."

"No running water, no electricity."

He stared at Meg for a long moment. "Well, then, you don't want it that close to the cabin. You'll be sorry."

"What about in the winter or in the middle of the night? I'm not walking far."

"What about in the hot summertime when there's a light breeze?"

She chewed on the end of the pencil. "Maybe I need a regular bathroom." She tapped the guest bedroom. "I could fit it in there."

"All the pioneers I know use pots in their cabins and then throw it out at a convenient time, instead of going outside in the middle of the night."

"They leave their waste . . . in a pot? Inside the cabin?"

"Sure."

She drew a line about one-third of the way through the guestroom. "It'll fit nicely right there."

"The pot?"

"The bathroom!"

"What are you going to have in the barn?"

"Livestock. You've got to have something to live on. Cows, pigs, chickens, etc."

"Yeah, I know; but what happens when it comes time to slaughter them?"

She was squeamish about this. "Somebody else will have to feed them and take care of them, because I'd become too attached. I couldn't eat anything I'd petted and I don't see me becoming a vegetarian anytime soon." She glanced out of the corner of her eye to see his look of amusement and gave him an elbow in the stomach.

"Ow! What was that for?"

"For making fun of me."

"Meg, I'm sorry. I simply can't picture you living in a cabin and living off the land. You're not cut out for the work. I see you in a huge house in the city–"

"I hate the city!"

"—with servants at your beck and call—"

"I'd be fat if I sat around all day. I help my mom."

"—and going to the ballet or plays on the weekends, high society crap, you know."

"What a bunch of hogwash!" she said. "I wouldn't be happy doing any of that. I don't think you know me as well as you think you do. I don't believe in ruining the environment and I love the woods—I respect it! I love being at one with nature. Have you ever read Laura Ingalls Wilder? That's how I want to live."

He rolled his eyes. "You just have this picture of what you think I should be, not what I am."

"Oh, is that so?"

"Yes, that's so."

"I know exactly what you are."

"Oh, really? What?"

"Mine."

April 26, 1967: Michael came over after his track meet. I had started drawing out my plans for the log cabin I want someday. I'm hoping Daddy will give me some land for graduation. Michael got a good laugh. But, I don't care--he says I'm his! I'm the only girl to be able to say she's Michael's girlfriend! He's never stayed this long with any one girl! Oh crap! It just dawned on me, I left my notepad with my cabin drawing in his car. Will have to remember to get it back from him.

Initially, Michael thought it would be awkward staying at Jim's house since he was dating Megan, but Jim had somebody new that he truly seemed interested in. It was such a relief for Michael to be able to walk into a house and not be worried about being yelled at or hit. For the first time in years, he was able to crawl into bed and know that he wouldn't be rudely awakened in the middle of the night.

Michael lay in bed that night smiling, thinking about Meg's log cabin and her living off the land. *Who was she trying to fool? I know you can generate electricity with a windmill, but what about running water? Was she planning on dipping a bucket in the stream every day or would she at least consider putting in a pump? I'm not excited about having to feed all the animals, but I'd be okay taking them to slaughter. How cheaply can one live that way? If the land was given to us, and we had no electric or phone bill, what would be left? I'd need a truck. Meg would need . . . something. Can people live off the land in this day and age? I might have to get a part-time job to have a little cash—stop! What am I thinking? Listen to yourself! This is not what you have planned for yourself. In fact, Meg is not in your plans at all! You are getting in way too deep. Don't do this to yourself. Dump her. Dump her, now. No, I can't. I made her break her date with Presulski. I have to take her to the prom. I'll break up with her after the dance. No, that won't look good. I'll do it the next day.*

No girl is going to make me change my plans.

"Why are you taking my head off? I just asked—"

"Why do you bug me so?"

Megan stared at him. "I'm sorry. I didn't know I was bugging you."

"Well, you are," yelled Michael. They were in the hallway after school. Michael was setting the hurdles up to practice. "My cast is slowing me down—and you bugging me is *really* slowing me down."

Jonesy walked by. "Has she dragged you out there yet?"

"Where?"

"Don't tell!" she yelled. "It's a surprise."

"And what a surprise it is," said Jonesy dryly. "I still haven't recuperated from yesterday."

"What happened yesterday?" Michael looked at Megan suspiciously.

"Jonesy, good-bye."

"Megan has a new little toy, or should I say two?" Jonesy continued. "She hauled Mandy out there the other day, and yesterday was my turn. You take a shot at it this time. You were wise to get a job."

"Jonesy!" warned Megan.

Michael turned around. "I'm not going anywhere with you until you tell me where we're going."

"It's a surprise, darn it! When can you go with me?"

"I don't know. You have to learn to practice some patience."

Oh, that is rich, coming from him. "So, I'll ask you again. Do you work today?"

He studied her. "No, but maybe I should. I'm busy. Get the message?"

She turned and walked out. He sighed. Michael hated when he was like this with her; but it was the only way. One day she would see that, one day she'd understand.

He was surprised to find Meg waiting for him after track practice. "Ready to go?" she asked.

He sighed inwardly. "Yeah, fine."

"You are going to love this!" she smiled at him. Several miles later, she pulled into a farm and got out.

"What are we doing here?" He stayed in the car.

"Come on." She opened up his door and hauled him out. She nearly ran to the far end of the barn, and waited impatiently while Michael took his sweet time.

"What?" he growled.

"They're mine. Both of them." She pointed to the adjacent stalls.

He stared at them and then at her. "You've got yourself two horses?"

"Yes! I have so bugged Daddy for them. Mom finally convinced him it was cheaper for me to have my own horses than to pay to have me ride somebody else's. Secretly though, I think he thinks I'll find it's too much work and decide to get rid of them and that way I'll stop bugging him."

"Why two?"

"I can't be expected to ride by myself, that's no fun. One's for you or Mandy or Jonesy or whomever I bring with me. My mom will probably ride some. Come on, grab a saddle!" She was so excited. To go horseback riding and to have Michael with her. She got Samantha saddled and turned to see Michael simply standing in the doorway. "Grab a—" she stopped. It had never dawned on her until then that perhaps he had never ridden a horse before. Or maybe he couldn't get the saddle because of his hand, but why not say so? She got Dudley's saddle and put it on the horse. "They're all set."

He stood there. "Your father bought you not one but two horses just because you asked?"

"Please, don't start in about money again—"

"My father has to work overtime just to get winter jackets for all us kids—and most of those are handed down."

The excitement was gone. She mounted Samantha and started out the stable door. "His name's Dudley."

"You expect me to ride a horse named Dudley?"

"He might surprise you." Meg rode out. *Why can't he enjoy what was presented to him? Jonesy and Mandy didn't act this way. Granted, they came*

from money too, but . . . what is the big deal? I don't have a hang-up about
money and sharing it, why does he?

A few minutes later Michael was beside her.

"I'm sorry," he said, although by now it didn't matter. Jonesy had been more fun—and he'd never ridden before. "I didn't know you rode horses."

"I have, for years. Last fall I was just too busy. I've been helping Dr. Thomas at one of the horse farms and I found I really missed riding. Plus, this way I've got to take care of them myself and I thought it would be good for me to see if I can handle it, you know, if I ever build my cabin and live off the land." He said nothing. just shook his head. "Have you ever ridden before?"

"Bareback, that's about it."

"You ride well."

"I don't need a compliment from you." They rode in silence.

"Why are you in such a bad mood?" she asked, while driving them back to the school where his car was parked.

"I've got a lot on my mind right now. For the first time in my life I've got to make a decision about something important, a life decision. Either way I look at it, I lose."

"Can I help?"

He turned and gave her a cold stare. "If I wanted to discuss it with you, don't you think I would?"

May 4, 1967: Daddy bought me two horses! They're named Samantha
and Dudley. Mandy has always wanted her own horse, so she's going
to help me by taking care of Dudley. It was just like old times when she
and I went out on the trails. Taking Jonesy though, was something else.
How come his sister has gone riding for so many years and he's never
been? I don't think he'll ever go again either.

Then, I took Michael. Dudley was perfectly fine with him and yet
Michael was nasty to me. He has been for a couple of days. I don't
know what's gotten into him. Is he worried he won't have enough
money saved for the prom? I don't dare offer to pitch in for that. Maybe
I'm worrying too much. Maybe his cast is bothering him. I know it's
slowing him down for track and that always upsets him. I'm sure it's
something that will blow over. It always does with him.

CHAPTER 12

PROM WEEKEND DAWNED. MEG HAD TO ADMIT IT DID NOT LOOK promising. Michael had not given her the silent treatment; but for two weeks he'd been pretty quiet. He'd come over to her house, but never had much to say. Occasionally he'd walk her to class; but again, he spoke little. He didn't seem angry; he seemed bored, which devastated Meg. "Don't be ridiculous," Michael had snarled when she finally found the nerve to ask him. "I just have a lot on my mind." That seemed to be his pat answer for everything lately.

In study hall on Friday, she asked him if she would be seeing him that night, since he had not made a date with her. "I'm working," he said, without looking at her.

"What . . . about tomorrow night?"

"What time do you want me?" Meg told him. That was the last conversation they had.

Saturday morning found Meg and Mandy eagerly having their hair done at the beauty parlor. In the back of her mind, Megan wondered if Michael was really going to show up. He had told her things were going well at Jim's house and that he was glad to be there; however, she was still convinced he was bored with her and would dump her.

As she waited for Michael to arrive, Meg wanted to cry—but she already had her makeup on. *He's not going to show. He's going to stand me up. I'll never be able to show my face at school again.* When he knocked on the door, she almost cried with joy and relief.

Michael was standing at the bottom of the stairs talking with her parents when she came walking down. He let out a low whistle and, for the first time in weeks, gave her a smile. "You're beautiful," he said.

"Thank you." *Whatever else happens tonight, at least he did not stand me up. And boy, does he look handsome in a tux, even with his hand in a cast.*

"I want you to know, I wouldn't do this for anybody else," he whispered to her as her dad snapped picture after picture. *He does care! He does.* Finally, they were free to leave the house.

They had agreed on dinner at her parents' private country club. Michael wondered what it was like to actually belong to such a place. When he drove to their make-out spot instead, Meg wondered if he was getting cold feet. *Is he looking to save some money?* She could feel her blood start to boil, when he reached in the backseat and proceeded to hand her a tall glass. "What's this?"

He smiled and produced another one for himself and then a champagne bottle. Her parents had let her have sips here and there, but never anything like this! "You're underage! Where did you get this?" she gasped as he poured.

"Older brothers do come in handy on occasion." He kept her glass full until she was seized with the giggles. "That's what I was afraid would happen. You're cut off."

"I like this stuff," she said, and threw herself into his arms. She began to kiss him passionately.

"Is this what it takes to get you in a loving mood? I should have thought of this before." He kissed her and then gently held her at arms length. "We've got the whole night ahead of us; maybe I'd better get some dinner in you."

"I don't want dinner," Meg said, trying to get back in his arms.

"I'm hungry. Besides, Jonesy helped me pick out this tux." Which meant it was expensive. He started up the car and then turned and faced her. Gently he traced a finger across her face.

"What's wrong?"

"Not tonight. This is your night. I want it to be special for you. You are so beautiful, Meg. Please believe me when I say that." *So, why do I feel this is the end?*

They went to dinner, which was great. Michael was glad Meg had shown him a formal table setting. From there, they went to the prom, which was being held at a rented hall. Meg danced with several other guys, although Michael did not dance with any of the other girls. "I don't want to," he said when she asked him. "It's kind of hard with one hand." She found he was using this as an excuse for a lot of things.

Meg's curfew had been lifted for this one night. They went to a party and then to the Hill's house for breakfast, along with eight other couples. They pulled into her driveway as the sun was coming up. After getting out of the car, they carefully made their way down to the stream. This had become their favorite spot and Michael brought along a blanket for them to sit on. He placed his head in her lap and they sat quietly, listening to the woods come to life at daybreak.

"Make love to me," he suddenly said.

She was startled and pretended she hadn't heard him. He sat up and she was forced to look at him. He cupped his hand around her face. "I want this memory of us," he kissed her, pushing her against the tree.

"Michael, don't," she whispered, as she kissed him in return.

"Honey, honey," he whispered, kissing her all over. She felt him tugging on her dress.

"Michael, no, not here . . . not now." *Why didn't he take me when I was drunk?*

"Stop denying what we both want." They wrestled back and forth for several minutes.

"Are you staying?" she asked. He stopped. "Is there an us, Michael? Are you staying? I don't want this memory if it means you're walking out on me. You're just using me then. What if I should get pregnant? What are you going to say to me then?"

"Megan, this isn't some sudden thought that's hit me. I did bring some protection with me."

"You . . . what . . . how . . ." she sat with her mouth open, speechless. Nice girls did not have these conversations.

"I told you. I have older brothers. Come on, honey," he kissed her again and she could feel herself letting go.

"This is wrong," she moaned.

"How? How can this be wrong?" *Oh, he feels so wonderful. His kisses, his caresses . . . Remember Marcy: "We just got caught up in the moment. It was not to be believed!" Then two days later: "He told me we're through! I gave him everything, and this is how he treats me? I'll never get another first time and he doesn't even remember my name!"*

"Michael, Michael, you need to stop."

"No, Meg."

"Michael, please stop!"

He stopped and looked at her. "Honey." *He has never called me honey so many times.* "I know you're scared. I promise, I'll be gentle."

"Do you promise to stay? Or am I just another number to you? Have you stayed around all this time because I'm the only one who's said no to you? Yes, we could have a great time right now--but what about tomorrow or next week? When you tell me you're done with me and you sit behind me in study hall, am I supposed to act like everything's okay? You've never said you love me. You have told me plenty of times though, that there is no us. I'm not free for your taking. Other girls may have been, but not me."

"Get dressed." He walked her to her door. "Good night." He looked around. "Good morning, Miss Becktame. Thank you for a very nice evening."

"Oh, Michael. Please don't—"

He walked off. "Someday you'll be sorry I wasn't your first."

May 27, 1967: Prom Night. Well, what can I say? I worried whether Michael would show up at all and, after spending the entire night with him until daybreak, I can still ask the same thing. The evening was wonderful. Michael showed up in one of his better moods. I guess that's because he planned on getting lucky. One of his brothers had gotten him champagne and that was fun. Then we went to dinner at my parents' country club. From there we went to the dance and then, because I didn't have a curfew, we went to a party at Trish's. Mrs. Hill had told Jonesy and Mandy that they could have a few friends over for breakfast. So, we went to that and then we took a walk in my woods. We went down to the stream and sat on a blanket. Michael really put the moves on me and I don't know even now how I got the strength to say no to him. He had thought of everything. It was so hard to stop him. It felt so wonderful being with him. We got pretty far when I stopped him and I know he's furious with me.

I have probably seen the last of him and I can't really blame him. Part of me is sorry that I didn't go all the way with him—but how would I feel come Monday when I see him? He'll be grouchy and I'll feel used and everybody will know.

I know that I did the right thing. I just don't feel like I did the right thing. I do feel though, that I've lost Michael for good this time. I console myself with the fact that he was going to leave me anyway. It was just a matter of time.

I just didn't want to remember my first prom like this.

Michael had not walked her to any classes; indeed, he had hardly spoken to her all week, so Meg was surprised on Friday when he tapped her shoulder in study hall. Since Miss Quinn was in the room, the best she could do was lean back. "I know I haven't spoken much," he whispered. *That's putting it mildly.* "And I left in kind of a huff last Saturday; but that medal still says you're mine." She shot him a disbelieving look. "Okay?" She went back to her book. "We need to talk," he said.

Meg wanted to tell him not to bother, because it hurt too much every time she saw him. Especially when he ignored her. Thank God she hadn't given in to him. Only a few more weeks of school left and then she'd never have to see him again. Of course, she could forget about dating her whole senior year, because no one was ever going to measure up to Michael. And, she was never telling anybody that she cried herself to sleep every night.

"You want to go to the show tonight?" he asked when he found Meg in the parking lot. Mandy quickly hopped inside Megan's car and sat.

Megan studied him. "Okay. Are we going to talk?"

He looked at the ground. "Yeah. It's time . . . I told you what's been on my mind."

She shook her head, got in her car, and drove off. "Other than his looks, what does he have to offer you?" asked Mandy. She had listened to Meg go on for months about how Michael was with her. She wouldn't have put up with it.

"We just have this connection," said Meg. "I can't explain it."

"I can. It's called puppy love. Infatuation. You'll get over it. Just don't do anything stupid with him."

"I know, I know."

"You haven't done . . ."

"No! But I wanted to."

Mandy sighed. "I was afraid you had it that bad for him. You *know* he's going to dump you."

"Yes. That's what keeps me in line."

They arrived at Mandy's house and she slowly got out of the car. She looked at Megan before shutting the door. "This is going to be a long summer, I can tell already."

"Yeah, you and me both."

Michael was back to his "yes, sir" and "no, ma'am" talk. She could tell this was not going to be a good evening. Although he opened the car door for her, he walked three feet away from her. He asked her what she wanted to go see. She answered him. There was no further communication.

He knew what she liked to eat at the show, so he ordered without asking her. He was paying when he glanced over and saw her smile for the first time. "What?"

"You've got money." *Not that I care, but you're always going on about not having any.*

He smiled back. "Never had a job before. I really thought I was going to hate it and it would mess up everything; but I found I like it. My hand in a cast was what really messed me up," he added bitterly.

"I'm sorry that you haven't broken any of your old track records."

"Not only that, but I was planning on setting some really great track records here that would be hard to beat in future years. I have one from before my cast ... Crichenton has the rest of them," she could see his black mood settling in—and what came out of her mouth next didn't help.

"Crichenton was going to be hard for you to beat anyway. He's always been really good. He has all the records at our old school." She thought about slipping her hand through his arm, but after the glare he gave her, she decided not to.

They came out of the theatre and she glanced at her watch. "It's still early. Do you think we could walk over to the next block and see if the fabric shop is open?"

He looked at her as if she'd just sprouted a face full of warts. "You want to go ... where?"

"The fabric shop. I sew. I need some fabric." He simply stood there, as people walked around them. "It's just another block. The walk won't kill you."

"No, but the shop might. Can you see me telling the guys that I went to a, a, I can't even say it!"

"Oh, honestly." She took off walking. He followed several feet behind.

She saw the relief in his face when he finally walked up to where she was standing. "It's closed."

"Thank God." He saw the disappointed look on her face. He smiled and wrapped an arm around her shoulders. "How about I buy you an ice cream to make up for it?"

"Okay." She wrapped her arm around his waist and they continued down the street. *I want us to stay like this forever.* She knew of two girls who were already discussing wedding plans. *They had each found someone. Why can't Michael see that we are meant to be together? Where will he ever find someone else to put up with his moodiness?*

They sat down with their ice cream. "Are you okay?" she finally asked.

He shrugged. "I am, in a lot of ways. It's great being out of the house.

Josh says things are okay with him. I don't see any marks on him. Jim's family has been great to me. I just have . . . a girl problem."

She nearly dropped her cone. *Has he been seeing someone else? And all the time he was telling me I couldn't date, like we were going steady but he didn't want anybody else to know? Or is this one of his old one-night stands who has come by with a bit of news?*

"A pregnancy problem?" The words were out before she even thought. The people next to them turned their way.

He chuckled. "No, definitely not. That's part of the problem. This girl keeps telling me she's not going to do that with me and . . . I just can't seem to get her off my mind."

"Oh, I see," she relaxed. "No, I don't see. What is the problem with that?"

"Well, she's told me that she loves me and, quite frankly . . ."

Oh, here it comes. Do not start crying. You know, you've always known that he doesn't feel the same way about you. Don't make a scene here; don't make one at the house. Wait until you are in your bedroom alone.

". . . I feel the same way." He saw the surprised look on her face. "But . . ."

But? How can there be a but after that? He's practically said—no he has said—he loves me! There is no but after that! He took a few more spoonfuls of his sundae. "I'm going to break her heart . . . just the same." His dessert became very interesting after that, and Meg was glad he wasn't watching her. She forced herself to take several deep breaths.

"Can we . . ." she stopped. Her voice was much too high pitched. "Can we start back to the car now?"

"Yeah, sure." She started to stand and fell back in her chair. He helped her up.

They drove to her house and they both sat in the car. "Meg," he started out softly, "I have to tell you something. I've known for a long time, but I could never quite bring myself to tell you. Another day was always better. But it's going to be in the papers tomorrow and I don't want you to find out that way." She could feel her face draining. What could he possibly be talking about? Whatever it was, it was not good. "Actually," he smiled, "it hasn't been in the papers all this time because of you. Whenever they would ask, I knew I couldn't tell you, so I wouldn't tell them. But, we're at the wire now."

"Just spit it out, Michael. This is driving me crazy."

"I accepted a football scholarship."

She started to laugh. "That's it? You're scared to tell me you accepted a football scholarship? You were offered some really great ones from around here."

"Yes, I was."

"So, which one did you take?" *What was the big deal about this? I've always known he was going off to college.*

He played with the radio. "Remember the weekend that I made a date with you and then you never heard from me?"

"Yeah, the weekend you stood me up."

He winced. "I . . . had another date and I thought . . . if I made the date with you then . . . I wouldn't go on the other date . . . but then . . . this is my dream, Meg." He looked at her. "I'm sorry, Meg. I've worked hard at this and I couldn't let my dream go. I went with it and . . . didn't show up for you."

"I never heard that you had another date. I see. Well . . . I don't see how that ties in with the scholarship but—" *I can't date because you gave me that medal, but it's okay if you do?*

"I flew to California that weekend."

"Michael, don't start lying to me now."

"I'm not lying."

"Where would you get the money for a round-trip ticket to California? I'm sorry, I'm not buying it."

"The school paid for it."

She was puzzled. "I never knew the high school paid for guys to fly."

"No, Meg. The college paid for me to fly out."

"Why would a college from here want to fly you out to—"

"USC paid, Meg!" He raised his voice and then quickly took her hand in his. "USC wants me and . . . I signed with them."

She stared. "The University of Southern California?" He nodded. "You're going to college on the other side of the country?"

"It's the most distance I can put between my father and me." All she could do was stare at him. "They offered me a full ride. I'd be stupid not to accept it."

"You are a stone's throw from two Big Ten colleges—and they offered you nothing?"

"No, they offered me full rides too, but they're not far enough away."

"So, basically your scholarship was based on your dad. That's great."

"I only had a year to go, Meg. Why? Why did you come into my life now? I have kept myself distant from everybody. I stopped talking to my friends; girls came and went. I had as little to do with my own family as possible, because I knew one day I would leave. I counted the days. I put everything I had into football. Not only to rub it in my old man's face, but because I wanted somebody from far away to notice me. When I leave here, Meg, I am never coming back. That was the promise I made to myself four years ago. That I would get myself out of here and I was—I am—never coming back. I'm sorry, Meg. I am truly sorry to be leaving you. I seriously considered a college around here, to be near you but . . . after the last fight with my father, I can't do it.

"There came a point in my life, a few years ago, when I swore I would never stay and that once I left, I would never return. And Meg . . . I'm not even going to do it for you. I had one more year! I was free of everybody! You're making me re-think my dream—but I'm not going to! This is what I've worked so hard for. I'm not quitting now. I'm not changing in midstream. Not for you, not for anybody.

"Please, don't stand in my way. Yes, I could stay here and be near you—and maybe that would be fine. But years down the road, how would I feel? I don't want to resent you. I don't want to resent you because I didn't pursue my dream. I have always wanted to go west, ever since I was a kid. It's not just the college or my father. I want to go someplace I've never been before. If I stay here, to be with you, I'd still be in the same place, even though I'd get a decent education.

"I want out of here, Meg. Except for you, I feel right about the decision I've made. It's exactly what I want. I don't want to resent you later in life, Meg, like my father does his family. That's why I've decided to go with my dream. I don't know what that SOB is going to do tomorrow when he reads the papers or somebody tells him."

She was numb. *You knew he would leave someday. What is the big deal?* He pulled her close and kissed her. "I'm sorry, Meg. We have the summer. Say something, please."

"Come back for me," she whispered.

"Meg . . . honey, you know I won't. You'll forget all about me in time."

"No, Michael!" She started to cry and then got a hold of herself. "I love you and if you feel the same way . . . I don't see why you can't come back and get me."

"Don't do this, Meg. It won't work. A long-distance relationship? No. It will never work. Let's just be happy with the time that we've had and will have this summer." He held her close. "I tried so hard to keep you out of my life. I warned you not to date me. I was nasty to you. I only had a few months to go! I thought about not dating you, but then I had to have you that much more. It was so much nicer to share my problems with you than to keep them bottled up inside, like I've done for so many years. It was much nicer to spend my time with you than with anybody else. I tried to warn you." He touched her cheek and felt the wetness on it. "I never meant to hurt you." He sighed. "Will you come to my graduation? I'm sure none of my family will be there."

"Surely Josh or your mom . . ."

"Maybe Josh will be able to sneak off; but I'm sure my father won't allow my mom so . . . no, nobody will be coming. I'd like you there. Please?" She nodded.

He held her while she cried.

June 2, 1967: I finally found out what Michael has been keeping from me. How could he? Now I understand why there has never been an us and why there can never be an us. He's headed to California! At least he warned me. I can't say he led me on, because he really has been up front with me from the beginning. He's been given a full ride to USC. That's the greatest distance he can put between himself and his dad. I really thought we had something special. Apparently, it's been one-sided. Mandy said this was going to be a long summer. She just didn't realize how long. I am sick at the thought of him leaving. Should I give myself to him before he leaves? Do I want that memory of Michael or will it only make things worse?

Graduation was one of those sad, exciting events. Megan went with the Hills and watched Michael, Jonesy, and the other guys and gals that she had grown up with graduate. Funny to think that after tonight she'd never see ninety-eight percent of them again—and she had known some of them since she was five. She knew Michael was in that group, too. Meg had cried nearly every night, hoping that would keep her from crying around him—and it seemed to be working—except for today.

Michael's mother, Josh, and a few younger siblings attended the ceremony, so Meg wasn't sure what to do or what Michael expected. She stayed close to the Hills and eventually Michael broke away from his family and came over to her. "You ready to leave?" he asked.

She looked at him and then scanned the crowd. "Michael, you can't leave."

"Why?"

"Well, for one thing, I see your family has not left yet; and two, several people are taking group shots and they are calling for you."

"Yeah, let's leave."

"No. Go have your picture taken. I'll wait here for you."

Reluctantly he went with Jonesy to some mutual friends. Megan glanced several times at the MacKenzie's, wondering if she should go over and say hi. She and Josh briefly made eye contact and then he looked away. *Okay, I guess I won't,* she thought.

Finally, Michael was done with pictures. He said good-bye to his mother and then came back to her. "Okay?" he asked. Meg turned to make sure his family was leaving, and then nodded.

They left. Meg could tell Michael wanted to say something, but he didn't say a word. Finally she looked at him and barked, "Spit it out."

He started to laugh. "That. Right there. Where do you get off telling me what to do? You always have. How can you get away with it? Why doesn't it bother me that you have me wrapped around your finger?"

"Hmph. If that was true, you wouldn't be leaving me," she replied.

"Meg—"

"I know, I know. We agreed to have a nice day. I'm sorry." *Why am*

I apologizing? "Just so you know—we have to go to my house at some point."

"Oh? Why?"

"Because my parents bought you a graduation present and they'd like to give it to you."

"What?" he nearly drove off the road. "What are you talking about? Why? Why would they do that?"

"Because they felt like it."

"I, I, I can't. No."

"Yes, yes, yes, you will."

He was uncomfortable with the idea of getting a gift from her parents; but after thinking it over for a few minutes, Michael decided to go to Meg's house now and get it over with.

"You don't have to sir and ma'am them, you know."

"Yes, I do."

"No, you don't. Please, don't. They like you. Just be yourself."

"They like me? Yeah, right." As they got out of the car, Meg could hear Michael mumbling; but he fell silent when he saw what her parents had bought for him. "I . . . I can't accept this." He stared open-mouthed at the three-piece leather luggage.

"Sure you can," said Mr. Becktame. "You're going to need it. Megan says you're going to USC. You need to arrive in style. Besides," he pointed, "it has your initials on it. Can't take it back now."

Megan didn't need to worry about any sirs and ma'ams; Michael couldn't get anything out. She disappeared in another room briefly and then came back out. "We're leaving," she told her parents. Michael was able to say thank you and then she helped him carry the luggage to the car. He noticed she carried a small wrapped box. When they got in the car, she handed it to him.

"What's this?"

"My present to you."

He opened it. "How much did you pay for this?"

"Why do you always look at everything as money? Why can't you be happy that I want you to have the best?" It was a watch. Not any watch, rather a Seiko with as many gadgets on it as Meg could find.

He put it on and suddenly grabbed her up. He held her for a long time. "I need you," he whispered.

Don't go. Don't leave me. Come back for me, she wanted to say; but couldn't. *What am I going to do without you?*

As they drove to a party Meg stared out the window. "Michael."

"Yeah."

"Besides money, do you see anything else in your future?"

Okay, where is this leading? "Like what?"

"All right. I don't think about money. I think about having a log cabin on some acreage, becoming a vet, someday I'll marry and have . . . How many children do you think I want?"

He glanced uncertainly at her. "You've thought about kids?"

"I think you'll find most girls do. The answer is four, by the way."

"You want four kids? Are you out of your mind? Want to try baby-sitting my brothers and sisters? That'll cure you of that."

"So, you don't plan on having any kids?"

He sighed. "I suppose down the road—the long road—I'll end up having a few; but at least I'll know when to quit. I do believe in birth control."

"Ever thought of traveling?"

"No. Well, yeah. Where is this conversation going?"

"Today is your graduation. This is a time for reflection and thought for the future. And, quite frankly, I know nothing about you in that department other than you wanting to make a lot of money. That's pretty shallow. So, I'm just wondering if you have any other plans for your life. You know, so years down the road when I think of you and wonder what you're doing I can say, 'He always said he wanted this or he was going to do that,' and I can think—"

"Stop it, Meg."

"—about you doing those things. Don't you want to someday imagine me surrounded by my four kids, living in the country? Or, when you think of me, is it just going to be a blank? 'I never knew what her hopes and dreams were for the future.' Or, are you not going to think of me at all?"

"Of course, I'll think of you." He pulled into the driveway and turned off the ignition.

"So, what are your future long-range plans?"

He stared out the window. He could feel himself getting angry and didn't want that. *Not today. Just answer the question and get it over with.* "I will get myself a good education, not exactly sure in what yet, but I will, and then I'll make good money in the pros—"

"The pros?"

"Yeah. The pros. As in professional football. I know I'm great."

Her mouth dropped. *The audacity. I have never met anyone so sure of himself.*

He saw the look on her face. "Meg, in all the years that I've played, I've been spiked once. That's it. No broken bones, no bad knees, nothing. I'm not going to get hurt. I was born to play football. I'm invincible. I am going to make a name for myself and when the time comes to end my football career, I will have an education and a name to fall back on."

"I see." She thought for a moment. "Okay, next question. Where do you think you'd like to travel to?"

"Actually, the West Coast. So, I've already accomplished two dreams. I've escaped my father and I'm going to college out West."

"You graduated from high school with honors."

"Yes, that's true. And I have a wonderful girlfriend, which was never in my plans. You were a surprise. A very nice surprise but . . . Australia. I think someday I'd like to go there." He saw Meg moving her finger around and around indicating that he should keep the wheels rolling and spit something else out. "So . . . where would you like to go?"

"Australia would be nice. I wouldn't mind going there, but my number one spot is Greece."

"See the ancient ruins, huh?"

"I'm into Greek mythology."

"Huh. Something I didn't know about you."

"Exactly, there's a lot about me you don't know."

"Really? Well, let's see. You want a log cabin with acreage. I'm sure you'll have animals around, like dogs and cats, besides your livestock. Four kids. I'm wondering if there's a husband in there, however . . . I won't be thinking about him. I have no doubt that you'll do well in vet school and be the best vet around. Actually, I see you traveling around the world. Maybe taking care of animals in different zoos."

She nodded. "Interesting."

"And what else? You, you like to do that . . . girlie stuff—sew and knit. And . . . you're a great cook. I do love your cooking. You want to go to Greece and you read Greek mythology. There, have I covered all the bases?"

She nodded. "What do you like to read?"

"Read?" he laughed. "For enjoyment?"

"Yeah. Jonesy reads."

"I always thought Jonesy was a little odd."

"I'm sure you're not into romance; but there are mysteries, thrillers, the classics." He rolled his eyes at this.

"Classics are for sissies."

"Classics are for . . . ever hear of *Twenty Thousand Leagues Under the Sea*? *Ivanhoe*? There are even some decent sports books."

"How would you know?"

"I've read them. I do a lot of reading. I bet you didn't know that." *And there's going to be a lifetime of you not knowing anything about me.*

"Can we go into the party?" She gave him a disgusted look and opened the car door. As they walked up the sidewalk he asked, "What do you know about me? How do you see me down the road?"

"I see you as Donald Duck's Uncle Scrooge: alone and surrounded by a lot of money."

June 10, 1967: I watched Jonesy, Michael, and the other kids graduate today. Funny to think that ninety percent of these people I have known all my life—I'll never see again, for the most part. I had quite a talk about the future with Michael, or rather, I tried to drive home the point that we had no future together with him going off to USC. I don't think he got what I was driving at. Oh well, what else is new?

He says we have the summer. I don't want to be a bitch and constantly be miserable around him; but every time I see him or think about him I just fall apart. How could he do this to me? To us? He's ruining everything to go after his dream! It's not fair! I have secretly thought about applying to USC and if accepted go to college there, but the best vet school is right here in my own backyard. And what if I got out there only to find that he has a girlfriend that he's serious about? I'd feel ten times worse and look like a fool besides. We have the summer together. I guess I'll just have to be happy with that. I'll be so happy and exciting and fun to be with that he will really regret leaving me behind. That will teach him.

Two days later, the receptionist at the vet clinic opened the back door and said to Meg, "Your boyfriend is here to see you." Meg smiled as the receptionist closed the door while muttering, "Why didn't they make them like that when I was growing up?"

Meg walked into the lobby. "Hey, what's up?"

Michael seemed agitated and he pulled her over to the corner of the waiting room. "Can you leave now?"

"What's the matter?"

"Can you leave now?" He gritted his teeth and glared at her.

"I'm in the middle of something. I can probably leave in fifteen, twenty minutes. Why?"

"I'll be outside waiting for you." And he was gone.

Meg found him in the furthest parking spot, away from all the other cars. "What's the matter?" she asked, coming up to him. He brought his hands up around her face and studied her. "You're scaring me," she said.

"My father came over to Jim's last night. It wasn't pleasant. I can't stay there, Meg. They've been great to me. Not just now, but my whole life. I can't put them through this. He'll just get drunk again and continue to come over as long as I'm . . . I'm . . . leaving tonight for California."

"No," she stood her ground. "You promised. We have the summer. No!" She shook herself free of him.

"Honey—"

"No! You promised, Michael!"

"Meg. I'm not happy about leaving either. I don't have a choice. That bastard will keep coming back until he knows I'm gone . . . or dead. I'm all packed. Let's go away today. The rest of the day is ours. Okay?"

Slowly she looked at him. "Go away where?"

"Any place you want to go."

She shook her head. "Where will you go in California? What will you do? How did you get a ticket so fast?"

"I called USC. They've ordered me a ticket. I'll stay in a dorm and they said they could find me work. Let's go away together for the day. We'll just go wherever we want."

"I'll have to tell my parents I'm going someplace."

"Meg, for once in your life do something spontaneous. You're always such a Goody Two-shoes. Just come away with me. We'll be gone, what? Six hours? I have to drop you off back here by seven in order to catch my plane."

"How are you getting to the airport?"

"I'll drive back to Jim's, leave my car for Josh to have, and Jim and his parents will drive me to the airport. Come on, Meg. Let's go. You're wasting time. Our time."

Never in her life had she ever done anything against her parents' wishes. She'd never lied, she'd never stolen, and she had always done what she was told. Always. Meg couldn't think of a single time of defying them. Well, except Michael driving her car . . . Michael coming in the house when her folks weren't home . . . this time wasn't exactly defying them— they'd probably never even know she was gone. "Okay."

They decided to take her car since it was more reliable, although Michael drove. When they got in, he gave her one long kiss and asked her where she wanted to go. "I don't care. I just want to be with you."

"I know where I'm going to take you, then."

She laughed and tucked her hand inside his when he parked and walked her up to the fabric shop. "Oh, Michael."

"I am *not* going in. I'll be across the street." Meg laughed and went inside. She soon came out, with nothing.

"Gosh, I thought you'd be a long time."

"I would normally, but . . . I can go any time. I don't want to spend the time away from you. Mandy and I will come next week. But, I appreciate the gesture." *You do love me, why don't you admit it?* They walked around downtown. They went to the mall. They got on the expressway and just drove. "I'm hungry. Why don't we grab some hamburgers and fries and go eat in a park?"

"Whatever you want." They didn't know where they were, but got off at the first exit that looked promising. They ordered their food, asked where a park was, and took off.

Megan grabbed a horse blanket out of the trunk and they found a secluded spot to eat. Afterwards they wrapped themselves around each other. No one had come by. "Take me," Megan whispered in his ear.

His lips ran along her neck, stopping here and there. "Do you know what you're saying?" he asked.

"Yes. I want this memory of us." She pressed herself against him for good measure.

"Stop that," he smiled, and brushed her hair back. "Why are you and I never on the same page?"

"What do you mean?"

"I would love to take you, but we're not going that far."

"It's all right. I've given it a lot of thought."

"No, honey. It's not all right. One, I didn't bring anything with me since I wasn't planning on going that far; and two, I don't want to be sitting in California wondering if you're pregnant. My father can't get to me—but yours still can. And, I know you. As time goes on, you'll hate yourself for giving in to me and then you'll start to hate me."

"I could never hate you."

"You say that now. But . . ." he smiled. "I do have a proposition for you."

"What?"

"You are not the only one who's been doing some thinking. How long can you wait for me?"

"What are you talking about?"

"We both know I can't make it without you. I kept thinking, when I'm out in California I need to find someone like Meg. Someone who can tell it to me like it is. Somebody who stands up to me. And then I thought, why am I looking for another Meg when I already have you? Yes, we'll be thousands of miles apart—but you'll still have my heart—and I have yours, right?"

She smiled. "Right."

"I'll be four years in college, then the pros. And when I start making decent money, I'll come back to get you. I always swore I'd never come back here; but I will, for you. Now, the problem is vet school. That's longer than four years."

She smiled. "Why don't we cross that bridge when we get to it? You promise to come back for me?"

He sat up and took off a ring she had never seen before. "This has been in my family for generations. It goes to the oldest son."

"That's not you."

"I know," he said. "I told you, my brother Dave is in the service. He's in Vietnam and before he left he gave it to me. He wanted me to have it, in case he didn't come back. Now, if something happens to Dave, I want it back because he gave it to me. And if he comes back alive, I need to get it from you to give it back to him so . . . this is your guarantee that I'm coming back."

"I'm not taking on the responsibility of a family heirloom. Are you nuts?"

"This is your guarantee, as the years go by, that I am coming for you."

"Well, I'll just take your word for it."

"Meg I want—"

"I am not going to take on that responsibility. What if I lose it?"

"I trust you."

"No. Absolutely not. I don't want that hanging over my head." He sighed and put it back on.

"I want you to promise me something."

"I won't have any trouble waiting for you." She kissed him.

"No, it's not that. Although, that's nice to know. Promise me you won't cut your hair."

She stared at him. "I can't let it go for five or six years. Do you realize how long my hair would be by then?"

"I expect that you'll keep it trimmed, but keep it about where you've got it now, okay?" It was halfway down her back and she was getting tired of it.

"I need it a little shorter, but I promise to keep it below my shoulders." She pulled at the front of her blouse, trying to get some air. "God, it's hot."

Michael grinned and peeled off his shirt. "You can do the same thing if you want. I won't stop you."

She saw his challenge and decided to meet it. She watched his face as she took off her blouse. He grabbed her up, peppering her with kisses as his fingers worked on releasing her bra. She ran her hands along his back. She had always wondered about the ridges beneath her fingers and realized that in the daylight she would be able to see them. She opened her eyes and looked down.

Michael felt her sudden tension and thought it was because he had gotten her bra completely undone. *What is the big deal, though? We've gone this far before.* As soon as he felt her hands come off his back, he knew what it was. Slowly he pushed her away from him and saw the horrified look and the question that she wanted to ask.

"Not pretty, is it? I didn't think." He grabbed up his t-shirt and pulled it back on, handing her blouse to her. "I've grossed out plenty of guys in the locker room, too. I'm sorry you had to see it."

"What . . .?" *What have my hands been running along all these months?* she wanted to scream. Instead, she sat silently with her mouth open.

"Let's just say it was a turning point in my life."

"Did you get burned?"

"No, Meg. Although it sure burned plenty at the time," he sneered. "Let's just drop it, okay? It's nothing."

"How did you get those marks, ridges, whatever you want to call them?" They ran every which way all over his back. His skin was a myriad of colors from white to red.

Why is it that whenever guys ask me and I say, "It's nothing," they drop it? Why can't she do the same thing? Maybe I didn't say it as forcefully as I do to the guys. Oh, that's right. The guys are afraid of me, she's not. "They're belt marks."

"From . . . from . . . your . . ." She could hardly get the word out, "Father?"

"Yes."

"Oh, Michael." He didn't want any sympathy from her; but suddenly she launched herself at him, nearly knocking him over. She held him tight. "Oh, baby. I'm so sorry! I understand. I understand now about your leaving." She cried for a couple of seconds and then got a hold of herself. "How many times did he hit you?"

"I couldn't tell you. I was a kid. I passed out at some point and when I came to, it was still going on, only my two older brothers had finally decided—I suppose because of my mom screaming—to put a stop to it. You've seen my father. That was no easy feat. Hmph. I've never told another living soul that story." Although he figured Jim had probably pieced most of it together. They held onto each other for a long time and then Michael told her it was time to head back.

Her car had bucket seats with a column on the floor, so she was not able to sit next to him, but she kept her hand on him. This would be the last time she would be able to touch him, see him for a long time, and she didn't want a second of it to pass her by.

By now everyone had left the clinic and his was the lone car in the parking lot. He pulled off a sheet of paper stuck in his window wiper, saw that it was addressed to Meg, and handed it to her. "Go straight home" it read.

"The one time I do anything a little out of the ordinary I get caught." She wadded it up and threw it in her backseat.

"Yeah, except you never get punished for it," he teased. "Okay, no long good-bye. One good kiss and then we each go our separate way."

He reached for her, but she put a hand out. "Wait," she rummaged around in her purse.

"What are you doing?"

"I need to give you my address."

"Ahh . . . no, Meg."

"Yeah. So you can write. I would think you'd have my phone number memorized by now, but I can write that–"

He took the piece of paper from her and then threw it back in her car and gathered her up. "No, a long-distance relationship isn't going to work. People have a tendency to start arguing on phones. You'll be mad that I don't write enough. I'm not coming back for vacations or holidays or anything like that. We won't be *seeing* each other. No writing, no phone calls, no contact. We're going to make a clean break with the promise of reuniting in five or six years."

"Why, you son of a . . ." she said softly. "You want to date. Be a man and just tell me."

"It's not something I plan on doing, but I don't see me being a monk all that time, either. I think that by keeping in touch, it will only make it that much harder on us. Once I break into the pros, you'll know I'm coming for you. But, there won't be any contact before then."

"What if you don't make the pros? What's my signal then?" He could feel her anger coming to the forefront, so he held her tighter.

"I will. I just know it, Meg. It's my destiny. I am excellent at what I do. I've never been seriously hurt. I'm invincible . . . I will make it."

"And, what am I supposed to do? Just sit here while you run around?"

"I suspect that you'll date, too," he smiled. "But you're never going to find another me—just like I'm never going to find another you. I wish you'd take the ring. You'd feel better about me coming back."

"No. I don't want the responsibility. Just promise—"

"I promise you, I'll be back. Promise you'll wait."

"I promise," she suddenly laughed. "Shouldn't we prick our fingers and mash the blood together or something?"

He laughed and kissed her. "I love you, Michael MacKenzie."

His eyes caressed her face and he brushed her hair back. "You know what? Until you said those words to me, I'd never heard them directed at me before. Thank you."

"Well, surely your mother . . ."

"No, no one. It's not something that's ever been said in my family." He knew what she wanted him to say, but the words were too foreign for him. "I'll be back, baby."

"Do you think you can handle a house in the woods?" she asked, trying anything to get him to stay longer.

"Yeah, I can. Can you manage without electricity and running water?"

"Maybe we won't go that rustic."

He chuckled and held her close. "Hey, here's an idea. I'll make money in the pros while you finish school and once you become an established veterinarian I can sit back and you can bring in all the money."

"Okay," she agreed. "You can stay home with the four kids."

He made a face. "Did I agree to four kids?"

She kissed him. "I'll get them out of you somehow."

"I bet you will," he whispered. "I am so sorry to be leaving you. Come on, I gotta go."

They each got in their respective cars. He waited for Meg to leave. She wished that Michael could have said those three words to her, but she tried to understand. Five, six years would be a long time. Well, she'd just keep herself busy. She had school, her friends, her horses, she could work as many hours at the vet's as she wanted. She would just make the time go by fast.

She pulled into her driveway and wondered about all the cars. *Well, at least with all these people, Mom and Daddy won't drill me with questions right off the bat.* She walked in to find a quiet house for so many people being inside.

"Meg's here." She heard Mrs. Hill's voice.

Her mother descended on her, eyes red and swollen. "Where have you been?" she screamed. Meg was startled, to say the least. She had never seen her mom like this.

It was embarrassing, with so many people standing around looking at them. "It's just a little past seven. It's no big deal."

"I've had Jeff out looking for you for hours!" Meg's Mom waved a hand towards the living room and Meg saw Jonesy and Mandy standing together, both solemn.

"I thought that was your handwriting," Meg said, looking at Jonesy. "Oh my God. You haven't all been out looking for me, have you? I'm home way ahead of curfew." She tried laughing it off. *What is going on?*

"Josephine, you really need to lie down," Mrs. Hill said, as Meg's mom continued to cry.

"I'm home. I'm fine. I'm safe. Nothing happened." Meg looked around the room. Her aunt and uncle, whom she hadn't seen in months, were there; neighbors; friends of her parents; and then she saw the three men in business suits. *Don't they work with Daddy?* Mandy had been crying. Neither her nor Jonesy would meet her gaze. *Why would men from Daddy's office be here, looking for me?* "Where's Daddy?"

There was silence. "Daddy?" she called louder. As she watched Mrs. Hill help her mother up the stairs, Mr. Hill came up to Meg and put an arm around her. "Daddy?" *Why doesn't he answer?*

"Megan, I'm so sorry," Mr. Hill said. *Where's Daddy?* She looked around the room. They were all just staring at her! "Your father had a heart attack at work today."

"No!" She flung his arm off her. She started breathing in short shallow breaths. "Then, shouldn't we be . . . we should go . . . to the hospital." She grabbed the door handle.

Mr. Hill was right behind her. "There's no need to go there. I'm sorry, Meg." He shook his head. "He's gone."

Meg flung open the door and ran into the woods. *It's not true! No! He was fine this morning. He'll come home!* "Dad, just let her go," she could hear Jonesy and Mandy outside with their father. Meg ran until she tripped on a branch and went sprawling to the ground. And then she just lay there.

"I told you . . ." she barely had enough strength to get the words out, "not to let him go."

"Megan, I'm sorry," said Jim at the other end of the phone. "I tried— my parents tried to get him to stay but . . . we couldn't sway him. I told him you just needed him to get you through the funeral and then he could leave but . . . he was afraid that if he stayed he would never leave. He said you had some sort of pact and that you'd understand. And to tell you that nothing has changed. Does that make any sense to you?"

"Yes, but he's wrong. Things have changed."

"He said to tell you—" Jim stopped. He was listening to the dial tone.

CHAPTER 13

2001

R OBIN SAT WITH THE DIARY ON HER LAP. SHE HAD GOTTEN used to her mother's handwriting, but these next entries were different. Although it frequently looked like her mom wrote in a hurry—there were often words scratched out here and there—this section contained entire lines and paragraphs that were obliterated with a pen. One section had been gone over so many times, the paper was ripped and ink marks were visible on the next page.

July 13, 1967: It has been a month since I've written in you. Let me just write it down and then, maybe, it will become clear. . . . Daddy and Michael are both dead. Daddy, literally; Michael, figuratively. I visit Daddy's grave every night that I work at the vets. . . . Michael left for California the same day Daddy died. I called Jim to tell him what happened and to make Michael stay until after the funeral. Apparently he thinks our pact will stand the test of time. And I was agreeable to that, but not the test of death. I was always there for Michael. The one time I needed him . . . If he thinks I am waiting for him, he's wrong! All that talk about caring and wanting to give me the family heirloom . . . a kick in the family jewels is what he deserves.

THE BASTARD ran out on me! Coming back for me! Yeah, right. To think I offered myself to him! I am so glad he turned me down. He can rot in California for all I care! Why should I wait for him while he runs around on me? I was so in love with him! I'll never get over losing Daddy. And, in all honesty, I'll probably never get over losing Michael. He was my big love. Everybody tells me "you always remember your first love, but you'll find your true love out there." No, I won't. I don't intend to ever fall in love again.

In all fairness, Michael did call from California to check on me. I wasn't here. Mandy had convinced me to get out of the house and we went horseback riding. The one time I leave the house, he calls! He did not leave a number. Another time I came into the house and I just knew from the tone in Mom's voice it was Michael on the phone. I yelled to her that I was home, but she hung up as I walked into the room. "Why did you do that?" I asked her. Apparently she never liked Michael. Truly, I would not have guessed that. She was always pleasant to him. She said she was never happier to see anybody leave this state. It was well worth the price of the luggage to make sure he left. That he was no good. Find myself a decent guy, like Jim. I guess she really liked Jim. That the Michaels of the world were beneath our social class. Social class? I've never heard Mom talk like that. Most of the kids I know, their dads are factory workers and farmers. Marcy lives in the trailer court. Mom has never had a problem with any of them. But, I'm not waiting for Michael. Then again, who am I saving myself for?

Robin closed the diary. She had never realized, never even thought about, her grandfather dying while her mother was still in high school. Robin's grandmother had shown her pictures and talked about him, but Robin had not realized that her mother was so young when her dad died. *Just like me*, thought Robin. *I have something more in common with her than just genes. She would have understood what I'm going through. Why did she have to die so young?*

CHAPTER 14

1967

MEGAN WAS SURPRISED TO OPEN THE DOOR TO JIM. "HI." HE stood there awkwardly.

"Hi."

They both stared at each other and then he studied the floor. "Would you like to come in?" Megan opened the door further.

Her mom came to see who was at the door. She was all smiles for Jim. She pleasantly chatted with him about his summer and where he was going to college. For the first time, Megan realized her mom had never stayed in the room to talk with Michael. She had been pleasant enough, but she never lingered; particularly if her dad was there. Then, her mom wouldn't even come into the room to chitchat. Megan wondered how her dad had felt about Michael. "Well, he certainly loved to brag that that was who you were dating," was her mother's only response to the question.

Finally her mom left the room, although not before sending Megan a look that clearly said "*He* came to say good-bye." *Yeah, well, so did Michael.*

The silence was oppressive. "So, how are you and . . ." *Dang, what is his girlfriend's name?*

"We broke up."

"Oh. I'm sorry, Jim."

He made a face. "I'm going off to college. I broke up with her. I figure I'll be meeting plenty of new girls." He smiled.

She chuckled. "New blood."

"Yeah, exactly. Listen," he struggled to pull something out of his jean's pocket. He held it out to her. He saw her eyes go wide and she stepped back.

"No."

"I take it you know what it is?"

"Yeah, I think so." She stared at the ring box.

Jim popped it open and they both looked at the ring. "Being the one to have to deliver this, I looked at it. I didn't want . . . I don't know . . . something jumping out at you or . . . oh hell, I was curious. This is Dave's ring. Why does Michael have it?"

"Is his brother still in Nam?" Jim nodded and Megan explained how Michael came to have it.

"If you don't mind me asking, since Michael wouldn't answer me, why is he giving this to you?"

Her breath came out ragged as she explained the pact that she and Michael had made.

"I see." Jim stood there in thought. "Well, now I understand what he meant. So, here's the deal. The night that Michael left, he gave me this for safekeeping and I was to give this to you when I felt it was appropriate. I don't know about appropriate, Meg. I just know that in two days I'm leaving for college and this can't sit in my room. My three sisters can't wait for me to leave. I haven't moved my stuff out yet; but every one of them has dibs on my room and they're hauling stuff in before the other one does. It's not a pretty sight." She smiled, visualizing the four of them crammed in his room.

"Michael says he has called here once a week since he left to talk with you and he can't get past your mom." He saw the surprised look on her face. "At first he thought, knowing that your mom doesn't like him . . ." *How did Michael see that and I did not?* " . . . that she was just putting him off. Now, he's beginning to wonder if you're standing by the phone, telling your mom you don't want to talk to him. So," Jim held out the box, "I told him I was bringing this over today and he is calling me tonight. And I will tell him whether or not you took it."

"Where does it go if I don't take it?"

"I'm to give it to Josh."

She looked Jim dead in the eye. "Then I guess that's who you need to give it to."

Slowly he brought his hand down. "Okay."

"Jim," she touched his arm as he turned, "I want you to go to college and find someone who is deserving of you."

He gave her a weak smile. "I don't suppose . . . that could be you?"

She brought her hand up to his face and pulled him down to her, giving him a kiss on the cheek. "Have yourself a great life."

"Yeah. You too, Meg."

He was almost to his car when he heard the front door open and Meg running out the door. "No! No! Jim!" For a split second he was hopeful that she meant she'd made a mistake turning him down; but he knew better. He was already starting to hand her the box when she ripped it out of his hand and clutched it to her chest. "Oh, please, Jim! Don't tell him! Don't tell him I nearly—please!"

He turned away as he saw tears streaming down her face. "I won't, Meg. Don't worry."

August 28, 1967: Jim came over today. He leaves for college in two days and wanted to deliver a message to me from Michael. Jim has had our pact ring all this time. He told me Michael has phoned my house at least once a week, but he can't get past Mom. Why would she do that to me? I know now that she doesn't like him, but to do that to him AND to not even tell me! I can't believe that of her! Here I've been going on and on about how obviously Michael doesn't care because he hasn't called except for the two times early in the summer that I knew about--and all along Mom knew he had been calling for me! All she has ever said to me is to forget about him, that he's no good.

Then I thought, maybe Michael is lying. I just couldn't believe that Mom would do this to me, so I confronted her with what Jim told me. She got really mad. As mad as I've ever seen her—and she said yes, it

179

was true. And that he had a hell of a lot of nerve to keep calling when she told him flat out to never call here again. Now he's demanding to speak with me. In the beginning, he asked, but now . . . He has no class, he has no manners, he has nothing! That if it hadn't been for Michael taking me away that day, I could have seen Daddy one more time. I could have said good-bye to him. That Daddy could have seen me one last time. Does she not know that I know the truth about that day or is that how she remembers it? The men from Daddy's office had come to tell us that Daddy was already gone. His heart attack was swift. He spoke to no one. Not even Mom. Even Mrs. Hill said she doesn't know what Mom is talking about. That Daddy was already dead when they came to the house.

Then Mom screamed at me: "You should be miserable because of your dad, not Michael!"

My God! Doesn't she know I am devastated at losing Daddy? He was everything to me! I probably visit his gravesite more than she does. But I can't get Daddy back, no matter what I do! I have a chance with Michael. As slim as it may be. I know I can wait for him—but I must admit I have my doubts about him.

Jim came over and told me it was my decision as to whether I took the ring or not, and that he would report back to Michael. I told Jim I wasn't taking it. Quite frankly, I've been so mad at Michael, I couldn't see straight. I also didn't want the responsibility of having 1) his brother's ring; and 2) a ring that's been passed down through the generations. And I meant it—but as I watched Jim leave, I couldn't do it. I couldn't let him get away and tell Michael that I wouldn't be waiting for him. Who am I kidding? I jump every time the phone rings, praying it's him. I want so badly to tell him off. I want him here! I want him to hold me! I can't wait five or six years. Maybe he can't either. He'll come back before that. Look at the other times he's dumped me and come crawling back. He'll do it again.

He just has to. He has to care. I know how hard it was for him to call and have to talk to Mom. But to find out that she told him not to ever call again and for him to do it anyway and demand to talk to me—he is worried about me. He does love me. I have the ring now. He has to at least come and confront me and get the ring back, one way or another.

Jim hinted that he's still hung up on me, and I feel really bad. He is such a nice guy. I hope he finds somebody who's just crazy about him in college.

CHAPTER 15

2001

"MICHAEL CAME BACK FOR HIS RING, DIDN'T HE?" SAID ROBIN to her godfather.

She was not prepared for the startled look on Jeff's face. "What makes you say that?" he said slowly.

"Well, because," Robin started to stumble. He looked upset. "I read about their pact ring in the diary and I went through what jewelry I had of Mother's and I didn't find it. All of the rings are feminine. I figured if it was his brother's ring and had been in his family for years, that it was a man's ring. Nothing Mom had was masculine. They were all tiny. They fit my finger. I thought . . ."

He chuckled. "You think you're quite the detective, huh?"

"Yeah," Robin relaxed. "I didn't find any wrestling medal either."

"So, what did you think of the diary?"

"It took me a while to figure out you were Jonesy."

He smiled. "A nickname your mom gave me that stuck until I went to college. I told people my name was Jeff, and half the time I didn't respond to it."

"It sounds like you were quite a playboy in your day."

"I had my women. Can't complain." Even today, Robin thought her godfather looked pretty good. He kept himself in shape and she had seen pictures of him as a young man.

"So, tell me. When he came for the ring, who told who off? I mean, obviously they didn't get married so . . . tell me what happened."

Jeff smiled at her eagerness and naïveté. "Michael went off to sunny California, your mom went to college here, and met your father and . . ." He leaned forward and took her hand. "Princess, I was hoping that by reading your mom's diary you would feel closer to her. That you could see how hung up she was on one person but that she found somebody else. That you will, too."

"You're talking about Matt breaking our engagement?"

"Honey, trust me. There will be others."

Robin looked at the floor. "I keep thinking I shouldn't have confronted him."

"It wouldn't have made any difference. It would have just prolonged things."

"Maybe we could have worked it out. I was just so stunned when I heard him on the phone saying, 'I can't tell her I'm leaving. She just lost her dad last month. She's all alone now. I can't do it.'"

"You're not alone, you know that." She nodded. He hugged her and she cried softly. He tried getting her mind back on her mother. "You know, your mom even found someone in between Michael and your father."

"Didn't marry him either, huh?"

He laughed. "No." He got up and strolled over to his desk. He opened the bottom drawer and took out a book. He walked back over and handed it to her. "One more. That's it."

Robin stared at the book for a moment and then carefully took it from him. "Mom wrote another diary?"

"Yep. This one is a little more explicit than I would like you to read— but it was the seventies. What can I say? With everything you kids see on TV and at the movies nowadays, I don't suppose there's anything in there that will shock you. But, this is the last one. Your mom met your dad, and I suppose she was too busy to write after that. I don't know. I do wonder what your grandmother thought though, if she ever read it."

He made a face and Robin laughed. What little she could remember of her grandmother was a woman who never smiled. She seemed to always be worrying. Robin knew that her father hadn't cared for his mother-in-law, but then, did anybody get along with his or her in-laws? Her other grandmother, her father's mother, had been strict. Robin thought she always looked down her nose at her only granddaughter. Gary, of course, could do no wrong.

Robin walked over to the bookcase and got down her godfather's high school yearbook. "Why are you looking in there again?"

"I want to see what Michael looked like. Oh . . . wow! He was good-looking, wasn't he?"

"The girls seemed to think so."

"Who was the other one—Jim? What was his last name?"

"Wagner."

She looked him up. "He's cute. He had it bad for mom, huh?"

"Yeah. But he's happily married now and has a couple of kids. Things do work out, I promise you Princess."

"If you say so."

CHAPTER 16

1967

M EGAN WENT TO THE FOOTBALL GAME BECAUSE THE GIRLS HAD bugged her to get out, and they promised they'd do something fun afterwards. *I doubt it*, thought Megan to herself. *And see, I was right. They want to go to the dance. I don't want to mingle with people. I don't want to dance with anybody—and if nobody asks me, I won't feel good about that either.*

Mandy had a date and as soon as Patti, Trish, and Marcy were on the dance floor, Megan walked out.

"You're leaving the dance pretty early, aren't you?" She turned to see a tall blonde walking her way. Her heart gave a leap. *Michael! Oh, no, little brother. Honest to Pete, is this my destiny—to be haunted by Michael's replica for the rest of the year?*

"Yeah, I am," Megan said over her shoulder. She opened her car door, only to have it suddenly slammed shut. She looked up at him. He was only slightly taller than her. Megan did not have to crane her neck like she had to with his older brother.

"Why don't we get something to eat?" Josh offered.

"I'm not hungry."

185

She watched his eyes rove up and down her. Not the same way Michael's did though. "You really need to eat." He took Megan by the elbow and led her to his car and helped her in. Megan was too flabbergasted to protest.

"Where would you like to go?"

"I'm not hungry. I'm not interested." She stared out the side window. *Well, this was a mistake,* she thought a few minutes later, when he pulled up to the pizzeria that she and Michael used to frequent. It was made even worse when Megan and Josh walked in and several people recognized them. *Yeah, I can imagine what they are thinking.* Megan gritted her teeth. *I will kill the girls next time I see them.*

Josh asked what she would like to eat. "Nothing." He ordered a large pizza. When it was ready, he pressed her to eat. Megan managed a few bites of her slice.

"You know, you look awful." She turned her Michael stare on Josh. "Just because Michael's not here doesn't mean you have to look bad for the rest of us who have to see you every day."

"I see you have your brother's charm," she said dryly.

"I noticed we've been together for an hour and you haven't asked about him yet."

She shrugged her shoulders. "So, how is the bas— How is Michael?"

"He's doing fine. Loves California. He's having a blast in college."

"How nice." *I just want to get out of here. Can't he eat instead of talk? Maybe I should do all the talking, that way he'll eat. Forget it, I don't feel like talking.*

"Too bad I can't report the same thing about you to him. But then again, that bolsters his ego, thinking you can't survive without him."

"What?" she was hot now. "How often have you heard from him? What did you tell him about me?"

"I told him exactly what I saw."

"And that was?"

"That you look terrible, are sullen, mean-tempered, and it's a good thing he got out when he did."

Megan was absolutely furious. She didn't remember ever being this mad at Michael. "You little . . . twerp! Where do you get off saying things like that about me?"

"It's true, isn't it?"

"No, it's not! We're done here." She grabbed her purse and flew out the door—only to realize that she did not have her car. Megan looked down the road towards the high school. *Should I walk? No, not a good idea.* Although she felt safe enough, it was dark outside, she was wearing dark clothing, and there were no sidewalks. A car could easily hit her. Plus, the walk would take almost an hour. *No, the jerk can drive me back. He is going to get an earful when he comes out.* Megan got in his car and waited.

Josh barely got the door shut before she let him have it. She'd had nearly twenty minutes to mull things over while he finished the pizza, paid the bill, and talked to some friends.

"You son of a bitch! How dare you tell Michael anything about me! You don't know me."

"Actually, I know quite a lot about you."

"Need I remind you that I lost my dad? And, unlike you and Michael, I got along with mine. I loved my dad! Nobody can replace—" Megan had to stop when she felt tears well up.

"Meg, listen."

"No, you listen to me! I lost Daddy, I lost Jonesy to college, and yes, I lost Michael—but if the two of you think that I am the way I am just because of Michael—well, the two of you have a lot to learn. How dare you!" she screamed. In frustration she took her fists and began banging on the dashboard. "How dare you!"

Megan pounded and screamed until she was spent. She put her face in her hands and sobbed hysterically. She felt his hand softly stroke her back. She whirled and knocked his hand away. *I am not taking comfort from this jerk.* She didn't know how long she went on like this, but finally she stopped. She felt numb. She collapsed against the car door. In the cool night air, they both listened to her ragged breathing.

After a moment, Josh started the car and they left the pizzeria. Quietly he said, "I do know that you lost your dad and that it was devastating. Michael knows that, too. I hadn't thought about you losing Jonesy, too. I know that changes a person—but you are not anything like the person I went to school with last year."

He brought up a hand as he saw he was going to get another verbal blast. "And yes, I do know a lot about you. Michael talked about you, he did care about you, but he's moved on—and you need to also." *What do you mean 'he's moved on'? He gave me a ring, proof that he was coming back. He's moved on already? No, I don't believe you.*

"You know, Jim stopped by to see me before he left for college and he told me that Michael was calling my house once a week." *And I've stayed home every day since then.* "Is he still calling?"

"No. He saw no reason to."

I see. "What do you mean 'he's moved on'?"

"He's dating again." *No. Not now, no. He wouldn't, not this soon. Yes, he had hinted that we should date—but that was down the road. Not right away. Like when we had been apart for a year or two or three. Not now! How could he?* At least as numb as Meg felt, she didn't hurt any worse with this revelation.

"He told you this?"

"He always asks about you, always," Josh continued. "He's worried about you ... but ... listen, Meg. He's not coming back. He swore years ago that once he left, he'd never come back—and that's exactly what he said to me the last day I saw him. He said he told you everything. You had to know that he had his plans laid out long before he met you. You knew things weren't good at home. You know, Michael was a different person after you came along. You're probably the only thing that kept his sanity together. I want to thank you for that, and I want to help. I know a few guys who would love to ask you out; but you're so unapproachable. You're like how they used to talk about Michael. You're always sulking and rude and quite unpleasant from the stories I've heard. You've got to snap out of this black mood you're in. You've got to start living again."

"God, I am so sick of everybody telling me what to do!" They were at the high school now so she grabbed the handle and slammed her shoulder against the door. It didn't budge. As Meg continued to slam her shoulder into the door, it dawned on her what car she was in. *Why didn't I notice before?* "I want everybody—*including you*—to leave me alone! I don't care about living anymore!" She remembered the trick to the door and pushed it open. "And, as long as you're giving Michael a daily report about me, give him this message from me: 'Up yours, MacKenzie'!" She slammed the door with all her might, got in her car, and left a patch of rubber in the parking lot.

September 22, 1967: The nerve of that little creep! He's got no more class than his brother! Tonight was the first football game I attended, even though we're well into the season. Mandy had a date with a new guy in school, someone all the girls are talking about. He really is cute and Mandy was thrilled that he asked her to the dance. Trish, Patti and Marcy have bugged me to do something with them, so I went to the football game. They wanted to go to the dance afterwards, which I was not up for, but they bugged the heck out of me. I finally agreed to go, knowing that I could lose them in the crowd and leave. Which is exactly what I did. I was out in the parking lot when I heard someone ask why I wasn't staying at the dance. I turned and for a split second I thought it was Michael, that he couldn't live without me and had finally come to his senses. But, as he walked up to me, I realized it was his brother Josh.

They both sound and look a lot alike. Michael is tall and broad-shouldered, while Josh is somewhat shorter and not quite so muscular. Michael's face is finely chiseled and, although Josh has exactly the same features, they are softer. Funny, although I had heard Josh's name a few times over the loudspeaker tonight during the game (he is not the athlete Michael is) I hadn't given him any thought.

He talked me into going out to eat with him. I suppose I really wanted to ask him about Michael. Where does he take me? The pizza place that Michael and I always went to. You should have seen the heads turn when we walked in. I wasn't hungry and pretty much just sat there. He starts telling me what a great time Michael is having in sunny California and how I look like shit! And I always thought he was a nice kid! He's got as much couth as his brother!

I was flabbergasted and furious! And then I find out that's exactly what he told Michael! With Michael's ego, he probably thinks it's because of him! I lost Daddy! I lost Jonesy when he left for college--and Michael thinks it's just him that I think about? I stormed out of the place, got outside, and then realized I had come with Josh. So, I had to wait while he paid the bill and took his sweet time coming out. When he got in the car I told him off but good.

We get back to the high school, I start to get out (oh, we're in Michael's car) and the idiot tells me to start dating because Michael has! He couldn't wait to get out of here! He never cared! I wonder if that "family" ring he gave me is real. Maybe he got it out of a Cracker Jack box and fed me a story? I fell for it hook, line, and sinker! He never cared! He NEVER cared about me!

It was a week since Megan had talked with Josh and she had mulled everything over that he had said to her. *Is he really telling Michael how awful I look? That I'm upset all the time and that I'm so depressed I don't know how I am going to make it through the day each morning I get up? Why would Michael think he is the sole cause of my unhappiness? Didn't it ever dawn on him that I miss my dad?*

Even her mom had sat down and talked to her. Daddy wouldn't be happy seeing her so unhappy, he always wanted Megan to have a full life. Her mom had bounced back. She was visiting friends, going shopping, and even talking about getting a job. Megan had gotten scared by this. Were they having money problems (wouldn't Michael love to hear that)? No, they were well provided for, but her mom needed something to occupy her days. Especially next year, when Meg took off for college, it would really be lonely for her. Meg told her mother she wasn't sure if she was going to college anymore and her mom threw a fit. Yes, Meg was going to college. She didn't have to go to vet school, but she had to go. Her dad would want her to. It was his dying wish. Meg decided not to point out that Daddy had died at work, so they didn't really know what his last thoughts were; and Meg hardly thought her going to college was utmost in his mind while going through a major heart attack.

October 11, 1967: Mandy, Trish, Patti and Marcy don't even speak to me anymore. I could care less. Mom even tried talking to me. I need to snap out of "my funk," as she calls it. I have decided I am going to stay right in the middle, not going to the left or to the right. My goal this year is to simply survive. At least Michael taught me that much: that it's not hard to just survive when one has no feelings.

October 16, 1967: Why did I even buy this stupid diary?

October 20, 1967: Mandy and Trish are on the Homecoming Court. The hoods in the bathroom told me that they think I would have been on it except that 'I've changed.' Who cares?

October 27, 1967: The football team lost out on going to state finals; but then again, I was expecting that. No disappointments for me this year. I neither hope nor expect anything good or bad.

November 8, 1967: I went down to the stream today. I haven't been there in months. I haven't been in the woods in months. What would be the point? But I looked down in the stream and saw a face. It startled me. At first I thought someone was with me—then I realized it was my reflection. I look awful! Just plain ugly! Last year it was so important to me to look good—and now look at me! No wonder I have no friends. I never have anything nice to say to anybody or about anybody. Daddy would be so terribly disappointed in me if he saw me now, and I don't want him to ever be ashamed of me.

And then I thought, is Josh telling Michael how terrible I look? That it was a good thing he got out when he did? What if Michael decides I'm not worth coming back for? Don't get me wrong. I don't want Michael back. I hate that man. When I think of what he did to me. But, I do want him to come back for me. Let him think that I waited all those years for him and then I'm going to crush him the same way he crushed me. I will get even with him if it's the last thing I do.

The best way to get even with him is to start dating. Maybe I could lose my virginity on the very first date—I don't care with whom. Then, I'll write Michael or tell Josh all about it and say that I'm not sorry that it wasn't him! That might be fun all the way around.

I have to clean myself up enough to start getting some dates. I don't want Michael to think I'm just sitting here waiting for him. Why should I let on for a minute that I'm unhappy at all? I've got to let him know that I've forgotten him as quickly as he's forgotten me. Maybe if he thinks I've forgotten all about him, then he'll decide he really needs me. Look how many times he dumped me and then came back. He'll decide he's made a terrible mistake and come back that much sooner. My revenge will be sweet.

Here's a thought: what if he showed up right now and I looked this bad? No, I have to look darn good when he comes walking through the door. I can't very well crush him if he's turned tail upon seeing me and runs out the door before I even get to tell him we're through.

Mandy only rode with Megan to school to avoid riding the bus. They barely talked, which for Megan had been just fine. But today was different. Today it felt awkward. *Why did I never notice the silence before?* Mandy and she had been best friends since they were three years old. *How is it I don't have a clue what Mandy has done the last couple of months?*

"Mandy," she hesitated, "I'm sorry that I've been . . ."

"What? Mean? Rude? Nasty?"

"Well," Megan was taken back, "I don't think I've been *that* bad."

"Why do you think we've started calling you Michaelina?"

"Michael— That's me? I heard that a few times in the hall, but I didn't know— That's *me* people are referring to?" She was appalled.

"Meg, you've been horrid to be around. I've tried to be understanding, but you know what? This is my last year of high school, too. I want to remember it as a fun time. Your dad would want you to live your life. And as far as Michael goes–I never knew what you saw in him. He's not the only fish in the sea. Jonesy, excuse me Jeff, wants us to come up for a visit. He doesn't want you to be rude to his friends though."

"I know. I've got to start being more myself. I'm going to try, all right? How about if I come over tonight, after I take care of the horses? We'll talk then, okay? I promise, I'm going to try to snap out of it."

"Why don't you try smiling today?"

"Yeah, okay."

The whole day felt awkward. *Who am I supposed to smile at?* Meg wondered halfway through the day. *Nobody will even look at me.*

Megan knocked on the Hill's side door after walking on the path through the woods. It was starting to become overgrown, which made her sad. Nobody had walked on the path in months; a path that had been well-worn for years. The woods even looked different to Meg; it had been nearly five months since she'd walked in it. She needed to do something about that, too.

Mrs. Hill opened the door and gestured for Megan to come in. "Oh, honey. It's so good to see you over to the house again. The girls are up in Mandy's room."

Meg had started through the house, then stopped. "The girls?"

"Yes."

"I didn't realize Mandy had company." *Of course, if I had walked down the driveway, I would have seen the cars.* "I'll just come another—"

Mrs. Hill stood in front of the door. "You're not going anyplace except upstairs. Go on!" She waved a hand at her.

Megan made her way uncertainly up the stairs. *Why didn't Mandy tell me she was having the girls over? I wouldn't have come. I wanted to talk with Mandy privately. Well, this is just great.* Megan knocked and the door swung open. Mandy, Marcy and Trish were on the floor eating popcorn and drinking sodas. "Come on in," Mandy said with a mouthful of food while Marcy cleared a spot for Meg to sit down. Meg felt the door suddenly shut behind her and she turned to come face to face with Patti.

"Gotcha," Patti said. *Huh?*

The next thing Megan knew, they were all pulling on her in every direction. Marcy had her hand. "I'm doing nails. What color do you want?" she asked as she held up three bottles.

"I'm putting on makeup," said Mandy as she grabbed Meg's chin. "Face me."

She felt somebody from behind grab her hair. "I'm doing hair."

"No!" Megan yelled as she heard Trish's voice.

"We made her promise not to cut it," said Marcy.

"You guys," pouted Trish, "I haven't done that bad of a job."

"Yes, you have!" they all chorused.

The girls sat on the floor, chatting away. "Ow!" yelled Meg as Trish vigorously brushed away.

"It's all snarly. Don't you ever brush it? If I could just cut—"

"No!" they all hollered.

They talked about boys, their classes, Jonesy . . . "You guys," said Mandy, "you've got to start calling him Jeff. He's really starting to harp on that." She made her arms like a body builder and, lowering her voice, said, "I'm the man about campus now. It's Jeff."

"I thought Suzann Cochran made him a man," said Marcy, and the girls broke out laughing.

"He never went out with her!" yelled Mandy.

"Yes, he did," said Meg. "One of my first conversations with Michael was about Jonesy having—" She clamped her hand over her mouth and looked toward the door. They had gotten pretty loud. Was Mrs. Hill listening? "Sex," she whispered. The girls screamed while Mandy sat open-mouthed. She picked up a handful of popcorn and threw it at Meg.

She felt Trish twisting her hair up. "Ow! That's attached to my head, you know!"

"All right," Trish got down near Meg's ear, still holding her hair taut in her hand, "tell the truth now. Did you and Michael do it?"

The girls turned and stared expectantly at Meg. "No. Ow!" The girls yelled and Trish pulled harder on her hair.

"Tell the truth!"

"Tell us what it was like!"

"How could you say no to him?"

"Trish, let go!" Meg tried turning to get a hold of her and suddenly there was a free-for-all. They wrestled and giggled until they were exhausted.

In the silence that followed they heard, "I did it." Slowly all eyes fastened on Patti. She shrugged. "Derek and I did it. Come on, he's two years out of high school. I didn't want him to think . . . we're probably going to get married."

"You have to?"

"No! That's not what I meant. I meant someday, so what's the big deal?"

"So, what was it like?"

She made a face. "I didn't think it was all that great."

Marcy put a hand to her chest and looked skyward, "Oh, when we made love—"

"Shut up!" yelled Meg and Mandy simultaneously, while grabbing popcorn to throw at her. They had agreed long ago that they were sick and tired of hearing about Marcy's ecstatic moment.

"Okay," Mandy stood up and dusted the food off her and looked at Megan. "Steps one, two, and three are complete. On to step four."

They all stood up, Meg last, thinking to herself, *I'm not going to like this.* "Come on." They marched out the door, went downstairs, grabbed their jackets, hollered to Mrs. Hill, and took off out the side door.

All the girls were familiar with the path through the woods. "This is getting over-grown." Meg could hear Patti talking to Mandy in the lead. "Hey, remember when . . ." They all had their own stories.

Mandy opened the door to Megan's house. "Hey, Mrs. B, we're here!" she hollered.

"In here, girls!" Even before they reached the kitchen, the aroma had already hit them. Chicken cordon bleu.

"I wonder who ordered that," said Meg, looking at Mandy.

"I haven't had it in ever so long," she smiled. Meg did not particularly care for her chicken this way; Mandy couldn't get enough of it. From years of experience, the girls went to the silverware drawer and talked amiably with Mrs. Becktame while they sampled the food that was on the stove.

"Okay, load up your plates and let's go to the dining room," announced Mrs. Becktame. As they sat around the table, Meg smiled. She hadn't had all the girls over at one time in a couple of years. One or two would visit; but they hadn't been together like this since they were freshmen. She could see that her mom was enjoying the camaraderie. The conversation flowed freely back and forth, with much laughing, joking, and teasing. The girls took their own plates back into the kitchen, scraped and rinsed them, and put them in the dishwasher.

"Okay, on to step four," said Mandy. They followed her up the stairs to Megan's room. *I can't wait to see what this is going to be.*

Mandy went immediately to Meg's closet and threw the doors open. She and Patti rummaged around. "I don't see anything new," mumbled Mandy.

Patti gave a shout of surprise, and pulled out several bags of new clothes that were on the floor. Mandy turned to Megan. "Your mom bought you clothes and you haven't even looked at them?"

"I told her not to."

"They've been sitting on the bottom of your closet since August?" asked Trish.

"What'd I get?" asked Meg, relaxing in a chair. The girls shook out the bags and held the clothes up to themselves while looking in the full-length mirror. Mrs. Becktame and Megan had gone shopping plenty of times, so she knew what her daughter would and wouldn't wear.

"Oh, I want to borrow this," said Marcy, pulling a sweater over her head.

"Not until I've worn it at least once," protested Megan.

"Here, I like this outfit," said Mandy, holding up a navy pleated skirt with a matching sweater and white blouse.

"Boring!" said Trish. She swapped out the blouse and sweater for some color.

"I don't like that combination," said Marcy, taking out the blouse for a turtleneck. Soon they were all arguing.

"Stop!" yelled Megan. "You take Monday, you take Tuesday, you take Wednesday, you take Thursday," she pointed to each girl. "And I'll finish up on Friday. Maybe by then I'll have the hang of it," she said dryly.

As she watched them putting outfits together she seriously considered making a deal with Trish: I'll let you trim my hair if I don't have to wear that combination on Wednesday. But, she decided against it. The outfit would only be for one day; the hair would take a lot longer to grow out.

November 9, 1967: I actually had fun today. I went to Mandy's and Patti, Trish, and Marcy were also there. They did my hair, nails and makeup. Then we came over to my house where Mom was already making dinner for everybody. Mandy said she did everything at lunchtime. She told the girls her plan and then they went to the pay phone and 'placed' their order with Mom. Mom said she had a good time and wants the girls to come over at least once a month, if not more often. "This is the last year you can do stuff like this," she says.

Mom bought me a bunch of clothes back in August that I hadn't even looked at. The girls got them out and I have a week and a half worth of clothes all laid out for me.

I had actually forgotten how much fun it is to do something with the girls. Patti let out her big surprise—she did it with Derek! Didn't seem to think too much of it, especially compared to Marcy.

So, tomorrow I will go off to school being a brand-new me. I'm kind of nervous. I'm sleeping on my rollers tonight so that my hair will be curled. I'll wear makeup for the first time all year. What will people think? And the girls said I had to smile and be pleasant.

CHAPTER 17

MEGAN SAW MANDY WAVING TO HER FROM THE FRONT PORCH, so she got out of her car and was halfway up the walk when she heard Mandy say, "Mom and I wanted to check you out. You look great."

Megan waved to Mrs. Hill, who was peering out the window, and the girls proceeded to the car. "I had to get out of my car for that?"

"If you didn't look right, we were going back to your house. This is a new day. Did you practice smiling last night?"

"I don't think I've forgotten how."

"Let's see." Megan stared at her. "Nope, that's not it."

"Look, I'm nervous; but I do want to thank you. Yesterday was great."

"It was a lot of fun, wasn't it? Can you believe Patti?"

Meg shrugged. "She's been dating Derek for two years."

"I suppose. Okay, Meg. It's just you and me in the car. You did do it with Michael, didn't you?"

"I really didn't," said Megan, looking at her. "We went pretty far, but I always told him no. He wasn't real pleased with me, to say the least. But,

the last day we were together I did offer to go all the way with him, and
he turned me down."

"He did not!"

"He did." Megan told her about their last time together.

Mandy digested this information. From what she knew of boys, they
never turned down an offer. "Just think," she suddenly said as they pulled
into the parking lot, "depending on what time it was, maybe your dad was
watching."

"Oh, gross!" screamed Megan. "God, the things you think of!"

"Well, I'm just saying—"

"Don't even think it!" They found a parking spot and Meg turned off
the car. "You thinking of doing it with Dwight?"

"No," Mandy shook her head. "I'd rather lose it when I'm off to college
than here. Here *everybody* will know. Look how the guys treat Marcy."
Megan nodded. "What about you?"

She shook her head. "I'm saving myself for Michael."

Mandy sat there for several seconds. "What?"

Megan hesitated. "Michael and I have a pact."

"About what?" Megan told her. Mandy sat up, "You don't seriously
consider that he's . . . that he will actually . . . Meg, he's not coming back."

Megan took a deep breath and let it out. *After my conversation with
Josh, she's right, but still . . .* "Probably not . . . there are days when I just hate
him. And other days, I can't wait to see him again. At least the thought of
him will keep me pure," she laughed. "Shall we go in?"

"Whenever you're ready."

All day, Meg received compliments and wolf whistles. More than once
she heard "Who's the new girl in school?" as the guys that she had grown
up with teased her. Even her favorite teacher, Mr. Mullins, leaned over to
her while passing out papers. "Nice to see you've joined the living."

*My word! Did I really look so bad before that everybody feels they have to
say something to me? And, if Michael heard how awful I was, what must he
be thinking of me?*

At the end of the day, Meg was walking down the hallway and saw a
tall blonde propped up next to her locker with his back to her. *Michael?*
Her heart beat fast. "Hey—Josh! Hi."

"I had to come see who everybody was talking about today." She could feel herself blush.

"You look gorgeous." He looked her up and down.

"Yeah, well, tell that to Michael." It was out before she could even think. *Well, what could it hurt? There had to be tons of pretty girls on USC's campus. I want to make sure Josh calls Michael with the news that I look great, so he hurries back here to claim me before someone else does. If he came or called, then I would know he really cares and then I can—no, I don't care. I don't care one way or the other.*

He nodded, "I will."

"I want to apologize for the last time—"

"No need. Gotta go."

She and Mandy went home, changed into jeans and sweatshirts, and headed out to ride the horses. *Now, this is the life.*

November 10, 1967: There was a new girl in school today—me! I have to admit, not only did I look a lot better than I have these last few months, I actually felt better. Josh saw me, too, and I told him to say something to Michael. I don't want him to think that I am just pining away for him. I want him to think I'm having as much fun as he is. Two can play this game.

On Saturday, Megan decided to take a walk down their private dirt road. In the summer, the trees provided a nice canopy; but they had dropped their leaves a month ago. Now they were just naked branches waiting for Mother Nature to grace them with her presence again.

Meg heard a motorcycle behind her and she turned to see who it was. She was surprised when it pulled up beside her and stopped. "Want a ride?" He smiled.

"Josh? What are you doing way out here?"

"It's supposed to snow tonight. Thought I'd take it out for one last spin and thought you might like to go." He tapped the helmet behind him.

Josh watched her face light up. "Yes!" Meg had never ridden a motorcycle before. She grabbed the helmet, snapped it on, and jumped on. She sat so close to him that their helmets constantly banged together. Eventually Josh turned onto a little used trail and stopped. They both got off.

"I love it!" she cried. "Could I try driving it?"

He laughed. "Of course not."

"Why? I'll be careful."

"You might hurt yourself or, worse than that, hurt my bike."

"No, I wouldn't."

"The answer is a definite no." She gave him her best pout, but he didn't give in.

"What was Michael like growing up?" She could see that she had taken him by surprise.

"Well, I know how rude he can be; but he's a really great brother. My other two older brothers are decent, too, I just really miss Michael. He and I did a lot together."

It had never dawned on her that anybody missed Michael besides herself. But, of course, Josh would. Michael had been with him his whole life. She remembered Michael being worried about Josh after he went to stay with the Wagners. "Are things . . . okay at your house?"

He made a face. "It's okay." Obviously he didn't want to talk about it.

"I don't suppose Michael is going to fly home for Thanksgiving?"

He shook his head. "No. Nor Christmas, nor next summer. You do know . . . he's never coming back."

She nodded. "He told me that. But think about it. By next summer, surely he will want to come home and see you guys."

Josh laughed slightly. "I don't need to tell you how bad it was between our father and him. Michael has always played football with the idea that some decent college far away would notice him and offer him a scholarship. He always said that if it happened, he would never come back. I believe him—and you should, too." She nodded but didn't say anything. They talked about things that were going on at school. He had done okay in football but certainly he was not anything like his older brother.

"I better get home before Mom wonders what happened to me."

"Okay." They hopped back on and he took her home. "I understand your woods is pretty neat to walk in."

She turned in surprise. "Did Michael tell you that?"

He nodded. "Yeah. He said it was peaceful, something he'd never experienced before. I . . . would like . . . to walk . . ."

She gave him a slow mischievous grin. "You let me drive your motorcycle and I'll let you walk in my woods."

He laughed. "Sorry. I'm putting this away until spring. I'll think about it over the winter." He turned the bike around and hollered, "Fat chance!" over his shoulder as he flew down the driveway.

We'll see about that.

November 11, 1967: Josh came by on his motorcycle today. I had never been on one before, but found that I loved it! I want to drive it; but he won't let me. I have all winter to bug him. He's certainly no Michael, but he is very good-looking. He's a lot more approachable than Michael and, therefore, the girls are always throwing themselves at him. I don't know if he dates or not.

November 26, 1967: Jonesy is home and he brought two guys with him who live out of state. Really cute!!! Mandy and I fought it out as to who we wanted to be hooked up with only to find out that the guys had done the same thing and we didn't match up! But they were both a lot of fun and I made out with Bryan. My first college kiss, so to speak!

Mom and I had Thanksgiving dinner at the Hill's. It was a full house, what with the guys and several of the Hill's relatives. It was really a fun weekend, although I don't think JEFF is going to forgive me—I slipped up and called him Jonesy and the guys have sure latched onto that. I don't see what the big deal is.

December 20, 1967: Christmas vacation is right around the corner. Big deal. I've been kind of hoping that Michael will break down and call me. For me to tell him off, that is.

I guess Michael thinks he's the greatest thing to ever hit California. He had a fairly good football season at USC as a freshman (everybody at school said 'spectacular'). Actually, I wouldn't know much about it as I listened to the gossip and newspaper reports . . . not at all. So, Michael's dream is starting to unfold, huh? I laugh every time I think about him telling me he's invincible! Just wait. Someday he'll get his and I'll be on the sidelines cheering! Think you can throw me over just like that, do you? You just try and call me this vacation.

I wonder what he's doing now. Not that I care, because I don't. I would feel better, however, if he'd had a rotten season or hadn't gotten to play at all. I guess he was even on TV, but I never saw him and I don't plan to. I hope he breaks a leg. Josh has already told me that Michael does not plan to come home for vacation, so I at least don't have to worry about him showing up on my doorstep.

December 25, 1967: Christmas Day has come and gone. This was a different Christmas with Daddy gone. Very quiet. Mom wouldn't have even put up a tree except that the Hills went out and bought one and came over with it. They helped us put it up on Christmas Eve.

It was a few days after Christmas when Megan heard the doorbell ring. She heard her mom answer it. Hearing a male voice, she assumed it was Jonesy and continued cleaning up the mess she had made in the kitchen. A few minutes later she heard, "Sure smells good in here."

She whirled. "Josh! This is a surprise." *He's come to give me a message from Michael. Surely Michael phoned his family for Christmas. He has a message for me. Mom, hurry up and leave.*

But Josh and her mother were having a regular conversation—not the guarded ones she had had with Michael. Josh was relaxed; he made her mom laugh. "Apple pie should be out in a minute."

"Michael told me you were a great cook."

"How would Michael know?" her mother asked. "He never ate here, and if he had, it would have been my cooking." *Great. As much as Mom didn't like him, now she thinks he's a liar, too.*

"I used to take cookies and brownies to school to give him whenever I made some. I'm sure that's what he meant." *Josh, please don't say a word.*

"That would be called baking." *And now you think he's stupid.*

"Cooking, baking. I'm sure it was all the same to Michael; he's a guy." Disapproval was written all over her mother's face. The timer went off for the pie. Megan thought she was going to scream when her mom hiked herself up on a barstool to sit and wait for the pie to cool.

"This is better than my mom makes," Josh said between mouthfuls.

"I'm sure that's not true; but thank you."

Her mother finally left, giving her a sign behind Josh's back that she approved of this one. *Yes, Mother, I got the message!*

"Well, I came over . . ." *Yes, yes.* "to see if you wanted to go skiing."

"Wh— skiing? Downhill? I haven't been in a couple of years."

"But you know how to, right?"

"Yeah."

"So, let's go. It'll be fun. I bought myself a pair of used skis for Christmas and I want to try them out."

"Oh, I don't know." When it came to downhill skiing, all Meg had were horror stories. The towrope that she got her pole tangled up in, and it lifted her into the air by one arm; the J-bar that somehow ended up in front of her, when it had started out behind her; and the chairlift that had caught her in the back and knocked her straight down between her skis, making it look like the Road Runner had plowed her over.

Her mom suddenly appeared. "Honey, I think you should get out. You need some fresh air. I notice you don't go out in the woods anymore."

"I go!"

"Not like you used to. You need the exercise. Just take her and go," she said to Josh. He grinned.

"Fine." She ran upstairs and changed her clothes. *This is killing me. What did Michael have to say?* She brushed her hair, put on a presentable amount of makeup so she would look decent, and sprayed herself with some new perfume she'd received as a Christmas present.

When they got outside she stopped. This was a car she'd never seen before. "Where did you get this?"

"It's mine. I traded Michael's in for it. What'd you think?"

Compared to Michael's it was. . . "Nice."

"At least now you can get the door open." The car didn't look in that bad a shape and it rode a lot nicer than Michael's did, even if it was ten years old.

"How was your Christmas?" she asked.

"Fine, how was yours?"

"Quiet . . . but nice. We spent a lot of time over at the Hill's." *Come on, quit stalling and just tell me what Michael said.* "Did you, um, hear from Michael?" she tried to sound as casual as she could.

"Yeah, he called. He's staying with his roommate's family. I guess they're loaded." *Well, that's right up your alley, isn't it Michael?* She waited. *That was it? He didn't ask about me? He didn't have a message for me?* Josh could feel her stare. "There was a nice article in the newspaper talking about how well Michael did for USC. Did you see it?" Of course, it had been hell for his family for a week while Mr. MacKenzie went on a binge.

"No," she shook her head. She waited for more. She glanced over at Josh again. Apparently he was done with the conversation.

Meg was uncomfortable having Josh pay for her rental and lift ticket. "I didn't invite you out expecting you to pay for it." He looked hurt.

"Josh, I know how expensive skiing is. You should save your money."

"I have been saving my money. That was a great idea you had."

"What?"

"Having Michael work for our uncle. After Michael left I took over his job. I've spent very little, so don't worry about today."

"But, still . . ." Josh was already putting his boots on.

Even though the slopes were packed, they spent several hours skiing. They ran into some kids from school and spoke to them briefly. Not quite out of earshot Megan heard one of the girls say, "Guess if you can't hang onto one, you might as well go after the brother." She was too embarrassed to glance over to see if Josh had also heard the remark.

Finally they both agreed they were hungry. "Let me take you out to dinner," offered Josh.

"No," Meg put her foot down. "I feel bad enough you paying for skiing today and the hot chocolate. Mom is fixing prime rib, my favorite. You're coming home and having dinner with us."

"I am not butting in on your dinner plans."

"I know Mom, she will make plenty and she loves it when my friends stay over. Please. It's rather quiet with just the two of us." Josh looked at her but said nothing.

"Perfect timing," hollered her Mom from the kitchen when she heard the kids coming through the front door. "Josh, you will stay and have dinner with us, won't you?" invited Mrs. Becktame.

"See, I told you," whispered Meg.

"Are you sure Mrs. Becktame? I don't want to put you out any."

Her Mom came into the foyer, where Meg was taking off her boots. "You're not putting me out at all. I already have the table set for three. Come on." She motioned for them to follow her. They hurried to get out of their outerwear as they could hear Mrs. Becktame still talking.

Josh was the complete opposite of Michael. He talked, he joked, and of course complimented her mother. Meg sat quietly and watched the two of them. Particularly her mom. *You never fixed a meal for Michael. You never sat and chatted with him, never made him feel welcome. Maybe if you'd been nice to him you'd have seen the side of him I saw!*

"What a pleasant young man," her mother said as they both watched Josh drive away.

Meg looked at her and decided it was best to retire to her bedroom.

December 29, 1967: Josh came over yesterday and took me skiing. I felt real funny about him paying for everything, but he says he has the $ since he took over Michael's job at their uncle's shop. I didn't appreciate hearing someone say, "If you can't get one brother, go for the other one." I hope and pray Josh didn't hear that. He's a great guy; but I am certainly not after him. He would probably know that though, since I have never gone out of my way to be with him.

Mom and I both invited him to dinner. With Daddy gone, the two of us just kind of look at each other. Josh was actually quite entertaining.

It's too bad Michael never learned to loosen up around my parents. I can still hear him saying, "Why am I the hated one?"

Guess my mom and his dad would have gotten along great.

Meg went skiing with Josh again, although this time Mandy came with them. "He's a lot nicer than Michael, isn't he?" Mandy said after Josh came to her rescue after a spill.

"I always found Michael nice." Mandy gave a snort.

"You two certainly get along."

"He reminds me of Jonesy." She wished Mandy would drop it.

"You may look on him as a brother, but I don't think he looks on you as a sister. After all, he's got plenty."

"We are just friends, and that is all."

"He's taking very good care of you for just being friends."

"And Jonesy didn't?"

"You two grew up together, like brother and sister. He looks at you . . . like Michael should have. Although, I must admit, you don't reciprocate. We'll pick up this conversation, in say, another month, and I bet you won't be able to say that nothing is going on between the two of you then."

"Mandy!"

"Hey, I think it's great, even if he is younger than us. He's pleasant, good-looking, and it's about time you forgot about Michael."

"You never did like Michael." Meg wondered why she was suddenly on the defensive. Still, when Josh joined them after skiing down the more expert slopes, Meg found herself looking at him in a different light. *Josh as a boyfriend? Hmm.* She almost laughed out loud. A sweet kid, but he hardly compared to his big brother.

January 6, 1968: We, meaning Mandy, Josh and I, decided to hit the slopes one more time before heading back to school in two days. I think Mandy is hopeful that I will "fall" for Josh. I'm not going to. He is nothing like Michael. He's not moody, he has his own set of friends, he's a whole year younger than I am, he doesn't have the build and strength of Michael, he only has a 3 point, therefore he's not nearly as smart as Michael--but he's kind, he's gentle and he makes me laugh. He's just not Michael. I look on him as a replacement for Jonesy, who I really miss.

If things had worked out between Michael and me I would have been Josh's sister-in-law. He's not going to do anything and neither am I.

"He walked you to class?" asked Trish as they entered French II.

"He was going my way. Would you stop listening to Mandy and listen to me? There is nothing going on."

"I think he's cute." Meg rolled her eyes.

Later, when school had ended for the day, Josh happened to be coming out the back door the same time as Meg and Mandy. He walked with them for a while.

"What are you going to do when he really comes on to you?" asked Mandy while they were driving out to see the horses. They had changed their clothes in the girls' bathroom.

"He needed to get to his car. And stop filling Trish's head with stuff."

"Yeah, she mentioned he walked you to class." Megan gave a little scream and shook her head.

Friday night Megan and Mandy met up with Trish and Marcy for the basketball game. Patti was going to the show with Derek. Mandy and Marcy had dates after the game with two of the basketball players, so the two that were dateless were trying to decide what they wanted to do. At halftime Megan ran into Josh, who was with his friends. "Want to go out and get something to eat after the game?" he asked.

"Yeah, okay." *That will be fun*, she thought. She knew Trish wouldn't care if she made plans without her; although on the way back to her seat, Meg knew she didn't want to hear the comments the girls would surely have about this. With any luck, they'd keep it to themselves.

Meg assumed that Josh had meant just the two of them would go out, so she was surprised to find that they were doubling with a buddy of his named Todd and his girlfriend. She felt a bit odd crawling into the backseat of Todd's car with Josh. She hoped none of the girls saw her.

The four of them got a bite to eat and then, instead of taking Meg and Josh back to their cars at the high school, Todd started driving around. *Oh no. I know what this means. Should I say something? No, these are Josh's friends; he will handle the situation.* Sure enough, Todd's girlfriend started to nibble on his ear. *Great! Can't she wait until they're alone?* Todd quickly pulled the car over and the two of them disappeared from view.

Megan stared out the window and felt Josh press against her. *He is not serious about trying anything!* She acknowledged him and then turned away, wondering how she had gotten herself into this position.

"You know," he whispered in her ear, "sometimes I find you as cold as Michael."

"Why would you say that?"

"Because it's true. Like right now. You won't even look at me."

She knew it was a mistake the minute she turned her head. "Josh, don't!" she hissed, thinking about Mandy asking her tomorrow if anything had happened. She turned her head quickly and received a kiss on the cheek.

Josh placed a hand under her chin and gently but firmly turned her towards him. "Why?"

"Because, it's not . . . I just don't think that . . . I don't want . . ." What was she mumbling about?

"Meg, what do you think Michael's doing right now?"

She stared at him and felt her heart thumping. "What do I care?"

"Don't try fooling me. You care. You always will."

"I don't! I don't care about him at all!"

"Then why are you so worked up? I can tell you what he's doing right now. The same thing he does nearly every night since he landed in California. He never looked back—"

"Stop it!" she yelled.

"No, you stop it! You tell yourself that you don't care; but you really do! After all is said and done, no matter what Michael did to you, you would go running back to him if he walked in here right now. Maybe you should know some more facts about Michael. He's out in California having a ball, literally, and loving every minute of it."

She turned away and, although she didn't make a sound, tears ran freely down her face. *Has Michael forgotten me so soon? I thought we had something special. But, he never said he loved me, did he? I should have known then. Oh Michael, if only you were here I would do things differently. I wouldn't be such a prude. What am I saying? He was only after one thing, and now I'm doubly glad I didn't give in to him. The prick.*

"Megan, I'm sorry. I don't want to hurt you," whispered Josh. "I just want you to know all the facts. I want you to forget about him and think about me." His lips brushed against her cheek and softly his tongue licked her tears.

For the first time in months, she felt something stirring inside the empty shell she had been carrying around. Slowly she turned towards Josh and he kissed her. He held her gently. *No, don't hold me like that; hold me tight. Let me feel your strength. Don't kiss me softly; kiss me hard. Let me feel something from you—some kind of passion. For all his coldness Michael had passion.*

Meg tried to convey her feelings with action. She pressed herself against Josh and ran her fingers through his hair. "I sure wish I had you alone," he said. Suddenly she realized what she was doing. It had been all right to act this way with Michael, after they had dated for a while—but this was her first time with Josh. *He is only a friend. She mustn't confuse him with Michael.*

She sat up. "I'm sorry." He looked bewildered at her sudden mood change; but the car was starting up and they were leaving. They didn't speak after that.

Todd dropped them both off at the high school to pick up their cars.

"I'll follow behind you, to make sure you get home all right," Josh offered.

"No, I'll be fine. But, thank you." *How did he grasp this concept but Michael never did?*

"Meg—"

"Josh, please. I'm tired. We'll talk another time, okay?" *Boy, will we ever have a talk.* She got in her car and left.

January 12, 1968: Okay, what am I doing? I went with the girls tonight to the basketball game and ended up going out with Josh. I thought we were just getting something to eat, but it turned out that we doubled and we got the backseat. We ended up making out. Big mistake. I don't want him to think that there is something going on between us! I think of him as a friend. Nothing more. And what am I going to tell Mandy when she asks me what happened with little brother MacKenzie? She's been warning me. I guess I was just hoping she was wrong.

January 29, 1968: It's been a few weeks and though I still see Josh in school and am civil to him, I think I have gotten the message across that we are just friends. Being involved with one MacKenzie has been enough, thank you. I heard through the grapevine that he's dating somebody else, and I breathe a sigh of relief. I did go out with two other guys, one last weekend and one this weekend but they're nothing to write about.

It was springtime and only a half day of school due to a teachers' conference. Megan found Josh leaned up against her locker. Other than to say hi they hadn't spoken in weeks. "It's gorgeous outside. How about a motorcycle ride?"

"Today?" She tried to think of an excuse; but she was not good at lying. Besides a motorcycle ride would be fun. "Okay. I'll pack us a lunch."

She hurried home, gathered up some food, and was ready to leave when Josh arrived. They decided to go to a park. They found a nice spot at the top of a hill and spread the blanket out to eat.

"You know," Josh said between mouthfuls, "it was you who made my first day at a new school so memorable last year."

"What?"

"Yeah. As a freshman I went steady with this one girl. I was really nuts about her, but when they split up the school district and I knew I was coming here and she was going to another school, I knew I'd lose her, and I did. I was real nervous coming to a new school, even though I'd know people. I mean, the school is huge, I didn't know where any of my classes were . . . I was just lost and . . . not happy.

"So, I'm walking along in the hall when I hear this crash and I turn around and there you are. You'd dropped all your books on the floor. All I could do was stand there and stare at you. I don't think you even looked my way. Even when I picked up some of your papers and handed them to you." Meg could feel her face growing warm with her own remembrance of that day. *The first time I ever laid eyes on Michael. No, I don't remember Josh being there at all.*

"I couldn't take my eyes off you. I just wanted to get to know you." She had no idea what to say to all this, so she just sat quietly. Josh didn't seem

211

to notice her silence as he continued. "You were so good for Michael, I could never be jealous. Michael's always had such a rotten home life, ever since I can remember. I was glad he had found someone he could turn to and that it was you. At least with Michael dating you, I got to know what you were like, instead of always watching you pass by and wondering. I would never have had the guts to introduce myself to you. You know, if it hadn't been for our dad, Michael would probably still be here with you. I know how much he really cared for you. Do you think you'll ever forget him, Meg?" he asked quietly.

Without even thinking she heard herself say, "No, never."

April 11, 1968: We had a half day of school today so Josh took me for a motorcycle ride. I packed us a lunch and we went to the park. Josh told me that he saw me the very first day of school last year and that he's had a crush on me ever since. I was thinking about Michael and seeing him the very first day and my own crush on him when Josh asked me if I'd ever forget Michael and before I even thought about it I told him, "No, never." There will never be another Michael. I will never love that hard again.

April 19, 1968: I decided today that for a change I would go to the track meet and watch Josh run. He's hoping to break Michael's one record because, as he said, "Michael had such a rotten season it shouldn't be hard to do." And he's right. Where Michael excelled in football, Josh is great in track. In addition to breaking Michael's one record, Josh has also broken several other ones and three long-standing conference ones.

May 19, 1968: I've been thinking it over and over in my mind and I was going to ask Josh if he would take me to my senior prom, but before I got the chance another guy asked me and I was glad to accept. Norm's a nice guy and we had a good time. But this year it was so totally different. Last year I was too excited to sit still, this year I simply wanted to go so as not to be left out. As good a time as I had, I continued to picture what it had been like last year and shooting myself for thinking that way.

When Josh asked her to the movies, Meg found herself accepting—and actually looking forward to the date. Josh picked two horrible monster movies at the drive-in.

The first movie was more comical than scary and they laughed through most of it; but the second one made Meg nearly leap out of her seat.

"If you're not enjoying this, maybe we should go," Josh offered when she hid her face again.

"No, you go ahead and watch it. Just tell me when the bloody part is over with and I can look again." She waited for him to say something, but he continued to stare at the screen. *Surely by now the bad parts are over.* She peeked between her fingers just as someone was getting a knife slit across their throat and their head tumbled down the stairs. She buried her head in Josh's chest.

He wrapped an arm around her chuckling, "You can watch now."

"I don't want to watch," she whispered, looking up at him. He kissed her, like she knew he would, and slowly they lay across the seat. *Why don't I think his kisses have any passion in them? Is it because he is gentle? Michael was always rough and bold, as if he knew he could take whatever part of me he wanted. His every touch excited me.* Josh caressed her gently and she found herself liking it—but was it Josh that did it or was it that she just wanted somebody after being so long without anyone? Josh looked so much like Michael in the faint light that came through the window, Meg could almost imagine Michael being here with her tonight. She knew that was fatal thinking, but she couldn't stop.

"Oh, Meg," he whispered, "if you only knew how I really feel about you."

She ran her nails across the back of his shirt. "Tell me." She needed to hear words of passion from somebody.

"No, not until . . . not until I'm sure. I'm afraid you're going to hurt me, Meg."

"No, I wouldn't do that to you."

"I wish I believed you. Damn, I saw you first. You should have been mine." He continued to kiss her until they both realized the show had been over for some time.

When they pulled into her driveway, Meg ran a hand through his hair. "Sunday's my graduation. Will you come?"

"I hadn't planned on missing it."

"Will you take me to the party afterwards?"

"Wouldn't you rather have a senior take you? You'll feel funny being with a junior."

"Don't be ridiculous. If I felt that way, I wouldn't have gone out with you tonight or asked you to take me. Can I count on you?"

"You can always count on me."

June 8, 1968: Went to the drive-in with Josh. Two awful horror flicks. We made out through most of the second movie. He so reminds me of Michael.

CHAPTER 18

June 10, 1968: I have 'done gradiated'. Finally, I can put my high school career behind me. In the fall, I will be off to college and I'm actually looking forward to it. So, I am going to spend a leisurely summer going swimming every day, riding Samantha and Dudley, and helping out at the vet clinic. They are even going to pay me over the summer to help out with college tuition. Not that I need it, but I thought that was really nice of them.

Mom says she's selling both horses at the end of the summer because she's not going to take care of them. This broke my heart, but I can see her point, even though she's ridden quite a few times. Trish and Mandy will probably take turns going with me. Patti is all wrapped up in Derek and got herself a full-time job and Marcy is scared to death of the horses.

Josh took me to my graduation party and I was glad when we could politely get away. I'll never have to see those people again for as long as I live. I'll probably always keep in touch with Mandy, Trish, Patti, and Marcy—we've known each other since grade school, but that will be it.

We had a few drinks at the party and I ended up in the car with my head on Josh's shoulder. I wasn't surprised when he found a place for us to park. It did dawn on me that I could do whatever I wanted now. I would no longer be part of the gossip around here. I can see me writing that letter to Michael—you'll never guess who I gave it all to! Your brother and I'm not sorry that it wasn't you. I still smile at the thought, although we didn't go nearly that far.

Josh gave me a present. I couldn't believe it. It's a camera. It's not a real expensive one, but it's not a cheap one either. I wish he hadn't spent the money on me. I feel terrible, although I'm glad to have it. I've never owned one.

June 14, 1968: Josh came over on his motorcycle. I took the camera with me and I made him go to the drugstore so I could buy more film. I can already tell I'm going to take a lot of pictures. We went to the stables where I snapped pictures of Samantha and Dudley and then we went riding. I took pictures of Josh and the trails we went on and flowers and everything. Why have I never had a camera before?

When we were done and walking out to the cycle I asked Josh if I could drive. There is plenty of open space right at the farm, so I didn't see how I could hurt anything. He told me no. However, after kissing him a few times he agreed as long as he sat behind me. Just because half the time I couldn't remember where the brakes were I don't think that makes me as bad a driver as he says I was.

July 12, 1968: Now that summer is here, Josh and I spend nearly every evening together and quite a few afternoons. We take the horses out, go motorcycle riding, go to the movies, whatever we feel like doing. So, this is what I missed out on with Michael. We do not speak his name, he has never written or called me. I am forgotten.

Sometimes we sit and watch TV, and if Josh is in an exceptionally good mood, he'll let me drive his cycle--provided he is on the back. I have to get myself one someday, although Mom has said a flat no to this idea. I love motorcycle riding!

Jonesy is home and we have, on occasion, doubled. From what he says, I think I'm going to really like college. He, Mandy and I will only be a couple of hours away from each other. Jonesy will have a car and Mandy and I are thinking maybe we can hop a bus to visit each other, seeing as how we're not allowed cars on campus our freshman year.

I have toyed with the idea of going all the way with Josh—what do I have to lose? However, I can never quite bring myself to do it—although we have gone kind of far. I just know that in the morning, I'm always glad we didn't do it. I had to laugh the other night when I heard him mumbling, "No wonder Michael took so many cold showers."

Josh has never said he loves me; but he does say that he'll never leave me. He treats me like he loves me. He's very attentive, does just about whatever I want to do, he's not moody like his brother, and he's around so much I'm sure he's not seeing anyone else. He does not like talking about me going away in the fall. Now, that's when I see him in a bad mood.

July 14, 1968: I think Stanley (the raccoon) was hit by a car. I was out walking along the road when I just happened to look in the ditch next to me and saw a bunch of fur. I got closer and realized it was Stanley. I grabbed him up and rushed him to the vet's. Dr. Thomas was able to fix him up; but he's going to be in recovery for a while. Jonesy made me a cage and I brought Stanley home. Josh has not been happy about this. He's sure we're both going to get rabies or something. I have finally gotten Josh to feed Stanley, so he's not quite so leery.

July 21, 1968: After all the fits that Josh has thrown about "catching something," I found him playing with Stanley outside his cage! Then, he tries to tell me how smart Stanley is and how once he's well he'll have to be released back into the wild and he thinks it's going to be hard on me because I'm so attached. Who's attached? I'll still see Stanley.

August 7, 1968: Josh and I released Stanley back into the woods. I think Josh took it hard. I told him Stanley'd be back, and I was right. Whenever we are out in the woods making out, all of a sudden Josh will jump a mile high with a yell and turn around to find Stanley looking at him. He's just tapped Josh on the shoulder. I find this hilarious.

Took in my sixth roll of film to be developed.

August 10, 1968: Josh is starting to get grumpy thinking about me leaving for college. I have told him and told him that we will see each other on the weekends. He seems to think that some college boy will steal me away from him. Tonight, for the first time, we talked about Michael. He wanted to know how I really felt.

I had to really think about that. Josh has helped me this last year to get over Michael. I don't think about him as much as I used to. And my stomach no longer does flip-flops whenever I think of him. Josh is really a great guy. He's so much more stable than Michael. He's nicer to me. He's stayed with me. And tonight he told me that he loves me.

I guess I've always known that. He's certainly showed it. Josh says he's loved me almost from the beginning, from when he saw me drop my books. And then, when Michael would talk about me, he always thought "that's who I want." He asked me if I loved him.

I couldn't tell him that I did, because truly I don't know how I feel. Josh has been so good to me, but to lie to him wouldn't be right either. So I told him, "When I fell in love with Michael, all he did was take it all and he left me with nothing. I told myself I'd never do that to me again. It hurt too much to love. I know that I care for you very much, and I don't want to date anybody else and that's the best I can give you."

He said that was actually better than what he was expecting.

Michael stood at the counter. He knew he wouldn't have to wait long. "Can I help you?" A girl hurried over.

"Ah, yes. I'd like to know if a Megan Becktame is registered here for the fall."

"Just a moment, let me look."

He waited nervously, fingers drumming on the counter. *I don't care if she isn't here, I don't care. I simply want to know if I should expect to see her on campus or not. I know we never talked about it but it would be something she would surprise me with and I don't want to be surprised. Should I have asked her to come? No, don't be stupid. If she wanted to come, that was her prerogative. She was free to go to any college she wanted.*

"No, there's nobody here with that name."

"Are you sure? She's from out of state. B- e- c- k–"

"No, I'm sorry. She's not here."

"Ah, well, thank you." He nearly slammed the door behind him as he left. *I don't care. I don't care!* He clenched and unclenched his fists. *So, what Josh told me was true. She's found somebody else. She didn't even wait six months, let alone six years! Boy, she really had me fooled. You told me you loved me. Well, let me tell you, I can forget you just as easily, Megan dear. I never said I loved you. Last year I had as good a season with the girls as I had in football—and this year I plan to have a great season in both.*

Starting right now.

September 3, 1968: I am on my way to college tomorrow! Hip, hip, hurray! I am so excited! I have been accepted to Michigan State University. I'll come home on occasion to see Mom, and Josh will come up every weekend he can. Other weekends, I'll go see Jonesy or Mandy, or the three of us will meet someplace. I am going to be meeting new people, making new friends. I can't wait. But, I must admit as much as I hate to, I cried about Michael last night. I don't think about him nearly so much since I have Josh, but last night somehow he just snuck in unexpectedly. I was crying about Daddy—he so wanted to see me off to college and then suddenly I was thinking about Michael. Why did he leave me when I needed him so? Somehow, I still believe that he loves me. Isn't that crazy? I've got to remember to hate him. That's the only way to get over him.

My heart has mended somewhat. He was always so cold, I should have known he'd leave no matter what. I guess it's my own fault. He warned me not to date him. Why did he continue to ask me out? You hurt me so much, Michael MacKenzie. I guess that's why I cried so hard. It still hurts because I still love him, even though I've denied it to everybody, including myself, all these months. But, I feel better now and Josh is so good to me. I couldn't ask for anybody better. It's hard to believe the two of them come from the same family. Josh is so gentle. I don't remember ever seeing him get mad about anything.

When Daddy and Michael left me, I thought my world was at an end; but Josh has shown me life isn't all bad. I'm finally picking up the pieces and I know now I'm going to make something of myself. Michael once said I'd be the best veterinarian around and I'm going to do my best to prove him right. Animals have always been my thing, and at last I'm finally going to do something productive about it.

Mom sold Samantha and Dudley to a really nice couple. I think they'll take good care of them and they told me I could come out and ride them anytime. I'll never do it, but it was nice of them to offer.

Daddy, I hope you're watching. I'm going to make you proud.

CHAPTER 19

YOU WOULD HAVE THOUGHT THEY HAD BEEN PARTED FOR YEARS instead of five days. "Why didn't you come up to my room?" asked Megan, smothering Josh with kisses in the lobby.

"I didn't know if I was allowed up," he answered.

"Oh, you silly. We'll get your suitcase later. You can spend the entire night here." The last part she whispered as she pressed herself against him, in a way he wished she wouldn't do right there in the lobby for all the world to see.

Josh was excited at the prospect of spending the night with Megan, until he discovered that it entailed two roommates. Sleeping two on a single bed was cramped and whenever either one of them made the slightest move, the bed creaked and the other two girls giggled.

Megan complained she always woke with him pressing her face against the wall and on Saturday night he rolled right out of bed. This brought on gales of laughter from all the girls and Josh stomped out of the room.

Megan found him a few minutes later in the study room. It was the only place a person could be alone since nobody studied on the weekends.

"I'm sorry," she said.

"All I've heard since I got here is college this and college that," he roared. "This isn't exactly how I planned this weekend. I can hardly give you a goodnight kiss without somebody giggling in my ear. Don't they ever leave the room?"

"I'm sorry," she repeated. "Once I get to know them better, I'll make some kind of arrangement with them; but I can't right now. I barely know them. I thought it would be romantic to fall asleep in each others arms and wake up the same way—"

"It might be, if you weren't talkin' all the time!"

"I'm sorry."

"I heard you the first time!" She wondered if he knew how much he looked like Michael when he yelled and paced the floor while running a hand through his hair.

"Why don't you turn out the light?" she whispered.

He turned and stared at her. She parted her robe slightly and smiled at him. Not quite giving in, he said, "Next weekend, it's going to be different."

"I promise," she whispered.

He snapped out the light and made his way over to her. The couch was no more comfortable than the bed, but at least they were alone.

It was a beautiful October afternoon. Josh could not make it up for the weekend, which was just as well since Megan had a big paper to write. But, at the moment, she hated sitting in her room. She should be outside on a day like today. The halls were quiet and she wandered downstairs, where she heard the TV blaring. "What are you watching?" she asked.

"Football. Run! Run!" The guys were yelling, while the girls sat and ate. MSU's football team was playing away this weekend and Meg assumed that's who they were watching. She walked further into the room. "How's the game going?"

"USC is up by nine," one of the guys answered.

She came to an abrupt halt. *We're not playing USC. I don't pay attention to football anymore, but I would know if we were playing USC!* Her heart was racing and she wondered why. *Why do I feel this way? I haven't thought of Michael in months. Well, weeks, anyway. All right, so it was only a few days—but there had been a day or two when I didn't think about him at all. I don't care about Michael. Josh is a much better guy; he loves me. He is much nicer to me. Besides, what are the chances of me seeing Michael on TV? He wasn't that great an athlete.* And then she heard the commentator. "A beautiful run by Michael MacKenzie of USC." *Oh my, God. It can't be! It's not him! I don't care. What do I care if it's him? It's all behind me now. High school crap. I'm a college student now, for God's sake.*

"Come and watch," said one of the guys who was in a class with Meg and had flirted with her several times. He offered her his seat.

"I can only stay a minute," she mumbled as she sat down. She watched the rest of the game in silence while the announcers discussed Michael.

"A fine athlete."

"He really proved himself last year as a freshman."

"Yes, I think you're going to see a lot of MacKenzie in these next three years."

"You remember, he's replacing Gilles, who was injured a few weeks back. With the job MacKenzie's doing, I don't think Gilles will be back with us."

"I think you're right. This sophomore is doing a tremendous job."

Meg nearly went through the floor when the camera zoomed in on Michael. Fortunately, he had his helmet on, so she couldn't see much of him, and then he turned his back on the camera. *Do you know I'm watching? Do you even care?* She stared at the number across his back and her heart pounded furiously. She felt her face grow warm.

Rich, who had given up his seat to her, noticed that her boyfriend was not around. Maybe this weekend was his chance to impress her. "Would you like to go get something to eat after—" He leaned over Meg and stopped. "Are you all right?"

"I'm fine, thank you," she stood up and made a beeline for the door. She heard a couple of the girls call her name, but she kept on going up the stairs and into her room. She threw herself onto her bed and sobbed.

For once, her roommates weren't around (the one weekend Josh doesn't show!) so she cried until she was spent. *Why didn't you write to me? Or keep calling until you got a hold of me? If you cared, you would have gotten past Mom! I took your ring. Didn't that mean anything to you? Or did Jim tell you that at first I refused? What difference does it make? I took it in the end!* It was in her mom's safety-deposit box. *He has to come back for it, and how will I face him then?*

I love you so much! How could you do this to me? I thought you cared! Where did I go wrong with you?

Finally, Meg drifted off to sleep and was awakened by the phone ringing. "Hello?"

"Hi, hon."

"Oh, Josh. I'm so glad you called!" she sobbed.

"What's wrong?"

"I'm just . . . lonesome. I feel so bad."

"You're sick?"

"No, no. I, I wish you were here, that's all."

"Oh, sweetheart. So do I. I'll be up first thing Friday. Before you get finished with all your classes, how's that? But, what are you so upset about? It's not like you to be homesick."

"No, it's not that. I watched TV today," she gulped.

There was silence for a moment. "Did you see the USC game?" he asked quietly.

"Yes." He felt his heart plummet. "It was on downstairs. I walked in and there it was. Oh, Josh. I thought I was over him. I really did. But God, it hurt so bad. I—" She realized too late that Josh was the last person she should be saying this to. *But then, none of my friends here would understand. I've never told any of them about Michael. Jonesy can never be reached on a weekend and Mandy is having problems of her own.* "I mean, I am over him. It just took me by surprise to see him. And you weren't here . . . oh, Josh. Can't you come up any earlier than Friday?"

"Why? What good would I do?" he asked dryly.

"I need you. You're the only one who can make me forget."

He sighed. "It doesn't look like I've done you any good so far. I don't know what to do any more, Meg."

She suddenly realized she was on the verge of losing Josh. This time it would be her own fault. *Damn you, Michael. If I lose Josh because of you* . . . "But I've forgotten him all this time because of you. It was just such a shock seeing him today, that's all. I hadn't realized I could see him on TV. I, I feel so much better already just talking to you." She grabbed for one last straw. "My roommates are going to be gone next weekend." *Even if I have to throw them out of here.*

"I definitely don't think I should come then."

"What? Why not? We'll do whatever you want. I promise. Anything."

"No. It's bad enough I'm emotionally involved with you; but to be physically involved . . . it would kill me if you left me."

"Who am I going to leave you for?" she screamed. "Michael's never coming back!"

"But if he did, you'd leave me, right?"

"No, that's not what I meant! There isn't anybody else I want but you."

"You know what? No matter what he's done *to* you and what I've done *for* you, he still has your heart. There's just no use pretending anymore, Meg."

"No, that's not true! Josh? Josh?" She listened to the dial tone.

October 6, 1968: What have I done? I saw Michael on TV today and fell all to pieces and if that wasn't bad enough, I told Josh when he called me! He hung up on me. I can't blame him. I can't lose Josh. He's the only one that makes me forget Michael. Somehow, I have to get Josh back. I've met my share of guys here, but I'm not interested in any of them. I'll show Josh when he gets here on Friday how much he really means to me.

Josh did not visit the following weekend.

Megan discovered that on any given Sunday she could pick up the newspaper and read all about Michael from the day before. Fortunately, none of her friends were into football, so she never had to answer any questions.

She should never have told Josh how upset she was upon seeing Michael. She should have known how that would hurt him—and she never wanted to hurt Josh. She knew how it felt. Finally, after two weeks of not hearing from him, she mustered up the courage to call him, hoping and praying that this did not get him into trouble with his father. Although as near as she could tell, Josh didn't have the problems with the man that Michael had had. His mother answered, he'd gone up north with friends. Hadn't he told her?

"Oh, that's right! What am I thinking of?" Meg tried to laugh. "You will tell him I called though, won't you?" *Please, Josh don't leave me! You're all I've got. If I can't have Mich— I don't want Michael. I want you.*

She finally reached Josh. He suggested they start seeing other people and she burst into tears. "There isn't anybody I want but you!" she cried. "Don't do this to me!"

"Well, I've already got a date for this weekend, Meg." Whether he was lying or not she couldn't tell—but her heart ached at the thought. "I'm sure you don't lack for dates up there."

"I've never cheated on you."

"Well, you're not cheating now, seeing as how I said it was okay. I'll see you around, Meg."

Once again she was listening to the dial tone.

November 1, 1968: I finally got a hold of Josh. We haven't spoken in weeks. He's been away with friends doing God knows what. He wants to start seeing other people. How could he say that to me? He was as cold as Michael. What was I expecting, when they come from the same mold?

J.T. glanced at Michael nervously. He could see the bad mood setting in. He knew all the signs. He'd known Michael for over a year now. The thing was, J.T. could never figure out what triggered them. Michael would be fine one minute and madder than hell the next. It didn't matter if he'd played a good game or a bad one, or if it was during the week. Michael would suddenly be in a bad mood and there would be no getting him out of it. If Michael asked J.T. to go drinking, then he'd know for sure he was in trouble—and anybody else Michael happened to chance upon.

"J.T., let's go drinking," said Michael, almost on cue.

J.T. groaned inwardly. If he said no, Michael would go anyway. That usually meant disaster. If he went with him, he had a fifty-fifty chance of talking Michael out of doing something destructive. Even after the night was over and Michael was in bed passed out or asleep, he was by no means quiet.

"C'mon, c'mon," said Michael, getting up. "The night's a wastin'." He walked to the door and turned, waiting for J.T. to follow.

Shit, thought J.T. Michael had been a bit arrogant last year when they first met, but he had at least been decent. This year, though, he was near impossible. It had started at the beginning of the school year. One of the girls J.T. knew had told him that Michael had come into the registrar's office where she worked and had requested the name of a certain girl, a Megan Becktame. *Yeah, I could have guessed that*, thought J.T. The name was not new to him. He had learned though, that one did not ask questions of Michael. She had to be his friend with money. Michael never spoke her name when he was sober; only when he had been drinking did he open up. And even then, it was on a small scale.

J.T. remembered the first time he saw Michael. They were to be roommates, but Michael was working and since he'd been on campus all summer had pretty much taken over their room. J.T. had been impressed with the expensive luggage he found in the closet; but was dismayed at the cheap, threadbare clothes. *Who was this guy?* The college was putting on a dinner for the football players that night. He supposed Michael would have to show up for it. J.T. had changed and headed over to the affair.

He had found Michael's nametag across from him at the table, so he sat down and talked to the other guys. Finally, Michael showed up. As soon as Michael sat down, the waitress appeared and spent her time talking with him. *Okay, what about the rest of us who have been here for a while?* His clothes were nothing to brag about, but the watch was expensive. *What's the story here?*

The dinner was formal, which was no problem for J.T. He watched as several of the guys waited to see what somebody else was doing. Raised in a family that was affluent, a formal dinner was no cause to be squeamish. J.T. had looks, a stellar high school football career, his own car, daddy's checkbook—in short, he had everything Michael longed for. J.T. waited to see what Michael would do. Michael was engrossed with a couple of girls, so it took awhile before he looked down at his place setting and noticed the soup. J.T. would have placed any amount of money on Michael not knowing what to do, so he was surprised when Michael glanced down and chuckling, grabbed the correct spoon and began to eat.

And after a year of being roommates, J.T. still knew little of Michael's background. Michael would skirt all questions asked and, if pushed, he could become belligerent. But when Michael drank, he was a little more informative and the name Megan had cropped up more than once. In fact, she was mentioned a lot once he'd had enough to drink.

"Look, she dumped you. Get over it!" J.T. yelled once when he'd also had plenty to drink and was sick of hearing the name.

"She didn't dump me," he remembered Michael slurring, "and I didn't dump her. It'll be okay in the end." Unfortunately, no further information was forthcoming as Michael had suddenly seen a girl who caught his eye.

"C'mon!" said Michael. J.T. sighed. He had no desire to go drinking; however, Michael had proved to be a decent person and a good friend. He would only get in trouble if he went off by himself. Slowly J.T. stood up and made his way to the door.

CHAPTER 20

MEGAN MADE JOSH PROMISE A HUNDRED TIMES THAT HE would not renege on his promise to come up and see her. "This is a very special weekend," she kept saying. Josh could not imagine what she had up her sleeve—not that it mattered. He had already decided that this weekend would be their last together, although he hadn't yet told Megan. He wanted to see her one final time. Plus, he felt he owed it to her to tell her in person rather than over the phone.

Megan met Josh in the lobby. She was smiling as she smothered him with kisses. She would not allow him upstairs. "Later," she promised, "but not now. I want to go out."

She dragged him, rather reluctantly, to get a hamburger and then to the show. Afterwards, they went to a party at one of Meg's friends. He could not understand why Meg had made such a big deal about him coming to visit this particular weekend; she could have done all this with somebody else—or alone. He started to make a sarcastic remark to her, but changed his mind. Meg was in an extremely good mood; it wasn't fair to ruin it.

He frowned when she made him wait outside her dorm room while she "went to check on things." *Have to tuck your roommates in?* he wanted to ask. Soon enough, he heard Meg holler, "Enter."

Upon opening the door, Josh was greeted by darkness. As his eyes adjusted, he saw a Christmas tree in the corner with small lights on it. He walked into the room and realized Meg was sitting on the bed. The furniture had been rearranged. Two single beds had been pushed together and the top mattresses turned lengthwise so one did not fall through the middle.

"Well, looks like I'll get a good night's sleep for a change," he commented.

"Yes, I think you will. I hope you will." She smiled and then added, "These last couple of months we've grown too far apart."

"You know why that is," he said as he started to unbutton his shirt.

"You've been seeing somebody else, haven't you?"

"Yes, but . . . I never looked at another girl once we started dating—until, well, you know."

"Do you love her?"

He stripped down to his shorts and then crawled into bed. "Don't tell me you haven't been dating," he stated.

"I haven't gone out on you, ever."

"It's your own fault then. I told you to."

"I don't want to. Josh, I blame myself entirely for what's happened between us. I want to make it up to you. I want to give you your Christmas present now; but I have to know if you still love me."

"Christmas isn't until next week. Save it for then." *Because by then I'll be long gone.*

"It won't keep. Do you still love me?"

After several seconds, he looked up at her. "I'm here, aren't I?"

"Then, my first present to you is to tell you something long overdue. I love you." His expression did not change. He did not believe her. "I really do, Josh. And that's why I want to give you something that I've never given Michael." She stood up and slowly started to undress.

When he realized she was going to strip completely, he said harshly, "What are you doing?"

230

"For your second present, I'm going to give you me." She had always been too modest to let him see her; but now she stood completely naked before him, with the lights from the Christmas tree illuminating her.

"Do you know what you're saying? What you're doing?" he asked hoarsely.

"I don't want to lose you, Josh. I've been such a fool. Not until I realized that I might lose you, did I know how much I cared about you. I guess, maybe it's a good thing you told me off. It really, really hurt thinking that I might never see you again . . . thinking about you with another girl. I didn't know I could hurt that bad all over again. That's why I know that I love you as much as I do. I want to prove to you that I do love you and that you needn't ever doubt it. And, what better way to prove it than this?"

She started to slip into bed. "Meg, don't." She looked at him with surprise and dismay. *Who said guys always wanted it? Am I going to be turned down for the second time? It never dawned on me that Josh would say no. Did Michael tell him that I offered myself to him? Does he not believe me? What's the deal here?*

"You don't love me?" her voice warbled.

"It's not that. But you'll hate yourself and me in the morning. Isn't that what you've always told me?"

What was this, a brothers' conspiracy? No, she wasn't going to panic just yet. She pulled the covers up to her waist. "No, I won't. I've thought about it for a long time." *I have a great relationship with Josh, something I never really had with Michael. It was never going to work with Michael, it will with Josh.*

Josh backed away from her. "Megan, what, what about protection? Your roommates?"

"I've taken care of everything. We're alone, all night long."

He sat halfway up in bed and stared in front of him. "No."

That had been definite. She turned her back on him quickly, so he wouldn't see her tears. She had made an absolute fool of herself!

"Don't cry," he said softly and rubbed her back. Her skin was smooth and warm against his hand. "I don't mean to make you cry—but I've got to start looking out for myself, otherwise I'm going to get hurt badly. Hell, I already hurt. Don't you see? I'd hurt all the worse walking away in the morning if we did it. I wish I could believe you, that you love me, and that everything is going to turn out all right in the end—but I don't."

"I thought you loved me," she sobbed.

"I do. Nobody can ever take your place; but I know somebody can take mine. Michael still has your heart."

She rolled over to face him. "That's not true. I've done a lot of soul searching these last few months. The Michael I loved in high school isn't the same Michael today. I've changed in just these last four months. How much has Michael changed living in California for over a year? If he came walking in here right now, I'd still stay with you. You're what I need and want. You are the constant one in my life. I've met a lot of guys up here, but they do nothing for me. What more can I do to prove to you that I mean what I say? Whatever you want, I'll do. I love you. I should have told you that a long time ago. I was just afraid to."

His hand caressed her face. *What more did he want from her? What better proof could he ask for?* "What about when you saw him on TV?"

"I was just startled. I've seen him since—" *And I read about him in the paper every week. No, don't tell him that.* "—and I've been fine with it. It's not there anymore. It's you I want." *Why should I wait for him to come back? Didn't you tell me he was having a ball, literally? Besides, no matter what he said when he left, I just don't see Michael coming back, ever.*

Josh bent over her and brushed his lips across hers. "I love you so much, Meg. Don't hurt me. I'm scared. If you ever left me now, I'd die."

"I'll never leave you. Just love me. Make love to me." She wrapped an arm around his neck and then felt him lift the covers between them as he pressed himself to her.

December 16, 1968: I did it. I did it with Josh. It was fine, really. We were each other's first, so it was very sweet.

I just wish I didn't hear Michael in my head saying "You're going to be sorry I wasn't your first."

Before they knew it, Meg was sitting in the stands watching Josh graduate. They spent the whole summer together, and Josh even mentioned

Michael's name a couple of times—just to see her reaction. Nothing. It was as if they were talking about Jonesy.

Josh had felt guilty in the beginning. After all, Michael had dated Meg first and Josh knew how much she had meant to him. But, he had dumped her. And, Michael was swamped with girls, what would he want with Meg? Michael no longer asked about her, which only proved he didn't care, right? Surely he wouldn't begrudge his brother having some happiness.

Still, when Josh wrote to Michael or talked with him on the phone, he could never quite get it out. In the back of his mind, Josh was still not certain how Michael would take the news. Especially if he knew how far the relationship had advanced. Josh was definitely happy with Meg. They made love whenever they possibly could and Josh always swore it was just like the first time.

Summer was over and Meg was mad at Josh. He had turned down several athletic scholarships to bum around for a year.

"I don't know what I want to do," he grumbled. Meg could not understand that not everybody felt compelled to further themselves.

"What if my college had offered you a scholarship?" she asked.

He smiled. "Then I'd be in your bed every night instead of hit and miss, like I get now."

"Oh, get away from me. That's all you think about."

"I do not!"

"If I cut you off for a solid week, you'd be climbing the walls."

"So would you." Josh started to nibble on her neck, but she pushed him away.

Josh had quit his uncle's shop in August because he "needed a break." He did find a part-time job though; thinking it would get Meg off his back. He visited her on weekends—the rest of the time he did whatever pleased him.

It worried Megan that Josh had no ambition and thought nothing about their future. They had not talked of marriage, but feeling the way they did about each other, wasn't that the next step? As much as she loved him, she wondered if she could marry a bum—for Josh gave every indication of becoming one. "I'll straighten myself out sometime, don't worry," he promised. But his words did not ease her mind.

August 23, 1969: I've had a nice summer with Josh—but what is he thinking? He turned down all scholarships to college and he had some really decent ones for track. The only constant thing he wants to do is take me to bed. If he isn't going to college, then at least a trade school or something. He wants to bum around for a year. He got a part-time job that he hates, so I know that isn't going to last. I just can't imagine that he doesn't know what he wants to do with his life. But he'd better straighten up because I don't plan on supporting him—though I was planning on marrying him.

Josh made sure Megan was out of her dorm room before he crossed over to the TV set to turn it on. He rarely got to see big brother play and he had some time since Meg was in the basement doing her laundry.

As he watched Michael running up and down the field, he wondered how it was that Michael knew what he wanted out of life, while he did not. The only thing Josh wanted was Megan, and she was becoming increasingly displeased with his lifestyle and starting to become a nag. He knew he shouldn't be surprised. Megan was used to money and was surrounded by future doctors, lawyers, and accountants. In Michael she had something to be proud of. What did she have to be proud of in him? But, come on, he was only eighteen. He had his whole life ahead of him. And who was she to tell him what to do?

He turned to find Meg entering the room. He started to turn off the TV but Meg said, "No, that's all right. It doesn't bother me."

"You sure?"

"I told you, I don't love Michael anymore. He can't possibly hurt me."

She sat down on the couch next to Josh and grabbed her knitting. He wrapped an arm around her. They sat quietly, watching the game . . . until the third quarter. They both sat up straight.

Although J.T. had never heard Michael yell in pain, he knew immediately it was him. It hadn't been so much a cry of pain as surprise. J.T. pushed his way through the players standing around him. Michael saw him. "Help me up."

"Would you hold still?" said the trainer.

J.T. dropped down on one knee beside Michael. "Just let him look at your knee, and then I'll help you up."

"There's nothing wrong with my knee," Michael declared through clenched teeth. The trainer shook his head. It did not look good.

"It's gonna be all right, Michael," said J.T. "It's gonna be all right."

Megan paced the floor while Josh sat on the couch. "Do you want to call California?" She motioned towards the phone.

"Where would I call?"

She shrugged her shoulders. "I don't know. Call home, then. Maybe they have some news."

"Michael would never call home. You know better than that." The few times Michael had phoned was when their mom had written, pestering him to call and telling him when it was safe.

"Yeah, I know. Oh, I feel so bad for Michael. He always thought he was invincible."

Josh gave a short laugh. "He told you that too, huh?"

It was late in the night when Meg rolled over to find Josh still awake. It was the first time he'd spent the night with her that they had not made love.

"Michael will be all right," she whispered.

"Yeah, I know," he pulled her close to him. "It's just put me in a dull mood, I guess."

"That's all right. I understand. Josh, I know how but I have always wondered why. Why did Michael get the scars on his back? What did he do that was so bad to deserve such a beating?"

She couldn't tell if Josh was surprised or upset by her question. He didn't answer for several minutes, and when he did his voice sounded strange. "That happened a long time ago. What did he tell you?"

"He said they were belt marks and that it was a turning point in his life. But, I always wondered what he did to make your dad get so mad at him."

Josh's eyebrows rose slightly. "A turning point, huh? Yes, I suppose it was. Michael wasn't the same after that."

"What happened?"

He hesitated. "We have a big sliding-glass door in the back of the house. We're not allowed to play football back there because my parents always worried we'd throw the ball through the glass. And . . . one day, Michael did. It was an accident but our father didn't see it that way. He took his belt to Michael's back." Josh stared off into the distance. "Beat him 'til he passed out, and kept right on going. I can still hear my mom screaming. My older brothers . . . finally stepped in."

"I don't need to know any more," she said quickly. It sickened her to think that anyone could do that to their child. To anyone. She couldn't recall her dad even spanking her. *How old would Michael have been at the time?* She remembered Jim telling her that Michael had been out of school for a while and when he came back he was different and remote. *Was that when Michael decided he was going to leave and never come back?*

September 10, 1969: Josh and I were watching Michael play football on TV when he got hurt. I think it must be serious as he was never put back in the game and whenever they showed the guys on the bench we didn't see Michael sitting there. The commentators couldn't tell us anything either. I'm worried, although I'm pretty sure I did not convey that to Josh. I tried to keep myself as neutral as I could. I just wanted to pick up the phone and call somebody at USC. Get a list of surrounding hospitals and start calling them. I am half tempted to do it still.

Josh filled me in on why Michael's back is so scarred. His father beat him over a broken window. I just cannot fathom that. And I know it never got any better for him. I think I understand now why Michael was so desperate, so set on leaving. That's why he always told me there is no us. Michael knew before he met me that he wasn't staying. He was determined to leave.

Is he also determined that he's coming back for me? He said he wouldn't write or call. He certainly let me know that he would be dating and for me to do the same. How many times did I think Michael had dumped me only to have him come back to me? I'm not happy with Josh just sitting around.

What would I really do if Michael came back today?

J.T. made his way quietly into the hospital room and sat down. Michael was still heavily sedated, so he decided to write him a note. Who knew when Michael would wake up? J.T. was not going to wait around to find out.

He found a napkin to write on. "Calmed your mother down, but she wants you to call home immediately. Your father? Stepfather? is also concerned and wants to know if he should fly out."

J.T. was confused. While talking to Michael's mom, he had heard a commotion and then a male voice had suddenly come on the phone demanding all sorts of answers. Who are you? J.T. had wanted to ask, since he had gotten the impression that Michael's father was dead. But that had seemed impolite, so he'd just answered the man.

J.T. signed the note and left it on the nightstand. He started out the door when he heard Michael mumble. Maybe he was coming around. "Michael?" he leaned over the bed.

"Meg?"

Oh shit, not her again! She had some kind of hold over him. J.T. sat down hard on the chair.

"Meg?" Michael began to stir.

Hmm, how much information could I get out of Michael, drugged up as he is? This might be my golden opportunity. J.T. stood over him. "All right, Michael. What about Meg? Tell me about her."

Michael's eyes opened briefly and locked on his. J.T. was positive that in that moment Michael was coherent. "Find her and bring her here."

J.T. knew Michael came from a large family; but the only one he had ever heard him talk about was his brother Josh. Well, it was a place to start. When J.T. phoned the MacKenzie's he reassured Mrs. MacKenzie that Michael was doing beautifully. He had come through the surgery just fine and would call her in a day or two when he wasn't so groggy. Could he possibly speak to Josh?

Josh knew who J.T. was. Not only was he a well-known football player in his own right but Michael had mentioned him several times. Josh could not imagine what J.T. wanted him for, except to deliver bad news to his folks. Josh had not slept all night. In fact, he had gotten up and left while Meg was still sleeping. Somehow sleeping with her while Michael lay hurt preyed on his mind. Now, he was glad to be home since he was needed. He was suddenly seized with panic. Michael wasn't dying, was he?

He grabbed the phone from his mother, "This is Josh."

"Yeah, hi. I'm a friend of Michael's and he asked me to do a favor for him but I don't quite know where to begin. I was wondering if you could help me?"

"Sure, what?"

"Do you know where I might find a girl named Meg?" There was dead silence. "Hello? Are you there?"

"Wh— what, what does Michael wa— want with her?"

"He keeps calling for her. He asked me to find her and bring her here. From what little information I have on her, I figure she must be from home. Do you know her?"

"Ah, I— I went to hi— high school with a Me— Meg," he stuttered.

"Do you know where I can find her?"

"She went— she left ah, for college, I think. She doesn't live around he— here anymore."

"Do you know what college?"

"Ah, well . . . I . . . no . . . some big university somewhere . . . out there. She doesn't live around here anymore."

J.T. frowned. After all the stories Michael had told him about his brother Josh, he had never let on that Josh was a halfwit. *Now where am I supposed to look?* "Is there anybody around there that would know? Her friends? Family? Anybody?"

"I don't know any of them. I don't . . . I know you mean well; but, but it's not a good idea to look for her," said Josh, making up his mind and taking a deep breath.

"Why not?"

"Ah, well, didn't you tell my mom that Michael was heavily sedated? I think once he comes around he won't make the same request." *Please God, don't let him.* "And I don't, I don't honestly think he wants her found; that's just his, what is it, subconscious talking. Ya know what I mean? The way things ended between them . . . he doesn't really want to see her again. I know."

"Maybe you're right," J.T. sighed. Michael never mentioned Meg unless he was drunk, and even then he would say the strangest things about her. And yet, when he looked at J.T. in the hospital room it had struck him that Michael knew exactly what he was saying. "I'll wait until he's fully awake and then ask him if he wants me to find her."

"No! No!" yelled Josh. "I mean, you don't want to do that because, well, the truth of the matter is that she doesn't want to see him ever again. She no longer feels the same way about him as she once did."

"You're sure?"

"Yeah. I've had a long talk with her about him . . . just recently, in fact. Don't let Michael get in touch with Meg and make a fool of himself. He's got enough to deal with, with his knee. I don't want her chewing him out and telling him off."

J.T.'s frown increased. Josh didn't know what college Meg went to, knew none of her friends--and yet had recently had a long talk with her about her feelings for his brother? Josh had also lost his stutter and was adamant that J.T. not bring her name up. "Okay, thank you."

J.T. hung up the phone. This girl was starting to mystify him. Well, at least he knew one thing for certain; there *had* been a Meg in Michael's life, something he had always vehemently denied when sober. J.T. thought about this for a moment. Maybe Josh was right. Maybe he should wait to see if Michael brought up Meg's name again. Yeah, Michael would probably be embarrassed if J.T. confronted him. He'd only deny it, like he did all the other times. He'd wait and see if Michael mentioned Meg when he had a clear head. He probably wouldn't even remember asking for her. It must have been the drugs talking.

Josh hung up the phone. He was shaking. *It wasn't possible. Michael couldn't still be thinking of Meg after all this time. He hadn't asked about her in months. Months! Maybe he meant somebody else with the same name? You're not going to buy that one are you? I should have told J.T. the truth. I should have let J.T. call Meg and let him hear for himself that she wants nothing to do with Michael. Or better yet, have Michael call her and have Meg tell him off herself. She'd enjoy that. But would she, once she knew that she was in Michael's thoughts? Our relationship is not as strong as it once was. Would it survive this? Maybe Meg would have second thoughts if she knew Michael wanted to see her. This would be the best test, wouldn't it? I'd know once and for all where her loyalty lay. Maybe I should get a job. A fulltime job that Meg would be happy with--but doing what? Where am I going to get a decent job with just a high school degree? Let's not panic, MacKenzie. Once Michael comes around, he will remember what I told him about Meg being so wrapped up in her new boyfriend that she is inseparable from him. Michael will never lower himself to call her. No, it's all right. Meg won't find out. I promised her after a year's time I'd look for a fulltime job. Well, my year isn't up yet and I'm having a good time doing nothing. Things will work out.*

J.T. walked in the hospital room and ducked when he saw the glass in Michael's raised hand. "Is my old man with you?" he bellowed.

240

"No!" Michael put the glass down.

J.T. straightened up and looked at him. "How many times have I told you you've got to stop throwing things?"

"You haven't seen me throw anything yet—like I'll throw that bastard if he walks through that door."

"So . . . that *was* your dad I talked to?"

"No. A dad is someone who plays ball with you, somebody you can talk to, somebody who's there for you. You, for instance, have a dad. I have a father. An authoritative figure. Somebody who only donated his genes. And I never want to see him again."

"He sounded genuinely concerned," countered J.T.

Michael laughed. "I'll tell you what he was concerned about. He's worried I might play again. I can promise you, he spent all Saturday night drinking to celebrate my injury."

"Michael . . ." he hated when Michael got in these moods.

"So, where is he? Waiting for me to send him money to fly him out here? Cuz he sure as hell can't afford a plane ticket himself." That was one of the beauties of his plan—his father could not get out here.

Okay, best not to say that his father thought USC should pay for it. "I . . . I talked him out of it. I told him you were getting great care and that there wasn't anything he could possibly do that wasn't already being done for you. Are you done yelling yet?" J.T. asked.

Michael smiled and cracked open the newspaper in front of him. "Did you read this?"

"Yeah, and you shouldn't." He tried taking the paper away from him, but Michael was too quick.

"MacKenzie Out For Season." He read the sports headlines out loud. "And, it says in here I'm probably never going to play again. What the hell do they know? What else would I do? Sit behind a desk at one of your father's plants?" Michael rolled this thought over for a minute. "How much do you think he'd give me to start?"

J.T. shook his head. "I don't know why my dad likes you so much. He's spoiled you just like the rest of us kids."

"He knows I'm great."

J.T. smiled. He supposed he shouldn't have been surprised when his dad first met Michael. All the kids in the family knew they could go to Daddy to fix any problem and never have to work. But Michael had asked—no demanded—a job immediately, since J.T. said he could get him one. He would not loaf around all summer like the rest of the kids. Michael had ambition, which was something J.T. and his brothers and sisters lacked and what his father admired. Now J.T. realized Michael needed a dad just as bad as his dad needed an ambitious son.

"Where did you get those flowers?" J.T. asked, pointing to the huge bouquet that took up an entire corner. Not that they were the only flowers. Indeed, the place was filling up as an aide came through the door with more. But, it was the largest.

Michael laughed. "Didn't you know I had a sweetheart?"

J.T. walked over and read the card. "Can I help it if my sister has a crush on you?" J.T.'s sister was ten years old.

"Listen J.T., you've got to stop your mom. She insists on bringing some specialist from New York City to look at my knee. I told her I already had a specialist looking at it; but she wasn't impressed."

"Mom's from New York. She thinks doctors on the West Coast don't know what they're doing."

"I told her I didn't think USC would want anyone else looking at it, so she's going to call the coach. You've got to stop her. I don't need anybody else looking at my knee."

J.T. shrugged his shoulders. "You're part of the family now. Nothing I can do about it."

J.T. had several more minutes alone with Michael before the well-wishers started to arrive. Not once did the name Meg pop up in conversation.

Meg sat at her desk, with pen in hand and paper in front of her. She was going to write Michael. She had to. She needed to tell him—what? That she understood once again why he felt he had to leave and get as far away from his father as possible? Meg didn't agree that he had to go to California, but now she was remembering their last day together. She hadn't thought about his back since that day—the day her dad died. It was while she was drifting off to sleep with Josh beside her that it had popped into her head. He said he would probably date other girls from time to time. Six years was a long time, but he'd be back. *No, I mustn't think that way. He isn't coming back.* And even if he did come back, it made no difference. She loved Josh. *Would it hurt to send a get-well card, though? To let him know that I am no longer angry with him?*

Meg read the newspaper article again. He had had extensive knee surgery. He would not be playing the rest of the season and it was extremely doubtful whether he would ever play again. Michael had been rated among the top college football players and USC felt his loss. *Oh Michael, baby, I'm so sorry. Maybe I should write to say that I don't care if he never makes it to the pros. No! No!*

She crumpled up the paper. *Are you never going to learn, Becktame? He has to know you're at Michigan State University, it's the only vet school in the state. He could have called Jonesy, or Jim for that matter. He could have tracked you down here; but no, he's never called or written. So what if he said he never would—if he really cared, he would have. He should have stayed and seen you through your dad's funeral. Michael doesn't care if you care whether he gets to the pros or not. He doesn't care about you anymore. When are you going to get that through your thick head? And remember, you're in love with Josh.*

October 12, 1969: I thought about writing Michael today or just sending him a get-well card—but what would be the point? I'm sure he doesn't care, and with all the mail that he's receiving, he'll never see mine even if I did send it.

I know I love Josh; but I wish to hell I could get Michael completely out of my system.

CHAPTER 21

WHEN J.T. ARRIVED TO TAKE MICHAEL HOME, HE DISCOVERED two other people had beaten him there. As he opened the door, he could hear his mother say, "Now, I'm not going to hear any arguments from you. You're coming home with us. Marc said you could have his room while he's away at Purdue, or you can have one of the guest bedrooms next to the gym, so you can work out when you're feeling up to it."

"Mrs. Keller, I appreciate the offer—"

"And, I'm going to have my specialist from New York look at you."

J.T. walked in to find Michael fully dressed and propped up on the bed with his ten-year-old sister Cecelia lying in the crook of his arm.

"Here's J.T., come to take me home to the frat house," Michael cried in relief.

"The fraternity house? All those boys will do is fill you with pretzels and beer. Dorothea will fix you three square meals a day."

"We have cooks at the frat house. Besides, I've gotten pretty far on pretzels and beer."

Mrs. Keller looked at him sternly. "Do you want me to go back and tell Dorothea that her food is only as good as a fraternity house cook?"

"Dorothea is a wonderful cook." Michael shot J.T. a look of desperation. "But I've already got everything lined up at school with the doctors, the trainers—I've got schoolwork to do—"

"You will get all that and much more at home. Michael, your parents aren't here to take care of you, but we are. Now, what kind of mother would I be not to haul you home and take care of you? You've got the swimming pool and a golf course down the street when you're feeling able. What more do you want?"

"And, I'm going to take care of you, too," announced Cecelia, for which Michael gave her a hug.

"Mom," said J.T. after watching Michael squirm for a while, "USC has a lot of money invested in Michael—three years worth. You can't just pull him out of here."

"And your father has poured a lot of money *into* USC," she shot back. "He'll get much better care at home—and that's where he's going."

"I'm expected back," said Michael. "I've got doctors' appointments already made for next week. J.T. might sell my room while I'm gone."

"Mom, it would really be better if Michael went home with me. I know you have good intentions, and Michael would get great care, but—"

"Besides, we'll be home soon . . . for Christmas." J.T. shot Michael a look.

"You boys tell me that every year, and every year you call from Aspen saying you're skiing and all I hear is a lot of giggling in the background. Frankly, I don't think either one of you knows how to ski."

"Of course we do," said J.T. "How else could we impress the snow bunnies?"

"I promise, we'll come home for Christmas," said Michael as J.T. glared at him.

Mrs. Keller looked at her son. "And you?"

Slowly he agreed. "I promise. We'll come this year."

She sighed. "Very well. If you feel more comfortable at a dirty frat house . . ."

Michael leaned over and kissed her affectionately. "We'll be home before you know it."

"He'll see that specialist at Christmastime," Mrs. Keller warned J.T. as she and Cecelia walked out.

As soon as the door closed, J.T. whirled on Michael. "Why did you give up our trip to Aspen?" he yelled.

"I can't go skiing with my knee like this. How am I going to impress any girl?"

J.T. smacked a hand to his forehead. "You idiot! With your name, you don't have to ski!"

Megan was home for the holidays and Josh soon began to resent the time she spent with Mandy and Jonesy. "But darling, I can see you anytime." He muttered a reply. "What's the matter with you lately?" she asked. "You used to be so sweet and kind and understanding."

"Maybe I've changed."

"Maybe I don't like it."

"Maybe I don't care," he retorted. He immediately regretted saying it.

Some of Meg's friends from college lived nearby and invited Josh and her to a Christmas party. Meg asked Josh if he'd mind going. *Why should I mind? They have better liquor than what my friends can afford.*

When they left the party they drove in silence, until Josh said, "Looks like you had a good time with Lance tonight."

She smiled. "He's a good friend."

"How well do you know him?"

"I met him last year."

"I asked how *well*, not how long."

"He's asked me out a few times, but I've never gone."

"Been to bed with him?"

"Certainly not!" Meg was outraged by the suggestion.

"Why not? I would think his type would be right up your alley."

"You don't care if I date?" she asked.

"Suit yourself. It's a free country."

"I don't understand you anymore. Ever since Michael got hurt you haven't had a decent thing to say to me; although you're still very willing to crawl into my bed. It's almost as if you blame me for his accident."

"I've changed, that's all," he said.

"It doesn't mean you have to change for the worse."

"You don't like me, leave me." Josh glanced over and suddenly realized the idea was not new to her.

Meg said nothing more until he stopped the car in her driveway. "I have something I need to give you. I'd like you to come in and get it, and then you can leave."

"You don't need to bother with a Christmas present."

"I'm not going to. I've had it for a while. I got it out of my mom's safety-deposit box. You need to take it home with you."

"Okay," he got out. He could not imagine what she had that she would want to give him; especially something from a safety-deposit box.

She went upstairs and came down a few minutes later. "Here." Meg handed Josh a ring box, which he slowly opened. She watched his mouth drop.

"Where did you get this?" he accused.

"Michael gave it to me. He said it belonged to your older brother."

"You're damn right it does—Dave. Why do you have it? It's never to go outside the family."

"I know. Michael gave it to me as a guarantee he'd come back to get me someday."

"Wh . . . what?" He stared at her in disbelief.

"Before Michael left, he said he'd come back for me in five or six years. I didn't believe him, so he gave me this ring, as security, so to speak. Now I'm returning the ring to you. I haven't heard from him in three years. It needs to be back in your family."

She was surprised at the look on his face. "You knew all this time . . . you knew all along that Michael was coming back for you . . . and you never ever said anything to me?"

"I thought Michael would have told you. You two were so close."

"No. No, he never did—and neither did you. Knowing how I felt about you, how could you be this cruel to me? You and Michael will make a fine pair."

"Michael's not coming back for me—we both know it. In the past, Michael always came to me when things went wrong for him. I really thought he'd get in touch with me after he hurt his knee; but he hasn't. He's not coming back and I've accepted that. I need to get on with my life."

"You bitch!" he yelled. "You really had me going. Luring me to your bed and everything!"

"Lower your voice," she hissed, and caste her eyes to the room above them where her mother slept. "I loved you, Josh. I really did. But I don't know you anymore and I don't know how I feel about you either."

His open hand came fast and unexpected, knocking her to the floor. Meg cried out. Not even Michael with his temper had ever hit her.

"You little bitch! You made me love you, when you felt nothing for me. You used me until Michael came back."

"You know that's not true. You and I had something special once. You've had too much to drink. Get out of my house."

He turned to leave; but then swung around to face Meg. "If Michael's coming back for Dave's ring, you'd better have it." He threw the box as hard as he could. She gave a sharp cry as it hit her squarely in the chest.

At the door he turned around again so that he would have the pleasure of watching her cry. He wanted that to be his last memory of her. Josh was surprised to see her standing, dry eyed—although the look on Meg's face was one he would never forget. An intense dislike was the nicest way to describe it.

December 16, 1969: I'm through with Josh. He has changed so much I don't even recognize him. He is not the guy I fell in love with. I tried to return the pact ring to him. I know Michael is not coming back. He always turned to me in times of trouble. With his knee the way it is, I was sure he would call. And I've quizzed Mom extensively. She swears he has not called--and she had quite a fit that I was still thinking of him.

Anyway, Josh threw his own fit. Not only did he call me several names, he hit me. Not even Michael has ever done that. He threw the ring back at me, too. I have a nice little black and blue mark where it landed. So, back to the safety-deposit box on Monday.

The last day of college for the semester and the whole town had turned out to get drunk. J.T. lost Michael somewhere along the way. Finally, in the early morning, he found him lying on his bed, still dressed.

"What'd ya leave for? I had a beautiful blonde lined up for ya," slurred J.T.

"You know I don't date blondes."

"Yeah, I know, just redheads. Over half the girls on campus have dyed their hair red. Why only redheads?"

"Beats me."

"Look, Michael, you've got to snap out of this depression. I know what you're thinkin'."

"But you don't know how I feel! All those years I played football and nothing ever happened to me. Now that we're going to the Rose Bowl, look who's going to be sitting on the sidelines."

"Maybe we'll win again next year—"

"I'm not waiting for next year. I'm going to play this January first."

"Michael, they've talked about you being a Heisman Trophy candidate. Don't throw everything away on one game; it's not worth it. I know you'll be with us in the fall if you don't do something stupid now. The doctors told you—"

"I don't give a damn what they said. I'm not going to sit and watch. I'm going to work out every day, swear off booze, swear off girls—"

"Ah, I think it's a little too late to swear off girls."

"What's that supposed to mean?"

"You shouldn't have left the party so soon. There was someone looking for you. When she found out you weren't there, she decided to announce it to all of us. Looks like I get to tell you the big news—you're gonna be a daddy."

As promised, they were home for Christmas. Michael sulked all the way there; not because he minded going—this was home for him—but because he knew without a doubt he would not be playing in the Rose Bowl. He also sensed they were ready to scratch him for next fall. Nothing had been said to him yet; but he could feel it coming.

Michael hid his disappointment well and put on a good front for the Kellers, who were delighted that the boys had kept their word this time.

On Christmas Eve J.T. walked into the den dressed for a party, only to see Michael slam down the phone. "I'll leave," he offered.

"No, that's all right. I . . . nobody was home."

"Why aren't you ready for the party? We're going to leave in a few minutes."

"I'm not going."

"What are you talking about? Of course you're going. Look—"

"J.T. I'm just not up for it."

"You? Not up for a party? You've got to be kidding me." Michael didn't answer. "Okay. You'll be sorry when I come home in the wee hours and tell you all about it." He turned to leave.

"I need a second operation."

J.T. stopped. This was the first Michael had indicated that all was not well with his knee. "When?"

"Soon. Ya know, the odds are slipping away from me."

J.T.'s mouth was dry. "It was the basketball game, wasn't it?"

Michael gave him a rueful smile. "It's all your fault, J.T. You told me not to play and you should know better than to tell me not to do something."

J.T. felt his blood boil. "You're old enough to know better! You're not a little kid. You knew you shouldn't be out play—"

Michael laughed sadly. "I know. You told me, the doctor told me, the coach, the trainer . . . I thought I knew my own knee better than anybody else. I just wanted to prove to all of you that I could play in the Rose Bowl—and now my chances of ever playing football again have just been sliced. The joke's on me, and now all of you can say 'I told you so'. That last time that I came down on my knee, when I went for the basket . . . the staple partially tore away."

J.T. had no idea what to say. Michael's whole life was football; this would destroy him. The thing was, Michael was smarter than that. There were a lot of other opportunities out there waiting for him—but he never looked their way. If only J.T. could make Michael see that football wasn't everything. Why did Michael insist on making football his career when he had the brains to go into any field he wanted? "Do you want to see Mom's specialist now?"

"No. And I don't want you telling the family until after the operation."

"It'll be in the papers before then."

He thought this over. "Yeah, I guess you're right. Well, I'll tell your parents the day after Christmas."

"Why don't you come to the party? Maybe you'll meet somebody there who'll make you forget your problems for awhile, huh?" smiled J.T. "Surely there's got to be one redhead in the crowd."

"No thanks. For once I'd like a quiet Christmas. Besides, I already promised Cec I'd read her a Christmas story and tuck her into bed tonight."

J.T. sighed. "This is the first time I've ever seen you miss your family."

Michael's face grew hard. "I don't miss my family. I just miss never having had a family."

Megan slammed the phone down and turned to Mandy and Jonesy. "Real nice, on Christmas Eve, too. That's the third time he's hung up on me in the last hour. Let's get going. I don't want to be here the next time he calls."

"How do you know it's a he?" asked Jonesy defensively.

"It's got to be Josh. Who else would call and then lose his nerve?"

On January first Megan watched MICHIGAN versus USC; but she had to turn it off when they showed Michael sitting on the sidelines. Her heart went out to him. She had never seen a defeated look on his face before. She knew he was going in for another operation soon. *Oh Michael, I'm sorry your dreams fell through. I really am.* She thought back to when he had first injured his knee and the letter she had been going to write. She thought about doing it now, now that Josh wasn't around. Would it hurt? She would send one simply as a friend, nothing more. But, the same pride that had stopped her before stopped her now. *You never wrote, you gave up calling me, you deserted me, deserted me when I needed you most. I just feel sorry for you, that's all. I don't love you anymore, Michael. I don't.*

January 1, 1970: I watched the MICHIGAN/USC football game today. It was awful watching Michael sitting on the sidelines. I just feel sorry for him, nothing more. I wonder if he ever thinks about me. Probably not, because if he did he'd have called me a long time ago.

Vacation was over and Megan had returned to MSU. Josh was standing outside her door. He had gotten this far, you would think he could get up the nerve to knock. Finally, he held his breath and raised his hand to the door. He couldn't have been more surprised when Lance answered his knock.

"Come on in," Lance gestured. "Meg, someone to see you."

Megan stood up as Josh came in. "Hi," he said. She stared at him. "I just came because . . . I wanted to talk to you."

"Hey, I've got to be leaving anyway," said Lance, grabbing some books off the desk.

"No, don't go." Josh noticed the way Megan touched Lance's arm. Lance shot a glance at Josh and then at Meg.

"What I have to say will only take a few minutes. I'd like to talk with you privately if I could. Please, Meg."

Meg looked at Lance who was drumming his fingers on his books. "Okay. I know you don't want to be late."

She walked Lance to the door and Josh heard him say, "I'll call you after class, okay?" There was a slight pause and Josh could imagine them kissing. Soon Megan was back in the room. With her arms folded across her chest, she leaned against the wall.

"What do you want?" He had never seen her so cold.

"To begin with, I wanted to apologize. I never meant any of the hateful things I said to you, and I sure as hell never dreamed I'd hit you."

"People change," she said simply.

"Meg, please." Josh came towards her and she stepped away. He stopped. "I'm not going to hurt you. Everybody has been on me so much about doing something with my life. I just got fed up with it and I guess I took it out on you. I knew how much you wanted me to do something with my life—and coming here all the time . . . seeing you and your friends, all knowing what they wanted to do . . . I guess I wanted to hurt you because it hurt me. I was really stunned when you told me that Michael planned on coming back for you. Until he hurt his knee, he was really having a fantastic time out there. Anyway, I thought you'd like to know that I've finally done something about my bumming around, as you call it."

"Well, don't keep me in suspense," she said sarcastically.

"I've joined the Army."

He saw her face register shock. "What? My God, Josh. There's a war going on!"

He shrugged his shoulders. "I know. My brother managed to come back in one piece. We'll see how my luck holds."

Slowly she sank in a chair. He kneeled down next to her, but was too afraid to touch her. "That's why I came here, Meg. I have a month before I leave. As much as you've hurt me, I want to spend that month with you, if you'll let me. There is nobody else I want to be with."

"You could be killed," she whispered.

"It'll be just four weekends," he continued. "Please, Meg. I love you. Even when I was at my worst, I never stopped loving you. Even when you told me about Michael." He waited for what seemed an eternity.

"I don't know what to tell you, Josh."

He felt his heart sink. "Lance?"

She shook her head. "It has nothing to do with him. I just keep thinking about the way you've been these last few months. I don't care to do that to myself again, not even for four weekends."

"But, don't you see? Things will be different now. I've got a purpose in life. I'll be the Josh you used to know."

"Of all things—how could you join the Army?"

"Please, don't start on that line, Meg. I've gotten enough of that at home. Just try to understand. The draft would have gotten me sooner or later. I've got no ambition in life. I don't care to improve myself. Maybe Army life will straighten me out."

Megan put a hand to her mouth and started to laugh and cry at the same time. "What?" he asked.

"I've played the game of love twice—and lost twice." She sniffed. "Three strikes and I'm out."

"Don't talk like that."

She put her head down on the desk and cried. "Meg, please don't cry. I— I thought you'd be happy I was finally doing something."

"You could have done something else!" she screamed.

He wrapped his arms around her, burying his face in her hair. She wrapped her arms around his waist and clung to him.

Later, when Lance got out of class and phoned Meg, nobody answered.

January 10, 1970: Josh came to my apartment to apologize and to tell me he's joined the ARMY! What the hell was he thinking? What if he gets sent to Vietnam? What if something happens to him? I don't think I could live with myself as I feel responsible for him doing such a rash act. I don't know how I feel about Josh. He's changed so much in the last few months—ever since Michael got hurt. It's like he blames me for Michael's knee and I swear I have not been in touch with Michael since he left me at the vet clinic the day Daddy died. The Josh I loved was sweet and kind and caring. I don't know this Josh, although he says he'll be the same old Josh if I just see him for the next four weekends—that's all the time he's got left. I'll see him; but I don't know how I feel.

I do know this though: if something should happen to Josh I can never go back to Michael. I would really feel like I betrayed Josh's trust. So, whether I like it or not . . . I'll never have either one of them. I just don't feel Josh will make it home alive. He doesn't have that basic instinct or desire or drive or whatever.

Something tells me that when I see him that last weekend, I'll never see him again.

CHAPTER 22

THE NEXT FOUR WEEKENDS WERE GOOD—IT WAS ALMOST LIKE
old times. Josh was as sweet and kind as he could be. He took
Megan to dinner, to the movies—anywhere she wanted to go. He
denied her nothing.

Neither one talked about the upcoming separation. *Why must you
leave like this?* Meg wanted to scream at him. *How can you do this to me?*
But it wasn't a decision that Josh could change his mind about.

On their last weekend, Josh announced they were getting a hotel
room. For two nights and three days they stayed in the room; calling room
service whenever they wanted something. On Sunday morning she heard
Josh in the bathroom. There was a loud crash. "Shit."

"What'd you do?" she hollered.

"Oh, I accidentally knocked over your cosmetic bag. I'm sorry."

"That's okay. I don't think I had anything breakable in it."

She could hear him picking things up off the floor. "Meg? Where are
your pills?"

He came out to the room where she was still in bed. "Ah . . . they're
in my purse."

"Don't lie to me. Where are they?"

She shrugged her shoulders. "Don't worry about it."

"What's that supposed to mean? Where are they?"

"Well, I ran out about the same time we broke up. There wasn't anybody else I wanted to go to bed with, so I saw no sense in renewing my prescription."

His look went from puzzlement, to disbelief, to shock. "Then, for this whole month that we've been together, you haven't been on the pill?"

"That's right."

"What have you been using?" He felt his panic start to rise.

"Nothing."

"Nothing? You've got to be kidding me! Are you out of your mind? Why didn't you say anything? My God! We could have stopped at the drugstore and gotten something! Oh, my God!"

"I wish you'd relax," she said.

"Relax? Do you know what this means? Meg, what if you're pregnant? Why didn't you say something to me?"

"Because . . . I didn't want to."

"She didn't want to!" he yelled to the heavens. He ran into the bathroom and came back with a cold towel pressed against his forehead. "I can't believe you didn't consult me on something like this. Oh, my God. I love you—but I don't want to be a teenage father. Oh, my God."

"You'd be twenty by the time the baby was born—and besides, we don't know that I'm pregnant."

"No? We've just had a marathon weekend of sex. I can't believe you'd do this to me. She never even consulted me!" he yelled looking skyward. "What time of the month is this for you? Good time to get pregnant or bad?" He peeked out from underneath the towel. "No, don't answer. I don't want to hear. Oh, my God!" *What difference would it make? We've been going strong at it the last month.*

Meg flounced out of bed. "I thought perhaps you'd carry on like this; but I didn't know you'd be this bad."

"Why did you do it?" he persisted.

"Because you're going away. I'm scared. What if . . . what if the unthinkable happens to you? I want your baby."

He stared at her. "You had no right to do this to me, Megan. I'm not ready to get married. How am I supposed to be a father? And how am I supposed to leave now? As if I've got a choice. I don't even have enough time to pick up a marriage license. I don't like the thought of you trapping me. I thought you were above that."

Her face went white. "I have no intentions of trapping you. The last thing I want is someone marrying me because they feel they have to. I never intended for you to know—and believe me, you'll never know if I have your baby or not." She ran into the bathroom and locked the door behind her.

He banged on the door. "Megan, you've done one foolish thing, don't do another. I don't want any child of mine running around being called a bastard. That child, if you are pregnant, was conceived in love. Now, open the door!"

She came out sobbing and flung herself at him. "Don't yell at me!"

He hugged her tightly; though he wanted to shake her. *Why? How could you do this to me, Meg? What am I supposed to do now?*

He felt himself coming back from a great distance. It felt as if he were being dragged down a long tunnel and his hand slipped from Meg's. "Meg! Megan!" he shouted.

"Let's wake up, Mr. MacKenzie. Your operation is all over." A nurse poked a finger in him.

"Meg," he said more quietly, more painfully. That look on her face; it said she didn't care. *How can you not care?* he wanted to scream at her. *You made me care—and now you don't? It's not fair. It's not right. You could have sent me a get-well card at least—for old time's sake—to let me know you were still thinking of me, keeping track of me. Would that have killed you? All I need is a sign from you that you still have feelings for me, instead of for your new boyfriend. I'd call, I'd write. You know I would if you weren't seeing somebody steady. I want you here with me, now! You could make the pain go away so easily. I trusted you. You told me you loved me. I gave you my word that I'd come back for you. Why did you find somebody else?*

Damn you! You'll never hear from me again—and it's your own fault. I meant for you to date a lot of different guys, not just one. If you'd dated around, I would have understood. That's what I'm doing. These girls mean nothing to me. They're just a fill-in until I'm back with you. How could you cling to just one guy when that one guy is supposed to be me? I believed you, like a fool. I trusted you. I loved you. I know I could never say it—but I felt it! You understood me. You understood that I loved you—whether I said it or not.

But no, you didn't wait, did you? Don't worry about me—you should see the girls I'm dating now. You don't even compare, Meg.

"Let's wake up, Mr. MacKenzie. You're having a bad dream. Wake up." Michael felt more pokes.

Damn you, Meg! I told you to stay away from me. Why don't you ever listen? What made you think I would even look twice at you? I never cared for you—do you hear me? Never!

"Mr. MacKenzie, do you hear me? It's time for you to come around. Don't move your knee. Do you hear me? Orderly! Don't move your knee!"

I've forgotten you. Do you hear? Not that I ever gave you a second thought. I just don't want you to get any ideas about us. There is no us. I don't need anybody. I never did. Michael screamed as pain ripped through his body. He felt tears sting his eyes. As he blinked, he saw the nurse above him.

"I warned you not to move your knee," she said. "Maybe next time you'll listen to me."

He turned away. *This is all your fault, Megan. Whenever I think of you—and I don't think that will be very often—I'll remember this pain, and remember that it was all your fault.*

Three months later, Megan was awakened by the phone ringing. "Hello?"

"Hello? Meg? Is that you?"

She heard commotion in the background then, "Just a minute." It gave her enough time to become wide-awake.

"Josh? Where are you?" The noise had lessened slightly but he still told her to speak up. "Where are you? Why haven't you called me before this? Or written?"

"I am in the only place where I could find a vacant phone booth—a bar. And I haven't had time to call or write before this."

"A likely story."

"I didn't call to argue." Meg cringed; she didn't want to argue with him either. She was relieved to finally hear from Josh. His voice softened. "I miss you so much Meg, you can't imagine."

"Oh? How do you think I feel? When are you coming home?" He felt the warmth of her smile as she said it.

"Not for awhile yet. Meg, are you pregnant?"

"No."

"Are you sure?"

"Yes, I get these little indications once a month."

"Meg, you told me you weren't going to tell me; but please—"

"Josh, I said that because I was angry. I would tell you if I was."

"Swear to me on your father's grave."

"Josh!"

"I have to be sure, Meg. I can't see for myself."

She sighed. "I swear on my father's grave, I'm not pregnant."

For a moment he was silent, and then Josh surprised her by saying, "Ya know, I was really starting to look forward to coming home and marrying you and being a father."

She smiled. "Well, come home anyway. We'll give it another try."

"No. I decided something a while back." He hesitated. "If you were pregnant, then I wouldn't tell you because it wouldn't serve any purpose. But, since you're not . . . then you have a right to know."

"I don't think I'm going to like this," she mumbled.

"I should have told you when it first happened; but I couldn't bring myself to do it. I'm a coward." He wished he could see her face when he told her what he had to say; then he would know for sure how she felt about him and about Michael. "When Michael first hurt his knee, a friend of his called me and wanted information about you."

"Michael's friend asked about me? Why?" Josh realized now that he knew her well enough. She was not a good actress. He did not need to see her face.

"Because Michael wanted you. He still has feelings for you, Meg. He'll be coming to get you, just like he said he would."

"But—I've never heard from him."

"It doesn't matter. He told you he'd be back—and he will. The family ring was a pretty good guarantee I'd say. I wish to hell you'd told me about it in the beginning. I could have saved myself a lot of heartache. I don't know that I'll ever forgive you for that."

"Oh, Josh, honey. I really love you. I never meant to deceive you. Truly, I didn't."

"I've got to go, Meg."

"What about us?" she cried. "I love you. I really do! What happened between Michael and me is in the past. You're my future."

"God, Meg. What are you thinking? I still haven't decided what I'm going to do with my life. What if I decide to make the Army my career? I could be traveling all over the world living in quarters that wouldn't suit you. You'd be constantly uprooted. That's no kind of life for you."

"Let me decide!" she screamed. "All I want is to be with you. Besides, I've never been around the world. You know I want to go to Greece—what's wrong with seeing the rest of the world? It would be a great adventure. Let me come with you."

"I can't ask you to throw your life down the drain with me. I'm never going to be anything. Wait for Michael, he'll give you everything. I never told him about us. I don't know that I ever could; he'd probably kill me. You were his first; don't forget. You needn't ever say anything to him about us. It'll be our secret, forever. I love you too much to drag you down with me. Good-bye, Meg."

"Josh, listen to me. It doesn't matter what he wants. What about what I want? What you want? I want you, not Michael. Neither one of you has ever consulted me on either of your decisions. Don't I get a say in anything?"

"Please, Meg. You know I'll always love you, I always have. But you loved Michael once. As soon as you see him again, it will all come back to you. He'll be able to offer you so much more than I'll ever be able to."

"No. Listen to me Josh—"

"Good-bye, Meg. I love you."

"Josh! Don't hang up. Josh? Josh! Damn you!" She stared at the phone. If Michael was really interested in contacting her, he would have done so by now. She had too much pride to write to him, and she had no way of contacting Josh. Meg was furious with both of them. She grabbed the telephone cord and ripped it out of the wall.

April 13, 1970: Josh finally called me last night. He told me a friend of Michael's phoned him when Michael hurt his knee last September. Michael wanted me. But Michael has been well for some time now, and he's made no attempt to get a hold of me. If he really wanted to, he could have tracked me down. And now, because of Michael, I've lost Josh. I am so worried about him. Michael is tough enough and he knows how to survive, Josh doesn't.

Face it. I've lost both of them.

CHAPTER 23

FALL 1970

O NCE MICHAEL PULLED HIMSELF OUT OF HIS DEPRESSION AND got his determination back, nobody was surprised to see him back on the football field come fall. It was his senior year and nothing was going to stop him, even though his doctors had not been encouraging.

Megan read about Michael every week in the newspaper. *Will you come back for me? Do you still wonder about me? If so, why haven't you gotten in touch with me? Did you really ask for me last year? I don't even know if I want you anymore. It's just not fair. What about Josh? I worry about him. I have no idea where he is; if he's safe or if he's found somebody else. Should I just wait and see which one of you comes back? But, why should I wait? What if neither one of you comes back? I've dated some pretty decent guys here.*

On the other hand, nobody's ever come close to claiming my heart—except you two. And you both left me. How could you? Michael, you're breaking records. Josh is going to travel the world. And all I'm getting is an education and crying myself to sleep most nights.

Michael had a terrific year. Certainly no one was surprised when he won the Heisman Trophy. Meg smiled as she read about it. She knew somebody who was famous. Not that she had ever told a soul about Michael, but just the same . . . She watched an interview of Michael on TV—and was glad nobody else was in the room. All she did was grin. *Eat your heart out girls; he's mine. Man, are you handsome in that suit.*

The season was over. Michael's knee did not seem to be bothering him—it was all happening just like he said it would. *I can transfer to a vet school out west. Almost four years of waiting are over. Michael will be coming for me soon!* Her pulse quickened. *I can forgive you for everything Michael, if you just come back for me.*

But what about Josh? I think about you just as much as I do Michael. I'm sorry that I nagged you into doing something with your life. I drove you to this, and I'll never forgive myself if something happens to you. Life isn't fair. Why did I have to fall in love with both of you? Josh, our love for each other was so much more than what Michael and I had. Sometimes I think I only think about Michael because I didn't spend as much time with him as you. You've got so many good qualities. Oh Josh, come back to me.

"I cannot understand you!" yelled J.T. throwing his hands up in the air. "Just an explanation, that's all I ask."

"I don't want to," Michael said simply.

"All I have ever heard from you was how you were going to make a lot of money playing in the pros. That was your goal! You made a terrific comeback this year and now you're refusing all offers. Do you really think if you hold out you'll get more money?"

"I'm not holding out for money, J.T. I've told you that. I just don't want to play football anymore. I could seriously damage my knee."

J.T. stared at him. When had Michael ever worried about his knee? "I don't swallow any of that."

"I don't understand why you're getting so upset."

"It's because I fail to comprehend your reasoning. You've been offered some of the biggest money ever."

"Your dad's offered me a good position and salary at his San Diego plant. I thought I'd take that."

"You hate that place!" roared J.T. "You love football—"

"All right! All right," Michael raised a hand to quiet him. He took a deep breath. "In the beginning, my goal was not to simply make it to the pros for myself—but for somebody else as well. But she didn't even wait a year before she found a steady boyfriend. It's been four years now and—"

Ah, am I getting a glimpse into the mysterious Meg? "Michael, as I recall, and correct me if I'm wrong, but you weren't in California twenty-four hours before you were in bed with some girl."

"So what? I never went with her. I don't even remember her name. I'd had some rather bad news just before I left home and I needed . . . a release. That girl was strictly a one-night stand. But *she* went with this guy steady. She was crazy about him. She never thought of me again once I left. I've never been serious with any of the girls that I date; you know that. That's the difference. I expected her to date—but I meant a whole lot of different guys—not just one."

"How can you be so sure that she was wrapped up with one guy?"

"Because I got it from a very reliable source—my brother."

"Josh?" asked J.T.

"Yeah. He wouldn't lie to me. Hell, he didn't even want to tell me. I had to pry it out of him." J.T. felt a bell go off inside his head; but he couldn't make a connection.

"Josh—he's the one with the stutter, right?" asked J.T.

Michael gave him a quizzical look. "No. Nobody in my family stutters."

Well, he sure was stuttering the day I talked to him, thought J.T. Michael had never once asked J.T. if he had ever tried to find Meg. And he was sure that Josh had never said anything to Michael about their conversation.

"Does Josh know . . ." He knew from experience that if he mentioned the name Meg, Michael would clam right up. ". . . this girl at all? Or is he getting his information secondhand?"

"No, he knows her. He went to high school with her. She was a year behind me and Josh was a year behind her. What's with all the questions?"

"Do you think maybe . . ." *How to phrase this nicely? Could one do that with Michael?* ". . . he's the one dating her?"

264

Michael roared with laughter. "No! Are you out of your mind? He would never cross me. Josh knew how I felt about her. No way. Why would you ask me something like that?"

The stuttering, the refusal to tell me where she was, but the certainty that she wanted nothing more to do with you. The fear in his voice. Maybe he was protecting a friend. "I don't know. But you're basing all this on one person telling you stuff. Maybe you should just go to the source and ask the girl."

"Forget it," his face was hard.

"Okay. Just a suggestion."

Michael sat quietly for a minute, reflecting. "Granted," he was talking to himself now, "I left her at a bad time. I made the wrong decision on that . . . but . . . I tried calling and talking to her but her *mother* would never put me through. Wasn't any sense in writing, her mother was sure to confiscate any letters I sent so . . . I just continued with our plan." He suddenly slammed his hand down on the table, making J.T., who was fixing a sandwich, jump.

"Well, getting back to what I was saying. It's not that important to me, personally, to make the kind of money I could make in a hurry in the pros," continued Michael. "It no longer has the appeal it once did. Her feelings changed, and so have mine. I'm not going to keep my promise to go back and get her. I'm sure she doesn't expect me to. I'm sure she doesn't even remember me. I'm not going back to make a fool out of myself by having her say she's got somebody else. Besides the fact that I don't care about her anymore. I'm not the same guy I was then and I'm sure she's not the same girl. Too much has happened since then and it can never be the same. I don't need those dreams of going to the pros anymore. I'm done playing ball."

Megan felt her blood boil every time she read the article about Michael retiring from football. He had ruined her life completely! And, thank you, Josh, for making your family swear they would never give out your military address to me. That must have been an interesting conversation. Mrs. MacKenzie, who was normally very nice to her, had been cold when Meg called her. What had Josh told her? Apparently, nothing good.

Meg wanted to hurt Michael as much as he had hurt her. At least she knew where he was. *It would even be worth the trip to fly out to California and back just to punch his handsome face. Michael MacKenzie has retired from football.* Oh! She slammed her fist on the table and ran her fingers through her hair in frustration. *I will get even with you, Michael MacKenzie, if it's the last thing I do. What can I do to really hurt you?*

> *November 12, 1970: I will kill Michael with my bare hands! He's RETIRED from football. What about our plans? Our pact? Not only did he leave me, but because of him, Josh has left me! I even called the airlines to get a price on a round-trip ticket to California. But who knows what he would say if I arrived unexpectedly on his doorstep? He can be really cruel. And I can see me walking in while he's got a couple of girls on his arm. I've seen pictures of him with "dates" and they are all gorgeous. But still, I need to let him know how I feel. I'll think of something.*

Josh didn't know exactly when his depression set in; in fact, he didn't even think about it. Everybody in Vietnam was depressed. At least the pills helped dull his brain. They were beginning to wear off though and reality was setting in. He groped in his pocket to discover it was empty. Josh started to panic as he remembered the last time he had been without his pills. He'd become separated from his unit and his supplier and he'd nearly gone mad. Stumbling through the swamps on his own, trying to remember instructions and directions, he'd finally decided to fall on his knife. *There wasn't anyone who cared, so why not?* But then, he'd heard voices, real voices, speaking English, and he'd been saved.

Josh swore he would never go through that hell again. The next time, he promised himself, he would take the easy way out. Only after Vern gave him the pills he needed, did his confidence return. No matter that he'd survived on his own in the wild for three days.

So, don't panic, he told himself. *You didn't pack Vern in a bag with the others today. He's still around; he hasn't let you down yet. Just stay calm and go find him.*

But he didn't find him. Vern had been wounded and was transported out. Josh laughed. The absurdity of it all struck him. Guys that didn't want to die, were dying; and he, who was ready to go anytime, was still in one piece. *I've got nothing to live for, why am I still here? I'm like Michael; I'm invincible. Why didn't Vern leave me something? If only I hadn't lost that packet. I only need a little something. Just a little.* He went to search for relief.

From somewhere close by, Josh heard artillery. He dropped, got up, and ran. He jumped in the nearest foxhole.

"Mac!" Josh turned to see Grif, a friend of his. "They told me you bought it."

"Not me, it was McGilley," said Josh. McGilley had come to ask him a question. A minute later, all hell had broken loose and McGilley had fallen into Josh's arms, mortally wounded. *It should have been me*, Josh thought, *it was meant for me. McGilley had a baby daughter at home he hadn't even seen yet. Why him?*

There was the sound of something flying overhead. It ricocheted in the foxhole. Josh felt it brush his leg. Instinctively he fell on it, while he sensed everybody else was jumping out.

Now that it was too late to jump out of the foxhole, Josh realized it was a grenade. *Well, at least it will be quick.* He held his breath . . . nothing. Slowly, he exhaled. *Is this thing going to go off or not?* He turned his eyes upward and saw Grif peeking over the top. He motioned for Josh to get up. No! he mouthed. If he got up it surely would go off. When he had jumped on it, he had been prepared to die. Now that he had time to think about it, though, this wasn't such a hot idea.

Josh didn't know how long he lay with the grenade pressing into his stomach, when he finally decided he wasn't going to blow up. "Grif?"

"Yeah?"

"Can you call ahead? I need a change of pants."

"Now this is what I call being famous," said J.T. as he carried in a box.

"What's that?"

"It says: 'To the Invincible Michael MacKenzie, Retired'." J.T. set it down on the desk next to Michael. "And to think that the post office found you."

Invincible? Michael frowned as he looked the box over. The words were in big bold print. He turned it over. Nothing. "That's all it says, and it arrived here?"

"That's fame for you."

Michael picked it up. Except for the fact that it had postmarks stamped on it, he would have guessed somebody had just dropped it off. There was no return address and the postmark was smeared.

He shook it. "I don't think there's anything in it."

"Yeah, I noticed it was pretty light. You want a beer?" asked J.T. heading for the kitchen.

"Yeah." J.T. was getting the beers out of the fridge when he heard a strangled cry come from the living room. He ran back in to see that Michael had opened the box and stood transfixed, looking down into it. From the look on Michael's face, J.T. didn't care to get any closer.

"Michael? What is it?"

"N— n — nooo!" he yelled. His face was white and his mouth hung open. "No!" J.T. watched as Michael slowly put both hands in the box and brought them out.

"What the hell is that?" asked J.T. Hair. Red hair. The box was full of it. J.T. picked up a few strands. *Somebody's been growing this for a long time. There's got to be two or three feet here! Gorgeous color.*

"What kind of joke is this?" asked J.T.

Instead of answering, Michael turned and walked out the door. He didn't return until days later, but the news had preceded him. Michael had signed one of the biggest pro contracts ever.

CHAPTER 24

1973

MICHAEL'S FIRST YEAR OF PRO FOOTBALL HAD GONE REASONABLY well; his knee had not given him much trouble. He was now in his second pro season and until now he had never questioned why he had decided to go on with football after his speech to J.T. It was as if he had been programmed. Somehow, Meg sending him her hair symbolized to him that she had been waiting all this time and that he had to continue with his original plan. So, he had.

Now would be the time to go back to get her. He hadn't seen her in six years. His heart quickened at the thought of seeing her again. *What would she be like?* It scared him a little. *Six years. What if I don't like what I see?* And then he analyzed what was really puzzling him. The pieces didn't fit. It was unlike Meg to not write or call, even though he had told her he wouldn't. It was not in her nature to do the same—especially after he had gotten hurt. He had half expected her to show up in his hospital room. Hadn't his heart jumped every time somebody had opened the door?

Of course, she is sore at me for leaving when I did. But still, when I was hurt . . . after all, I promised to go back and get her. So, the explanation

269

for her silence has to be her steady that Josh told me about. Meg has found someone new.

Michael was surprised at the physical pain the news caused him when Josh admitted he'd found out for sure that Megan was heavily involved with one guy. *Why did she send me her hair to indicate she has been waiting for me all this time? Why? Did her boyfriend drop her and now she is telling me she'll take me as second choice? Never!* He felt his blood rage at the thought. *Maybe she realized her mistake with the guy. Maybe she dumped him.*

But why didn't she write and explain herself? Did she think I wouldn't find out about her steady, with Josh right there in the same school? Does she think I am ignorant? Or maybe, just maybe, her boyfriend isn't out of the picture at all. Maybe Meg hasn't forgiven me for running out on her, even with the promise I made. Maybe she and her boyfriend are waiting for me to return and claim her. Michael sat up. *That would be like Meg. To throw somebody else in my face and say, "Are you kidding? What would I want with you?" No. I won't give her the satisfaction of having the last laugh at my expense. I will out-smart her once and for all. Who does she think she is playing games with?*

"Hey kid, wake up." Josh felt someone shake him. He tried to brush the hand away. Someone was going through his shirt pocket. Josh opened his eyes slightly. "Look," the man said as he pulled Josh into a sitting position and pointed his finger at the runway. "You just missed your plane." The man held the ticket up to his face.

Josh stared for some time at the plane that was bound for home. He watched it get smaller and smaller. "I missed my plane," he announced out loud to no one, as the man had given up on him and walked away.

Josh sat for several more minutes, his brain registering nothing. "I missed my flight home," he announced again. *Should I do something? Like . . . ?* He sat there as his brain wandered around in a maze, searching. *Well, the first thing to do, is to get to the bathroom, pop a pill, and hit the bar. That is the most sensible thing to do.*

1976: I just found you and dusted you off. I tried reading this, but it's too painful still. I have waited nine years. Neither one came back. I need to get on with my life. I know that Josh returned from Vietnam, but I understand he's not in the best of shape. Michael, of course, is just fine. He is making good money, his knee doesn't seem to be bothering him any, and did I mention all the women I've seen draped on his arm?

Dr. Thomas would like me to work for him, but I can't go home. I have been offered a job at Bryce and Manns vet clinic on the west side of the state. Far enough away so I won't hear anything; but close enough so that Mom can visit regularly.

Jonesy—oops, force of habit—Jeff and Mandy are both married. Patti and Derek are on their third kid. Trish, of all people, is living in Australia. Marcy is divorced with one child and working as a waitress. And what is Megan doing?

Let's see. I dated some really great guys. A couple were marriage material; but no, Michael was coming back. The one person I've never been able to forget. If I was nice, I would mail his brother's ring back to him, but I'm not. The son of a bitch can either face me or face the consequences from his brother. Hmm, I wonder how big his brother is?

I am packing up and moving to the other side of the state, so this is all I plan to write.

CHAPTER 25

2001

T HERE WERE TWO NEWSPAPER ARTICLES IN MEG'S DIARY. Michael made headlines in the sports world with the discovery that he was back in football. His team was expecting great things from him. And the news of Josh receiving a Silver Star Medal for valor was a small item near the back page.

Robin closed the diary. She sat for a long time. As the sun went down, she continued to sit in the swing. She and her mom had something in common: both had been dumped.

Mom, just to let you know, it wouldn't have been any fun if Michael had come back. Matt came back to me. He came to tell me he'd left a few things behind and wanted to get them and—surprise—he was engaged. He was so happy. He hoped I'd find the kind of happiness that he had finally found. Yes, thank you. I needed that, Matt. Robin didn't notice the cold breeze as she thought about the mother she had never known.

I never thought about Mom being a veterinarian. I knew she went to college; but I didn't know she actually did something with her degree. All this time I thought she met Father there, and that they married and had me—and then she died. I can't imagine someone as passionate as Mom being with Father, who had no emotion at all. Did she die of a broken heart or was she really in love with Father?

It was hard for Robin to imagine anybody being in love with her dad. She had been in love. It required passion and commitment. You were happy and smiled all the time. Robin had never seen that in her father. He was remote and distant, like Michael. Robin smiled. *Yes, Father must have been similar to Michael. Mom had found happiness once again.*

And I will, too.

Robin was grateful that her grandmother and Uncle Jeff had given her the two diaries. She had read her mother's thoughts, had been close to her. Her grandmother had also given her the few pictures she had of Robin being with her mother. *I want more. I don't want it to end now.* She fingered the two newspaper clippings tucked in the diary that her mom had cut out.

She sat up. *Newspaper clippings. The newspaper office! It would be full of stuff on Michael, wouldn't it? He was a talented athlete in high school and a Heisman Trophy winner. Josh was a war hero. It would be fun to look them up, get my mind off Matt—hey, maybe investigative reporting could be my new major at college since I can't find anything else I like. If only Father hadn't been so dead set against me taking finance and business. Let it go. Go to the newspaper office. Do something positive with what's left of the summer.*

Funny, neither Aunt Mandy nor Uncle Jeff has ever mentioned Michael or Josh; and they seemed to be a big part of Mom's life. I wonder why that is. I wonder why Mom quit writing in her diary. I wish she had written about meeting Father, something about me.

Oh, well, the newspaper office beckons.

CHAPTER 26

1977

M R. BEECHUM, WHY DIDN'T YOU BRING IN YOUR DOG A FEW days ago? I could have maybe helped him then. I'm sorry. All I can suggest now is that he be put to sleep."

"Okay," he shrugged his shoulders. "But I will talk to Dr. Bryce about your handling of this situation when he gets back."

Meg stared at him. He had done nothing but complain about the fact that Dr. Bryce was on vacation and that she was a woman. This upset him more than the dog's health. She felt sure he thought she was an assistant trying to pawn herself off as the real thing while the good doctor was away. *Somebody, make him go away! He's a royal pain and I've got other patients to see.*

"Perhaps you'd like to get a second opinion," Megan suggested as calmly as she could.

"Yeah, that's what I thought. Not quite sure what to do now, huh, honey?"

He watched as Meg looked at the needle she was holding and slowly turned a cold stare to him. "Oh, I'm quite sure what I want to do."

He stepped back from her; but no woman was having the last word with him. "I hope that's full of vitamins, because that's all he needs and then he'll be back on his feet in no time."

"Okay," she agreed. "Now that we have the second opinion, what would you like me to do? I hate to see an animal suffer when nothing more can be done for him."

"You're cute," he sneered. He looked around the room until his eyes lighted on her diploma. "Let's get something straight, Megan—"

"That's Dr. Becktame to you."

"Oh, I see. A bit uppity, are we?"

A bit of an asshole, aren't we? Meg bit her tongue.

"All right, Becktame." Obviously he felt she didn't deserve the title. "I'm in a hurry. I'm a busy man. Let's get on with it."

Meg paused. He had not touched the dog since bringing him in. She hadn't expected the man to break down and cry, but usually owners gave their pets one final pat.

"I'm ready," she announced, thinking he would say good-bye.

"So, go to it—unless you don't have the stomach for it . . . doctor."

She started to explain that this was the part of vet practice that she didn't like, but then changed her mind. It would be wasted conversation and she wanted him out. Meg looked at the dog, gently put her hand on him, and said, "It won't be necessary. Your dog has died on his own."

There was no reaction. "I suppose you want me to pay you for an exam."

"Actually, I thought I'd just charge you for your bad attitude. How long did you have him?"

"Five years."

"Five years and you don't feel anything?"

"For God's sake, it's a dog!"

"Good day, Mr. Beechum." He turned to leave. "Wait! Your dog."

"I don't care what you do with him."

"Well, we can cremate him for you, but a lot of people take their pets home and bury them."

For the first time, his face changed. He was horrified at the thought. "Look here Becktame, there is no way I am going to carry anything dead in my car!" He walked out.

Meg was tempted to bill him a hideous amount for funeral services, but changed her mind. Let Dr. Bryce take care of it. Mr. Beechum had left and he was no longer her problem. *What an asshole.* She hoped she never laid eyes on him again. *Arrogant, conceited . . .*

When she came out an hour and a half later, he was waiting for her.

"Oh, God, not you!" The words were out before she could stop herself. No matter, she quickly decided. Now that he had no dog, there was no reason to treat him like a paying customer. God forbid, he should get another one. The receptionist had informed her earlier that Mr. Beechum had paid his bill in cash before leaving. She turned her back on him and walked to her car. It had been a miserable week.

"I thought maybe we could have dinner tonight." He smiled for the first time at her.

"I don't think so."

"Have to wash your hair?" he smirked.

She smiled to herself, thinking he probably heard that line a lot. "Something like that."

"I don't take no for an answer easily. I promise to treat you to only the best."

"I promised myself that, too . . ." *Which is probably why I'm still by myself.* She smiled back and got in her car.

He leaned down. "I'm afraid you've got the wrong idea about me. Give me a second chance. I can be pleasant. I just lost my dog. Tomorrow night?"

"Mr. Beechum—"

"Ben."

"Mr. Beechum, my mother is getting married this weekend—"

"Oh. For the first time?" Meg started to roll up her window. "Hey, I'm sorry! Poor joke, okay? You don't have any sense of humor!" he yelled as she roared off down the road.

Michael woke to the sound of drawers being opened and closed. He cracked an eye open and then sat up.

"Anne, what are you doing?" he asked.

"What does it look like? I'm packing."

"What? Why?" He jumped out of bed.

"I just figure it's time for me to move on, Michael."

"What are you talking about? Would you stop with that?"

"I'm sorry, but I simply won't compete anymore. I'm done."

"Compete? Compete with whom? I have not been with anyone since you moved in here." She continued to pack. "Answer me!" he roared.

"I've lived with you for almost a year and every time it's the same. I thought if I stuck around long enough, she'd go away. I thought I could get you to love me; but whatever kind of hold she's got on you, I can't break it and I'm done trying."

"Who? What are you talking about? Nobody's got a hold on me except you. I swear to God I have not been—"

"Do you know what it does to my ego when you make love to me and then afterwards, when you drift off to sleep, you call out for Meg? In the beginning, I thought I could make you forget."

"I don't do that!" he hotly denied. "I don't think about her, ever! She's nobody!"

"Funny, you deny it just like J.T. said you always did with him."

He clenched his hands. "And what have you and J.T. been saying about her? You two don't even know her. You don't know what she's—"

"And you can't forget her. The same with that watch of yours that has her name on the back. You've broken it so many times it can't be fixed anymore—and still you won't throw it away." She picked up her suitcases and headed for the living room.

"Anne, don't go. Please," Michael said, trailing behind her. "I'll, I'll really try to forget her. You're the only one who's come close to helping me forget."

"What happened between you two?"

He hesitated. "I left her."

"Why?"

"Because at eighteen I thought I was too young to be in love. I thought there was something better out here. I guess, I really thought I could leave her behind. I mean, after all the girls I've met, why does she still stick in my mind?"

277

"I can't answer that Michael. Did she love you?"

"Anne, for—"

"I'm curious. Tell me about her."

"She said she loved me, but that was years ago."

"And what happened to her after you left?"

"I don't know. She was planning on going to college to become a veterinarian. I suppose she did."

"Don't you ever wonder if she thinks about you as much as you do her? Don't you wonder where she is? What she's doing now?"

"No, never!"

"Oh, Michael. You don't need to lie to me. I'm leaving you, no matter what your answer is." Anne turned away, and then hesitated. "You know I love you, but before you, I loved someone else. I loved him very much and he loved me. We got into a silly argument. He didn't like the dog I'd picked out—can you imagine? He felt he should have been consulted. One word led to another and the next thing I knew, we broke up. It all seems so stupid now. I wasn't all that crazy about the dog, it was the principle of the thing. We weren't living together. I should be able to pick out the dog I wanted. Anyway, a few days later, he came back. He was sorry and wanted me back. But I was still mad and I thought this time I'm going to make him pay for the hurt he's caused me. He sent me flowers, candy, called me—and as much as I loved him, I wouldn't let him near me. I was going to teach him a lesson.

"Of course, I always intended on taking him back. If he had quit phoning me, I would have called him immediately." It took her a moment to compose herself. "He's dead, Michael. And I never got the chance to tell him how I felt, how much I really loved him. He died thinking I didn't care what happened to him."

"I'm sorry, Anne," he said quietly. "I never knew."

"But you still have a chance, Michael. At least, I hope you do." She turned towards him. "Go back, find her, and tell her how you feel."

"No! I left her ten years ago."

"So?"

"She's, she's sure to have forgotten me by now. She's probably married and has our four kids at this date."

Anne's eyebrow arched. "Our?"

"What?"

"You said 'our four kids'."

She saw the color rise in his face. "We had this ridiculous plan. We were only kids."

"Go back, Michael," she said softly.

He dropped onto the sofa. "I can't. I can't imagine that she ever forgave me for what I did to her."

Anne sat down next to him. "What did you do to her?"

He studied the floor for a long time. "Our last day together . . . I had this great idea to just get in the car and go. We went wherever the wind took us. Spent the whole day together. I had a plane to catch that evening. We promised we'd be together again. We . . . made a pact. We each had our own plan. I was going to make it to the pros and she would get a degree, become a veterinarian. And then we'd get back together. Start our lives together. She got in her car and went home and I got back in my car and . . . I wasn't living at home; I was staying with friends. They were going to take me to the airport. When I got there . . ."

Anne sat and waited.

"When I got there . . . Meg had called to say her dad had passed away suddenly, quite unexpectedly, and nobody had been able to find her because they didn't know where she was. She was very close to him."

"Oh, Michael, that wasn't your fault."

"Yeah, it was. If we'd stayed at the local hangouts, Jonesy—her neighbor—would have found us. I called her house for several weeks after I landed here. To find out how she was doing, to explain to her why I left instead of seeing her through the funeral, like she asked. Her mom wouldn't let me talk to her, and finally she told me . . . that Meg had missed the opportunity to talk to her dad before he died because I had taken her where nobody could find her."

"So, she blamed you?"

He gave a wicked laugh. "I'm assuming so, seeing as how she never came to the phone. Not once in all the times I called. Meg wanted me to see her through the funeral . . . just three days. And I didn't do it. I got on the plane and came here—and I've never gone back. And there hasn't been one day that I haven't regretted my decision." She rubbed his back.

"Go back, Michael. If for nothing more than to tell her that. Get *that* off your chest at least. You know, if she became a veterinarian, maybe she hasn't married. She wouldn't be dependent on a man to provide for her. We women aren't marrying as young as we used to. But as far as four kids—her clock is ticking. I know the feeling." She stood up and unconsciously ran a hand along her stomach.

Anne looked at him. "Whenever I've mentioned children, you've been pretty negative on the subject. Did you plan on having four kids with her?" He didn't answer. "I see. You owe it to yourself and her to go back and find out if she's still waiting for you. How can you *not* go back?"

He nodded. "I've thought about it. Between the ring and her hair."

"Excuse me?"

"I had a family ring that's been handed down for generations. I tried to give it to Meg that last day, as my promise that I'd come back for her, but she was worried she'd lose it. The fact that I had offered would be good enough for her. When I got back to the house where I was staying and they told me Meg's dad had died . . . I decided to leave the ring with a friend of mine, Jim. I told him to give it to her when he thought it was appropriate. That way she'd know that our pact was still on, and if she took it I'd know she was still with me."

"Oh, I see. She didn't take it."

"No, she did."

"Then, Michael, she forgave you. Why have you not gone back?"

"You know, it's a two-way street. She could have come to me, too. Especially when I got hurt."

"Why? By your own admission you ran out on her. You're the one who needs to apologize. She may not come to you, but it sounds like she's forgiven you. And you know what? You've been photographed with a lot of women on your arm. You think she didn't see at least some of them? As a woman, I wouldn't be too sure of the reception I would get. You are always looking for her in everybody else. Don't wait another day—another minute. Find her."

He shook his head. "I haven't in all these years. I never will."

"You're a coward, Michael." She picked up her bags. She didn't bother to ask him about the hair. She'd already heard the story from J.T.

"Anne, please. I don't want you to go. I'll really try . . ." *To love you.*

She smiled. "I'm sure within the week you'll have found yourself another roommate. There were plenty here before I arrived."

CHAPTER 27

1978

WELL, MEG?" ASKED JEFF. HE HAD TAKEN HER OUT TO DINNER. She looked up inquiringly at him.

"Well, what?"

"Are you going to marry this Ben guy?"

She laughed. "I've hardly mentioned his name. What makes you think I'm contemplating marriage with him?"

"Mandy told me. She said he was nice and was bonkers about you."

She laughed some more. "He's been proposing to me since he met me ten months ago. I don't know what I'll do."

"Do you love him?"

"I don't believe in love, you know that. Love is a fairy tale," she scorned. "He's a good man . . . I guess. He has different priorities than I have." She sighed and said quietly to herself, "The man has no sense of humor."

"Meg, do you remember when we all went out and celebrated you being offered a job with Dr. Bryce? You got pretty snookered and you told me Michael was coming back for you. You don't still think he's going to come back, do you? I mean, that's not what you're waiting for, is it?"

"No," she shook her head. Jeff was relieved to see that she didn't fly off the handle at his asking. "Michael's making a helluva lot of money right now. If he wanted me, he would have been back long before this. It's been eleven years and I'm all right now, really. I enjoy being a career woman, being on my own and independent. I love what I do. I don't know what I'd do without it. But . . . I would like to have a couple of children and I'm not getting any younger . . . decent guys to meet are getting scarce." She made a face at him. *Still,* she wondered, *why did Michael join the pros after he said he was retired? Why did he continue with our plans and then not include me?*

"You know, I'm really proud of you. Your dad would be proud. In talking with Dr. Bryce, he can't speak highly enough about you. You are going to be a great—you are a great—veterinarian."

She smiled. "Thanks for the support. Ben is a firm believer that women should not be part of the work force." Meg sighed and stared past him. "I don't have anything else to do, Jeff." He had constantly harped on being called by his given name and yet it saddened him when Meg did it, as if to remind him he was getting old.

"What about Ben? Mandy says he's great. That he treats you like a queen."

"Oh, he is great in a lot of ways . . . if I think about it hard enough. I could do worse, I suppose. What, are you worried I'm going to be an old maid?" she teased.

"No, that doesn't worry me. It's you always dwelling on the past that worries me."

"I know. You're right. Well Jonesy, how would you like to give this bride away?"

He smiled at her. Megan had matured into a beautiful woman. He didn't wonder why his wife was always furious when he took Meg out alone. Unfortunately, Peggy had not liked Meg from the start and she could not accept the fact that Meg and Jeff had a strictly platonic relationship. No amount of talking would convince her. Peggy demanded Jeff not see Meg anymore; but he refused. Meg was like a sister to him and he wasn't going to leave her because of Peggy's jealousy. Peggy was welcome to come along with them anytime she wanted, although she always declined. Megan was just as glad. She could talk more freely to Jeff when they were alone.

"I didn't know I had such persuasive powers," he said, pleased with himself.

"Not to deflate your ego any, but you don't," she reached across the table and put her hand over his. "Congratulations, Jonesy. You're going to be an uncle."

Michael stood in what he decided was pretty much the center of his newly acquired property: five hundred acres of Canadian wilderness. It felt good to be out of the city.

He took his compass and a map and started walking. *God, I haven't done this in years.* Supposedly there was a building somewhere around here, although in what shape nobody knew. It took him most of the day to find the dilapidated log cabin. It stood in what was once a good-sized clearing. He would set fire to it. But the barn didn't look too bad. It appeared to have been built later and only needed some minor repairs.

Michael waited until the next morning, rose at daybreak, and got to work. He reached for his wallet and slowly pulled out a sheet of folded paper. He opened it carefully, so the lock of red hair didn't blow away. The paper revealed the crude sketch of the cabin Meg had drawn years ago. He had ripped it out of her notebook and filled in what each room was. He didn't know what had possessed him to do it, but now he was glad he had. If he was going to go back and try to win her heart all over again, then he had to have something to win her over with—to entice her. He couldn't show up and tell Meg he had nothing to offer in the way of their plan. He wanted her to know that he did remember, and that he had thought of her every day since he'd left. And that he'd always dreamt of what their time would be like once they were reunited.

He cut down trees during the day and passed out from exhaustion in his camper trailer at night. He relished the solitude.

A week passed. The next day he saw a young woman on horseback headed towards him. With her wavy dark hair and brown eyes she had caught many an eye; but Michael paid no attention to her.

"Hi!" she hollered. "I'm Lisa Townsend, your neighbor."

He grumbled a greeting and continued with his work.

"What are you doing?" she asked.

"I'm building a log cabin." *Stupid broad, what does it look like I'm doing?*

"By yourself?"

"You see anybody else here?"

"It'll take you awhile to do it by yourself."

"Gee whiz, you're a big help. And me with just my college degree."

His sarcasm did not seem to affect her. "I have five brothers and a father. I'm sure they'd be glad to come over and help you."

"Thanks, but I'd rather do it myself. Now, if you'd care to get lost, I'd think you were a real nice neighbor."

As soon as she left, Michael had second thoughts about his rudeness. He had no idea how many people his age were nearby. *What if she is the only female around for Meg to socialize with?* He supposed he shouldn't ostracize himself before Meg arrived. He'd try to be a little nicer next time . . . if there was a next time.

Eighteen hours later, Michael got a second chance when Lisa showed up with her five brothers and father in tow. She saw his anger start to rise, but then he reluctantly showed Mr. Townsend his sketch. In only a few days, the cabin was done. Lisa brought the men lunch every day and Michael found it was much better than what he had packed. The Townsends told him about the few neighbors that were around and the nearest place to get supplies.

As they were putting the finishing touches on the cabin, Michael looked at Lisa—really looked at her. She knew that look. There wasn't a boy or a man around that didn't eye her up and down like that. Michael smiled at her for the first time. She smiled back.

Perseverance had paid off. She'd caught herself another one.

Ben and Megan made their wedding plans. Megan sternly told herself that she was going to go through with it—and be happy about it. Everyone was thrilled for her. He was such a great catch, they all said.

So, why hasn't somebody caught him before this? she wondered.

Ben had looks, money, he was crazy about her—and he was thrilled about the baby. They were going to be one big happy family, he said. *So what if he scoffs at my cabin in the woods? So what if he hates animals? So what if he wants me to quit work? It doesn't mean I have to give in to all of his demands. Michael isn't coming back, Josh isn't coming back, it is getting harder and harder to meet decent men. Who else is there?*

When Meg left for college, her mom had kept her bedroom untouched. Meg had only been back a handful of times. Now, she gave her bedroom one last look. All reminders of Michael and Josh would have to go. *My word, look at you Becktame. At your age, still hanging onto high school memorabilia. You certainly didn't lead a dull life in college. God, why didn't I marry one of those guys? At least I felt something for a few of them.*

Slowly she dropped the items in a box. She couldn't bring herself to throw any of it out; she'd put the box in the attic. In later years, she'd get it out and laugh to herself, she hoped. Meg's heart leaped when she came across the photo album of all the pictures she and Josh had taken when he'd given her the camera. She tried to thumb through it, but couldn't quite manage it. Tears welled up.

Don't be an ass, Becktame! This marriage isn't the end of the world. Ben has a lot to offer. You'll learn to love him. He's a good man . . . in some ways.

What to do with the photo album? It can't stay here. It's too painful. It will have to go; but I can't throw it in the trash, either. Meg had a sudden inspiration and knew if she thought it through, she'd decide not to do it—and yet, it was the only sensible thing to do. She packed up the album and dashed down to the post office before she had a chance to change her mind.

Not having any other address, she mailed it in care of his parents. It had given Meg immense satisfaction to cut her hair and send it to Michael. She hoped she'd feel good at sending the photos to Josh. Although, she still felt guilty about him. *Why didn't I tell Josh in the beginning that Michael planned on coming back for me?* She told herself it was because she didn't believe Michael and that it was a secret between the two of them—plus the fact that her feelings for Josh were real. *Knowing how he felt about me, how could I have nicely put it that he would make a good second if Michael didn't happen to show up? I should have been upfront with Josh from the start. He deserved that much.*

Meg felt the blood drain from her face when she thought about Josh jumping on the grenade. She wished her mom had never sent the newspaper clipping. That was one piece of news she could have done without. To Meg, it was not an act of bravery but one of suicide. Thank God he had survived. She didn't know what she'd have done if he'd been killed.

Lord knows if you'll ever get this Josh; but it's just not something that can be put in the attic. I hope you understand.

Michael was settled inside the cabin, with a roaring fire, when he heard a soft knock at the door. He looked at his watch. Anne was right. He couldn't bring himself to throw Meg's watch out—but he'd done the next best thing when it couldn't be fixed anymore. He'd bought another one just like it. It was late and he decided to wait for the second knock. When it came, he slowly got up and answered it. Lisa noticed he was not surprised to see her.

He was, however, surprised to see her dressed up. She wore an evening dress and a shawl. Her hair was cleaned and pulled back instead of lying on her shoulders. "I wear jeans and t-shirts for months on end, and then sometimes I feel like dressing up. But there isn't anybody at home to notice," she explained sweetly.

Lisa unwrapped the shawl to reveal that the dress could be buttoned its entire length; however, few holes were filled. She obviously wore nothing underneath.

"You look very nice," he said. "I'd offer you a chair but ..."

She smiled. "Oh, I knew you didn't have any furniture. I just thought I'd stop by to . . . chat."

"That is next on my list. Do you want to go with me and help pick out furniture?"

She smiled. "I'd love to." *Because I plan on living here.*

He had brought in some of his belongings from the camper and was able to find something for them to drink. Michael sat down next to Lisa by the fire. She was disappointed when he made no advances towards her. *Why does he think I'm here? Certainly he isn't naïve enough to buy my line? Hasn't he ever been with a woman before? Is he one of those guys who doesn't care for women? No, I'm sure I didn't mistake the look on his face. Maybe he is just shy.*

Finally, when Lisa could stand it no longer, she decided to fling her fate to the wind. She put her arms around his neck. For a moment, he acted as if nothing had happened and continued to stare at the fire. Suddenly he laughed, the first time she'd ever heard that sound from him. "I wondered."

"You wondered what?" she asked, removing her arms from him.

"You're very much like Meg."

"Who's Meg?" *How dare he compare me to some other girl! Doesn't he know how many men would give anything to be in his shoes right now?*

"Someone . . . someone who was very close to me," he said softly.

"Was she your wife?"

"No, but she should have been." He looked startled when he glanced over at her.

Lisa felt her anger subside, although she still stood up and made her way across the room. "Then, it's a compliment?"

"Yes, it's a compliment." He watched as she hesitated at the door.

"It's getting late. I should be leaving."

"It was late when you arrived." He stood up. "Come here."

Unlike Megan, Lisa nearly ran to him. Although Michael felt a sense of disappointment, he nevertheless pulled her to the floor to do whatever he wanted with her—as he knew she'd let him.

CHAPTER 28

1979

"MICHAEL?"

"I'm right here." He got up and walked across the room to stand at the foot of the bed.

"How did you get here?"

"I live here."

"You live . . . in Germany?"

"No, Josh, in Canada. Don't you remember anything? I got a call that you were in the hospital. You had been discharged from the Army and they wanted somebody to take you home. Remember, I came and got you? The flight back here? Has your mind deteriorated that much?"

"Oh, yeah." Josh spoke slowly. He tried to sit up but it took too much effort. "Have you . . . have you got anything for me?"

"Yeah, I have orange juice."

"I don't want . . . Nothing else?"

"No," said Michael firmly. "If you want, I'll fix you a solid breakfast."

Josh groaned. He didn't want that garbage. He just needed a little something, not much, and then he'd kick the habit.

"Mom thought it was so nice of me to fly to Europe to spend my vacation with you—and now she's mad at me. 'Why did you talk him out of the Army? He had such a *wonderful* career going'," Michael mimicked their mother. "Let's hope she doesn't find out what really happened."

"I don't give a shit," muttered Josh. He rolled himself out of bed.

"Why don't you take a look in the mirror?" offered Michael.

Josh stumbled into the bathroom. For a few minutes he didn't recognize himself. *It's not the drugs; it's the hospital stay that did this to me!* His clothes hung on him. There were dark circles underneath his eyes. His hair was unkempt. *I'll go out today and find what I need to get back on my feet.*

"Breakfast is served," announced Michael.

Josh sat at the table, looked at his plate full of steaming food, and stood up. "Eat it."

"I don't want to."

Michael grabbed Josh by the collar and slammed him down in the chair. "Eat it. It'll be the first decent meal you've had in years; but I think you'll survive." Slowly and with shaking hands, Josh ate.

They dined in silence. Josh swore he was hiking it out of there the first time Michael turned his back. *Big brother to the rescue, just what I need. Everything came easy to you, Michael. Don't you dare sit there and judge me. While you were running up and down a football field trying to win games, I had to run for my life.*

"I think I'd like to take a walk," Josh said cautiously.

"If you feel up to it, go ahead."

Good, this is going to be easier than I thought. Josh gathered up his jacket, hoping he had a couple of bucks in it, and casually walked outside. He smiled. *Michael was such an idiot.* He closed the door behind him and stopped dead in his tracks. Green. Everywhere he looked there was foliage. Trees. Grass. Bushes. For miles and miles. Josh started to hyperventilate. "What kind of place is this?" he hollered over his shoulder.

"It's my cabin in the woods," Michael said, stepping outside and propping himself against the doorframe.

Oh, my God. This is Meg's cabin. This is Meg's cabin in the woods. Was she here? Has she seen me like this? "Is . . . is there anybody else living here?"

"Not at present . . . no."

Josh suddenly had flashbacks. There was a girl, something about a girl ... "Is there a girl ... who comes around here?"

"Yeah, her name is Lisa."

"Not—okay. Who ... what ... why ...?"

"What are you mumbling about?" asked Michael.

"Why is she ... is she my nurse?"

Michael laughed. "No. She's a neighbor. Is there anything going on in that brain of yours? Do you remember anything from the last few weeks?"

This is Meg's cabin in the woods, I'm sure I remember that. Where is Meg? I can't let her see me like this. I need to get cleaned up. "Where ... how do you get out of here?"

"You," Michael pointed a finger at him, "don't."

"I'm a prisoner?" For a minute Michael thought he was going to burst into tears.

Michael softened as he saw the defeated look on Josh's face. He had always protected Josh from their father and bullies when they were younger. How Josh had survived Vietnam, Michael had no idea—and he knew he shouldn't condemn him. Michael had no right; he'd never served. He could only take care of Josh as best he knew how ... and with help from talking to doctors, nurses, other soldiers who had been there, and friends of Josh's. "You're not a prisoner. Look at this as a place to clean yourself up. Fresh air, decent food, no drugs, no cigarettes, no booze."

"Oh, God!" Josh crumpled to his knees. "I've landed in hell, and you are the devil!"

"I don't think things are quite that bad." Michael tried to reassure him. "There are a couple of gals about your age around here that aren't bad looking. I got you a horse—"

"A horse?" Josh stared at Michael with a puzzled look on his face.

"Yeah. Do you remember what a horse is?"

"No, Michael. I have completely and utterly lost my mind. How I am stringing these words together is beyond me. A horse?" He pondered this a moment. "Is that similar to the jackass I'm looking at?"

"Good, good," said Michael, unperturbed. "You're getting your sense of humor back. That's a good sign."

291

Josh slowly picked himself up off the ground. "What do I need a horse for?"

"To get around. It's a lot easier than driving."

Josh looked at his surroundings. "Where's your car?"

"That's not your concern. But it's not here." There was no way he was going to let Josh sneak out and take his camper. "Josh, listen to me. This is the first time you've been able to carry on any kind of a conversation—a conversation that makes sense, anyway. You were released to my care because of who I am, because of the people I know, and the fact that I live out here in the sticks where you can't hurt anybody. Or, if you prefer, you can go back to the mental hospital I hauled you out of. You decide."

"I am never going back to that hospital. The things they did to me. *That's* where I started losing it."

"Yeah, right. You've completely wasted your body. It's a wonder you're alive. They found you in a ditch—half out of your mind. You'd been AWOL for days. You were taking so many different drugs, you didn't respond to anything. You've been delirious for weeks. Do you know how long you've been here?" Josh glared at him. "Do you remember any of this?" More silence. "Do you know that you didn't even know who I was when I came to get you? Even when I told you I was your brother?" he started to yell. "Ya know, if you're not happy here, I'll be glad to take you back. You've been a royal pain in the ass and I don't see any other family member or friend offering to help you out. You go for a walk and then come back and tell me your decision." Michael slammed the cabin door shut.

Josh couldn't even make it out of the clearing. He lay down, huffing and puffing. *What kind of crap is Michael trying to pull on me? I'm fine, just a little tired. I'm just out of shape is all.* He looked around. *My God, it's summer.* He sat up. *Summer? In Canada?* Panic seized him. *What happened to Christmas? The snow? No, it can't be true. I haven't been out of it all that time. There has to be another explanation. Michael must be lying. So, I popped a few pills here and there, big deal. Who didn't? They just made me feel good, that's all. How can it be summer?*

CHAPTER 29

1980

MEG LAY AWAKE LISTENING TO BEN BREATHE. *HOW DID I GET to this point?* she screamed at herself, as she had for months. She could feel tears welling up. She needed to get to another part of the house where she could really let loose.

Quietly she crawled out of bed. She didn't even grab a bathrobe. "Where are you going?" Ben asked gruffly.

"I . . . thought I heard Robin cry—"

"I didn't. Get back in bed."

"Yes, Ben." *Am I allowed to do nothing on my own? I can't work. I rarely get to see my friends. I'm not allowed a pet. You never let me out of your sight. And now, I'm not even allowed to see my own child?* The only bright spot was getting pregnant again. Ben demanded that they have another child and Meg had prayed to get pregnant, because then he'd leave her alone. Oh, he'd still tell her what to do—but at least he wouldn't touch her. That alone was a major blessing. *I can't stand you touching me.*

She remembered a few months ago, when she calmly explained to Ben that they had nothing in common except their daughter. She did not want alimony or child support. She simply wanted a divorce. Meg had even gone so far as to wonder if her mother would give her some of her acreage, so that she could finally build her log cabin. And, Meg had spoken with Dr. Thomas. He was willing to have her work for him. Her bags and Robin's things were already packed and in her car. Ben had stood there so calmly, Meg actually thought that he was happy she had taken the initiative.

The beating he gave her was incomprehensible to her.

Oh, he was the dutiful husband and visited Meg in the hospital after her "fall." He brought flowers and candy and, when no one was around, stood next to her and said, "Do you really need to be told why we are *never* getting a divorce?"

Meg simply stared up at him with dull eyes.

"As I have told you several times—and you'd better start listening to me—I have political ambitions. Senator, governor, president. People I consult with say I need a wife. You have what I need. Breeding, money, looks, a nice figure, and an education. A divorce is not in my best interests nor, I guarantee you, is it in yours.

"You may not love me, but honey, you better learn to. I'd like to know what there is about *you* to love. You're lucky I wanted to marry you. You were destined to be an old maid—nobody wanted you. And you know damn well I didn't marry you for your money. I do very well in the lumber business. Now, you are going to be the obedient wife and stand by my side. If you find that you're not capable of that, well . . ." He leaned over and whispered in her ear, "Widowers get a lot of sympathy I'm told."

And where had being the good wife gotten her? Yes, she lived in a huge house. Yes, Ben took her out to plays, ballets, and expensive dinners to meet and impress people. Yes, she had charge cards with no limit imposed on them—but now that he realized Meg was afraid of him the slaps, shoves, and punches came more frequently. Meg was never able to toe the line because the line always changed on her.

Once she had gone out with one of the neighbors. The woman discovered that Meg's birthday was in a few days, so as a present she paid for lunch. Later that evening, Meg found Ben going through her purse.

"How stupid do you think I am?" he asked.

Meg was completely baffled. "About what?"

"Tell me again what you did today."

"Sandra and I went shopping and had lunch." *My word, I was only gone for three hours.*

"And yet, you still have the same amount of money you started out with—and no credit card slip for food."

"That's because Sandra paid for my meal—" The back of his hand came up hard against her face.

"Let's try it again. Tramp that you are. Who did you pick up?" He always had this line of thinking. Ben had no illusions about his marriage. Meg had made that perfectly clear. And, if she wasn't happy with him then she had to be looking for it elsewhere. Of course, he had no proof of this—and never would. Meg knew there was nothing to gain by having an affair.

The constant physical and verbal abuse was beginning to erode Meg's self-confidence. She was beginning to give in more and more to his demands: it was just easier. And the more she did, the less she thought of herself.

She had slowly walked over to the phone. Ben ripped it out of her hand. "Sandra charged it. She'll have proof she paid for two meals."

"And when she asks you why you're asking for this information, you'll probably say something stupid like 'my husband wants to see it because he thinks I'm lying,' which makes me look like a jealous husband and then she'll come over and see the mark I just left on your face. Can you never think ahead? God, you are totally worthless to me." This was a common phrase of his.

Then let me go! Let me go!

As he raced after Josh in the pre-dawn hours, Michael was sorry that he hadn't kept in shape. Josh wasn't hard to follow though. Shouting, snapping twigs, and occasional gunfire let Michael know where his brother was. Michael was scared, though. He was responsible for Josh. *What if he shoots someone? How am I going to get the rifle away from him?* The medical professionals had warned Michael; but he did not have the heart to put Josh away in a mental institution. Obviously, he hadn't realized how bad Josh really was.

Michael believed that after Josh dried out, they could start life anew, together. Josh had dried out—but his mind was gone—at least it was right now. *And yesterday, Josh had carried on so normally. How could I have been so careless as to not lock the rifle away when I was done with it?*

"Halt!"

Michael ran into the small meadow to find the rifle leveled at his chest. "Josh—"

"State your name, rank, and serial number."

"What? Cut the crap, it's me."

"Now, soldier!" Michael didn't know if there were any bullets left in the rifle or not. He raised his arms up slightly.

"Michael MacKenzie, aw, sergeant . . ." *Maybe being a rank or two above him will encourage Josh to hand over the rifle.* Michael gave his social security number.

Josh's eyes narrowed and he stared down the sight at Michael. "Josh, listen to me—"

"I'm General MacKenzie," Josh roared. "You, shut up!"

"General?" Any other time Michael would have found this humorous.

"You are to be executed for desertion," announced Josh.

"Ex— for des— Wait, for God's sake!" yelled Michael, sensing Josh's finger on the trigger. A million thoughts raced through his mind. "I— I get a last cigarette, don't I?"

Slowly the rifle came down. "Yeah, I guess so. One."

Michael felt foolish going through the motions of getting out, lighting, and smoking an imaginary cigarette.

"You should never have left her!" yelled Josh across the meadow.

"Left who?" Michael was shaking. *How am I going to get the rifle? Should I gamble that it's empty?*

"When she needed you most, you deserted her. And desertion calls for execution!" his voice was getting louder.

"What?" Michael felt his heart quicken.

Josh brought the rifle back up to his shoulder and Michael dove. There was a single shot.

As he landed on the ground, Michael realized the shot had come from behind him. For a split second it was quiet, then Josh let out a terrifying scream, danced around in circles, and shot off the rifle until it was empty. Michael jumped up and ran at him, trying to tackle him. But Michael was not trained like Josh was for hand-to-hand combat and Josh had put on some weight. The unexpected blow that Josh gave Michael sent him reeling, knocking the breath out of him.

"Stop it! Stop it!" Lisa screamed. "You're surrounded, general. Put down your rifle!" Josh threw it down and put his hands over his head.

Lisa made her way over to Michael. "So help me, I'll shoot!" she sobbed, keeping her gun pointed at Josh.

Slowly Michael got up. "Thank you, Lisa."

"He's crazy! He would have killed you! There's nothing more you can do for him, Michael. He's threatened you for months and one of these days he's going to succeed. You either shoot him here and now and put us all out of our misery, or you have him locked up where he can't hurt anybody!"

"Calm down." Gently Michael took the gun away from her, afraid that she might take it upon herself to shoot Josh. Then he walked over and picked up his own rifle. He was still shaking.

"He's dangerous! You can't go on living like this! I am not going to stand by and watch anymore!"

"Just stop, Megan," Michael didn't even realize what he had said, but it had its effect.

"Michael?"

"What Josh?"

"Is there any apple pie left?"

CHAPTER 30

O NE OF US IS LEAVING," STATED LISA. THEY WERE BACK AT THE cabin. Josh was sleeping contentedly in his bedroom.

"Honey, you don't mean that."

"Yes, I do! I was willing to sit by when I thought you were making some progress—but he's slipping away again. I go cold every time I think about—"

"Lisa, I'm grateful that you showed up when you did, but I promise it won't happen again."

"How? How are you going to stop him, short of tying him up for good? He needs professional help. It's not as if you haven't tried! There's nothing for you to feel guilty about."

"He'd die locked up somewhere."

"It's either you or him. Now, who do you think is the better man? What does your brother have to offer mankind?" She ran a hand over her face. "God, I should have shot him myself when I had the chance."

"You don't mean that," he said again.

"Yes, I do. I can't sit by and watch anymore. We had a good thing going before he got here. You spend all your time with him, and none with me. So, you decide right now, because I promise you, I will pack up and leave."

"Except for this morning's incident, he's been doing okay. I'm afraid that if I send him away—" Lisa stood up and headed for the upstairs bedroom where her things were. "All right," he sighed. "Josh goes."

She wrapped her arms around Michael and hugged him. "I was beginning to doubt whether you cared about me the way you said you did." *Although, he still hasn't gotten those three little words out.*

He held her tightly. "Don't doubt me, babe."

"Don't let anybody come between us again like that," she whispered, thinking of the slip-up he'd made in the meadow.

"I won't. Just give me a week or two to find a decent place for him. I'm not sticking Josh just anywhere."

"A week," she stated, "and then I'm going to make you forget all about . . . everybody."

"Didn't I tell you that you'd make me the perfect wife?" Ben said delightedly. *Yes, when you're not yelling "tramp" and "whore" at me.* "You were superb tonight."

Meg waved a hand at him, wishing he'd just shut up and leave her alone. Lucky for him (and for herself, she supposed) she enjoyed going to parties and mingling with other people.

She wondered if she could plead sleeping in the guest bedroom again since it was cooler in there. It had worked a couple of times, but Ben was becoming suspicious. Of course, he wasn't getting suspicious that she didn't want to sleep in the same room as him. No, he suspected that she was secretly meeting another man in there. *How insane is he? I'm six months pregnant. I can really attract men like this. As if I want to have sex in this condition. And, as jealous as he is, does he really think I am stupid enough to do it right under his nose, where he could walk in at any time?*

"Come over here," he patted the bed.

"Oh, God, please! I'm exhausted. I don't feel that well." *I don't want you touching me!*

He looked hurt. "I was only going to give you a back rub."

"Oh. I can get up for that." She slowly got out of the chair and held her stomach as she lay on her side on the bed. Ben did, in all honesty, give the best back rubs and she needed and deserved one tonight.

"See, life isn't so bad with me when you're good, Meggie," he stated after a few minutes.

"Yes, Ben." *God, I hate that name, Meggie!*

"I come from a wealthy family. At least you know I didn't marry you for your money. A lot of guys would have, you know. I mean, let's be honest. You didn't have much else to offer." She gritted her teeth. *And yet, you had a list of reasons as to why I was the chosen one when I balked at marrying you.* "We go out a lot. I don't mind you sewing and knitting and doing all that womanly stuff. You shop at the finest stores with unlimited charge cards. You have a healthy daughter, thanks to me ..." *Yes, of course, there's no thanks to me!* "... and another on the way." He kissed the nape of her neck. "As long as you're good, Meggie, you've got nothing to complain about. I haven't had to beat you in months. Months. You've been just splendid. And, there's no reason why things can't go on this way." *Right. As long as I never leave the house without your trusted friends or you, you don't have to give me the third degree when I arrive home. You don't have to grill me to see who I've picked up. You don't have to call me all sorts of awful names.*

She sighed. She had to stop thinking like this. For her own sanity, and for Robin's and the baby's sake, she had to try to find the positive in her life.

Okay. As long as everything goes Ben's way, our life together is ... well, livable. All the things he mentioned are true. When it comes to money, he has yet to deny me. Plays, ballets, movies, dinner out, vacation spots—they are mine for the asking—as long as they don't interfere with his plans. The cabin, he laughs at. Greece, well, someday when he has the time. I don't dream about either one anymore, so it really doesn't matter. Well, Michael, I ended up with everything you said you thought would make me happy. Want to ask me if I'm happy? Want to know how happy I am now, Michael?

"Meggie, I've never cheated on you." *Only because you don't want to be caught in a scandal.* Ben was running for state representative at the moment. An affair would not look good, would not get him votes. "I have no reason to. I'm very happy with you and I don't see that ever changing. I've always known the type of woman I wanted--and you're her. You're everything I ever dreamed about."

"Thank you, Ben. You're very good to me." *If I ever get out of this marriage, I am never marrying again.*

＞　＜

He woke up screaming, threw the covers off, and started to run. He felt strong arms holding him. "Run, you idiot! They're dropping!" he yelled, trying to get away.

"No, Josh. Stop! You're safe. You're home. You're fine. Stop running. You don't have to run anymore."

Josh fell sobbing against Michael's shoulder. "Don't put me away, Michael! I can't go back there, please. I heard you and that bitch talking."

"Stop right there, Josh."

"I have the same nightmare over and over again—but not as often as I used to. It'll go away soon, I'm sure. But if you send me back, I'll be lost there. Nobody will look after me there. I'll just be a number. Please, Michael. Please—"

"Josh, just calm down."

"I know what a pain in the ass I've been—but that's because you ruined my life and I was getting back at you. If you're going to put me away—"

"I flew to Germany and hauled you out of the loony bin—and it's my fault?" yelled Michael. "This is the thanks I get? Well, you're welcome!"

Josh stopped and looked at him. He had never told Michael about being involved with Megan. He wasn't about to explain it now either. "I . . . I don't know what I'm saying. I'm sorry. Of course, you saved me. I'm grateful you took me out of there. I'll straighten up, I promise. I'll . . . I'll go do those chores you've been after me to do. I'll go do them right now. I'll—"

"Sit down, Josh."

"Please, Michael. I'm begging you. I can't go back."

"Josh, calm down," said Michael. "I'm not thinking of putting you in a mental institution . . . where you won't get any help. There are some decent places that I'm willing to pay for."

"No! No, Michael. Please! I can't! I can't do it! How will you tell Mom and Dad that you locked me away forever?"

"I want you to calm down!" yelled Michael. He took a deep breath and let it out slowly. "I would like us to have an adult discussion about your future. I can't do it with you becoming hysterical. I am willing to listen to you. I want to do the right thing for you, Josh. But I'm not going to do it if you don't hear me out!" Josh sat quietly with his lips pressed together.

"Now, we're going to try this one more time," said Michael as calmly as he could. "I'm not sure how or why you blame me for the fix you're in. I didn't tell you to join the service. Hell, as I recall, Dave tried talking you out of it. I never pushed the drugs on you; I keep my liquor locked up . . . As far as Mom and dead-beat Father are concerned, I would simply tell them the truth. I won't have a guilty conscious about that. I brought you here because I honestly thought I could help you. Getting you away from your pals and the drugs was a big plus. I find working here on the farm to be therapeutic; I thought you would, too. But it hasn't worked out that—"

"Yes, it has! I've been so much—" Josh saw the hard look on Michael's face and shut his mouth.

"I admit you're better than when you first arrived. I've seen a lot of improvement but . . ." Michael saw the worried look in Josh's eyes. ". . . maybe you need more help; something that I can't give you. You won't be put away forever—only until you're better. I'll see to it that you get the best treatment. I'll visit you and make sure that you're being taken care of. I promise you, I'm not locking you away." He could see that Josh was about to burst. "I don't want to hear any whining or sniveling. Just tell me what you think."

"Okay," said Josh. He thought for a moment before he spoke. "I— I think I am better just being here. I know I've done some really stupid stuff . . . and I'm sorry. I don't . . . like Lisa. I know that's none of my business, but if this is the only time I get to speak . . ." He stared at Michael, who said nothing. "God, I still crave the drugs. It just kind of drives me insane sometimes. But I'm having more good days than bad. I . . . would like to stay here, please. And I will really, really try to straighten myself out. I haven't given it much effort but . . . I can't go back to a hospital. You've had it so easy. You always got the girls, you've got money—you have everything! I have nothing!" The two of them stared at each other. "Oh, sorry. I guess that falls under whining and sniveling."

Michael shifted in his chair. "I had no idea you resented me. All this time, I thought I was the big brother coming to the rescue. I've always protected you and now I find out . . . well." He leaned back, away from Josh.

Josh laughed slightly. "Trust me, Michael, when you stepped in between Dad and me, I appreciated it. Let's face it, I've made a mess of my life and if you hadn't come along . . . I'd probably still be there. I do appreciate you getting me out. I know I sound like an ungrateful brat. Can we . . . can we please start over? I'm going to really try this time. If I don't straighten up, then you can put me away. Please, Michael. One last time."

Michael looked at the floor for a long time. "Lisa doesn't exactly care for you either. What if . . . what if we fixed up a room in the barn for you?"

"The barn? You want me to live with the animals?" Josh was mortified.

"It will give you a little space. Some place to get away from the two of us. Gain a little independence."

"Oh, God. The barn . . . Lisa gets the house while I get the . . . fine. Yeah. Okay."

"You want to build your own place?" Michael asked. Josh looked at him to see if he was joking. He appeared to be serious. "I built one-third of this cabin by myself, before Lisa's brothers and father showed up and helped me finish it. I could have done the whole thing. There was something about doing this with my own two hands . . . for all the things that I have done in my life, here, I finally have a feeling of accomplishment. You need a goal, Josh. You need something to occupy your hands and your mind. It doesn't have to be big. Just a room. I'll help you. Something big enough to fit a bed, a dresser, and a desk, maybe. A fireplace for heat. You can get your meals over here."

For the first time the worry left Josh's face. He nodded. "I might like that. I'm willing to try that."

"This is the last option. If this doesn't work . . ."

"I know."

They lived peacefully for a time. Lisa moved her belongings out, taking all the guns with her. She also lectured Michael on the danger of knives and ice picks. Josh continued to live in Michael's cabin until his own was ready. Once Josh realized that Lisa was only waiting until he moved out before she moved back in with Michael, Josh took his sweet time finishing his cabin. But, with Michael's help, it was eventually ready. Occasionally, Josh had nightmares, which scared Lisa out of her wits. The two of them barely spoke to each other.

Josh wondered what Michael saw in Lisa. He had met her kind before and was surprised that Michael couldn't see through her. For Pete's sake, the man had plenty of experience! On the other hand, maybe his tastes had changed. *What about Meg?* The question burned in his brain morning, noon, and night. *If it hadn't been for you saying you were coming back for her, she could have been mine. I wouldn't be in the state you see me in now. You ruined my whole life! Everything I've done to you, you've deserved. I think about her all the time, don't you? How could you not?*

Lisa was not in the cabin. Michael was exceptionally cheerful at breakfast. "I'm finally going to take the plunge, Josh."

"Oh, what plunge is that?" Josh tried to match Michael's lighthearted mood.

"I'm getting married."

Josh's spoon stopped in midair. "To . . . to . . . Lisa?" He could hardly get the name out.

Michael laughed. "Of course, Lisa. Who else?"

"Meg." It was out. He hadn't been able to stop it.

Michael sat rigid, his eyes flashing. He looked at Josh and said in a low even tone, "You won't ever mention that name again on these five hundred acres."

They glared at each other across the table. *I gave her up for you. I wish you could see the look on your face. You still care about Meg. Marry Lisa? That bitch. She doesn't hold a candle to Meg, and you know it!*

"You promised you'd go back for her. Why didn't you?"

"That is none of your business. Drop it, Josh," Michael warned as he clenched his fists on the table. There hadn't been this much tension in the cabin since the day Josh arrived.

"I'll tell you why," said Josh quietly. "My famous Heisman Trophy winning brother, who I've worshipped since I can remember, is a coward."

It was quiet for a second, and then Michael leaped across the table at him. *I'm going to kill him! Josh has been nothing but trouble since the day he arrived.* But, Josh was too quick and moved out of Michael's reach. Experience with reading people's faces had taught him well.

"You're afraid to go back and face her," continued Josh. "Afraid she's forgotten all about you. Afraid she isn't waiting patiently for you—that maybe she never did. How would you feel if I told you—"

"Stop it!" yelled Michael. "She means nothing to me! She never did! That's why I didn't go back. Why the hell are you dragging all this up? That was years ago. What do you care? Why are you doing this to me?"

Do you want me to tell you why? I'll tell you why. Something I should have told you years ago: I could have had a life with her. She'd have had my children by now. She wanted me. Josh looked around him. "Who did you build this cabin for, Michael? Lisa?"

"Don't. Don't do this to me, Josh," Michael pleaded. "It's all in the past. There's nothing to be gained by this conversation. I haven't had the easy life you think I have. I made one mistake in my life—one that I've always regretted. Let's not hash it around. Lisa helps me to forget, she—"

"Because she's so much like Meg?"

"No!"

"Yes. I know what you see in her. I see it, too. But she's not Meg, and she's got certain qualities that definitely aren't Meg's." *Was Meg still waiting for Michael? Would she accept me instead, if I went back? She always said she loved me. That she would take me over Michael. I was a fool to leave her. And to think I thought I was being honorable by bowing out to you. What a laugh. The only thing is, I haven't kept in contact with Meg either. I never sent even one letter, although I wrote many. If only I'd kept in touch with her. Or Michael. Yes, if I'd only kept in touch with either one of them, I would have known Michael wasn't going back.* "Why did you quit the pros? You had some terrific years."

Michael was suspicious at the sudden shift in conversation. He straightened up. "I decided to get out while I was still healthy. I've got all the money I need. I just sit back and invest it now. I work this farm here for something to do. It's good hard labor; it relieves my tension and boredom. And, quite frankly, I enjoy the solitude. I love it here."

Josh nodded. "You've got an education, a name, and money. I wonder how many people would understand this." He held up his hands to the room. They had no electricity, only a pump in the kitchen for running water and a wood-burning stove for cooking. The two fireplaces, one upstairs and one down, served for heat. "And to think I had to make a name for myself by dodging bullets."

Michael had never seen Josh so bitter. Somehow, he imagined Josh would be the same happy-go-lucky brother he had left behind. "I don't have any money, and now I don't even have a job."

"You know you can stay here for as long as you like," said Michael hoarsely.

"Go back, Michael."

"Go back where?" *He's not serious!*

"Go back and find her. You've got all this acreage and this cabin. You're only missing one thing, and Lisa's not the replacement you're looking for. I know it gets lonely out here. I understand—"

"I can't go back! She has to be married by now! I'd look the fool going to her. Like some heartsick boy who can't go on living without the one he loves. What a bunch of rubbish."

"But what if she's not married? What if she's waited all these years for you? You've never married," he pointed out. "You want her, you know you do. You've wasted all these years, when maybe you didn't have to. Are you going to waste the rest of them, never knowing what might be? It's your own damn fault you didn't go back before this. You've only yourself

to blame for looking the fool. Go back and suffer the consequences—
whatever they might be. How can you go through life never knowing
what's killing you? Are you being fair to Lisa?"

"I left her when she needed me most. I walked out on her—after
all she did for me. Even if she weren't married, even if she hasn't found
somebody else, which I find hard to believe, she'd never come back here
with me. She's had all these years to build up her resentment against me,
and frankly, I don't blame her."

"But, what if she understood your leaving? What if she's sitting
somewhere right now, waiting for you to come back?"

"What do you care? You told me yourself she had a steady boyfriend.
That she was crazy about—"

"Oh, that didn't last long. Didn't I tell you?"

Michael's eyes flashed. "No. No, you never did. When? What . . . oh
shit, what does it matter now? I've got to stop living in the past. I'm
going to live for the here and now, with Lisa. It's easier for me this way,
Josh. Now I can think of Meg as always waiting for me. I'd rather think
that then know that she's happy in somebody else's arms. I couldn't take
that. I haven't been able to stand the thought of it all these years. Do you
understand? I'm all right not knowing."

"What about getting the family ring back? What are you going to tell
Dave?"

"I've already told Dave I was sorry; that with all the girls running in
and out of my life, one of them must have lifted it."

"How do you think Dave would feel if I told him where it was and
that you could get it back if you had the balls?"

The two of them looked fiercely across the table at each other. Michael
gritted his teeth. "Understand me, I am not going back."

"Then you're a coward—and a fool," said Josh, "and no brother of
mine."

CHAPTER 31

2001

ROBIN ENTERED THE HOUSE SHE CALLED HER "MICHIGAN HOME." When she was young it had been Godfather's and Mrs. Hill's house. But Jeff had divorced his first wife, Peggy, some time ago and a few years later married Sheila. Sheila was much warmer than Peggy ever was.

Robin's first memory of Aunt Sheila was running into the Hills' house unannounced to find Jeff in the embrace of a woman she'd never seen before. Robin was sure she was in trouble, but Uncle Jeff smiled and yelled, "Hey, Princess!"

The woman disentangled herself from him and walked over, bending down to Robin's height. "Oh, Jeff. She's as darling as you said she was. What do you say? Should we ask your godfather to take us girls out to get some ice cream?"

And, from then on, whenever she was allowed, Robin spent her free time and vacations at their home.

"Look at all the stuff I found on Michael," Robin said, setting down a manila folder. She pulled out sheets of copied articles. "There wasn't anything on Josh."

"Michael? Josh?" Jeff was staring at her. "What are you doing?" She looked up at the sharp tone in his voice. "Where did you get these?" he demanded.

Robin stepped back. She had never seen Uncle Jeff angry, at least not with her. "I . . . I got them at the newspaper office in town."

"You went—" He glanced over his shoulder as he heard his wife, Sheila walk in. Seeing the look on her face he stopped, took a deep breath, and let it out slowly. "What do you plan to do with these?"

"I don't know that I was planning to do anything with them. I just thought it'd be fun. My mom knew somebody famous . . ." Her voice faded as Jeff grabbed the papers, thumbed though them quickly, and threw them down.

"How far—what dates have you looked at?"

"Well . . . Mom's diary started in 1966, so I started there. But then it dawned on me that Michael was a really good athlete, so I went back to his freshman year in high school."

"What about the other way? How far did you follow his career?" *Why is Uncle Jeff mad at me? What have I done that's so wrong?*

"I know about the girls he had . . . all the pictures show him with different ones. Obviously he never came back, never thought of Mom again."

"How far did you go?" he yelled.

"Jeff," Sheila said quietly.

Robin looked from one to the other. "He retired from the pros in 1977. I looked in the sports section for 1978; but after he retired from football there wasn't anything more on him. Why was it he quit football right after college, but later signed? Does he know my mom's dead?"

Robin stared at her godfather as he paced the room. Walking near Sheila she grabbed Jeff's arm. Although she whispered it, Robin heard her just the same. "You need to tell her."

"No!"

"Is this how you want her to find out?"

"What?" yelled Robin throwing her hands up. "What have I done wrong? They're a bunch of old news articles. Big deal. It's not like I'm going to confront the man and ask him why he never came back. I think it's pretty obvious he forgot Mom . . . didn't care anymore . . . just like Matt." She sat down on the sofa and looked up to see her aunt and godfather scrutinizing her.

"What would you do with the truth?" asked Jeff softly.

"What do you mean?"

"What would you do if . . . I don't know, Robin," he sighed. "I don't know what's best for you. We love you as our own. You know that, don't you?"

"Of course I do."

"I wouldn't want you to do anything rash. You've been so depressed. I don't want to send you over the edge."

"I'm okay. I'm much closer to you than I ever was with Father. And the guy that helped me find all this is really cute. He asked me out," she smiled.

"Oh. Are you going?"

"Yeah."

"So, things are looking up?"

She nodded. "I think so."

He smiled for the first time. "Well, good. I'm glad."

"That's wonderful, honey." Aunt Sheila sat down next to Robin and put an arm around her.

"I don't suppose," said Jeff, "that if I asked you to not go through anymore files that you would stop."

"Not now," Robin answered.

Jeff turned and slowly made his way over to his desk. He extracted an old newspaper that was tucked way back in the drawer. It was rolled with a rubber band around it. He walked over and stood in front of Robin. She felt Sheila's arm hug her tighter. "I never thought I'd see the day when I gave you this." Robin could barely hear him, he spoke so low. "But, I definitely don't want you finding this on your own. I hope I'm doing the right thing," he said, handing it to her.

The rubber band was so old it broke as she tried to roll it off. Robin lay the newspaper down on the coffee table and ran both hands across it to hold it in place. **WOMAN VANISHES FROM REUNION** read the headline. *What has this got to do with anything?* Then Robin's eyes lighted on the woman's name: Megan Becktame Beechum. Her head jerked up. "Mom?" Jeff nodded. "You told me she died of cancer."

"It's what your father demanded we tell you. You read the article— then we'll talk."

Robin sucked in her breath sharply. *No, don't even think it,* she told herself. *Uncle Jeff isn't saying that Mom is still alive . . . is he?*

Discover the truth behind the headlines as Jeff continues the story of Meg, Michael, and Josh in the forthcoming sequel, *All's Forgotten Now,* available in 2010.

To purchase additional copies of *Owe It To The Wind*, to read about the author, and to check the status of the sequel, please visit:

www. jrarmstrong.net

Or you may write to the author at:

Willowrose Publishing
P. O. Box 1187
Fowlerville, MI 48836